DIRTY BOSS

MANHATTAN BILLIONAIRES
BOOK 7

LILIAN MONROE

Cover design by Maria at Steamy Designs
Editing by Shavonne at Motif Edits
Proofreading by Paige at PK Edits

WANT THREE BOOKS DELIVERED STRAIGHT TO YOUR INBOX?
HOW ABOUT THREE ROCK STAR ROMANCES THAT WERE WAY
TOO HOT TO SELL?

GET THE COMPLETE ROCK HARD SERIES:
WWW.LILIANMONROE.COM/ROCKHARD

ONE
ALBA

IT TOOK three days for my life to be ruined so completely that fourteen months later, I barely recognized myself when I looked in the mirror. Gone was the carefree, privileged woman who thought she could dance through life, having her cake and gorging herself on it too. In her place was a haggard, aching wreck teetering on the edge of total ruination, one of millions in the city. I was one of the people that I wouldn't have even noticed before, like the person who'd done my laundry or brought my food to my door. I'd lost everything and turned invisible.

Maybe I got what I deserved.

As yet another suit-wearing patron snapped his fingers at me to get my attention, I pasted a smile on my face and shoved my disdain somewhere deep, deep down inside me where he wouldn't be able to get a whiff of it.

Most customers I served were normal, polite enough people who just wanted to eat and go about their days. A small portion of them were complete jerks who seemed to enjoy making my life as difficult as possible in order to make themselves feel better. They'd send back food multiple times. They'd talk down to me and treat me like I didn't have two brain cells to rub together. They'd hit on me and occasionally try to grope me.

The men from my previous life had groped and leered and harassed too, but I'd been protected from them by my name, my family's money, my status.

All that was gone now.

I *hated* working here. I hated being treated as lesser. Hated that all those people felt like they could harass me just because they were sitting at the table I was serving.

But this was my life now. Wasn't it time I accepted it?

A worse question lingered at the back of my mind: Is that how I used to act?

When I got to the table of the finger-snapper, I forced my lips to curl into a pleasant, bland smile. "What can I do for you?"

"You can tell me when you get off work," the old lecher replied, smiling at me with stained teeth. He leaned back on the cushioned chair, the buttons of his bespoke shirt proving their value by keeping the flaps of fabric closed even under considerable strain. The diamonds on his watch twinkled in the light, and even at a distance, I could tell his suit cost more than three months' worth of my pay. I could tell because those were the types of clothes I used to wear.

God, I missed my old clothes. I missed having places to wear my old clothes. Now my clothing itched and tugged and didn't fit quite right. They weren't tailored to sit exactly right on my body, weren't handmade from the finest materials.

I still owned some of the old stuff—what I'd been able to pack into bags before being thrown out of my home—but wearing three-thousand-dollar pants to work where they'd get grease-stained and damaged beyond repair didn't seem like a good idea. Besides, even though the old clothes fit my body perfectly, they didn't seem to fit *me* anymore.

It was like clinging onto jeans from high school for decades in the hope of buttoning them up again. My expensive designer clothes hung in my too-small closet, taking up space, reminding me of a life that was gone forever.

Now the cheap fabric of my work pants scratched against my legs as I shifted from foot to foot and tried my hardest to keep my smile in place. "I'm sorry, we're not allowed to give out personal information," I told the old man, revulsion turning my gut. I pasted that cardboard smile on my face again when I noticed it had slipped, then turned to his companion. This man wore an off-the-rack suit that was a little too narrow in the shoulders. It was lined with cheap fabric, and I could tell his shirt needed a date with an ironing board.

He was just like me, begging for scraps from the bigwig in the expensive clothing. Except in his case, he had the possibility of ending up in the chair across the table one day.

I, on the other hand, had dreams of getting out of the city and never having to interact with anyone ever again.

Cheap Suit's face made up for any beauty lacking in his garments. Chiseled jaw, cut cheekbones, and the kind of lips that made women weep. Eyes of ice blue that watched me, something like pity swirling in their depths.

I didn't need or want his pity. If he was sitting at this table, no matter how cheap his suit was, he was part of a world that had closed its doors in my face.

A year ago, men like him had circled me like vultures. My ego had loved the attention. I'd guzzled it like it was water. I'd craved it. All my worth hinged on how much other people valued me; it's how I'd been raised to see myself. Now I couldn't stand even the barest brush of an attractive man's gaze over my body.

I turned back to the first creep and did my very best to not let any hint of my thoughts show on my face. I tilted my head and blinked at him like a pilot could land a commercial jet between my ears. After getting fired from my first three waitressing jobs, I'd finally discovered that people preferred it when they thought their servers—or was it servants?—were dumber than them. Or at least when we had the good sense to pretend. "Was everything okay with your food?"

I knew before he opened his mouth that he wasn't done harassing me. It was always the same with the lunchtime business crowd. They made passes at me to impress their clients and board members. They talked down to the busboys and clicked their fingers in between making billion-dollar deals.

This wasn't a fancy establishment. I wasn't a good enough waitress to serve in those kinds of places. But it was a hidden gem with really good food, and a lot of businesspeople came here when they wanted to impress each other with their secret knowledge of the city. So although the billion-dollar-deal crowd didn't make up the majority of our patrons, they weren't exactly rare.

It disgusted me. I couldn't believe I'd been part of their world before, even if I'd just been a pretty accessory on the periphery.

The old man tried again, his gaze raking down my body and back up again. "Pretty girl like you shouldn't be working in a place like this. I could give you a job." He grinned at me like he wasn't thinking about offering to make me wait tables.

I stood on aching legs as my feet pulsed in pain with every heartbeat, wondering if I should pick up his knife and stab him in the eye. Surely prison would be better than this.

"Roger," the other man growled, and I gritted my teeth. I didn't need him to come to my defense. "Let the poor girl go."

My gaze flicked to his pale blue one. I wondered if he meant "poor girl" literally, and resented his attempt at playing the hero.

"I'm happy here," I said breezily, ignoring Cheap Suit's attempt at saving me from his companion. "I'll send the chef your compliments," I said, managing a coy smile and a wink as I whisked the older man's plate away.

The old creep laughed, pleased that I'd capitulated that far. I'd played his game, made him feel like he had a chance with me. Power over me.

It made me feel dirty, but I couldn't afford for him to stiff me on the tip. So maybe he did have power over me, after all.

The vulnerability of my situation hit me then, and I couldn't stand the clinking of utensils on plates and the low murmur of people schmoozing over overpriced sandwiches.

My fall from grace had been abrupt, and I still hadn't quite stuck the landing. I existed paycheck to paycheck. I worked two jobs and lived in a shoebox. Actually, the shoeboxes of my old life were far nicer than my current accommodations—but I couldn't complain. The alternative was the street, and January in NYC wasn't exactly hospitable.

Dumping the plate in the dish pit at the back of the restaurant, I ducked into the walk-in cooler and leaned my head against a metal shelf. The door closed, and the din of the kitchen was abruptly muffled. I exhaled a puff of white breath, opening my eyes to stare at the container of limes directly in front of my face.

A little over a year ago, I was rich, I was engaged—and I was in love. Not to the same man, mind you. My engagement was essentially a sham, but I knew my duty to my family, and I was ready to keep up appearances by tying my life to Cole Christianson's. He was the darling of my father's company, and our union was supposed to make us Manhattan's newest power couple. Or, if I were being honest, it would make him a powerful man and me the woman along for the ride at his side. I'd learned just how little agency I'd had over my life when I'd been ousted from it.

Cole and I would've each gotten to live our intimate lives in private, away from each other and from prying eyes. He could have had his own fun on the side, and I could have had mine.

Until I went and fell in love, like the idiot I thought I'd never be. The fact that he did too had felt like a blessing—it meant we could finally stop lying to each other and break up. No need for a sham wedding after all.

Ha.

That hadn't gone over well with Mommy and Daddy Dearest.

Love, as far as I was concerned, was what had started this descent into near-poverty, this crash from the upper echelons of Manhattan society into the subsistence that passed for my life now.

Love is what bit me in the ass and made me throw everything away. And then love laughed in my face and turned its back on me. The man I thought I loved didn't love me back when I didn't have access to Daddy's purse strings anymore.

That was a slap in the face like I'd never experienced before.

And Cole? Well, last I heard, he reconnected with The One Who Got Away, and they were blissfully happy and recently married.

That hurt too, which I knew was pathetic and selfish of me.

I took a deep breath, squeezed my eyes shut for a moment, then squared my shoulders and walked out of the fridge. I grabbed a couple of plates on my way out of the kitchen and brought them to the hungry patrons who had ordered them, smiling like my life depended on it.

In a lot of ways, it did.

When I glanced over at the far side of my section, the old lecher had disappeared. A red-stained wine glass remained at his seat, and his companion in the cheap suit now wore a troubled frown as he leaned his chin on his palm and stared out the window at the city rushing by outside.

My first thought was that I was glad I wouldn't have to interact with the other man again. My second was that I'd wasted all that effort resisting the urge to stab him in the eye when he wasn't even the one who was going to pay the bill.

At least when I flirted back with them, they tended to pay me for it. This guy didn't look like he'd bother. Cheap Suit glanced up when I stopped to clear the other man's wine glass.

"Can I get you anything else?" I asked.

His pale blue eyes met mine, and he shook his head. "Just the bill." His voice was pleasantly deep, and it annoyed me. Just another handsome, entitled man who lived life on easy mode.

Business lunches and bottles of wine. Money flowing through his hands like water. A devastating smile and a trail of heartbreaks behind him.

Yeah, I knew his type.

I was so *tired.*

"I'm sorry about that, earlier," he said, motioning to the other side of the table, and a flash of annoyance went through me. He didn't have to pretend to care. No one else did.

"Not your job to apologize for other people's actions."

He tilted his head. "Still. Not the kind of thing I like to endorse." A sigh left his lips, and his gaze slid away from me as he said, lower, "So I guess it's a good thing he walked."

I arched a brow, and a scoff slipped through my best defenses. "Meeting didn't go the way you wanted?"

I knew the moment the words came out of my mouth that my tone was way out of line. Too much sass, not enough deference. All the judgments that were supposed to be bottled up inside me had been folded in that question, barely hidden just below the surface.

Like how little I thought of him and how much I'd faked it with his lunch mate. How much he and his ilk disgusted me. How much I resented his kindness.

There went my tip.

He leaned back in his chair, the seams of that polyester suit straining at his shoulders as he stretched his arm out across the seat next to him. His dark hair was tousled, but not in a thousand-dollar-haircut kind of way. More like "I buzz my head every four months over the bathroom sink with clippers I bought at Walmart, and I'm due for a chop" kind of way.

He didn't look *bad*. He wore it as well as a guy could. But if he was attempting to rub elbows with the kind of man who had just walked out of this lunch meeting, he had entirely the wrong look.

Not that I cared. I wasn't part of that world, either. Not anymore.

The man looked at me, and I felt like a bug under a microscope. "You don't seem surprised," he noted.

"That he walked out on you and left you sulking?"

"Sulking?"

"What would you call it?" I picked up the empty bottle of wine and put it on my tray beside the other man's glass, arching a brow at him. Cheap Suit hadn't partaken in the wine that the old lecher ordered. He hadn't even pretended to indulge, the fool.

"I'm not sure I like your tone," he said, and there was a warning in his eyes.

I held the tray in one hand and planted the other on my hip. "I'm sorry to hear that," I replied, and smiled.

His eyes narrowed. "It's one thing for an investor to tell me that he's passing on my company," he rumbled, "but being patronized by the fucking waitress is not why I came here."

I reared back, and the empty bottle on my tray wobbled. I

grabbed the neck of it and held it in my free hand, glaring at him. "'The fucking waitress?'" I repeated.

"Pardon me. The fucking server."

A squeak escaped me, and my temperature went up a few degrees. I ground my teeth. "I see. You were made to feel small and now you want to turn around and do it to someone else. How utterly predictable. I guess you being my valiant defender was just an act earlier?"

He scoffed and leaned forward, eyes boring into mine. "You couldn't wait to walk over here and point out that I got rejected."

"Sounds like you enjoy making up stories in your head, buddy."

"Sounds like you don't like being called out on your shit."

I opened my mouth. Closed it. My breaths came fast and hard, and fantasies of eye-stabbing returned. My grip on the neck of the wine bottle tightened.

The man smiled and leaned back. "The bill, princess. And if you wouldn't mind, make it quick. I need to get back to work."

I clomped away from him, rage boiling in my gut. How *dare* he. How dare he!

I mashed the screen on our cash register and ripped the bill from the printer. The leather bill fold snapped closed in my hand. I glared across the dining room, ready to march back over there and—

"Alba."

I turned to see the front-of-house manager staring at me with narrowed eyes. Elena was a short woman with ink-black hair and skin a few shades darker than mine. She'd been in the service industry since she was twelve years old, and she terrified me a little. Misbehavior was not tolerated on her watch. Lord knew why she'd given me the job. Nothing I did was up to her standards.

I stood up a little straighter, swallowing past the constriction in my throat. "Yes?"

"Take five," my manager said, and held her hand out for the billfold. Her head angled toward the back, where she wanted me to go.

"I'm fine," I ground out.

"It wasn't a suggestion."

I bit my lip and handed her the check, then watched her walk toward my table. Then I took a deep breath and went through the swinging door into the kitchen. I ducked through the hectic space, calling, "Behind!" as I passed each of the cooks, and then pushed through the door to the back alley.

Winter wind bit at my neck and face, and I gulped down a deep breath of cold, garbage-scented air. I wanted to cry. Leaning my hands on my knees, I parked my butt against the brick wall of the restaurant and stared at the icy, gravel-encrusted ground between my feet.

I wanted to cry, but I wouldn't. I'd done enough of that, and I was sick of feeling weak.

Salvation was one phone call away; all I had to do was call my mother and tell her I was ready to kowtow to her and Dad. I was ready to admit that I'd been wrong, and I would do whatever it took to salvage our reputation in the eyes of society.

To hell with that.

They had turned their backs on me, just like James had when he realized my family's money wasn't in fact mine. My dad had flung insults at me when he found out about the man I loved. The man I'd thought loved me back. I was a worthless whore, and I'd go out and earn money like one before he let me parade myself around in front of all of New York with James. That's what my father had said, his face purple with rage, my mother crumbling in on herself in the corner of the room, her eyes baleful as they daggered into me.

I hadn't played by the rules, and I'd been excised for it. Poof! Life as I knew it, gone.

I thought James would be there to help me pick up the pieces. Ha. It surprised me how naive I was, sometimes. How utterly stupid.

No, I wasn't going to grovel. Humiliation on that level wasn't something I was willing to endure—not again.

If I went back, what would happen? I'd be handed off to some other man to marry. I'd make a baby or two, and smile for pictures at glitzy events. I'd find solace in the bottle, or maybe prescription pills. I'd be yet another too-thin, zombified woman who'd sold her integrity for a plush bed and a closet full of beautiful clothes.

I couldn't do it. A part of me was surprised by that, as I was sure my parents had been. But I just couldn't spend the next several decades of my life living a vapid existence, even if it was more comfortable than this. At least here, with my nails worn down to nubs and my body aching with every movement, I knew I was alive.

Another deep breath of fetid air, and I stood up straighter. The chill in the air pierced my thin white button-down, and I glanced sideways at the street. People and cars rushed by, oblivious to me. Oblivious to my pain.

I was going to get fired. Again. I wouldn't be able to make my rent. None of my friends or acquaintances from my old life spoke to me anymore—and I'd been too focused on survival to think about making any new friends this past year—so there wouldn't even be a couch or a spare bedroom for me to crash on.

I was out in the cold, on my own, and I'd just messed up *again*.

Sighing, I pulled the door open. Might as well face the music.

But when I made it back to the dining room, Elena just handed me the billfold from my table and looked into my eyes.

"Better?" she asked.

"Yes. Thank you."

"Good. You've got a four-top on table seventeen. The old man with the gold watch used to be a regular; treat him like it. His name is Wentworth."

"Sure," I said, and I peeked in the billfold, expecting a whole lot of nothing, and half looking forward to cursing Cheap Suit for the next few days. It was nice to have a target for my aggression.

Instead, a crisp, fresh, hundred-dollar bill fluttered out of the leather holder and landed between my black shoes.

Moving slowly, I picked it up and held it like it was a dead rat that I'd been charged with removing.

"Something wrong?" Elena asked, a brow arched.

"The guy on table fourteen left this...for me?"

Elena nodded.

"Did he say anything?"

"Not a word."

I crumpled the bill in my fist, scowling. That asshole was rubbing my face in it! He *knew* I was broke, and this was a message. I was the dirt under his shoe. I was the uppity waitress who would take his money because I needed it more than he did.

Damn him! Damn his arrogance! Damn him for being *right*!

An image flashed through my mind: me, rushing out of the restaurant, catching him before he disappeared. I'd put a hand on his arm and make him turn, and then I'd stuff his filthy money down his throat and make him choke on it.

God, that would feel so good.

Unfortunately, it would also mean I couldn't pay my overdue power bill. Apparently, when you didn't pay it, the power company shut your electricity off. This was something I'd learned when I first moved into my own apartment after my life fell apart. I hadn't realized I needed to open an account in the first place, let alone pay for electricity myself.

I know. I *know*. I felt as out of touch and pathetic as I should've. Real life *sucked*.

Swallowing past the constriction in my throat, I stuffed the money in my belt and ignored Elena's questioning look.

I painted my best smile on my face and went to greet the four new customers at table seventeen.

BY THE END of my shift, I was a tiny bit richer and a whole lot achier. My lower back pulsed as I slid on my jacket, and all I wanted to do was head home, collapse on my couch, and get real intimate with both Ben and Jerry.

Unfortunately, rent was due in a few days and even with an extra hundred bucks in my pocket, I was still short. So I couldn't crash out and gorge on ice cream. I had to go to my second job.

The hundred-dollar bill burned in my pocket. A year and a half ago, a hundred dollars would've been nothing to me. I hadn't even carried cash; I probably wouldn't have even stopped to pick the money up if I'd walked by it on the street. I'd swiped my credit card and bought whatever I'd wanted, and someone else had handled the bills.

Now the money was necessary. And the man in the cheap suit had known it, and that *galled* me down to the tips of my toes.

I'd changed into my cleaner's uniform in the staff room at the restaurant, so all I had to do was head a couple of blocks over to the familiar, glass-encrusted tower where I worked in the evenings.

Even though it was after hours, the automatic doors slid open at a swipe of my card, and I nodded to the security guard behind the front desk.

Then I made my way to the forty-second floor, where I opened the cleaner's closet and strapped the vacuum to my back.

"This is temporary," I promised myself, same as I did every evening. Just until I could find a better-paying job. Until I figured out what I could do with two years of a liberal arts college education, no degree, no useful training, no money, and no contacts.

Until I decided to grovel, to debase myself and go back into the family fold. If they'd have me.

As I checked the levels in the spray bottles of cleaner, I wondered what it would take for my parents to take me back. Would they have someone else lined up for me to marry? Someone appropriate? Would I have to endure endless humiliation? What lies would they have told their friends and acquaintances about my absence in order to save face?

I was irrationally angry at my parents for not preparing me for the world. But I was thirty years old, so a lot of that blame rested on my own shoulders. Besides, they *had* prepared me for the world —just not this one.

They'd shown me how to smile and how to sit. They'd taught me which forks to use at a formal dinner. They'd explained the politics of society, told me to keep track of who was cheating on whom and who would stab whom in the back. I knew how to dance and how to smile so a man would pay attention. I knew how to use clothing and hair and makeup and accessories to make a statement. I knew who was on the cusp of a big business deal, and who to turn to if I wanted to stop it.

Fat load of good that did me now.

Tightening the straps on my vacuum, I closed my eyes and took a deep breath. My hip ached. After the car accident that had kicked off the worst week of my life, my body hadn't quite been the same. My back ached all the time, and my hips clicked when I got really tired. And my feet—forget it. They just throbbed all the time now, but maybe that was because I was on them for thirteen hours a day.

Maybe this was all a dream. Maybe I was lying in a hospital bed, in a coma, and I'd wake up to see my parents beside me. They would still love me even if I didn't marry Cole. They would support me even though I refused to keep up appearances by sacrificing the rest of my life for a sham marriage. My father wouldn't have said those awful things to me, and my mother wouldn't have stood by and let him.

And James—James would still be in love with me, even if I was dirt-poor.

But when I opened my eyes again, I was still in a dusty closet, surrounded by cleaning supplies.

I found the outlet at the close end of the hallway, plugged in my backpack vacuum, and got to work.

When I entered the corner office at the far end of the hall, my shoulders dropped. Once again, the big shot who inhabited the space had tossed his work boots in the corner of the room, where all the dirt and grime and slush and salt from outside leaked into the carpet and caked itself there.

Grumbling to myself, I knocked the dried dirt off the boots and vacuumed up what I could, scowling at the tan footwear. Then I scowled at the desk, where heaps of paperwork threatened to topple over every time the HVAC system turned on.

Typical, wasn't it? There was always someone to clean up after him, so he didn't bother to do it himself. He probably didn't think about me for even a second, so he had no idea he made my life more difficult every single night.

Guilt squirmed through me. How many times had I made a

cleaner's job harder in my lifetime? I'd never even thought about the army of people that cleaned my family's properties, the people who landscaped our lawns, made our food...

I was ashamed of my former self. I wished I could go back in time and change the way I'd acted.

But I couldn't—and I still had to clean the carpet.

I vacuumed and scrubbed and vacuumed some more, but the salt from the road must have damaged the carpet fibers. A patch of discoloration remained. Would it be enough to get me fired? I stared at the salt stain as pressure and heat built up in the middle of my chest.

In the fourteen months since my fall from grace—if grace was what you could call the life of privilege I'd been ousted from—I'd been fired from a total of nine jobs and rejected from even attempting to work at countless others.

All those people had looked at me and found me lacking.

Nine people had asked me to do the most basic tasks, and I'd failed. I couldn't scrub dishes, or serve coffee, or mop floors. I couldn't file paperwork or keep up with the speed required of a cashier.

Elena had given me a shot. The cleaning company had given me a shot. But mostly, people had told me I wasn't good enough.

The stain on the carpet stared at me, and I could almost hear it laughing.

Without connections and money, I was nothing. I could hardly take care of myself. I was a terrible cook and a worse cleaner. Navigating insurance and utilities and leases had almost made my head explode. Without the insulation of my parents' wealth, it was plainly obvious how useless a human I really was.

I couldn't even get a stain out of a carpet.

Would this be my tenth firing? Would whatever bigwig who

kept the messy desk walk in and decide to call the cleaning company to get rid of the faceless cleaner that he'd never interacted with because of a stain *he'd* made?

I'd have to save every penny from the restaurant if I wanted to cover rent and bills and hope that I could steal a few fries from the expo line to feed myself during my shifts.

The heat built up in my chest, and I squeezed my eyes shut. When I opened them again, I stared out the tinted windows at the silent winter beyond. This far up, the snowflakes whirled and danced, caught up in the various wind currents swirling between high-rise buildings. Night blanketed the city, lights dotting the skyline like glittering jewels.

I thought of the men at lunch today, and I gritted my teeth. They found it so easy to speak down to me. One of them enjoyed watching me squirm in the face of his advances, and the other took every opportunity to remind me how small and pathetic I really was.

How dare they.

Anger sizzled through me, chasing away the chill of desperation. When my eyes landed on the stained carpet again, I couldn't help the hiss that slipped through my clenched teeth.

What did I care if I got fired? I'd pick up more shifts at the restaurant. I'd find a way.

I would *not* go back to my parents. Not after what they'd said to me. After how they'd treated me. And I would not let yet another man make me feel worthless and small and useless.

Sheer, pathological stubbornness was the only thing that had gotten me through this past year. It would see me through whatever came.

Marching to the mess on the desk, I glanced at the single framed photo of a little girl, and I huffed. I bet he loved looking like a family man, but how often did he see his kid? Was she growing up like I had, with all the privilege in the world and not an ounce of real affection?

If I lost my job for this, it would be worth it. I snatched one of the papers from the stack on the leftmost edge of his desk, flipped it over, and grabbed the first pen I found.

TWO
VAUGHN

I SHOVED my tie into my pocket and shouldered my way through the front door of my Upper West Side townhome. Another investor had passed on the company, which meant I'd have to go begging again. My construction company was stagnating. Stagnation was as good as shrinking, and shrinking was as good as failure.

Failure was unacceptable.

It was only one of my companies, but I couldn't bear the thought of failure. Most of my fortune had been made off a patent for a specific type of scaffolding connection. From there, I'd grown my one-man-van general contracting business to a multimillion-dollar corporation. Now I had the construction business, the patent money, an equipment rental company, and a labor hire company. If the construction business plateaued or even collapsed, it would be a rounding error in my total wealth.

But I couldn't let it happen. It wasn't about the money. It was about achievement. About controlling every possible outcome to make sure that me and mine were always taken care of. No matter what. To give my people the stability I'd never had.

And to do that, I needed an in. I needed someone who moved in circles above my own, who had politicians' ears, who would introduce me to the true power brokers of the city.

Then my future—and my daughter's—would be secure.

"Daddy!" a familiar little voice called out moments before the pitter-patter of a five-year-old sprinting echoed down the hall.

I dropped my laptop bag and knelt. Charlotte collided with me, her little arms circling my neck. I stood as her legs hooked around my waist, squeezing me tight with all the love in her little frame. Her hair was wet and she was in her PJs. She smelled like overly fruity hair products, and she held onto me like she never wanted to let go.

Charlotte was the reason I did this. The reason I *kept* doing this.

I'd bought this four-bedroom townhome before Charlotte existed—before her mother and I even knew each other—and spent a year and a half renovating it into the light-filled beauty it was now. It was in a good school district, and I'd imagined a wife and multiple kids filling the rooms with life and joy.

I hadn't imagined being a single dad and only getting snippets of time with my daughter two weeks at a time when I had custody of her, carving out evenings and weekends in between trying to grow the company and solidify my legacy. Lately, it felt like my snippets of time with her were getting shorter and shorter—something my ex-wife loved to point out. She didn't tend to point out that my work was what let her live in a paid-off house with a lifestyle multiple levels above what she and her new husband would be able to afford without me.

But even with everything else I'd accomplished, being a father was the best thing I'd ever done.

"Hey, turkey. Did you have fun with Billie?"

"We made a fort! Come see!" She wriggled until I let her down, then clamped a hand on my wrist and towed me deeper into our home.

In the mouth of the living room, the nanny who had been a lifeline these past couple of years smiled. "Hi, Vaughn. Charlotte had two servings of spaghetti tonight, and a yogurt with orange slices for dessert."

"I was hungry," Charlotte confirmed with an exaggerated nod.

Billie smiled, then looked at me. "I have to run. I have a dinner to get to tonight."

"Still dating Finance Guy?"

Billie laughed and shook her head. "That didn't work out. I met a guy at my climbing gym, though, and he seems nice. Down-to-earth."

"Enjoy. Thanks for your help today," I said, and nodded toward the door with a smile.

The nanny disappeared, and I crouched down into the fort that now dominated the living room. Charlotte gave me a tour of the space, including the area she'd reserved for her dolls. I sat with my knees scrunched up at my chest, letting the tension of the day drain away.

When I told her she was allowed to sleep in the fort tonight, my daughter gave me the kind of smile that felt like a punch to the chest. One of those moments that made me sure I'd do anything for her.

A little while later, when Charlotte was asleep with one arm curled around her pillow and her favorite blanket wrapped around her legs, I leaned against the kitchen counter and ate leftover spaghetti noodles, mulling over my options.

I had to attract some serious money if I wanted to keep the

business growing and be able to bid on the kind of jobs that meant something in this city.

But every time I met with an investor, I was told some variation of "no, thank you." It's like they looked at me and didn't believe I belonged in the same room as them, even though my wealth often elapsed theirs. The company didn't match the risk profile they were looking for. The construction industry was too volatile. I wasn't offering anything different in a crowded market.

Maybe I was too dumb, or too crass, or too blue collar. I couldn't hear the language I was supposed to speak, even when it sounded like we understood each other. I was missing something, and I had no idea what it was.

Actually, I knew exactly what it was. The moneyed class were a bunch of shallow, vain liars who licked each other's boots for fun. They could tell I had a speck of integrity, and they weren't interested in having anything to do with me. I'd learned that young, when my coward of a father had begged, borrowed, and stolen everything he could to try to be one of them. He'd ruined our family chasing get-rich-quick schemes, and my mother had indulged and enabled him.

It had been a childhood of instability. On multiple occasions, Mother had woken me in the middle of the night and told me to pack my bags, and then we'd be sneaking out of a home we could no longer afford. Moving every time one of my father's ventures went south. Dodging loan sharks—and being caught by them.

I'd made sure I would never, *ever*, go back to that life. Now I just needed to take one last step to ensure it for my daughter, for her children, for good.

So what was I missing? Why didn't any of these bigger fish want to take a bite?

Frustration couldn't even begin to describe what I felt. Even the waitress at lunch treated me like some kind of fraud. Sassing me as she flicked that blond ponytail over her shoulder. Looking at me like I wasn't worth the gum stuck to the bottom of her shoe.

What the hell did she know?

Some pretty little waitress who knew just how to keep a dirty old man on the hook, like she had with Roger at lunch today, thought she was better than me? She didn't know anything about me or my life.

My bowl clattered against another as I put it in the dishwasher, frustration making me clumsy. From the living room, I heard Charlotte stir.

I gripped the edge of the counter and breathed out my anger. My daughter was the reason I'd done all this. I wanted to give her more than what I had. Every opportunity, every chance, every leg up. She would never wonder if she'd have to be the new kid at school for the umpteenth time. She'd never have to wear clothes three sizes too small and eat peanut butter sandwiches three times a day for a week straight until some money came in.

All I could do was keep trying. I stalked to my home office across from the living room where Charlotte slept, opened my laptop, and went back to work.

IN THE MORNING, after eating breakfast with Charlotte and greeting Billie, I stopped at one of our construction sites in Midtown. My company had won the bid to build a twenty-seven-story building, and we'd successfully got it out of the ground before winter. It was meant to be a stepping stone to bigger jobs. It was supposed to be the kind of project that put my company on a powerful investor's radar.

There was an important concrete pour happening to start

forming some of the structural columns, and I stayed long enough to make sure that things were going smoothly.

They were not.

Concrete trucks had to be rejected for quality defects, one of the subcontractors had brought on unsafe equipment, and one of our engineers had caught a mistake on the drawings we were supposed to be casting in concrete that very morning. The weather was colder than forecast, and it was teetering on the edge of too cold for the concrete to cure properly.

In other words, the morning was an unmitigated disaster. My control of the project was slipping, which made my skin itch.

By the time I made it to the office, it was just before noon and I felt like I'd been awake for days. If we couldn't pull off the Midtown job, all hope of finding an investor would be lost.

The elevator opened onto the forty-second floor that I'd leased and renovated in the first big company expansion. The company logo welcomed me on the wall across from the elevators, and then glass doors slid open to allow me entrance to the executives' wing. It smelled like recycled air and old coffee. I waved at my CFO, Jim Davis, through the glass wall of his office, and then ducked into my own. I kicked off my work boots and noticed my second pair in the corner. I'd have to remember to tell my assistant to bring one of them back down to the car.

My chair squeaked when I dropped into it, and I braced myself before booting up my computer, knowing from the buzzing of my phone that I'd have an avalanche of emails to attend to.

I was *tired*.

And that's when I saw it.

Scrawled on the back of the quarterly finance report was a note. The handwriting was neat, but whoever had written it had pressed so hard that the paper had deformed, and the imprint of their words was visible on the blue folder beneath. The note read:

Mr. Big Shot,

For three days, I have cleaned the mess made by your dirty work boots. Tonight, I find myself unable to remove the stain from the carpet. If you insist on keeping your boots dirty as some macho show of being "one of the guys" when you leave your fancy corner office and go on site, I would appreciate it if you would at least knock the salt and gravel off before traipsing across the carpet. If that's too much to ask for, look forward to more salt stains around your office. I will not be cleaning them any longer.

Signed, Your Friendly, Invisible Cleaning Woman

I read the note three times. She didn't sound fucking friendly to me. I crumpled the note and chucked it toward the trash. The ball of paper bounced off the rim of the basket and fell on the floor, just a few feet away from the salt stain that had offended her so much. I made to get up so I could throw it away properly, then reconsidered. Maybe when she saw the crumpled paper, she'd get the message. I didn't have time for yet another snippy woman who thought she was better than me.

Which made it even more inexplicable that I found myself at Carmine's once again for lunch. My eyes tracked the swinging blond ponytail across the dining room, and I asked the hostess to seat me in her section.

Maybe I knew how much I'd enjoy the look on her face when she saw me. The shock, quickly followed by disbelief, and then the gratifying clenching of her jaw and narrowing of her eyes.

She'd be beautiful if her attitude wasn't the size of a small planet. I enjoyed watching her march over to my table and paint an obviously false smile on her face.

"Hi. I'm Alba. I'll be your server today."

I hadn't registered her name yesterday, but I made a note of it now. "Hi Alba," I said, and put a hand to my chest as I introduced myself. "Vaughn. Good to see you again."

"We both know that's a lie," she shot back, then clamped her lips shut. Her face went faintly red, which was lovely. The blue in her eyes shot thunderbolts at me, and I watched her inhale, then exhale. The vapid smile returned to her face; her mask was back on.

I didn't want the mask. I wanted the real her. I wanted her to antagonize me so I could spar with her and feel better about the shitshow of my life.

I gritted my teeth in my best approximation of a smile, and I knew it hadn't reached my eyes. "I'd like to hear the specials, please."

Her mask dropped, annoyance flashing, and a rush of pleasure went through me. "They're the same as yesterday. They're weekly specials, which means they only change once a week. I can try to explain it in smaller words if that's still too complicated for you." Her smile was sharp as a blade.

I braided my fingers and leaned my forearms against the table, holding her gaze. There were so many ways I could've let off some steam to relieve the stress of my company's current predicament. I could've gone to the gym to run it off, or boxed one of the heavy bags. I could've had a few drinks and called one of the friends I'd neglected. I could've found some woman willing to roll around in a bed with me.

But I was here. Antagonizing a waitress who clearly hated my guts.

I arched an eyebrow. "My memory isn't what it used to be. Remind me."

Another deep breath, and then she rattled off dishes and their prices. There was a steak sandwich, a seafood dish, and a starter that included some kind of duck. I listened, and when she was done, I said, "I think I'll have the chicken breast I had yesterday."

Frustration laced her every expression, from the pinching of her lips to the flashing of her eyes. All she said was, "Of course," and took the menu from me.

I watched her walk away, admiring her long legs and utterly straight spine. She moved like a dancer, graceful, strong. But the weight of her pride kept her from gliding the way she might've otherwise.

When I paid the bill at the end of my meal, she flicked her gaze over the receipt. A muscle jerked in her cheek.

"Something wrong?" I asked, leaning back in my chair.

"No," she said, then dragged her gaze up to mine. "Thank you."

Oh, that sounded like it hurt. So it *was* her pride that weighed her down. And my generous tips were rubbing her the wrong way.

Good.

I grabbed my jacket and scarf, nodded to her, and walked out of the restaurant.

THREE

ALBA

I STARED at the ball of paper on the office floor, and my temperature went up a half dozen degrees. He hadn't even bothered to throw it in the trash can next to his desk. And a few feet away, the boots I'd cleaned had multiplied. There were *two* sets of dirty work boots, and they'd leaked their melted, dirty snow into the carpet fibers again.

Argh!

I vacuumed the office and straightened the boots, but I refused to clean the carpet under the footwear. After all, I'd promised I wouldn't. And when I bent over to pick up the note I'd written him, I paused with my hand hovering over the scrunched-up paper. Then I stood and stared at it for a second.

And I left it there.

He wanted to tell me how little he thought of me? Well, two could play at that game.

Sure, I was the one with the entry-level job who couldn't exactly afford to get fired, but who was keeping track, anyway? Not me. I was willing to find out how much further I had to fall.

I finished cleaning the office, then continued on to the rest of the floor. When I got home, I showered, punched my pillow into submission, and glared at the wall, willing myself to fall asleep.

And I thought of him. The guy from the restaurant, who'd come back and sat in my section again. Vaughn. He was such a jerk.

And I'd...liked it?

After he'd left, I'd felt a little lighter. The annoying customers with their unrealistic demands hadn't bothered me quite so much. Some of the aggression I'd felt had dissipated.

At least he'd been good for something. I closed my eyes, wondering if I'd see him again, then caught myself. My eyes popped open again and I glared at the wall.

No. No, I didn't want to see him again. Sure, he was attractive and I enjoyed the way he gave as good as he got. But I'd learned my lesson with James. I was done with men. Especially the beautiful ones who lived in a different reality from me.

James had wanted me for my money. I knew that now. But I'd believed his pretty words about our future and our love. I'd been so starved of affection that I'd convinced myself it was real. I'd thrown my life away to declare my love for him, and it had turned out to be pathetically delusional and one-sided.

I was so, so ashamed.

We hadn't gotten physical until after I broke it off with Cole, because I'd asked my fiancé for the same courtesy and I had a *shred* of decency. But it had been an affair. I'd been engaged to a man I didn't love, and I'd poured my affection into the text messages and late-night phone calls and stolen dates at dive bars, hoping my friends and acquaintances wouldn't see me but secretly thrilled that they might. James and I kissed and pawed at each other, whispered in each other's ears.

And it had all been a lie.

Vaughn had money, so if he was interested in me—which he wasn't—he'd want me for something other than my parents' fortune, but he'd still want to use me and discard me. To remind me that I was small and weak and pathetic.

Both of them would toss me aside—or already had—as soon as I was no longer useful to them. Just like my parents had done.

I wouldn't put myself in that position again.

THE NEXT DAY was my day off from the restaurant. I woke up aching from head to toe, bleary-eyed and shivering. My blanket wasn't cutting it, and I knew I couldn't afford to put the heating up any higher (I'd learned this last winter, when I got an eye-popping bill that took me weeks to pay off).

What I could afford was an overpriced coffee and maybe a pastry from the café down the block. As a bonus, the café was warm, and it had comfy couches that might be vacant on a weekday like today. My feet hit the floorboards, and I shivered. I pulled some jeans and a long-sleeve top from my pile of laundry on the floor, then stared at the tangle of garments. They were work clothes mixed with a few of my favorite sweaters, all of which were starting to smell a little musty. And in a tiny studio apartment, with a kitchenette within arm's reach of the bed, there was no escaping musty. Ugh.

"Fine," I grumbled to myself, and I gathered the whole mess into my laundry basket and humped it to the basement so I could put a load on before getting my coffee.

I left my basket on top of the machine, then bundled myself up to face the elements and went outside. The espresso machine hissed as soon as I entered the café, then stopped to let me listen to the low murmur of conversation and the ambient music in the background. I got in line, ordered my coffee and a cinnamon apple braid, then scanned the space for somewhere to sit.

At one of the long purple sofas on the far side of the room sat a woman on her own. Black, industrial-style light fittings shone down from above her head. Her hair was piled high on her head, brown streaked through with highlights of blond. As I approached, I noticed her ears were adorned with dangles and studs all the way up the shell, and her lips, painted dark red, pursed as she frowned at her laptop screen.

"You mind?" I asked, pointing to the opposite side of the couch.

"Be my guest," she replied with a casual wave.

When my name was called, I got up to get my drink and came back, then moved to sink into the cushions—and bashed my foot against the table leg.

I yelped and stumbled, and my coffee cup wobbled on a saucer that clearly hadn't been designed for that specific mug. The clinking of ceramic on ceramic was the only warning I got before the tall, slender mug tipped and spilled all over me. I swore, grabbing the cup when only a sip of two of my drink remained. The rest of it stained the front of my clothing.

I stared at myself, and my shoulders dropped. A groan slipped through my lips. Tears prickled, and heat crawled up the back of my throat. I *hated* that. I didn't want to cry—not in public. Not over spilled hot milk.

The woman with the earrings leaned back on the sofa and looked at me. Sympathy shone through in her smile. "Tough morning?"

"Tough year," I replied.

"Let me buy you a new one. What are you drinking?"

"You don't have to do that—"

"I want to," she said, and smiled again. "I've had bad days where a tiny act of kindness would've made all the difference."

"Do I look that bad?" I said, forcing a laugh.

"Honey," she said, "you look awful." Her smile was bright, and it was impossible not to huff a laugh in response.

I relented. "It was a latte with half a pump of sugar-free vanilla syrup."

She smiled at me, got up, and came back a few minutes later with a drink for herself—and one for me. In the meantime, I dabbed my clothes and wiped my jacket off, and then I was able to sit semi-comfortably despite the stains.

At least I hadn't worn any of my good clothes.

When she handed me the new drink, I almost started crying. "Thank you," I said.

"I'm Deena."

"Alba," I replied, and we shook. She adorned her fingers with rings the way she did her ears—maximally. Three out of five fingers on each hand had at least one ring on it, a mix of gold and silver, some of them featuring semiprecious stones in bezel settings. Her clothes were easy and comfortable, and they looked like a mix of vintage and decently made basics.

She wouldn't have fit in with my previous social circle—too few designer labels—but she oozed style. I wished I'd put more effort into my appearance, but Deena didn't seem to mind.

"What are you working on?" I asked after taking a sip of my fresh latte.

She waved a hand. "Boring work stuff. I want to know why your year has been so terrible."

I groaned—and she laughed. My own lips curled into a smile, and I realized it was the first time in over a year that it had felt easy to talk to someone.

"I had a falling out with my family," I admitted, my throat

tightening even with that vague mention of what had happened. "They kind of...disowned me."

Her eyebrows shot up. "For real?"

I nodded.

"Ouch."

"The guy I was dating then dumped me, because apparently he was only with me for money and connections. Of which I now have none."

Deena leaned her elbow on the back of the couch and crossed her legs as she angled her body toward me. "I recently got dumped," she told me. "It wasn't anything serious, but it still hurt."

I ran my finger along the handle of my mug and stared at the drink Deena had bought me. Then I looked at her. "Why do guys suck so much?"

She snorted. "One of life's mysteries. Maybe one day I'll learn."

I grinned. "It's like this guy who came into the restaurant where I work yesterday. He totally got off on tormenting me."

Deena arched her brows, and I told her all about my interactions with Vaughn aka Cheap Suit. Then I found myself telling her about the crumpled ball of paper in the executive's office and was gratified when she laughed so hard tears formed in her eyes.

"And you just left it there?"

I nodded. "I haven't gotten any angry phone calls this morning, so I'm guessing he hasn't called to have me fired."

"I like you," she declared. "What are you doing this weekend?"

"Working, mostly."

"Well, we need to get together." Deena pulled out her phone and gave it to me, telling me to put my contact details in.

I felt...nervous. A shy smile kept teasing the corners of my lips, and it wasn't just the temperature in the coffee shop that made me feel slightly flushed.

I'd lost all my friends over the past year. Without money, I couldn't dress like them, or go to the same events as them, or meet them on impromptu international vacations. The friends I thought were close with me drifted away from me over the weeks that followed my parents' disownment. It was like my fall from grace was a communicable disease; they might end up poor if they spent too much time with me.

So, for the past year, I'd been largely isolated. Deena was the first person to actually treat me like a person who had value. I had coworkers, sure, but most of the time I was so clueless about how things worked that they treated me like the village idiot. I treated me like the village idiot. It was hard to feel confident when it felt like I'd been thrown on another planet and expected to know how to survive.

Deena was cool and confident and kind, and her offer of friendship made me feel like for the first time in a long time, I had something to lose. I *really* wanted to meet up with her again, if only to have someone to tell about my unprofessional antics.

We parted not long after. My laundry had been moved out of the washing machine and tossed into my laundry basket on top, which felt slightly violating, but what didn't feel slightly violating these days? It's like the whole world was designed to make me feel less than human.

I put the clothes in the dryer and went up to my apartment to make myself some food and grab a nap before my cleaning shift.

When I woke up, my clothes still weren't dry. I frowned, put some more money in the machine, and turned it on for another ninety minutes. The next time I checked them, same deal. Growling in frustration, I took my still-damp clothes, brought them back to my apartment, and laid them over every available piece of furniture before rushing to get ready in time for work.

And realized I hadn't made myself any food for dinner.

For the millionth time, my eyes prickled at the tiniest thing.

How did people do this? How did the majority of the population stay on top of everything that needed to be done?

I'd grown up with cleaners, nannies, gardeners, drivers, cooks, and assistants. There had always been a whole team of people ready to do all the things required to make life function, and sometimes I'd still found it hard.

Now I only had myself.

In a way it felt good; I'd learned just how much I could rely on myself in the past year. I'd figured it out. I'd survived...but I was exhausted. It was all the cooking and cleaning and rushing and work. I had to organize all my bills and utilities. Then I was supposed to work out, take care of my health (with what money?), and somehow form social connections?

Impossible.

By the time I made it to work, the glow of my interaction with Deena had faded. I was back to the reality of my daily grind. A sleek black sedan idled in front of the building's entrance, and I hid my grimace at the sight of it. I used to have a driver who would sit there waiting for me. Now I had a subway card, a hip that clicked, and feet that always ached. I swiped my after-hours access card and entered the building, trying not to think about all the things I'd left behind.

The elevator doors closed as I pressed the button for the forty-second floor, and I squared my shoulders to ready myself for another body-breaking shift.

FOUR
VAUGHN

IT WAS DARK OUTSIDE, and the building was quiet. I tried not to work late on weeks that I had Charlotte, but these days I couldn't seem to get away before her bedtime. Guilt tightened my throat as I checked the time. She'd be asleep by the time I got home. Again. I walked out of my office and pulled on my jacket, then called the elevator. I watched the little screens above the elevators and stood next to the one most likely to arrive first. While the far car zoomed up from the lobby, the doors in front of me opened.

The stress of the business was getting to me. I'd actually gone back to Carmine's like some sort of desperate stalker, wanting a hit of snark from my favorite waitress. Verbally sparring with her always made me feel better.

But she hadn't been there today, so my stress had only wound itself tighter.

I made it to the lobby, and my phone rang. It was Jim, and he delivered news I'd already predicted: "The Midtown job is hemorrhaging money," he told me. "Unless we turn it around, and quickly, nobody's going to touch us."

I grimaced. I could inject some cash into the company myself to get us through a rough patch, but that would be a red flag for any investor. I had to present a healthy company if I wanted access to bigger jobs.

"The subcontractor with the faulty equipment?" I asked.

"Legal has just sent them a breach of contract notice."

My grimace tightened. Just what every investor wanted—legal troubles. "Can we paper over the Midtown problems with some of the other jobs?"

"I'll find out. It isn't guaranteed to stand up to scrutiny, though. Especially not the people you're courting."

"All right. Thanks, Jim."

If I didn't fix these problems—and quickly—there would be no access to back rooms and politicians' ears. There would be no security. The company would stagnate, maybe even crumble. No one would want to hire us—we'd be radioactive after such a big and public failure.

Charlotte's future would hang in the balance, and I'd be the deadbeat who ruined it all.

Just like my own dad. The pattern I'd sworn I'd never repeat. I'd watch him gamble our family's money like a man with his eyes glued to the roulette wheel.

And here I was, repeating his mistakes. Promising my daughter the world and unable to deliver. Letting her nanny take care of her while I spent my evenings locked in my office. Maybe my ex-wife was right about me, after all.

As I reached the lobby doors and flipped the collar of my jacket up against the blast of cold wind, my driver jumped out of the car and moved to open the back door for me. I nodded to him and slipped inside.

The future seemed bleak, apart from three things:

First and most significant would be the sight of my daughter, safe and sleeping, when I got home this evening. That would heal almost everything.

Second, the cutting remarks that Alba would have for me when we next saw each other. I could fling harsh words back at her and watch the gratifying way her eyes would narrow. The perfect pressure release valve.

And third, the anticipation of whatever my snarky cleaning woman would do when she entered my office tonight and saw what I'd left for her.

FIVE
ALBA

THE BLACK SHOE tray gleamed with newness from its spot of honor next to the door. Two pairs of boots—cleaned of any remaining gravel and salt—sat in perfect alignment on top of the plastic tray. And in the corner closest to me, a note leaned against the steel toe of the nearest boot. It was addressed to "Ms. Cleaning Woman."

I scanned the room. The balled-up note that I'd written was gone. The desk was relatively tidy, with stacks of files lined up and a few square inches of desk showing in the gaps between them. There was a scent in the air—rich male cologne that made me want to inhale deeply—as if someone had only just left the room.

I hesitated on the threshold of the office, knowing I'd already overstepped with the first message I'd left here. I'd gotten carried away by the injustice of my life these days, the difficulty of scraping by.

But he hadn't demanded that I be fired.

And he'd bought a shoe tray.

Tiptoeing inside, I bent over and picked up the note:

Ms. Clean,

I trust this is a satisfactory solution to our mutual problem. Please refrain from leaving paper debris on my office floor.

Regards,

V.A.

My heart thumped. This was exactly like the hundred-dollar tips that Vaughn insisted on leaving me. A gift wrapped in disdain.

I gritted my teeth and scribbled my own words below his, then left the note in the middle of his desk.

Then I got back to work.

SIX
VAUGHN

THERE WAS a note when I got back to the office. Scrawled under mine, she'd written:

The tray was the least you could do. And I feel the need to remind you that the paper debris was not left on the floor by me.

I huffed a laugh. She had me there.

A few hours later, when I went out for lunch, a tingle of pleasure zipped through me at the sight of golden hair wrapped in a high bun. I unbuttoned my jacket and nodded to the hostess, who brought me to my favorite server's section.

When Alba saw me sitting at her table, she stopped dead. "Again?" she snapped. "Don't you have somewhere better to be?"

"Nice to see you too, princess," I replied.

The hostess's eyes bounced between the two of us, and then she slowly backed away.

My waitress cocked her hip and leaned her tray against it. "Let me guess. Chicken again? We all know how adventurous you are."

"I don't know," I said. "I might want one of the specials."

"Has anyone ever told you that you're unbearable?"

"Not recently, why?"

She rolled her eyes, and I watched the way the light played on her cheekbones, her clavicle, her hair. Some of the tightness between my shoulder blades eased, and I leaned back in my chair.

I knew, in some corner of my mind, that I was acting like an ass. I knew she probably just wanted to do her job, and I was antagonizing her. But everyone else in my life—other than my five-year-old daughter—tiptoed around me like they were afraid of me.

I liked Alba's sharp words and unimpressed looks. It brought me back down to earth. Reminded me of where I'd come from. It wasn't the oozing, slimy smile that men like Roger gave me. It wasn't the odd deference my employees seemed to adopt around me.

Her attitude was real and raw, and it made me feel like I was just a one-van contractor scraping by in the city again. I was nothing special, and neither was she, and that was just fine.

With a sharp smile, she rattled off the specials. Then she added, "No creepy bigwig to impress today?"

My own smile matched hers. "Just me."

"What happened? He decided you weren't worth the trouble and now you're sad that he hasn't opened the purse strings for you?" When my smile slipped, hers widened. "Oh, I'm right, aren't I? Ha!"

"I think I'll have the chicken," I said.

"Mm-hmm," she replied, grabbing the wine glasses I wouldn't use from the place setting in front of me.

I watched her move through the restaurant, gliding between tables and effortlessly charming the other patrons. She caught me watching a few times and scowled at me.

When she stopped at my table with my food, I couldn't help asking, "How did you guess?"

She blinked at me. "You've ordered the chicken every time, big guy. It wasn't rocket science."

"Not about the chicken. About the investor I was meeting with last time."

"Oh," she said breezily and waved a hand. "You didn't stand a chance. Enjoy your lunch!"

"Wait—" I said, but she was already gone.

I chewed and swallowed, but my mind wasn't on the food. When she stopped by a few minutes later with a saccharine sweet "How's everything tasting today?" I couldn't help setting my fork down and leaning forward. "What do you mean, I didn't stand a chance?"

"Oh, did I huwt your feewings?" She pouted, blinking big blue eyes at me.

Insolent woman. I wanted to put her over my knee. My cock throbbed, and I realized it wasn't just the pressure release valve of sparring with her that brought me back here, day after day. It was the fact that she made my blood thrum in a way nothing else had in a long, long time. I was no better than Roger, was I? "I want to know what you noticed," I insisted.

And I did. I had to have a gaping blind spot to have failed to snag an investor after all this time. I needed to know what it was. I needed to fix it, so I could shape the business—and my life— exactly how I planned.

Alba knew something I didn't. That was unacceptable.

She dropped the mock-sympathy act and shrugged. "He probably saw that polyester suit and four-in-hand tie knot and dismissed you before you even sat down. You look like a little boy playing dress-up. Then you declined to share that bottle of wine he ordered, and he decided to milk you for a free lunch."

I won't lie; I was offended. I leaned back in my chair and scowled at her. "What's wrong with my suit?"

The waitress looked me up and down, arched a brow, and shook her head. "If you have to ask, I'm not sure I can even help you."

And she walked away.

My suit? The wine? What the hell was she talking about?

I watched her disappear into the kitchen and looked down at the tag sewn into the side seam of my suit jacket. I pulled it across and squinted.

100% polyester. Well, damn.

Frowning, I picked up my knife and fork again to finish my lunch. When she came back with the bill, I met her gaze.

"Yes?" she asked, brow arched.

"Why was it a mistake not to order wine? I don't drink when I have to go back to work in the afternoon."

"That's very responsible of you, but it sent the message that you don't want to be part of his little club."

"'His little club?'"

"You know, the boys' club. You told him loud and clear that you won't play by his rules."

"I just don't like drinking during the day." Not when I had to work—and not since I'd become a father. I didn't like drinking in front of my daughter, and I'd vowed a long time ago that she'd never see me drunk. I'd watched my father buy bottles for men he tried to impress, watched him drink himself into a stupor whenever his latest business venture failed. I'd found it pathetic then, and I found it pathetic now. I wouldn't become him. "I don't see how that would have made him decide not to invest when he had the potential to make bags of money off me."

"Men like that don't only care about the money," she replied, and I knew it was true. After all, I didn't only care about the money. She went on: "They want to feel superior. It's why he hit on me. It's why his suit was probably bespoke, and his watch was worth forty thousand dollars. Everything he did was designed to make you and me feel inferior. Mostly you. I was just a bonus." She said it casually, like it was the most obvious thing in the world. Then she grabbed the billfold and peeked inside. She obviously saw the tip I'd left her, and for some reason she looked annoyed.

"Were you expecting something else?" I asked, nodding to the leather folder.

"I don't need your pity," she shot back.

"Of all the things I feel about you, pity isn't one of them."

She scoffed. "Oh yeah? What do you feel about me?"

"Annoyance, mostly." Sort of. Among other things.

"And yet you keep coming back."

"It's more fun than a punch in the face."

"High praise." She rolled her eyes.

I laughed. "I can take that back if you prefer," I said, nodding to the tip I'd left her.

She snapped the billfold closed. "No. You keep coming here every day just to piss me off." She lifted the leather folder. "This is the least you could do."

The words echoed through me, and I frowned. The cleaner had said the same thing in her note. Before I could answer, Alba had walked away.

I gathered my things and headed back to work. I'd only walked through my office door when Jim knocked on the jamb. "Can you talk?"

I gestured to one of the chairs in my office and took a seat behind my desk.

Jim, a tall, lanky man, stood behind the chair I'd gestured to. He pushed his wireframe glasses up the bridge of his nose before moving his hand to the back of the chair. "We just heard back from Arlo Noble. He's interested; he wants to meet."

"The solar panel guy?"

"Solar panels, early cell phone components, dabbles in conductor parts... Bit of everything."

"And he wants to get into construction?"

"He's got money to burn."

A flutter went through my chest, blood rushing to my extremities. Could this be it? The saving grace we'd been looking for? "Okay," I said, "let's set it up."

Jim patted the back of the chair and strode out. I stood, combing my fingers through my hair as I paced my office.

Arlo Noble was a big fish. After he'd sold his last company, he'd taken time to be with his family, but I'd heard he was looking for a new venture. He was the kind of guy who took big risks.

I was a big risk.

My assistant, Hillary, poked her head in. "Jim just told me about Arlo Noble. You want me to set up a meeting? Lunch at the usual place?"

I thought of Alba watching and silently judging the whole thing. "No," I said. "Somewhere new. Somewhere nice."

"Got it," Hillary said. "And Billie just called; she just picked Charlotte up from school, and Charlotte's running a low-grade fever."

I swore softly. "I'll work from home for the afternoon."

My assistant nodded and checked her tablet. "Nothing else is pressing."

I grabbed my things as Hillary went back to her desk. My

heart beat faster than usual. For the first time in a long, long time, I felt hope. I could *not* screw this up. I stepped out of my office door, then veered left toward Hillary's desk.

She looked up. "Yes?"

"My suit," I said, spreading my arms. "What do you think of it?"

"What do I think of it?"

"Yeah. Be honest."

Hillary tilted her head. She'd been with me since my contracting days, and I trusted her implicitly. Her pause told me that she was frantically trying to find a diplomatic way of telling me that my suit was awful.

"It's...okay," she said.

"Hillary."

"It could be better. The shoulders..."

I arched my brows.

"It doesn't really fit." She cringed. "You know?"

"No," I said. "I don't know. That's the problem." I tugged at the suit jacket, then straightened my tie. "Polyester," I said, looking at her. "Is polyester a problem?"

"I mean, it's not the most comfortable, that's for sure."

"Could you tell that this suit is made of polyester?"

"Yes..." she said, frowning. "Why?"

"Shit." I groaned, then pointed at her. "Find me a tailor. Or a suit store. Or... Where do I get a good suit?"

Hillary's shoulders eased down from her ears, and she smiled. "I'll send you some options this afternoon."

"Good," I said, and marched out the door.

SEVEN
ALBA

Ms. Clean,
   Please accept this tribute as a sincerest apology for
my previous transgressions.
   V.A.

I TOOK the little box of gold-wrapped chocolates between my
fingers, eyes narrowing. Sincere apology, or snarky gift?

Unwrapping one of the treats, I took a seat at Mr. Big Shot's
desk. I kicked my feet up on his desk as I bit into the chocolate,
gooey caramel dragging out the other half as I pulled it away from
my lips. Delicious.

I uncapped his pen as I chewed the second half of the chocolate and scribbled my response:

Tribute accepted.

The sugar hit got me through the shift, but I still woke up the next day with an aching body that had to be forced to do the mounting list of chores before being dragged into the restaurant in too little time.

So maybe I was a little snippy when a familiar broad-shouldered man sat down in my section and opened the menu like he was going to order something other than the chicken breast.

"The specials are the same as last time you were in," I said in way of greeting.

"Hello to you too, princess."

"Please don't call me that."

"How about sunshine? Because of your disposition, you see."

"Har har. How about you call me nothing?"

He grinned. "Chipper as always, huh. So the first few times weren't a fluke."

"And yet here you are."

He tilted his head. "You seem more irritable than usual though. Is everything okay?"

I'd had a terrible morning. There didn't seem to be enough time to get through all the drudgery, let alone leisure or recuperation. My resolve had slipped while I ate breakfast, and I'd thumbed through the society pages of online magazines to look at all the people I no longer associated with. I'd seen photos of my mother at a charity auction, dressed in Valentino, smiling with her paddle in her hand. She'd bought artwork for the Hamptons house, apparently, which meant she was redecorating it again. Good for her.

And then my clothes had been damp, and they'd frozen hard on my way to work. The heat of the kitchens had thawed them again, but they hadn't dried.

My life could be summarized into one word: discomfort. Maybe the sincerity of Vaughn's question is what made me slip up and tell him a partial truth: "Everything's fine, except that my building's dryers don't seem to be working properly so now I'm stuck working in damp clothes for the next six hours." I smiled at the man who seemed to want to contribute to the discomfort whenever he could. "But now you're here, so at least everything is a little bit worse."

He laughed. It was a rich, warm sound that made a tingle go through my stomach. I liked making him laugh—except, no. He was the worst. I didn't like him at all. A scowl drew my brows low, my fingers tightening around my tray.

I didn't want to like the man. He represented everything I hated. He reminded me so much of James, in that there was something magnetic about him. Everyone in the room glanced at him at some time or another. When he walked in, people noticed.

He wasn't the top dog—yet—but he had that special something that turned heads. Not just his good looks; it was his bearing, his ice-blue gaze that seemed to pierce through you, his confidence. If he got clothing that actually fit him properly, he would be unstoppable.

And I would still be here, serving him chicken breast for lunch, looking at photos of a life I didn't want anymore but couldn't seem to forget.

"Damp clothes," he mused, wrinkling his nose. "That's unfortunate. I won't ask you if you cleared the lint trap," he said, like we were sharing some kind of joke.

My brows tugged together. "The what now?"

He blinked at me. "The lint trap."

"Oh." I chuckled. "Right."

"You know what a lint trap is, don't you?"

"Yeah, sure," I answered, waving a hand. "It traps lint."

53

"Yeah."

"Yeah." I smiled brightly, dying inside.

This was something else I'd discovered over the course of the past fourteen months. There were countless things that I didn't know. Obvious, normal things. Things that were second nature to most people—things that made me feel like a bumbling fool who was too dumb to make it through a day unaided.

I had no fucking clue what a lint trap was, nor did I know how it related to my clothes.

But I'd be damned if I ever let him see it. I pivoted to asking him if he wanted the chicken, and he handed me the menu with a nod. I scurried away, my chest hot, my cheeks burning.

Ducking into the staff room, I pulled out my phone and Googled "lint trap."

Within a fraction of a second, I learned that apparently you were supposed to be cleaning this thing out with every single load of laundry. Major fire hazard. Freaking wonderful.

At least I hadn't burned my building down.

Sighing, I leaned my phone against my thigh and lightly bashed my head against the wall.

"Hey, Alba!" Daisy, one of the other waitresses, said as she walked in, smelling of the outdoors with patches of bright red on her cheeks.

I faced her and held up my phone. "Do you know what a lint trap is?"

She unzipped her jacket and hung her purse up in one of the empty lockers. "Like, in a dryer?"

"Yeah. Never mind." I put my phone away and shoved my embarrassment deep down, then squared my shoulders and went back out into the fray.

Vaughn's food was ready, so I grabbed it from the expo and brought it to his table. That stiff smile was in place on my face, and

I said my usual, "Did you need anything else?" before turning away.

"Alba," he said, and the sound of my name on his tongue froze me in my tracks.

I turned, still feeling the burn of my embarrassment, and smiled at him. "Yes?"

"Other than my suit and the wine, what else did I do wrong?"

"Sorry?"

"The other day. My business meeting. What else did I screw up?"

I shrugged. "How am I supposed to know?"

"Don't give me that," he snapped, and the command in his voice made all my nerve endings sizzle.

I reared back. "Excuse me?"

"You knew about the suit. My assistant agreed, by the way."

"Well, duh." What was he getting at?

"So, tell me. I have another meeting coming up, and I don't want to get dismissed before I even open my mouth to make my pitch."

I rocked back on my heels. "Are you being serious right now? You really want my advice?" The girl who didn't even know that lint traps existed or that they needed to be cleaned? He was asking *me* what I thought?

That hadn't happened in...way longer than fourteen months.

"Alba," he cajoled. "Come on. Be brutal. I know you want to be."

I huffed a laugh despite myself, then shifted my weight and bit my lip. "Well..."

"You won't hurt my feelings."

"Your hair," I said.

Vaughn's brows slammed down. "What's wrong with my hair?" he demanded.

I laughed, and the outrage on his face grew. I held up my hands to stop him, and I said, "The cut is just a little...rough around the edges."

He stared at me for a moment, then glared out the window. "My hair."

"You have a nice, thick head of hair," I added, not wanting to be *too* harsh. "It's just a little scruffy looking."

A long sigh slipped through Vaughn's lips, then he met my gaze again. "All right. The suit, the hair, the wine. What else?"

"Well, it depends on the person, but I got the sense that you launched into business way too soon. I was pouring you guys glasses of water for the first time, and you were already telling him about project pipeline projections, or whatever." I waved a hand.

"It was a business lunch," he growled. "I was talking business."

"The man ordered a three-hundred-dollar bottle of Italian wine. He clearly wanted to be wooed."

Vaughn rubbed his chin with his finger, his gaze falling to the table. "I misread him," he said.

"I think so."

"And you think my clothes would have made a difference?"

I shrugged. "They would've stopped you from being dismissed in the first five seconds."

It was a sad but true fact of the elite world into which he was trying to break. You had to look right, and act right, and talk right. Only then would you be taken seriously. That either meant expensive designer clothing, custom pieces, or unbranded clothing that was tailored to perfection. Once you were in, you were allowed to engage.

"So, my hair," Vaughn said, lifting his head to look at me. "What would you change?"

Before I knew what I was doing, I reached over and ran my fingers through his strands. By the time I realized I was touching him, all I could do was brazen it out by acting casual and tugging at his hair slightly. He grunted in response, his head tilting toward me.

The noise sent a wash of heat through me, a tingle that started in my chest and moved down between my thighs. I dropped my hand to my side and took a step back. "A little off the sides. And maybe"—I let out a theatrical gasp—"some styling products."

Vaughn's eyes were pale and blue and intense, his throat bobbing as he swallowed. My heartbeat thrummed, and I hoped the heat crawling up my cheeks wasn't accompanied by redness. He couldn't know how much touching him had affected me.

He leaned back in his chair. "I've been cutting my own hair since I was sixteen."

"Yeah. Don't do that anymore," I said.

His smile was wry, and I couldn't help flashing one of my own in response.

For the first time, my grin was genuine. Our gazes lingered on each other, and then I cleared my throat and turned away to keep doing my job.

Mr. Big Shot,
    Your desk chair squeaks when it tilts back. I've taken the liberty of oiling the mechanism.
    C.W.

Ms. Clean,

Sitting in another's office chair is bad manners. Shouldn't you be scrubbing the carpet?

V.A.

I WAS WORKING evening shifts on Saturday and Sunday at the restaurant (I only cleaned the offices during the week), so I agreed to meet up with Deena for brunch on Saturday. The extra tips I'd gotten at work this week were a big help; I wouldn't be able to afford to eat out without Vaughn's passive aggressive tipping strategy. I begrudgingly thanked him in my head, then opened my closet and turned to the section of clothing that I hadn't worn in months.

Clothing from my old life.

My fingers lingered on the fine fabrics, the delicate details, the solid stitching. The closures of one shirt caught my eye; I'd never noticed the golden sheen on the pearlescent buttons. I'd worn these clothes without a thought, without worrying about threads snagging or oil splashing. All of it had been replaceable. Not anymore.

But Deena was stylish, and despite myself, I wanted to feel pretty. I wanted her to notice my clothing and compliment me. It was shallow and vain, but I hadn't had the luxury of dressing nicely in so long that I couldn't resist the urge. I chose a pair of navy wide-leg trousers and a cream knit silk turtleneck. My hands trembled slightly as I clasped one of the necklaces that I used to wear daily, a thin gold chain with a cluster of diamonds as a pendant.

I'd styled my hair in waves, and when I stepped back to look in the mirror, I hardly recognized myself. It felt like I was playing dress-up with someone else's closet.

In a lot of ways, I supposed I was.

I grabbed my bag and jacket and headed out the door. When I got to the brunch restaurant, Deena was already waiting. She put her phone away when she saw me and greeted me with a smile and a hug.

"You look amazing!"

I ran my fingers over my pants' legs and gave her a smile. "So do you, as usual!"

Deena wore layers of cream fabric, all different shades, draped over her body like she'd just decided to go to JoAnn's and throw on a half dozen bolts of fabric. An oversized wool coat rested on the back of her chair. Her earrings were dramatic dangles. She looked fabulous, and not because she'd walked into the Gucci store on Fifth Avenue and dropped the equivalent of a median salary on her outfit. She looked better than that.

We sat down and ordered mimosas. I learned that Deena worked as a freelance travel agent and had found a niche organizing flights for corporate clients. It was wildly impressive to me that she had her own business and that she'd built it herself—from nothing. I could hardly understand how someone would start something like that, let alone make a success of it. I was embarrassed to tell her that I was a waitress and a cleaner, that I was barely scraping by.

She didn't ask me about my family, about the disownment I'd alluded to the first time we met. I appreciated her tact.

Our food came, and I made a point to notice our server. She was an older woman with short hair and a kind smile. Someone I wouldn't have even seen two years ago. Not because I didn't come to brunch restaurants, but because she wouldn't have even registered to me. I'd been a horribly self-centered person. I wanted to be better.

"You okay?"

I blinked and turned back to Deena. "I'm good," I answered, trying to smile.

"Your expression changed just then."

I took a breath, intending to brush her off, and then reconsidered. Deena was the first person to befriend me in a long time. She hadn't judged me when I'd spilled coffee all over myself, or when I told her what I did for work. If she judged me for who I used to be, maybe we weren't meant to be friends.

So I admitted, "I was just thinking about a couple of years ago, how I wouldn't have even noticed a server coming to my table at a restaurant. Not as...as a real person."

Deena nodded. "I see."

"Sometimes..." I tried to snort, to play it off like a joke. "Sometimes I think my current life is some sort of karma for growing up rich. I'm struggling in exact proportion to the privilege I never acknowledged."

"Or maybe it's just another chapter. It's a challenge for right now, and all you can do is see it through. Maybe even make the best of it."

"Are you one of those 'everything happens for a reason' people?" I asked, skeptical.

Deena laughed. "Maybe. Mostly I don't believe in karma. There are way too many rich assholes who die as rich assholes for your suffering to be some sort of karmic justice."

Oddly comforted, I tucked into my food. By the time our lunch was over, I felt lighter. I went to work and pretended I wasn't disappointed when Vaughn never came in. But why would he? He never came in for dinner, and he didn't eat here on the weekends.

I threw myself into work, and by the end of the night, was surprised with the amount of money I made in tips. Even Elena came up to me and told me I'd done a good job.

When I left the restaurant, it was dark out—but I felt better than I had in a long time. I slept like the dead, and I woke up thinking the light was a little brighter than it had been before.

EIGHT
VAUGHN

CHARLOTTE HAD RECOVERED from her fever and woke me up on Saturday by jumping on top of me in bed. "Wake up!" she screamed, lips approximately a quarter inch from my ear.

Groaning, I rolled onto my side and caught her in my arms. She squealed and giggled as I tickled her, and then I planted a kiss on the side of her head and lay back on my pillows. "I need your help with something today, turkey."

Charlotte flopped down with her head next to mine on my pillow. She petted my face and smiled. "Okay. With what?"

"I need a new suit, and I need a haircut. Maybe you can help me decide what to get."

My daughter sat up, intrigued. "I can help you."

"Good. Now it's time to get up."

Our Saturday morning tradition—when I wasn't at work—was pancakes and bacon in our pajamas. I served it up on her favorite plate, then sat down across from her with my own breakfast. Billie had arrived midway through the pancake making and was sitting next to Charlotte at the table.

"The barber will be here in an hour, and then we'll be visiting the tailor," I told Charlotte before biting into a strip of bacon. "You can help me decide what color suit to get."

"Blue!" my daughter decreed. "To match your eyes. And mine." She opened hers wide and looked at me, then at Billie. "See?"

I huffed a laugh. "All right."

An hour later, the doorbell rang, startling me from an email-induced trance. I glanced over at my daughter, who was playing with dolls by herself close by, and tried to squash the guilt that sprouted. I had so little time with her; I had to stop working during it.

We both glanced up when Billie appeared, two men in tow. The barbers I'd hired to make a house call. A man with a full beard and a sharp haircut entered with another, shorter guy, and I directed them to the second living area on the ground floor. They set up their gear, and I sat down in front of a tall mirror in a chair they'd carried in.

Charlotte hovered around us, bouncing from one leg to another. "What are you going to do? Are you going to shave it like usual?"

I glanced at the barber, brows arched.

He shook his head. "We'll do a fade on the sides and keep your length on top," he said, running his fingers through my hair to check the length. "We can grow this out and go for a more textured cut in a few months."

His touch was professional, but it reminded me of the last time someone had run their fingers through my hair. When Alba had reached over to touch my head, a bolt of lightning had gone through me. She'd tugged at my hair and then dropped her hand, and my entire body had buzzed for an hour afterward.

The logical thing to do was to stay away from her. The last

thing I needed right now was a distraction. Between meetings with potential investors, my daughter, and the mountain of work required to keep my businesses going, I didn't have time to add a woman to the mix.

But logic wasn't driving my new lunchtime ritual. Every day, I woke up with an itch under my skin that only seemed to ease when her eyes landed on me and rolled. In a world of work and teetering business empires and over-budget projects and sick five-year-olds and custody drop-offs, Alba was a simple, bright spot in an otherwise drab week. Could anyone blame me for wanting more?

Besides, she was the one who'd pointed out my hair—and when the barber revealed my fresh cut in the mirror, I had to admit that she was right. I angled my head from side to side to have a better look and couldn't help the smile that curved my lips. He'd shaved my beard as well, and the line of my stubble defined my jaw.

I looked good.

Charlotte threw herself at my legs and beamed at me. "Daddy! You look so handsome!"

I laughed and ran a hand over her little head, feeling the soft, fine strands of her brown hair. "Thanks, turkey."

"Are we going to get you a new suit now?" she asked, big blue eyes shining with excitement.

"Let's go," I told her. She ran out to go find Billie, and I shook the barber's hand.

"Same time next week?" he asked.

"Can you come to my office during the week? I like to keep my weekends free for my daughter." Or I tried to, when work wasn't as crazy as it was now.

"No problem," the barber replied. "I'll talk to Hillary and set up a time."

I saw them out and then caught my reflection in the foyer mirror. Alba was right. I'd looked scruffy and unkempt before. It worked fine when I was a contractor, walking around dirty construction sites all day long—but I was a business owner now. If I wanted to attract big money from investors, I needed to look the part.

We took a cab to the tailor. The front of the shop was fairly unassuming, with gold lettering on the window and green trim around the door. But the inside oozed style. Bolts of fabric lined one wall, with the other dominated by various suits, shirts, and silk ties.

Even from a distance, I could tell there was no polyester in the building. The tailor, Mr. Koval, looked up when we entered, and nodded. "Mr. Avery," he said. "Right this way."

He was a short man with salt-and-pepper hair that was combed back from his face. He had a slight Eastern European accent and wore a measuring tape draped around his neck. Charlotte's eyes were big as saucers, and she darted to the side of the room to touch one of the suit jacket's sleeves. "I like this one," she told me in her version of a whisper, which wasn't much quieter than her speaking voice.

Mr. Koval led us to the back room, then he gestured to the dais in the middle of the space and began measuring me. "You need the suit for Monday, yes?"

"Yes. Monday morning if possible."

"No problem," he said, taking meticulous notes in a tiny notebook. Then he looked up and speared my daughter with a look. She sat back on her chair next to Billie, looking nervous. "You," Mr. Koval said, and Charlotte leaned farther back, as if she wanted to get away from him. "Show me the jacket you liked."

Charlotte looked at me. I nodded. My daughter slithered out of her chair, and I watched her and Mr. Koval go through to the front room, where she pointed out the navy jacket she'd shown me on the way in.

The tailor grabbed the coat hanger on which it was draped and gestured for Charlotte to head to the back room again. She rushed back to her seat, where Billie smiled at her.

"Your daughter has good taste," Mr. Koval announced, entering behind her. "This is good fabric for an everyday suit. Plain weave wool, soft touch. Feel." He presented a sleeve for me to touch, and I did, nodding.

"It's nice," I said, not really knowing what I was supposed to say.

I was way out of my element here, but I didn't hate it. Mr. Koval recommended a similar wool for my new suit, and he let Charlotte choose the color from a selection of fabric bolts on the wall. When she chose a dark navy, he gave her a solemn nod—but I saw the twinkle in his eyes. He liked children, and I appreciated him including my daughter.

"Come back tomorrow for a fitting, same time," he told us, then waved us away.

We walked to a nearby coffee shop and Charlotte bounced next to me, her cheeks red in the January cold. "That was fun!" she announced. "You're going to look so handsome, Daddy."

I put my arm around her shoulders and smiled. "I hope so."

THE NEXT DAY, I went in for a fitting. It was mostly me standing on the dais while Mr. Koval grunted and scowled at me, moving pins around and making notes.

"Tomorrow, I deliver," he said, then made a shooing motion toward the door.

And deliver, he did.

I got into the office around noon, after a long visit to the Midtown construction site, and found a garment bag hanging on a hook behind my desk.

Hillary poked her head in and smiled. "Nice hair," she said, then nodded to the garment bag. "And that looks nice too. I've emailed you notes about Arlo Noble ahead of your meeting this afternoon."

"Thanks, Hillary," I said, eyes on the bag. I closed the door to my office and kicked off my boots.

Then I looked down at the carpet and swore. I'd forgotten to brush them off again. I quickly put them on the shoe tray next to the door and scanned my desk. Nothing from my snarky cleaning woman—until I pulled back my desk chair and found a gold wrapper right in the middle of the seat. One of the wrappers from the chocolates I'd given her. That's what she thought of me chastising her for sitting in my chair. I laughed, delighted.

It reminded me of Alba, snarky and resentful as she dropped my food off, lobbing advice over her shoulder like it was nothing.

I glanced at the garment bag—a suit bought on her advice. Unzipping the bag, I touched the navy fabric inside, begrudgingly admitting that it felt a lot nicer than the suits I already owned. I hadn't known wool could be this soft.

I changed in the private bathroom attached to my office, then stared at myself in the mirror. Almost without my conscious input, my shoulders rolled back and I stood straighter. I hardly recognized the man looking back at me. I looked broader, more imposing. Even the crinkles around my eyes looked less obvious. I looked like I belonged in some fancy boardroom in a skyscraper.

I caught myself at the thought.

I was already in a skyscraper, and much of my day was spent in a boardroom. So why did it feel so weird to finally look the part?

Mr. Koval had thrown in a free tie with the suit, which was

nice of him, except for the fact that his suit cost more than what I would've considered a reasonable mortgage payment before I made it big. The tie was dark navy as well, with black thread forming a subtle pattern. I wrapped it around my neck and started to tie it—then stopped.

The four-in-hand tie knot was unacceptable, according to a certain opinionated waitress. But she hadn't told me what tie knot I was supposed to use.

I checked my watch. I had time to spare.

I grabbed my jacket and left the office.

NINE

ALBA

MY DAY HAD STARTED off on a bad foot. I'd finally got the dryer in the basement working and had done another load of laundry, only to discover that the beautiful silk turtleneck I'd worn to meet with Deena was now the size of a doll's.

I won't lie; I cried when I pulled it out of the dryer. I cried real tears, because the top had been one of my favorites and now it was ruined—and also because I felt stupid and useless and foolish. Bested by a load of laundry—*again*. How useless could one woman be? There was no way I could afford to replace it, which made me sob harder, but then I had to wash my face and get ready for work.

When Elena had asked me why I looked so sad, I told her about the top, and she looked at me like I was the stupidest person in the universe. She asked if it was dry clean only, and then I had to admit that I'd never understood what people meant when they talked about dry cleaning, and then she'd given me that look that I'd become accustomed to—the one that showed me just how little everyone really thought of me.

Coming from Elena, who was the very definition of competence, it hurt.

But how was I supposed to know laundry had so many freaking *rules*? Every time I learned a new one, I messed something else up. My entire life, I'd put clothes in a hamper and they'd magically appeared in my closet the next day, clean and pressed. I hadn't known to separate colors, to dry things flat, to freaking dry clean. What did that even mean? I still didn't know!

I'd been so sheltered and so naive, and now I could barely function in the real world.

Then at the restaurant, we'd been slammed from the moment the doors opened, and the kitchen had run behind. Customers were irate, and I'd gotten the brunt of their anger. I'd clung to my cheery, dumbed-down waitress persona with the force of my will, but when the fifth person complained that their food had taken too long and that I must be the worst server they'd ever had, I nearly lost it.

Was it worth going back to my family on my knees? Was it worth the groveling I'd have to do for the rest of my life if I did?

No.

I wouldn't be sold off to some other man in a pseudo-business deal. I wouldn't let my family push me into a marriage because that's what worked for them. I wouldn't get on my knees and beg for their protection after what they'd said and done to me.

Now that I'd spent some time away from that world, it was too easy to see how vapid and soulless it really was. What if I met another James and fell in love, only to discover that he was after my family's money again? What if I *didn't* meet another James, and I lived my life in a gilded cage, feeling nothing but bitterness?

It wasn't worth the risk. At least here, sweating through my uniform and praying for the end of my shift, I had integrity. For once, I was proud of the person I was becoming.

Now it was just after noon, and things weren't looking like they'd slow down anytime soon—but an old lady had given me a sympathetic smile and a fifty percent tip, and that had given me the energy to keep going a little bit longer.

I was aching and stressed and I'd just realized that I forgot to put deodorant on that morning—and then I saw him. At first, all I saw was a vision in a perfectly tailored suit. Silhouetted by the light behind him, he was broad-shouldered, sharp-jawed, all male confidence with a cocky smirk.

Then the smirk registered, and I stumbled.

Vaughn spread his arms when he saw me. "Better?"

"Um," I said, catching myself against the hostess's stand. "Yes."

He twirled for me, slowly, so I could see every perfect seam on his suit and admire the sharp-as-a-blade line of his haircut against his neck. He looked *amazing*. He looked like he had money and time and could get anything he wanted with a snap of his fingers.

My heart thumped as he spun back around to grin at me, blue eyes twinkling in the warm light of the dining room. I gripped the hostess's stand a bit harder to keep my balance. He smoothed the lapels of his jacket, and my gaze snagged on his hands. They were big, with prominent knuckles and long fingers, tendons and veins pushing against his skin as he adjusted the quality fabric of his suit. Small scars crisscrossed his fingers, his palms like he'd spent years working with his hands and had the wounds to show for it.

A man's hands. The kind I'd love to see gripping my thighs, spreading them open. I blinked away the image and focused on the man before me.

Vaughn was gorgeous.

I'd known he was an attractive man, obviously. From the moment I'd seen him the first time, I could tell he was handsome. But dressed like he was, there was no denying it. He was other-worldly. He could walk into any room and turn heads. He would have women and men staring, and if he played his cards right, he could get them to do anything for him.

Finding an investor would be a breeze if he acted like he belonged in the clothes he now wore.

"It's wool," he said, extending his sleeve toward me.

I let out a laugh that sounded a little high-pitched. "I can see that," I replied, and reached over to feel the fine fabric between my fingers. The lining was silk, and it teased my fingertips. The wool was buttery-soft, its weave perfectly uniform. The shoulders sat at just the right position on his frame, and the jacket showed off his trim waist.

Suddenly my throat was tight. Vaughn stood in front of me, broad and handsome and smiling, and I felt very small. The weight of his gaze made me want to crumple.

I wasn't the kind of woman who stood beside a man like that. Not anymore. Maybe in my previous life, I could've wrapped a hand around his elbow and entered the rooms he was sure to be invited into. The galas and charity balls, the boardrooms and private dining affairs. The private jets and secluded beachfront properties.

Now I belonged nowhere near any of those places. I belonged right here, sweating through my work uniform, wondering if it was worth selling my soul to get a bit of comfort back.

"Did you come here to show off?" I asked, recovering myself and taking a small step back.

He looked almost sheepish when he pulled a tie out of his jacket pocket. "Actually..."

I crossed my arms and popped a brow.

He flashed that grin at me again. The wicked, teasing one. His beard had been shaped to emphasize the strength of his jaw, and somehow it made his eyes seem more piercing. My knees wobbled a little. "You said my tie-tying skills weren't up to scratch, so I was hoping you could help me out."

"You came to my workplace in the middle of my shift so I could tie your tie?"

He shrugged, unfurling the tie and letting it dangle between us. An invitation. A trap.

The smart thing to do was to stay away from him. He was a reminder of everything I hated—the luxurious, expensive world that had thrown me out. But I'd discovered, over these past fourteen months, that I wasn't exactly as smart as I'd once thought. All it took was one handsome man's attention to lure me back in.

I took the tie between my fingers and was unsurprised to find it was made from the softest silk. Squinting up at him, I felt the need to put up walls between us. "You realize we aren't friends, right?"

He shrugged, nonplussed. "You're the only person who had the balls to tell me why I wasn't getting any joy with investors."

I tilted my head to concede the point, then gestured for him to approach. My fingers shook slightly as I fastened the last button on his shirt—a beautiful, thick shirt with a button that slid through its hole with ease—and tried to ignore the thumping of my heart. I could feel the warmth of him this close, and the press of his gaze above me was a physical weight. My knuckles brushed against his freshly shorn stubble, the rasp sending little bolts of sensation through my fingers.

He smelled divine. The scent twigged in my memory, but I couldn't place it. His cologne was rich and woodsy, utterly male. I inhaled, and immediately felt weak in the knees. It was the first time I'd been this close to a man since James. The sounds of people eating and talking and laughing faded to nothing in the crowded dining room behind me. All I could hear was the rushing of the blood in my ears.

He was tall and broad and male. He was beautiful—and he was staring at me. It wasn't the first time an attractive man had looked at me, but it *was* the first time since my ousting from society. Sure, patrons at the restaurant sometimes harassed me, but that was a power play more than anything. No one had looked at me and seen me the way it felt like Vaughn was seeing me now.

Like I was worth something. Like he wanted to know more.

I wrapped the tie around his neck and focused on the movement of my fingers against the silk fabric, going for a full Windsor knot. My mother had taught me how to tie a tie. She used to do it for my father before one of their many social events. It felt strange to be doing this for a man. It was intimate—and it wasn't.

This wasn't my husband, standing before me while we got ready to go to some ball or another. It wasn't a man who would bend down and press a soft kiss on my lips once I was done, his eyes promising more later. This was a man I'd verbally sparred with a handful of times at work. He enjoyed having a consistent routine, eating chicken, and annoying me. It wasn't some grand romance for the ages.

Soon, when he fully embodied his new look, he'd realize he could have whatever he wanted. He'd buy a dozen more suits and he'd find someone else to tie his ties.

And I'd be here, serving him chicken for lunch.

Unless I crawled on my hands and knees back into the family fold.

Vaughn watched me, and when I tightened the knot and smoothed his tie, he adjusted his cuffs and spread his palms again. "How do I look?"

He looked incredible. Unbearably handsome. Devastating.

I squinted. "It's better," I admitted. "The hair is nice."

The grin he flashed me made my stomach clench. "Wish me luck."

"You don't need luck," I told him, and couldn't resist the urge to lean over and pluck a piece of lint off his shoulder. Vaughn stood very still as I brushed it off and straightened his lapel. I looked up at him and stepped back. "All you need is to act like you belong."

"That's it, huh."

I shrugged, smiling sadly. "You look the part now. Assuming your company is worth investing in, then all you have to do is act like that investment is coming, one way or another. Someone will bite."

"Would you?" His lips curled, eyes flashing with dark amusement.

My heart rattled, heat rushing up my neck and over my cheeks. "Only if you were very, very lucky," I shot back before I could stop myself.

His smile widened, and then he winked and gave me a little two-fingered salute before turning for the door.

When I faced the dining room again, Elena was frowning at me from the kitchen door. I lifted a hand to wave at her, then scurried to my tables to check on the patrons. My steps were unsteady, and my heart still thumped.

I didn't know what to think. I didn't know what it meant, that he'd come here. That he'd taken my advice. That he'd wanted me to tie his tie and see him looking like that.

I didn't know what to think about the fact that I'd liked it. A lot.

All I knew was that it was bad. It made me look up from the drudgery of my life and think about maybe, someday, somehow... wanting more. It made me remember what it felt like to be wanted.

I'd been tossed aside like garbage. Shunned. Treated like I was worthless. I'd been in a daze my entire life, conditioned to think I was chattel that could be married off to the most suitable man.

Then it fell apart, and I realized how alone and vulnerable I really was. The past fourteen months had been cold, hard, and hungry.

Vaughn made me feel warm and buzzing and pathetic because I wanted this all the time. I wanted him to look at me and smile at me and touch me and kiss me and fuck me until I felt alive again.

I felt raw and exposed for wanting those things.

I could never, ever let him know.

TEN

VAUGHN

ARLO NOBLE WAS a broad-shouldered man with a thick head of salt-and-pepper hair. He greeted me with a firm handshake before we sat down across from each other. The crisp white tablecloth brushed my knees as I took my seat, the glassware on the table shining under the multitude of chandeliers in the space.

Hillary had chosen well. The Italian restaurant was formal enough without being stuffy. The staff wore crisp, clean uniforms, and the kitchen was visible from the dining room through a long rectangular opening. The movements and voices of the cooks provided a counterpoint to the clinking of dishes and murmur of low conversation.

When the waitress asked about drinks, Arlo ordered sparkling water for the table, and I breathed a sigh of relief. I hadn't been looking forward to nursing a drink when I had to go back to work later. The waitress left, and Arlo faced me.

"Thank you for meeting with me," I started.

"Of course. I'm always willing to listen to an intriguing business proposition." He smiled, and I saw a shark in his eyes.

Nerves gripped me. Here was a man who'd started and sold half a dozen companies. He was a visionary. I was just a contractor who'd traded his steel-toed boots for shiny leather shoes, pretending to belong in the boardroom I rented on the forty-second floor of a building that never felt quite comfortable.

Money poured in from my various ventures, but it still felt fake. I still wondered if it would crumble away to nothing one day, the way it always had in my childhood.

Then I remembered Alba's words. *All you have to do is act like that investment is coming, one way or another. Someone will bite.*

She'd been right about the suit; there was a marked difference in the way the maître d' had spoken to me, the way doormen stood straighter when I walked in, the way a few women's heads had turned when I strode down the street.

It made me feel slightly sick. I remembered my father donning his one nice suit before any big business meeting, my mother fussing over him as he promised that *this time*, things would work out. *This time*, his ship would come in. We'd be rich, and all our troubles would go away.

But *this time* never came—not until I made it happen for myself.

Now I was dressing like him. Dressing better than him, truthfully, and people were treating me like I was somehow superior to the man I'd been before. I didn't like it. It felt like a lie. It felt like everything I'd resented about my father, tailored to fit my frame.

It hadn't felt like a lie when Alba looked at me. I'd seen her stumble and been darkly satisfied. I'd watched her watch me, and I'd felt the air between us spark. Then her fingers had brushed my throat as she'd buttoned my shirt and tied my tie. Her breath had ghosted across my jaw, and I'd curled my hands into fists to stop myself from resting them on her hips.

I refocused on the man across from me. He watched me with

dark brown eyes, leaning back in his chair, looking at ease as he studied me.

"The growth of your business has been impressive," Arlo said. "Fifteen years ago, you decided to expand your steady, successful one-man-van operation. And the last five years have been meteoric."

My instinct was to jump into the numbers, to try to convince Arlo with logic that my company was worth his time and money, but Alba's words still echoed in my head. If this were a done deal, what would I say?

I'd tell him the truth, I realized.

So that's what I did: "Fifteen years ago, my father died, and I realized I didn't want to end up like him," I told Arlo. "And five years ago, my daughter was born, and I realized I'd do anything for her."

Arlo hummed, head tilting. "When Will, my son, was born, it changed my entire worldview. Everything I did took on a new meaning. Then I had my daughter Becca, and everything changed again."

I nodded, immediately calmer. "It's not just a business anymore. It's her college fund and her safety net. It's everything I was never able to have as a kid."

"The last five years of your growth makes more sense now," Arlo mused. "I wondered what had changed."

"We were aggressive," I conceded. "And with another set of eyes—someone who sees business and growth and gets excited—I think we could go even further."

Arlo smiled, but he didn't have a chance to respond. The waitress appeared to take our orders, and we settled into a more casual conversation. I let him circle back to business, remembering what Alba had said about my meeting with Roger. When our meal was done, Arlo set his glass of sparkling water aside and looked at me.

"I'm interested," he said bluntly, "but I need time to review your financials. I'd also like to make sure that our values align."

"Of course."

"My foundation is having a charity gala in a few weeks. We're holding it early this year, at the beginning of March—venue problems." He flicked a hand. "I'll have my assistant send you the details. We still have a table or two available, if you were interested in attending."

Ah. A shakedown. *Donate to my charity, and I'll look at investing in your company.* I respected the hustle, and it was further than I'd gotten with any other potential investor, so I nodded. "Sure."

"Good," he said, then he shook my hand and left the restaurant. I sat back in my chair with a sigh, my legs suddenly feeling like wet noodles. All the tension in my muscles disappeared in a rush, and I scrubbed my face to try to get some life back in my body.

I'd passed the first hurdle, but now I needed to clear the second. The thought of his fancy soirée made my heart speed up. Attending a charity gala was not in my wheelhouse. It presented endless opportunities for me to mess up. Would I need a tux? Would there be food? Was I meant to bring a date? Was Arlo serious, or did he simply want to extort me for his charity?

I had no idea. I was out of my depth—but this was the best shot at a business deal I'd gotten since I'd started looking for an investor. A familiar need rose up inside me: the need to control every possible outcome. I needed to learn everything about charity galas. I needed to gather every bit of information I could so that I could control what happened next.

Failure was not an option. I would do everything in my power to make this deal go through.

"All done here?" the waitress asked, pointing to my plate. A few pasta noodles remained, but I nodded.

And I wished it was Alba standing at my table, because she'd know what I was supposed to do. Hell, maybe she'd even agree to be my date. At least then someone would know how to tie my tie properly.

I shoved that dangerous thought away. Alba's contempt for me dripped from every word. She rolled her eyes at the sight of me. She'd never agree to coach me through some fancy charity event.

But there'd been that catch in her breath when she'd tied my tie...

The slap of cold air on my face when I finally stepped outside the restaurant brought some sense back into my thoughts. Alba would never agree to be my date, and it would be inappropriate to ask.

Besides, if she said no, I'd never be able to eat at Carmine's again—and they made really good chicken.

AS IT TURNED OUT, I didn't get to eat at Carmine's for a while, regardless of Alba's thoughts toward me. The Midtown job ground to a halt, with the subcontractors who'd had the faulty equipment walking off site when our quality assurance team flagged a few issues and demanded they rectify them. I was pulled into countless emergency meetings with my legal and procurement departments, trying to simultaneously bring the subcontractor to heel so they'd finish the job, and frantically searching for someone else who could if they didn't.

Lunches were hastily catered sandwiches delivered to conference rooms, with crumbs brushed off draft letters of demand passed back and forth between me and the lawyers.

And maybe it was for the best. My custody week was coming to an end—Charlotte's mother would then have her for two weeks —and the extra time in the evenings would allow me to rescue the Midtown job and hopefully save my company. A distracting blonde with a sharp tongue was the last thing I needed. I could use my hand to let off some pressure when I needed to.

That, and the small jolt of pleasure I got every morning when I saw a new note from my cleaning woman. It was perverse, to enjoy her attitude as much as I did—but then, I had a type, didn't I?

She wrote me one evening:

Your guest chair is all wrong. It should be stiff and slightly uncomfortable to discourage your visitors from thinking they can walk all over you.

My response was a quick scribble below her neat handwriting:

Why should I take advice from a cleaning woman who doesn't clean? The windows need a wipe, sweetheart.

And they did. I glanced at the wall of windows that let me see out into the hallway beyond, frowning at the smudges left by a dirty rag hastily smeared over the glass. My private bathroom hadn't been restocked with hand towels or toilet paper in weeks, and I wasn't sure she actually knew how to vacuum properly.

She was terrible at her job—but I didn't want to have her fired. The notes she left me were one of the only things that felt honest about my life now, other than Charlotte. The cleaning woman's attitude felt real the way Alba's eye rolls had felt real.

When everything else in my life felt like chaos, I needed the tiny bit of grounding her notes gave me.

On Friday, after dropping Charlotte off at her mom's in the early afternoon, I drove back to work and slumped into my office chair. My head pulsed with pain, and I could see at least half a dozen urgent emails about the Midtown job that I needed to respond to.

I always felt slightly emptier when I dropped Charlotte off with Tiffany, knowing I wouldn't see her for two weeks, thinking about the empty townhouse, the lifeless rooms.

The thought of jumping right back into a crisis at work just made me feel tired. So, as the workday ground onward, I opened up my web browser—and hesitated.

I'd already decided I wouldn't go see Alba. She was a distraction, and I needed a distraction like I needed a hole in the head.

But there was something about her that niggled at me. So she knew good clothes? Fine. That could be explained in a hundred different ways. But she also knew business, and she talked about Roger like she was familiar with his type. How would a waitress at a hidden gem of a semi-casual restaurant know that? I couldn't think of an explanation.

Who *was* she? How did she know the things she knew?

So I typed the only thing I knew into the search bar—her first name—and decided that a few minutes spent prodding at my curiosity would allow me to refocus on work once I was done.

I was wrong.

ELEVEN
ALBA

VAUGHN DIDN'T COME into Carmine's for the rest of the week. It disappointed me more than I cared to admit, but I wasn't surprised. Why would he come in? Just to see me?

All I'd done was tell him his suit sucked, which anyone with eyes could have done. He didn't owe me anything.

But the rejection stung—even though it was familiar.

A little over a year ago, I'd been rejected by the man I loved. Rejected by my family. Hell, I'd even been rejected by Cole, even though I was the one who broke it off in the end. From the moment we'd started planning the wedding, a part of me knew he didn't want to marry me.

The only reason I'd wanted to see it through was because I thought we understood each other. I thought he was incapable of love, and I was willing to set my selfish desires aside to marry him.

But he wasn't incapable of love. I watched him fall—and fall hard—right before my very eyes.

How could I *not* break off our engagement?

It was still a rejection, even if I was the one to end it. He'd wanted her more than he'd wanted me. When I'd finally told him I hadn't wanted to marry him, he'd looked *relieved.*

Ouch.

Now, something as mundane as a semi-regular customer skipping a few lunches at my workplace hurt. I needed a thicker skin. It annoyed me that I cared.

Elena noticed, and she warned me to fix my attitude. Then I messed up an order or two, and she pinched her lips. And on Friday, I sniped at a rude customer when she was within earshot, and I found myself dragged into the back office at the end of my shift.

"We have a culture of respect here," she lectured, and I knew what was coming. "I like you, Alba," she said, her eyes resigned, "but I have to put the work first. I'm taking you off the schedule."

My nod was a quick dip of my chin. "You're firing me." It wasn't a question.

"I'm sorry, Alba."

I said nothing, afraid she'd hear the devastation in my voice. My movements were mechanical as I packed my things, changed into my cleaner's uniform, and left the restaurant for the final time.

Ten firings in a little over a year. I was terrible at everything I tried. I walked into the cold January wind and let the chill seep down my bare neck and into my chest.

I was almost out of options. Terrified, broke, broken.

Maybe that's why, when I started my shift at the office and found that one of the conference rooms was full of old, half-eaten takeout containers, rage detonated in my gut.

I was already on the precipice. I was tender and sensitive, with my emotions on a hair trigger. No one wanted me or cared about me. And the messy conference room? It simply proved that no one even considered that I existed at all. Their mess would magically get cleaned up, the way my messes had before.

Did these people not *think*? Did they not even consider that they might gather their trash into a pile, at least? Or that they could throw it away themselves?

Of course not. How many times had I left my bedroom littered with clothing on the rug, the bed linens thrown any which way, and come back to a pristine room? How many times had I dropped dishes into a sink and walked away without giving them another thought, without thinking of the hands that would be washing them?

Lo mein noodles littered one of the place settings, and whoever had sat there had rolled over a few of them. Old, sauce-encrusted noodles were now caked into the chair's casters and into the damn carpet.

I couldn't do this. Staring at the mess, I reached my limit. I'd been berated, harassed, fired, and ignored. I'd fought and fought to keep going, to prove to myself that I was more than my parents' money.

But what if I wasn't? What if all I was good for was a marriage to a man I didn't love in the name of family status?

Maybe it was time I accepted it. I couldn't hack it in the real world. I wasn't smart enough, or driven enough, or determined enough. That's why I'd been rejected so many times, by so many people. They could see how little I was worth—wasn't it time I admitted it to myself too?

My fingertips tingled as I pulled open the conference room door to walk out into the hallway. Unsteady breaths sawed in and out of my lungs, and I turned for the supply closet. I'd drop this annoying backpack vacuum, call the elevator, and leave. I'd tell my manager that I quit over text. I didn't owe them anything else.

This year had been a gauntlet. I'd learned that I was wholly unprepared for real life. I had no idea how to take care of myself. Without the insulation of my parents' money, I was looked down on, sneered at, and derided. I'd been rejected by jobs, by my peers, by every single person that I came across, and I was *done*. I wouldn't get on my hands and knees and scrub their carpets too.

But I would get on my hands and knees and beg my family to take me back.

My eyes stung with unshed tears. I had no choice. I had to go back to my family. I had to crawl back to them and debase myself to be welcomed back into the fold.

They'd said horrible things to me. They'd shown me that their love was conditional on my good behavior. They'd tugged on the leash and reminded me that I would never escape it, and now I knew for sure that they were right.

It made me feel dirty and small and ashamed to think of making that call, of begging my father to open his wallet and his home again.

But wasn't it better than *this*? I'd lasted fourteen months out in the cold on my own; that was something, wasn't it?

The vacuum clattered when I dropped it on the supply closet floor. My little caddy full of cleaning supplies and microfiber cloths landed beside it, and I stretched my back from side to side with a sigh. My hip clicked; my feet pulsed.

I was getting sorer by the day, and I couldn't take it anymore. My body was breaking. My spirit was already shattered.

I would sell my future for a few creature comforts, and it would be worth it. The humiliation of crawling back to my family after failing to make it on my own wasn't as bad as the humiliation of being invisible and broken and alone.

The fact that I was disappointed that Vaughn hadn't come in for lunch just proved how low I'd fallen. Those were the scraps I was clinging to in my attempt to survive on my own. A few moments of kindness from Deena, a woman I hardly knew, and the contrived attention of a good-looking customer at work.

Pathetic.

Prostrating myself on the floor in front of my parents would be no worse than *this*.

My jacket was still damp with melted snow, and I shoved my arms through it as I exited the supply closet. I turned for the elevator—and saw a light on at the end of the hall. It wasn't the overhead lighting, but it still shone from the interior windows like a beacon.

Mr. Big Shot didn't care about power bills. Of course he didn't. Why would he?

The ball of humiliation and defeat in my gut suddenly felt like lead. It weighed me down—and made me angry. I'd never come back here again, so I had nothing to lose. I marched down the hall, mentally composing the note that I'd leave on Big Shot's desk.

Asshole, I'd write. *Tell your staff to clean up after themselves. Picking noodles out of carpet fibers isn't part of my job description. Enjoy the stale smells of rotting food, you inconsiderate fuck.*

Never mind that picking noodles out of carpet fibers probably was part of the job description. It was just rude, and I was done.

Stomping down the hallway, I huffed. I needed an outlet for my rage. I needed to scream into the void, to tell *someone* that they were wrong, damn it. That this wasn't fair. That life *sucked*.

The light spilled out from his office's glass wall, and I sped up. His door was closed, which wasn't unusual, but it did slow me down slightly. The handle was cool as I slipped my fingers over it, the door a solid weight as I shoved my shoulder against it.

I was halfway across the room—my mental note having tripled in length and increased in vitriol—when I noticed the body behind the desk.

The only light in the room was the screen in front of his face.

I froze. He looked up from his computer. It took me a second to understand. My pulse sped up and slowed down. My emotions reeled, my vision going fuzzy at the edges.

"Alba?" Vaughn asked, brows drawing together.

Reality came into sharp focus. "What the hell are *you* doing here?" I demanded.

Vaughn looked at me like I had three heads. "This is my office. What the hell are *you* doing here?"

"This isn't your office. This is Big Shot Asshole's office."

"'Big Shot Asshole?'"

I clamped my mouth shut as logic pierced through the haze of rage that had obscured my thoughts. Oh. *Oh.*

Vaughn stared, the blue glow from his screen giving his skin an eerie pallor. Without a word, he stood up and began circling his desk.

I sipped in breaths through my constricted throat and whirled for the door.

His fingers closed on my wrist, and he tugged me back and kept me from escaping. I spun and crashed against him, my fingers curling into the luxurious fabric of his partially unbuttoned shirt. This one was navy; he must have bought multiples. His free arm clamped around my waist, and we stood there, staring at each other, saying nothing.

His body was a warm wall, and I fought the urge to melt into it. I stood there trembling like a trapped bird, saying nothing.

He was the first to break the silence. "I know who you are."

My body locked up. I stared at the weave of his shirt on his shoulder as emotions slammed into me, incomprehensible in their intensity. Everything I'd felt thirty seconds ago was still there, but now I was also afraid. And mortified.

"Alba," he said, his thumb stroking the inside of my wrist, his other arm drawing me closer to his chest. He was so warm, so broad. He smelled so good, *so* good—and I realized why he'd smelled familiar. I'd been inhaling the scent of him every night, right here in his office.

I know who you are.

He knew how far I'd fallen. My breaths were still unsteady, my heart beating so hard I knew he could feel my panic thrumming against the thumb he held at my wrist.

I marshaled my emotions into line and forced my lips to smile. Then I met his gaze. "You read all the sordid details, huh?"

There hadn't been much in the papers about the end of my engagement to Cole. My family was wealthy, but we weren't in the public eye. A couple of pictures on social media, some chatter in a few forums that followed the lives of Manhattan socialites a little too closely for my liking...nothing that had me plastered on every tabloid the way a celebrity would be.

But the broad strokes were there, if you went digging. I didn't know how to feel about the fact that Vaughn had done so. Ashamed, of course. And oddly flattered?

He'd looked me up. He'd wanted to know more about me, even though he hadn't come into the restaurant to see me.

"I read that you were engaged, and now he's reunited with an old flame. And you're working at Carmine's, even though your last name is Enders and your father is a successful financier on Wall Street."

A grimace twisted my face despite my best efforts to stop it.

There was a silence. Vaughn's thumb stroked my pulse point, and I stared at his shirt collar, his stubbled throat, the little divot in the middle of his chin.

"Do I need to send someone to murder your ex?"

I jerked, eyes snapping up to meet his gaze. "What?"

"He hurt you."

The darkness of his voice sent warmth flooding through my

center. It wasn't a question, but I still answered. "Yes, but not the way you think."

"What do I think?"

"That he tossed me aside to reunite with the mother of his child and then left me out in the cold."

His eyes were icy blue, intense. "And that isn't what happened?"

"What kind of company is this?" I asked, suddenly breathless. "How many hitmen do you know? Who *are* you?"

"Answer the question, Alba."

"Yes, he was in love with another woman, but I was the one who ended it. I..." My voice caught. I couldn't tell him about James. I couldn't tell him about my parents. The end of my engagement hurt my pride, but it hadn't hurt *me*. Not the way the rest of them had. I took a deep breath, and the scent of his cologne went to my head. "I was glad when our engagement ended."

Vaughn hummed. His thumb stroked. His other palm spread out, so I could feel the warmth of his hand against my waist. The heat of him seemed to chase away a chill that had sunk down to my marrow a long time ago, so long that I didn't remember the last time I'd felt warm.

His head dipped slightly, and the stubble on his jaw brushed my temple. I closed my eyes and leaned into him, my head angling up. His cheek touched mine, the corner of his lips ghosting across my jaw.

I felt...safe. I also felt raw and naked, and I wondered what would happen if I let go entirely. Maybe Vaughn would move his head a fraction of an inch, and I'd move mine, and then we'd be kissing. Maybe those big hands would circle my waist, and he'd back me up so my thighs hit his desk. Maybe he'd turn me around, bend me over, and fuck me so hard I'd forget my own name, forget everything that had happened over the past year.

Maybe I'd like that, my cheek pressed against the papers strewn all over his desk, my hands gripping the edge, my voice raw from crying out his name.

Then, quietly, with his lips close to mine, he said, "Tell me why you're here."

I opened my eyes. My panties were wet. "I work here," I whispered.

He frowned. "No, you don't."

I pulled my body away from his, pulled my jacket open, and gestured to the logo on my uniform. "I do. I'm the cleaner."

He stared at my shirt, then snapped his eyes up to meet mine. Then he went to his desk and pulled open a drawer. A moment later, a stack of half-crumpled papers landed on top of his desk.

My notes. My heart was a trapped bird, flapping in my chest as it tried to escape. If the ground had opened up and swallowed me whole at that very moment, I would've welcomed it. I stared at the notes, then at him. "Um," I said, and stopped.

"This is you?"

"You ruined the carpet!"

"So quick to go on the attack, princess." His voice was like soft velvet. I shivered.

Then I crossed my arms. My nipples were hard points, and I was glad for my jacket to hide them. "Am I wrong?"

"Why did you march in here like you were about to set it on fire?"

"No reason."

"You didn't look like you were going to clean. So what were you going to do?"

My hands landed on my hips, and I glared at him. It was easier to be outraged, to be angry. Then I wouldn't have to think about how much I wanted him, how good he looked with his collar open, the shadows in the office carving out his features.

I moved forward and stood with only his desk separating us. My index finger speared the stack of notes. "I was going to write exactly what I thought of you and your staff."

His brow arched. "Which is?"

"That you're a bunch of messy pigs, and that I refused to clean up after you any longer."

He reared back. "That's a little harsh."

"Have you seen the conference room?" I demanded, glaring.

When he combed his fingers through his hair and let out a tired sigh, I realized I wasn't quite as full of rage as I'd been when I walked in. I was fighting with him...but there was no heat behind it. And when he leaned his knuckles on his desk and pinched his lips, a little piece of me melted.

"I bought dinner for the team. They've been working late all week. I'll tell them to clean up after themselves. It won't happen again."

"Well, that's great, but I won't be the one to see it. Good luck with everything."

He stood straighter. "What do you mean?"

"I'm quitting. I can't do this anymore."

"This as in cleaning? Or the restaurant?"

"Both!" I exclaimed, then took a breath and forced a smile. "Goodbye."

It was high time I got out of here. He was too attractive, too dangerous. He made me want things that I knew would only hurt me in the end. Better to scurry back to the gilded dungeon from whence I came and forget that Vaughn existed at all.

Once again, I turned for the door. This time, he stopped me with his voice.

"Alba," he said. "Wait."

I didn't want to wait. I wanted to run. My heart was beating unsteadily, and I felt weirdly embarrassed. He was here, in this fancy office at the top of this building, and I was...

I was the cleaner he hadn't even thought about until I wrote that silly note. I was the waitress who brought him his lunch, except when he was too busy doing important things to stop by and annoy me. I was nobody. I was the woman who couldn't hack it in the real world, who was running back to Mommy and Daddy as soon as life got too hard.

"You were right about the suit," he said.

I angled my body so I could see him over my shoulder. "Well, yeah."

Vaughn huffed, scrubbing a hand over his jaw. "And you were right about the hair."

I waited. I didn't know what he was getting at.

He moved slowly, circling his desk once more. In the gloom, his movements seemed almost predatory. He stalked toward me, slow and steady, and I could do nothing but tremble as I stood there.

The urge to run fought with the urge to go to him. I wanted those strong arms around me, the warmth of him melting the ice that seemed to cling to my pores. I wanted to feel safe.

And I wanted him inside me. For the first time in over a year, desire snaked through me. His body on top of mine, his hands claiming me, his mouth—

When he reached me, his hand landed on my upper arm, then slid down to my wrist. His thumb brushed against my bare skin there, and I couldn't help the shiver that went through me.

"You were also right about how to act with potential investors. To pretend that it was already a done deal." He spoke with a low voice that seemed to twine around me, drawing me closer to him.

I gulped. "Fake it till you make it," I said. "That's pretty basic stuff."

His smile was a flash of white in the darkened office. With my wrist still manacled by his fingers, I had nowhere to go. Nowhere I wanted to go. Vaughn's free hand rose up to brush against my cheek and tuck a strand of hair behind my ear. The touch sent sparks through me. It was soft and intimate, and it made my heart ache for the old me—the one that believed in love.

"Why do I get the sense that I'm never going to see you again?" he asked, voice so low I hardly heard it over the hum of the computer and the rattle of the air vent.

I didn't know why it felt like a dangerous question. I didn't even know why I told him the truth. I lifted my gaze up to meet his and whispered, "You probably won't."

His gaze landed on mine, then dropped to my lips. "I wanted to come see you at Carmine's," he said. "Thank you properly for your advice."

I snorted, pretending like his words didn't send a wave of relief crashing through me. He'd wanted to see me. He'd thought about me. It hadn't been the rejection I'd imagined.

And how silly was I for thinking those things? Why did I even care?

I pulled my wrist from his grasp, but I didn't step away. "If you don't have a single person in this company who is able to tell you when you're wearing a bad suit, then you need to find someone who will."

His eyes narrowed slightly. "Did you get another job?"

"What?"

"You said I'd never see you again. That means you're quitting this job and the one at Carmine's. You found something better?"

That made me laugh. "I guess you could say that." If "something better" was selling my soul for a life of ease. Giving up the shitty independence I'd found scratching out my existence this past year in exchange for the money and privilege I'd grown up with.

I couldn't do it anymore. The long hours, the body-breaking work. The endless tunnel with no light in the distance.

Turned out my integrity did have a limit. I'd finally reached mine.

"Work for me instead."

My gaze, which had wandered down to study the stubble on his jaw and the movement of his throat as he spoke, snapped back up to his eyes. "Excuse me?"

"An investor is interested. Arlo Noble. But he wants me to attend his charity's fancy gala thing. I have no idea how to...be. How to act. What to wear. You do. You could coach me."

My heart thumped.

I could do that. I could make this man into a titan. He had the looks and the money and the bearing; he just needed a few tweaks. It would be so easy. I'd have to go nearer to a world where money was no object and privilege was a given. A world I'd almost been shackled to by marriage.

But even if I worked for Vaughn, I wouldn't be part of that world. I'd be the little matchstick girl, freezing in the cold while I watched from outside the window. Watching *him* from outside the window.

I blinked back to myself and forced myself to stand taller. "Maybe you're not coachable, Vaughn." I said it flippantly, because my heart had started to race.

Even if I'd forever be on the outside looking in, working for Vaughn gave me what I needed most: another option. I could work for him...and then who knew? Maybe something would come of it. I wouldn't have to call my mother. I wouldn't have to get on my knees and beg.

And I wanted to see Vaughn again. I wanted to feel the buzz

of our banter, to see the line of his jaw and the way his face lit up when he smiled. I wanted to feel my heart thumping the way it did when I saw him walk into the restaurant in that suit. I wanted to make him laugh again. If I worked for him…

Oh my God, no. I was so, *so* attracted to him. Working for him would be disastrous.

"I got new clothes, didn't I? And my barber comes to the office every week." He ran his fingers through his hair. "That's coachable."

"I'm not interested."

"You're lying to me." His eyes sparkled. Working for him would be my downfall. I had to get out of here before I made the worst decision of my life—and that was saying a lot.

"You know what? This is over. Goodbye."

He beat me to the door and stood in the opening, palms braced on the frame. "Alba," he pleaded.

"Get out of the way."

"I need you."

"No, you don't. Let me leave."

"You'd be hired as a consultant. Name your price."

I crossed my arms and arched a brow. "Dangerous words."

"I mean it." He dropped his arms from the doorjamb and let out a long breath. "I've made no headway in finding an investor. None. Until you."

He closed the distance between us. His cologne smelled rich and masculine, and it took all my self-control not to lean into him. His blue eyes looked darker in this light, and I could tell he was serious.

It was another option. A way out. If I could resist him…

"Name my price?" I asked.

His eyes flared, and the corner of his lips lifted. "Anything."

"I'm going to need a written copy of the job description."

He dug through his pocket and pulled out his phone. "Put your contact details in there. I'll have something to you by the time you walk through your front door."

This was such a stupid idea. He was a shiny lure, dangling just beyond my reach. He was the illusion of the life I left. Working for him would only remind me of everything that I'd lost.

But if he was serious about naming my price, it meant working for him would also buy me time. It would buy me my independence for just a little bit longer.

I could resist my attraction to him if it meant keeping my freedom. Couldn't I?

My father's words rang in my ears, the ugly way his lips had twisted when he'd called me a whore. Yes, I could resist my attraction to him if it meant staying away from *that*.

I handed him his phone back, and he tapped the screen. My own phone started buzzing in my purse. I arched a brow. "Really?"

"Just making sure," he said, smile flashing.

I tried not to acknowledge what that smile did to my stomach. I marched past him and didn't look back as I walked to the elevator. And when the doors closed and I was finally alone, my hand lifted up to touch the spot on my cheek where his fingers had brushed.

TWELVE
VAUGHN

I'D WANTED to kiss her when she stormed into my office, spitting mad and ready to rage. I'd wanted to kiss her when she softened, when she hesitated, and when she got that glint in her eye at my job offer.

Alba intrigued me. That's why I'd spent valuable time scouring blogs and forums and social media search results for her, and why my heart had thumped when I'd found oblique references to her from a little over a year ago.

I still didn't know why she was run off her feet working two jobs when her father was Ted Enders, but at least it made sense why she'd never heard of a lint trap. And it made sense that she knew suiting and tie knots and how to bag an investor. She'd been born into that life, not this one.

My discoveries about her only left me wanting more. Why had her engagement broken down, and was she telling the truth about being relieved? Why wasn't she already attending galas like Arlo's every week? Why was she *working*?

It was a mystery I wanted to unravel, even though I knew hiring someone I was attracted to was a bad idea.

I could resist attraction. I wasn't in the market for a new relationship; I'd learned my lesson, and my priorities were my daughter and my business. Besides, my time with Alba would be spent talking about clothes and appearance and putting on a persona that was uncomfortable and hollow. My attraction to her was almost certain to fade. I was hiring her to teach me about everything that reminded me of my father. Everything I strove not to be.

Not only that, but she came from a family that represented everything I despised. She *was* everything I despised—except she wasn't, was she? She wasn't hollow and false and vapid. She was intriguing and unsettling and quick-witted. Raw and real in a way I hadn't thought her ilk could be.

I finished the task I'd been working on and opened up a blank document. At the top of the page, I wrote JOB DESCRIPTION.

My fingers drummed against the edge of the desk. I stared at the blinking cursor, and then wrote, "Etiquette coaching. Style advice. Image consulting. Any other skills required to not make a fool of myself at the Noble Foundation Gala."

That was basically it. I needed Alba to teach me how to act so I would seem like I belonged in the rooms where real money was made. It made me feel slightly sick to think about it, but I had no choice. If I wanted to grow my company and provide for my daughter, I had to play the game.

I stuck the paltry job description on company letterhead, added some conditions: that she'd train me in preparation for Arlo's soirée, and that she'd be available to coach me on any other events and meetings, as required.

I sent it to Alba. Ten seconds later, she replied: "Sure. $500/hour. Four-hour minimum. All expenses reimbursed."

I couldn't help the laugh that burst out of me. She had promised me that asking her to name her price was dangerous, and I knew now that I could take her at her word. I liked that about her. There was no pretense, no fakeness.

Thousands in outgoings to an image consultant wouldn't look good on the company books when Arlo's team started scouring them. Besides, this wasn't strictly related to the construction business. I'd have to pay her from my personal fortune. Easy enough.

I answered with one word: "Done," and then I left the office and headed home.

THE NEXT TIME I saw Alba was the following week. Charlotte was still at her mother's house, so I booked a private room at a five-star restaurant for Wednesday evening, as per Alba's instructions. As I checked my watch, I mentally calculated how much this dinner would cost me.

And I smiled.

It wasn't money itself—or spending it—that bothered me; it was the subterfuge that did. My father promising the world, then going to my mother, hat in hand, to tell her he'd spent all their savings. He'd rocketed us from lobster and steak to instability in a blink. I'd spent my childhood bathed in anxiety and started working as soon as I was able. Then I kept working, and working, and working. I wasn't sure I knew how to do much else.

Alba was the opposite of my father. She had set clear expectations, and she was going to deliver a service. It was clear-cut and direct. I liked that she knew her worth.

The private dining room was warmly lit, with sconces dotting the walls around the table, plush, comfortable chairs, and double wooden doors through which I'd entered. The table was draped in crisp white linen, and my place setting had multiple utensils, a side plate, and two wine glasses. I drummed my fingers on the edge of the table with one hand while I rested my chin on the palm of the other.

Then the door opened.

"This way, ma'am," the waiter said in a deferential tone.

"Thank you," came Alba's voice a moment before she appeared in the doorway.

My mouth went dry.

She wore a dark burgundy dress that skimmed her body and moved like water. It was cut high on her neck and had long sleeves. She wore a gold necklace and thin bracelets on top of the fabric, the metal shimmering in the buttery light spilling from the sconces.

The dress highlighted the willowy, curvy shape of her. Her legs were bare, and she wore simple black heels.

It was the first time I'd seen her with her hair down. Blond waves fell down to her chest, framing that face that had plagued my dreams for days.

Suddenly, I was standing, though I had no recollection of getting to my feet. I gulped, blinking rapidly, and said, "Alba."

She smiled, her lips shining with some subtle makeup. "Good evening," she said, and nodded to the waiter as he pulled the chair out for her. She timed it perfectly to sit as he tucked her chair, like she'd done it a thousand times before.

This was a different woman from the snarky, opinionated waitress and the furious cleaner. I'd never met this one before. A niggle of disquiet went through me. Was she as real as she'd seemed, or had it all been a lie?

"Who are you?"

Alba arched a brow, a grin teasing at the corners of her lips. "You know who I am."

"I don't think I do."

She took the menu that the waiter handed her, her eyes still steady on mine.

I'd never seen someone so beautiful. It dazzled me to look at her. She moved differently here than she did when she was at work. There was subtle tension in her body, but she didn't look uncomfortable, as if the very way she held herself put walls up around her. It made me want to lean in and break them down.

She ordered wine and thanked the waiter, then turned back to me when he stepped out after having cleared one of the two wine glasses from each of our place settings. Her eyes were sharp. She was unbelievably beautiful. I couldn't breathe properly.

"You stood when I entered. That was good."

"Right." My voice was a croak. I still hadn't recovered.

Alba was all business. "Hillary sent me the invitation from the Noble Foundation Gala. It's a white-tie event this year," she noted.

The fact that she said "this year" implied that she knew about previous years' dress codes. Unsurprising, but it still sent a thread of insecurity through me. If this was the type of person I'd be surrounded by, how could I possibly hold my own?

"What will you be wearing?" she asked.

"A tux," I said, shrugging slightly.

Alba arched a brow. "With an evening jacket, waistcoat, and white bowtie?"

"Sure."

"The correct answer is, 'Yes, absolutely.'"

"Yes, absolutely," I parroted.

She huffed, and I could tell she was holding back from laughing. "We'll have to have a look at your outfit. And your date will have to be in a floor-length gown, maximum formality."

"Right," I said, not mentioning that I didn't have a date, nor did I know anyone who would be comfortable at that kind of event.

I was out of my depth—again. But I was here to learn.

I watched Alba when the waiter came back. She was unfailingly polite, but she didn't treat him like an equal or a friend. There was no joking the way customers did at the restaurant where she'd worked.

The waiter showed her the bottle of wine, then opened it tableside. He poured a drop into her glass, let her taste it, then poured mine and topped hers up.

When we were alone again, I took my glass and said, "I don't know anything about wine."

Her eyes twinkled with a teasing light. "I can see that by the way you're holding your glass."

I looked at the glass, cupped in my right hand. "What's wrong with the way I'm holding my glass?" I demanded.

"Do it like this," she said, gripping the top section of the stem instead of the bowl of the glass. "That way you won't get dirty finger marks all over it." Her tone was wry, teasing, but it wasn't mean.

I did as she said. It felt awkward and pretentious. I grimaced.

"Vaughn, holding your wine glass differently doesn't make you a bad person."

My eyes snapped up to hers. "You can tell I'm uncomfortable."

She arched a brow. "I don't have to be a psychic to know that."

"This all seems like a lot of bullshit just to have a drink and a meal."

She tilted her head, conceding. "It is, mostly. But it's convention, and you'll stick out if you don't follow it."

"How did you learn all this?"

She smiled, eyes flashing. "We're not here to talk about me."

In the intimate, low light of the private room, I very much wanted to talk about her. I wanted to know where she'd gotten that dress, and how she'd learned to move like that. I wanted to know how she'd grown up that she looked completely at ease here, when I felt the itch of every thread against my body.

"Vaughn."

I looked up. Alba had set her glass down and was leaning forward. Her hand reached across the table, and her fingertips brushed against the top of my palm. I let out a long sigh at the touch, shaking my head. "I wish I didn't have to do this."

"Learn table manners?"

"Play this stupid game. My business is solid. It shouldn't be a stretch for someone else to see it."

She hummed.

"I didn't grow up rich," I admitted. "I..." My voice trailed off, and my gaze slid to the side. "My dad always had a new business venture, but most of them didn't pan out. All this... It just reminds me of him. He always wanted to be part of this world, and he'd drag us along, but it never felt natural. I feel like I'm playing dress-up."

"It's uncomfortable."

"Very."

Her fingers brushed my palm once more, and then she pulled away. "What's your reason for wanting to find an investor?"

"To grow the business more than I'm able to grow it myself."

"Why?"

"What do you mean, why?"

She shrugged, an elegant movement. "Why does it matter that your business grows?"

"If I don't find an investor, I'll have to sell off chunks of the business. Shrink. We might never grow again, if my reputation takes a hit."

"But you won't be destitute." She arched a brow, and I could see in her face that she'd done her research on me since we'd seen each other last.

"Well. No." I blinked. "I..." Trailing off, I cleared my throat. "I want to give my daughter everything I never had. I want to provide for her."

"You can't do that already?"

"I want her to have the best."

"That's what my father used to say, and yet I ended up here."

I sat up. That was a rare crumb of information about her, directly *from* her, and it made me hungry for more. "You did. How?"

"We're not here to talk about my family." She looked at me. "You need to decide if you're willing to play this game, and if the discomfort is worth the outcome."

"You don't think it is."

"I never said that."

"I won't be a failure," I said, and it came out bitter and harsh. I felt exposed, like I'd cracked myself open by accident and showed her a part of me that was supposed to remain hidden.

Alba didn't react. She watched me, cool and aloof.

The doors opened, and our waiter came back to take our orders. I watched the way Alba acted, how she held the menu, how she moved. She encompassed everything that made me uncomfortable about the monied class. Her bearing was all superiority and elegance, and I felt like an ogre in comparison. I shifted in my seat and tugged at my tie.

"Vaughn," Alba said, "stop fidgeting."

"You're making me nervous."

She laughed. "Now you're the one who's lying."

I grinned in response, and her eyes lingered on my lips before climbing up to meet my gaze.

She took a deep breath, then gestured to the place setting. "Let's go over the function of each utensil."

Alba spoke, and I listened. She showed me how to hold my

VAUGHN

fork, how to cut with my knife. She instructed me on safe topics of conversation and when it would be acceptable for me to bring up business.

"I've broken a million rules in my meetings so far," I admitted.

"They probably weren't formal dinners," she said. "I'm trying to get you up to speed for a white-tie event. Business lunches at Carmine's are another thing entirely. Those are mostly about bravado and confidence."

"And avoiding polyester."

"That's just a good life strategy in general."

I laughed. By the time our meal was done, I was exhausted—but I wasn't uncomfortable. Alba had managed to demystify some of the table manners that I'd encounter at the Noble Foundation Gala. I felt incrementally more prepared. I probably wouldn't fit in, but I might not make a fool of myself in the first ten minutes, either.

We walked through the restaurant and stood on the street. I hailed a cab and opened the door for Alba.

"Thank you for tonight," I said as she walked around me toward the open door.

"We have a lot of work to do," she said. Her jewelry glinted under the streetlights between the open flaps of her long wool jacket, her breath puffing in a cloud of white. A few flakes of snow landed on her shoulders.

She looked otherworldly. Untouchable. I wanted her desperately.

Our eyes met, and I cleared my throat. "What's next on the agenda?"

"Dancing."

"Dancing?"

"You heard me. You'll want to take your date onto the dance floor at least once."

I groaned, and Alba grinned.

"You're enjoying yourself," I accused.

"Immensely. Goodnight." She got into the cab, and I closed the door and watched the car drive away.

And when I closed my eyes that night, I saw Alba painted on my eyelids. Her smile. Her hair. The way she moved in that dress.

Dancing with her wouldn't be so bad.

THIRTEEN
ALBA

MY FIRST PAYCHECK from Vaughn hit my account that Friday. I lay in bed and stared at my phone screen, heart thumping.

It was more money than I'd had in my account since I'd been excommunicated—and all I'd had to do was go to dinner at one of my favorite restaurants.

When I'd walked into the crowded dining room, I'd scanned the space as my muscles twitched like they were preparing to bolt —and been relieved to see no one familiar.

And then the door to the private dining room had opened, and there he was. Obviously uncomfortable, unbearably handsome.

I'd forced myself to stay professional. He was my ticket to a bit of stability, my second chance at independence. I wouldn't ruin it by acting on base urges.

Now I climbed out of bed and stretched my neck from side to side, groaning at the ache in my spine. Maybe if I worked for Vaughn for long enough, I'd have enough money to go see a physiotherapist.

For the first time in months, I was able to roll out my yoga mat and stretch my body. I ate a leisurely breakfast, then headed to my favorite coffee shop for a treat.

Deena wasn't there today, but I ordered at the counter and took a seat at the same sofa where we'd met. I got up when my coffee was ready, then settled against the cushions with a book. Minute by minute, my body relaxed.

It had been a little over a week since I'd marched into Vaughn's office, wanting to leave him a rude note, and I'd had time to quit my one remaining job, complete all my errands, clean my apartment, and do some much-needed grooming. My legs were shaved, my toes were painted, and my hair had been conditioned with an extra-hydrating mask. My entire body was exfoliated, and I'd managed to actually complete a basic skincare routine every evening for a week.

I almost felt like myself again.

After turning a page on the romcom in my hand, I curled a leg under my opposite thigh and leaned forward to grab my mug. I took a sip of the vanilla latte and hummed. Delicious. For the first time in weeks, maybe months, I felt calm and almost hopeful.

Then I heard my name. "Alba?"

All the tension that had melted out of me locked my muscles up once more. A woman glided toward me, all glossy dark hair and expensive clothes.

"Yvette," I said, forcing a smile. "I didn't know you drank the coffee here."

"I don't, normally, but I was across the road meeting with my financial advisors and was desperate for a cappuccino." Her eyes were sharp as they swept over me, and I regretted my choice to wear old jeans and my comfiest, rattiest sweater. The designer clothes hanging in my closet still felt like someone else's.

"It's so good to see you. We missed you at Ryan's this year."

Ryan was a mutual friend who was famous for throwing extravagant, multi-day birthday parties. The location changed every year, from one exotic destination to another. Even if I'd been invited, I wouldn't have had the money to go.

"I'm sure it was fabulous," I said, standing to kiss the air on either side of her cheek. "How have you been?"

"Oh, I'm so *over* the winter. I was just thinking I need to get out of the city for the weekend, at least."

"You still have that place in...Jamaica, was it?"

"Oh"—she waved a hand, laughing—"we sold that place last year. We're looking at buying in the Bahamas, but you know, the hurricanes are getting worse..."

"Uh-huh."

"How about you? I heard you were *working*...at a *restaurant?*" She laughed, frowning, but interest sparked in her gaze.

"Who told you that?" I asked with a coy smile, forcing myself not to squirm.

At dinner with Vaughn, it had been so easy to put on the persona I used to wear all the time. The poised, effortless, carefree woman whose chief worry was booking her next blowout at the salon. It was harder now, in the face of a woman who delighted in spreading malicious gossip. I knew she'd be on the phone before she left the café. Then I thought of Vaughn's discomfort—and the way he'd braced himself, straightened, and forced himself to pay attention—and I figured if he could push past it, so could I.

So, I smiled at Yvette. "It was fun," I said breezily, waving a hand.

Her catty smile turned confused. "Fun," she repeated, like she'd never heard of the word. Or maybe she'd never heard it in relation to actual work.

I smiled. "Very."

"Your ex-fiancé seems to be doing well. I ran into him and his new woman. They're madly in love."

As far as daggers to the chest went, that one wasn't subtle at all. My smile remained in place only because I had years of practice. "I'm so happy for the both of them."

"And...what was his name...James?"

I tilted my head. Apparently news of my connection to James had gotten out. "What about him?"

"Are the two of you blissfully happy as well?"

"I haven't seen him in over a year, so I can't speak for him, but I'm doing well. Was that your name that was just called?"

Yvette glanced at the counter, where the barista placed a steaming drink. She turned back to me with a razor-sharp smile. "Nice to run into you. We should catch up sometime."

"Absolutely," I said, knowing she wouldn't call me and I wouldn't call her, and we'd both be happier for it.

As she walked away, her designer shoes clip-clopping on the café's tiled flooring, I turned back to my book. The words scrambled on the page, my attention on the sound of her heels as it moved toward the door. When she was gone, I blew out a breath and slumped on the sofa.

I'd been wrong last week, when I thought I was ready to grovel my way back into the family fold. I missed my clothing, my driver, my ready-made food, my cleaner, my beautiful penthouse apartment. I missed all the things that had made life easy.

But I didn't miss *that*. The fake niceness, the subtle and not-so-subtle jabs, the constant put-downs and one-upmanship.

None of the people in Yvette's and Ryan's social circle had spoken to me when I was thrown out of my family. None of them so much as sent me a text message. They weren't my friends. I knew that now.

And I knew that I didn't want to go back to that world, even if it meant doing it tough for a while longer.

My coffee was cold, I couldn't focus on my book, and it was about time I started getting ready for my next session with Vaughn.

I could thank Yvette for one thing: she was the perfect reminder of what was at stake if I messed things up with my new boss.

I'D RENTED out a small dance studio in preparation for our session. Dressed in leggings and a loose tee, I leaned against the wall of mirrors and scrolled through my music app for something appropriate.

It was dark out, with the lights in the studio reflecting against the glass and blocking the view of the outside. The minutes trickled by, and I wondered if Vaughn would call to cancel, if he'd tell me he'd changed his mind.

At least I'd get paid, I thought. At least I had a tiny cushion in my bank account. Not enough to last more than a couple of weeks, but enough to get me to my next job.

Worry gnawed at my stomach. Yvette's face loomed at the back of my mind. How many more old acquaintances would I have to face? Maybe I should've moved out of the city.

And then he was there, filling out the doorway, his blue eyes snapping to mine. He scanned the room briefly, as if to check that I hadn't laid any traps in the corners, then crossed to where I stood. He smelled of the cold and a hint of his cologne.

"Alba."

"Vaughn." I fought the smile that tried to curl my lips. "You look nervous."

"I haven't danced since middle school Phys Ed class," he admitted.

"I'll go easy on you," I promised, and my heart jumped at the spark in his eyes.

"Not sure I want you to."

Dangerous—he was dangerous. I ducked my chin and put my phone next to my bag, leaving the music off for now. "Get comfortable. We'll start with a waltz," I told him, and gestured to the middle of the room.

I tried not to stare at him, but the studio was full of reflective surfaces. The darkened windows, the wall of mirrors—they all conspired to make me ogle.

He shifted those big shoulders and let his jacket drop off, his back to me, his front reflected in the mirror. His hair and beard were groomed to perfection, his body shifting and tugging the fabric of his shirt tight across his back and arms as he laid the jacket down next to my bag. Then he turned toward me, but his eyes were on the cufflinks he unhooked and tucked into a pocket, then on the work of rolling up his sleeves.

I'd never seen his forearms before, and I found myself unable to look away. They were thick and corded with muscle, veins popping out as he moved those big hands. Obscene.

There was heat swirling all through me, coalescing down below my navel and tingling down to my extremities. I swallowed convulsively, angling my body away so I could gather myself.

I was providing a professional service, and ogling was not part of the job description.

That was just a perk, I thought, then braced myself and turned to face him. He was done with his sleeves and he spread his arms out toward me, open and waiting.

"Over here," I said, "arms like this."

I demonstrated the position, and Vaughn approached. His belt buckle gleamed, his shoes shone, and his pants did nothing to hide the strong thighs they covered.

This would've been easier when he'd looked like a bum who'd raided a smaller man's closet. I lifted my chin and stepped into the frame of his arms, one hand nestled against his palm, the other resting on his shoulder. Through the fabric of his shirt, I felt the hard muscle of his shoulder shifting, and then his hand was just below my waist, fingers dangerously close to the waistband of my underwear.

"Hand higher, about mid-back," I said, arching a brow, "unless this is you trying to cop a feel."

His eyes sparkled, and his hand slid higher. His fingers pressed into my back, palm warm against me, and that pooling heat pulsed between my legs.

I ignored it.

This was my stability, my second chance. This was my only hope at not having to crawl back to Mommy and Daddy Dearest and discover that I really wasn't so strong and independent, after all. I could *not* mess it up. Not until I had some sort of financial safety net. A plan. A direction.

"The waltz is in three-four time, meaning three beats per measure."

"Uh-huh," he said, nodding, but I could tell he had no idea what I meant.

I bit back a smile and explained, "*One*-two-three, *one*-two-three."

"Got it," he said. His hand splayed a little wider, and I found myself leaning a tiny bit closer, like my body wanted us chest to chest.

Resisting the urge, I demonstrated the basic steps. To my surprise, Vaughn caught on quickly. Within minutes, he was leading.

"Stop trying to throw me around the room, Vaughn. Gentle pressure on my back will do."

His version of gentle pressure was an undeniable demand to move into the cage of his arms. Our bodies drew closer, and it was only a slight stumble from him that jarred me back to myself.

I stepped back. "Good," I said. "Let's try it with music."

My hands were trembling as I picked my phone up off the floor. It was still plugged into the sound system and I'd cued up the music, so all I had to do was unlock it and press play.

I looked up and, in the mirror, saw Vaughn practicing his steps to the music, his face screwed up with concentration, his arms out, steps slightly awkward but not quite off-beat. The wrinkle between his brows and the slight parting of his lips made me melt a little. A big, broad man, trying his hardest.

It said a lot about him, that he was throwing himself into this. He was determined and unafraid. It made me like him a little more.

It also made me wonder *why*. I'd looked him up, and *Forbes* estimated his fortune somewhere in the high-hundred millions. He didn't need to go to this gala or get an investor. He could fund whatever venture he wanted himself. But he'd made that comment —*I won't be a failure*—like it meant something. He was chasing something, and I couldn't figure out what it was. Entry into the world that had ousted me?

Then he glanced at me, and his lips quirked.

My mouth was dry as I stepped up to him, our bodies fitting together like we'd been dancing together for years and not minutes. My heart thumped hard as his scent enveloped me. The smell of the outdoors had dissipated so all that was left was the scent of him. His hand found the small of my back and slid up, like he liked the feel of his fingers running along my spine.

I tilted my head and found his eyes on me. Our chests were

nearly brushing. My nipples were hard points under my sports bra.

For just a moment, I wondered if he'd take me here, hard up against the mirrors, my leggings around my ankles. If he'd bite my shoulder and shudder as he emptied himself into me, hands holding my hips still until the breath returned to our bodies.

Then I blinked, and rehearsed the litany of reasons I could never have him. The reasons why I didn't *want* him.

By the time our hour was up, I was flushed. Vaughn had unbuttoned another button on his chest, and the space between his shoulder blades was damp. The world outside the windows was dark, snowy, and cold. It might as well have been another planet.

"What?" I asked as Vaughn studied me while I handed him a bottle of water from the studio fridge.

"I'm imagining a little Alba learning to dance so she could fit in at society balls, and how different that must have been to the way I grew up. You were a natural, I assume?"

I snorted. "My dance teacher went gray trying to get me to stop leading."

"That tracks."

I smacked his shoulder. "What's that supposed to mean?"

He gulped his water, his eyes sparkling. When he'd swallowed, he gestured toward me with the mouth of his water bottle. "You don't like people telling you what to do."

"Does anyone?" I protested. And that was unfair. I didn't *like* having to fight to be allowed to make my own decisions. I didn't *like* that when I tried to decide for myself who I'd spend my life with, the rug was pulled out from under me in punishment. Of *course* I hated people telling me what to do.

"So I'm right?" he challenged.

I lifted my chin. "And what, you're any better? When I told you to get a new suit, you nearly bit my head off."

"'Told me to get a new suit?'" Vaughn protested, laughing. "You said I looked like a little boy playing dress-up."

I had said that, hadn't I? I waved my own bottle of water at him. "Potato, po-tah-to."

His laugh was velvet wrapping around my body, raising goose-bumps over my skin. "I don't mind," he said, voice quieting. "You were the only one with the balls to say it out loud."

"You must work with a bunch of invertebrates."

"Engineers, mostly," he replied. "I'm not sure they know anything about suiting either."

"Good thing you've got me, then."

His eyes roamed over my face, flicking down to my lips before coming back up to meet my eyes. "Good thing I've got you," he agreed, and the tenor of his voice sent a shiver through me.

Too much. Too close. Too dangerous.

I painted a bright smile on my face—one of the ones I'd used at the restaurant to put walls up between me and too-forward customers that wouldn't lead to me losing out on much-needed tips. Vaughn saw it, and frowned.

He cleared his throat and leaned over to pick up his jacket. "I've got my daughter for the next two weeks, so I won't be able to do evenings. I'll have Hillary send through my availability during the day."

Just like that, the teasing and camaraderie was gone. It felt like a slap, but I was the one who'd put my walls up first.

I nodded as I gathered my own things. "Sure," I said. "I'll be in touch."

FOURTEEN
VAUGHN

WE MET at Koval's the following Monday. Alba wore wide-leg pants and a crisp blouse tucked into them, the collar open to reveal that gold jewelry. Her hair was wrapped in a knot at the base of her neck, and I found myself staring at the line of her jaw, the hint of clavicle.

She and Koval spoke in another language, one with hems and seams and knits, waistcoats and lapels. I stood there, pretending to listen but mostly looking at the way the light caught Alba's hair, the way her hands smoothed over the fabric Koval presented her, delicate and sure, the purse of her lips when she mulled over the older man's options.

"I can rent a tux," I said, when they were arguing over evening jackets.

Two heads whipped toward me. Koval looked ready to throw me out of his shop. Alba looked exasperated.

"Quiet, you," she snapped.

"Listen to your woman," Koval suggested.

"I am not *his woman*," Alba said, rounding on him.

The older man shrugged. "Then let him rent a tuxedo from a mass-market shop," he said mildly. "Makes no difference to an old man who knows nothing about anything."

"You are impossible, Mr. Koval," Alba said, releasing a sigh. "We'll go with the peaked lapel."

"You'll see," Koval replied, satisfied that she'd gone with his suggestion. "Big man. Big lapel."

"Or he'll look like he's playing dress-up," she muttered.

"Wouldn't be the first time," I couldn't resist saying. The venomous look she threw me was worth it, and I flashed her a smile.

From Koval's, we went to lunch at a French restaurant called Rebellieux. Alba glanced around the dining room, eyes scanning furtively, and I wondered if she was looking for someone, or simply embarrassed to be seen with me.

This time, I ordered the wine, and the rigamarole with the pouring and the tasting fell to me. Alba watched me, then nodded when the waiter left, both our glasses filled. "Good," she said.

"I still feel like I'm playing pretend."

She shrugged, unsympathetic. "Don't we all?"

"It never bothered you? Feeling like you weren't being yourself?"

She fingered the stem of her wine glass, her nails painted a soft shade of pink. "I'm not sure I even knew what being myself really meant," she admitted.

"You seem to know yourself now."

"A year of suffering will do that to a person." Her smile was a bitter twist.

Another crumb of information, rare as a precious jewel. I stared at the red wine in my glass, tilting it the way I'd seen her do, and asked, "Has it been that bad?"

"What exactly did you read, when you were doing your creepy

little internet stalking session about me?" Her eyes were narrowed when I met them.

I huffed. Shrugged. "Not much. Your engagement ended. Your parents are wealthy. I still wonder how you ended up at Carmine's and cleaning an office building."

She stared at me for a moment, and I stared back. I wasn't sure why she decided to tell me anything, but she did. "Cole, my ex-fiancé, worked for one of my father's companies. We were supposed to be a power couple, bringing together our families. I... didn't go along with the plan."

"Doesn't seem like your ex did either," I said, frowning.

She snorted, that twist in her lips deepening. "No. He didn't."

"But he gets his happily-ever-after, and you end up working yourself to the bone for a year?"

"My parents weren't happy that I didn't toe the family line. They cut me off."

I was struggling to understand. "You didn't... You didn't have work to fall back on? A career?"

Her spine straightened. She touched the stems of her silver-ware, straightening them with sharp, precise movements. "I know to a self-made man like you, it seems pathetic that I'd still be relying on my parents for money at my *advanced age*." Her words were precise, and she wouldn't meet my gaze. "But I grew up in a different world than the one you know. I was a pretty object, and I was expected to behave. Marry. Make babies. I didn't."

"And they threw you out."

Her eyes finally lifted, and they were hollow, dead. "They did."

Part of me wanted to scoff. She was a grown woman, and she wasn't an idiot. Why would she rely on her parents' handouts? I'd known from a young age that I couldn't rely on my parents for anything. Everything they touched turned to shit. My father, especially. My mother was mostly along for the ride, blinded by her love for him.

But then I thought about the way Alba moved when she was in a restaurant like this one. The things she'd known to ask Koval. The practiced, automatic steps of the dance she'd started to teach me.

Her whole life, she'd been molded to be the perfect little society woman, and then she'd been handed off to a man to marry. It was outdated and insulting and wrong. It made me angry for her. A woman who couldn't stand to be told what to do, who was hard and driven and *mean*. How did she stand it? How did she *survive?*

Her eyes still held that horrible blankness, and I wanted to chase it away. I wanted to drag her over to my side of the table and needle her until she bit back or smiled or stabbed me.

I wanted to smooth my hands down her spine and draw her close, but I had the feeling that if I tried to be soft with her right now, she'd close herself off and never let me in. That was unacceptable.

...and when had Alba letting me in become a goal of mine? I forced myself not to look at that too closely and instead picked up my wine glass (by the stem) and leaned back in my chair to take a sip.

"So, your ex, your parents...who else?"

"Pardon?" she asked, brow wrinkled.

"People I need to kill."

A surprised laugh fell from her before she could clamp her lips shut. Her eyes sparkled, and satisfaction coursed through me. "Stop it. You wouldn't murder a fly."

"Big concrete pour happening at our Midtown job at the end of the week," I said casually. "Good place to dispose of a few inconvenient bodies."

The older couple at the table next to ours glanced over, no longer pretending not to eavesdrop.

We both ignored them, eyes locked. Alba's lips twitched. "Don't slouch, Vaughn."

I nudged her knee with mine and grinned. "Yes ma'am."

She rolled her eyes, but her cheeks were flushed and a small, pleased smile haunted the edges of her mouth.

When we were done with our meal, I couldn't resist the urge to guide her from the dining room with a hand on the small of her back. Our coats were checked in the lobby, so I could feel the knobby bones of her spine above the waistband of her pants. My hand splayed out as we went through the double doors into the lobby—and it was that touch, that closeness, that alerted me right away when she stiffened.

A brown-haired man stood at the coach check counter next to a woman with long, dark hair. The man glanced up when we entered, recognition flaring in his green eyes.

"Alba," he blurted, and the woman with him spun.

Beside me, Alba turned to stone. "James," she replied. She was frozen on the spot, tension thrumming through her back beneath the pressure of my palm. I eased my hand around her waist—it looked like she might need someone to hold her up—as she nodded to the woman. "Yvette."

"Twice in a month!" the woman exclaimed, a smile curling her lips while her eyes went sharp and black. "What a surprise to see you *here*. Did your shift just end?"

I nearly choked on my own spit.

"Lunch at Rebellieux isn't exactly surprising," Alba replied, ignoring the woman's final jab. Her voice was high and tight, and she swayed slightly on her feet. Her eyes flicked to the woman, then back to the man.

He cleared his throat, sidling closer to the brunette. "Long time no see," he announced. I didn't like the way he was looking at Alba, how his gaze raked down her body and back up again, openly assessing, almost possessive. Then he looked at me.

I let him see exactly what I thought of him, all the anger and aggression and territorial possession, and he replied by arching a brow.

"New pet?" the woman—Yvette—asked with a mean smile.

"Who, yours?" Alba shot back, then lifted her chin. "Excuse us." She motioned to the coat check, where the attendant was doing her best to look like she wasn't gobbling up the interaction. Alba's back was straight as she swept past the couple, her movements sure. I stared at the couple as they went through the lobby doors, then turned to Alba, who was handing her coat check ticket to the attendant with a polite smile.

While the attendant looked through the racks for our jackets, Alba stared straight ahead. Blotches of red bloomed on her cheeks, her neck, and I could see the thrumming of her blood in her neck.

"Who were they?" I asked quietly.

"Old friends," she clipped. "Don't worry about them. You did well today."

"Alba—"

"Your jacket," she said, nodding to the attendant as she handed mine over and grabbed her own. She still hadn't looked at me.

"So. I'll send through the details for our next session. I've got a train to catch." She looked down at the closure of her jacket, her hands steady as she did up the zipper.

If I hadn't spent time studying her every move, I would've thought she was okay.

But she wasn't. Her mask was on—the one she wore in society. It was on tight, except for the very slight twitching at the corner of her eyes.

"Alba—wait." I followed her out the door. "Hang on. Talk to me."

"We're both busy, Vaughn," she called over her shoulder. "I'll see you soon."

I jogged to catch up, the bottom of my jacket flapping around my thighs. "*Alba.*"

She spun when I curled my hand around her arm. Her eyes remained downcast, her breaths gusting out in big puffs of white. It wasn't snowing, but the sky was overcast and oppressive above us. Cars went by, the sound of wet slush and melted snow squelching under their tires.

"Let go of me," she said quietly, and I did.

With my arms hanging uselessly at my sides, unable to hold her to me, unable to draw her in, I asked, "Who were they?"

"I told you that already."

"Tell me again. Tell me to go in there and punch him in the mouth, and I will. Tell me, Alba."

Finally, she looked at me. Her eyes were blue, blue, blue, and terribly unhappy. She was beautiful and sad and I wanted to fix it.

"He's the reason I broke off my engagement. I thought—"

"I'll kill him."

She rolled her eyes. "Stop it."

"I'm serious." And I was. I'd been joking before, mostly, but if she told me he hurt her and she wanted revenge, I'd walk right back into that pretentious fucking restaurant and stab him in the neck with his own fork.

But then her gaze was on me, and some of the sadness in her eyes had ceded to faint amusement. "You'll never convince me you're some kind of crime lord, Vaughn."

"Plausible deniability. Smart."

Her lips tried to curl, and she shook her head. "I'm fine. I'm good. I just—I wasn't expecting to see him. Them, together. I'm sorry."

Unable to resist any longer, I lifted my hands to rub her upper arms. "Don't apologize. Not for that."

She swallowed, and when she leaned into me and rested her forehead against my shoulder, my breath caught in my lungs. I was afraid to breathe in case she backed away again. Moving slowly, I wrapped my arms around her and felt her sigh, her breath warm against my neck.

"We were...seeing each other," she said, her voice so quiet I had to strain over the sound of the cars beside us. "James and I." She sighed, her body slight and fragile in the cradle of my arms.

"Did he hurt you?" I asked, my voice strange even to my own ears.

Alba shook her head, her forehead rotating on my shoulder. "Not the way you mean. He just—" She gusted out another breath. "I thought he loved me, but he really just wanted my parents' money. I got in a car accident and ended up in the hospital, you know."

I nodded. I'd read about that.

"I wasn't seriously hurt, but it clarified a lot of things for me." She shivered, pressing herself against me. "I knew I couldn't marry Cole. I thought James... I thought James and I would be together. He wasn't from a well-to-do family. He didn't have much. But we were happy. Or so I thought. Our relationship was all phone calls and messages. We'd only actually seen each other a handful of times. But he came to see me in the hospital the day I broke off my engagement. Got there just minutes after Cole left. He met my mother for the first time, and it was a disaster. She was distraught about Cole. James was polite, and I thought... I thought..."

She closed her eyes against the memory.

"He broke up with you after?" I asked, voice low and angry.

The laugh that came out of Alba was so bitter it was almost unrecognizable. She shook her head, her forehead rubbing against my shoulder. "No. He slept with me, and then he broke up with me. He made me feel like what we had was real long enough that I'd finally get in bed with him after all those months of talking and dreaming and wishing, and then when we were still lying there, naked, he told me it wasn't going to work between us. Said he'd call me a ride so I could go home."

A low, burning anger built in my gut. "Coward."

"Opportunist, mostly."

"Shameless, spineless worm." I lowered my head so my face was next to hers, so I felt the bunching of her cheek as she smiled. My arms were still around her, and she'd stopped pretending not to lean on me.

I felt the rightness of her here, in my arms, and I never wanted it to end. When she pulled away a fraction to look up at me, I didn't give her space. Didn't step back.

Instead, I lifted a hand to her cheek and swept the moisture from beneath her eye with the tip of my thumb.

"Thank you," she whispered.

"I haven't killed him yet."

A wry smile. "Please don't."

"Only if you insist."

In my arms, she felt slight and fragile. Nothing like the whirlwind of personality and snark and wit that I'd come to know. It was like that one interaction had sucked the life out of her, and it wasn't right.

My hand was still on her cheek. Pedestrians passed by us on either side; cars slowed to a stop when the lights turned red behind me. Her lips were inches from mine, her lashes clumped together with the tears she'd tried to squeeze back from falling.

Beautiful, strong, brittle, breakable woman. I'd never met anyone like her.

I dipped my head, the side of my nose touching the side of hers.

"Vaughn…" Her breath shivered against my lips, but she didn't pull away.

I brushed my mouth against hers, a whisper of a touch. Barely a kiss. She shivered, her eyes falling closed, and I pulled away an inch. Her clumped, wet lashes left smudges of mascara on the high points of her cheeks, and when she looked up at me again, I knew I had to stop lying to myself.

I wasn't going to be able to keep my hands off her, and I was sick of trying.

Eyes on hers, I lowered my head again and kissed her. She let out a sigh, her fingers curling into the lapels of my overcoat, her mouth parting to let in my delving tongue. She tasted like red wine and the pepper from her meal, and I wanted to kiss her until I tasted only her.

I groaned as she curled her hands around my neck, her fingers stroking my nape, nails digging into me. I wanted her to mark me, to leave half-moon indents in my skin so I'd feel the sting of her for the rest of the day. I wanted her angry and snarky and mean, because it was better than hollow and dead-eyed and running away from me.

Her body melted into me, and I forgot about the cold nipping at my ears and the cars spraying slush over the curb.

Yes. This was right. *She* was right.

I would let her distract me until my business fell down around me, because kissing her made me feel like I was flying.

She pulled away first, dazed, panting, her hands still on my neck. "We weren't supposed to do that."

"I know," I said. "Let's do it again."

FIFTEEN
ALBA

FOR THE FIRST time all year, warmth and safety penetrated the chill in my bones. I clung to Vaughn, fingernails digging into his skin, body leaning into his bulk. His arm tightened around me, his hand angling my head to deepen the kiss.

When we pulled apart again, I was dizzy. Then reason returned to my buzzing mind, and I put a hand over my mouth. "Oh, no."

"Not the reaction women typically have when they kiss me," Vaughn answered, a brow arching.

"I—"

"Whatever you're going to say, Alba, just—don't."

"We can't—"

"Don't say that either."

"I'm not—"

"Unless you're going to tell me you want me to drag you to bed and have my way with you, I don't want to hear it."

"*Vaughn.*"

His eyes were devilish, his arms still holding me close. He'd dropped the hand on my cheek to my waist, his other hand sliding across my back to band me to him.

I had to pull away. I couldn't leave the warmth of his arms.

"Erase the last ten minutes from your memory," I demanded.

"No can do, princess."

"I quit."

"I reject your resignation."

My hands were on his chest. When had my hands landed on his chest? I pushed away from him, and his hands dropped from my waist. We still stood close, the world around us a haze. My chest heaved; my mind spun.

He kissed better than I'd expected. Like he'd known exactly how to take charge, how to make me melt, how to make me want more.

I didn't want more. I was desperate for more.

"I have to go."

"Alba—wait."

"We shouldn't have done that. I can't get involved with you."

"We're not involved."

"So what, you kiss all your consultants?"

His jaw bulged as he clenched it. Then he spread his palms. "It won't happen again."

Was that disappointment making my chest feel tight? I gulped. "Good. I'll see you later this week."

I turned on my heel and walked away before he could call me back. My head remained full of cotton balls all the way home, and I found myself standing in my kitchen, staring at dried-on egg yolk smeared on one of my plates. How in the *world* did people get egg off their dishes? The stuff was like cement.

The ceramic clattered against the stainless steel of my sink, and I slapped my hands over my face. I'd screwed up. I shouldn't have kissed Vaughn. I shouldn't have reacted that way to seeing Yvette and James.

Yvette and James. My God. She'd smiled at me last week, pretending like she didn't remember his name. How long had they been sleeping together? How long had it taken him to jump from me to his next gravy train? Had they been fucking when I was with him? Why did that sting as much as it did? I didn't even *like* him anymore, let alone love, and we hadn't actually *been* together. But we'd spoken like we were. I'd been wrapped up in the dream of having my own independence, of finally feeling like I had agency over my own life. And he was just playing me.

How had I been so *blind*?

A buzz sounded from my purse. I looked over my shoulder at the table where I'd dropped it. Desperate to get out of my own head, I clawed at the zipper, opened my purse, and pulled out my phone.

Vaughn had messaged:

VAUGHN

I'm sorry.

As if it was all his fault. As if I hadn't leaned on him, clutched at him, kissed him back.

As if I hadn't enjoyed it.

I threw the phone down on the bedspread and paced my apartment. It was one room, and it only took five long strides to cross the whole space. I paced them, over and back, over and back. My skin was on too tight. My heart beat far too fast. For the first time since I'd left both my jobs, I missed having something to do. There were hours ahead of me with nothing to do but *think*.

Frustrated, I marched to the bathroom and turned on the shower. I stripped off my clothes—expensive, designer clothes from my old life—and left them crumpled on the linoleum floor.

Steam filled the small room, fogging up the window that had been sealed shut by some overzealous landlord with a gallon of white paint.

I stepped over the lip of the tub and yanked the curtain shut, careful not to let the wet, nasty bottom of it touch my legs. I missed glass walls, huge cubicles, luxurious rain showers overhead. But this one would do.

I'd be red as a lobster by the end of it, but I tilted my head toward the spray and let out a breath.

And I still wasn't as warm as when I'd been in Vaughn's arms. I still felt like I wanted to burst out of my skin, like I'd never be able to sit still. I could still feel the band of his arm around my back, the force of him tugging me closer. Shivering, I leaned my head forward to wet my hair.

His palm on my cheek, thumb brushing under my eye. His stubble against my temple. His lips, soft, demanding, delicious.

The light in his eyes when he'd promised to murder everyone who'd hurt me.

I wasn't sorry he'd kissed me. I wanted it to happen again. My hand was between my thighs before I could think to stop myself, and then my imagination ran away from me.

Those big, scarred hands spreading my knees. Ice blue eyes flicking up to meet my gaze, his dark head framed by my thighs. A wicked tongue, flat and hot as he tasted me. A low, satisfied groan. Fingers delving. The weight of him on top of me. The stretch of him inside me.

I gasped as heat washed through me, my hand scrabbling at the wet tile in front of me. Water pelted my back, my sodden hair shielding the world from me on either side of my face. Gulping down steamy air, I trembled under the spray and tried to remember the reasons I wasn't supposed to want him.

I stayed in the shower until the water went cold, and then I bundled myself in my comfiest clothes and slept.

———————

I WOKE up the next morning and immediately wrinkled my nose. The musty odor in my apartment seemed to be getting worse. Flopping onto my back, I stared at the ceiling, then cast my eyes around the single room that made up my home.

There were drifts of laundry gathering in the corners of the tiny two-seater sofa along the wall next to the front door, and drifts of dust in the corners of the room. When I turned it on, the light flickered overhead, as it had since I'd moved in. There was a persistent chill in the air and that now-familiar musty dampness that made me think of abandoned places.

But it was mine, paid for with money I'd earned myself. Besides, it was all I could afford.

I shifted in bed, and my thoughts turned to Vaughn. The ghost of his touch lingered on my back, my cheek, my waist.

I should never have kissed him, but I couldn't quite bring myself to regret it.

He was my boss now, my ticket out of instability. I couldn't go and ruin it by hooking up with him. And more importantly, he wanted entry into the life I never wanted to live again. The glittery, empty existence of a Manhattan socialite.

We were on different paths.

And yet—I was drawn to him. I wished he were here, so I could roll into him and spend the next three hours in his arms. I wished I could taste his lips again, lose myself in the warmth and safety of his arms.

Snorting out the moldy odor that seemed to cling to the inside of my nostrils, I swung my legs over the edge of the bed and stretched. My hip clicked, pain shooting up my back. Wincing, I curled in on myself and breathed through the pain. After almost a year and a half, I was mostly used to it. It would dull to a throb eventually, and I'd be able to move again.

It was yet another reality that had taken me a long time to accept, but I finally had. I'd be in pain for the rest of my life, because I could no longer afford adequate medical care. With a deep breath, I forced myself to straighten and used my arms to push myself off the edge of the bed.

Water and painkillers would help—or at least they'd make me feel like I was doing something about it. I shuffled the scant three feet from my bed to the kitchenette and tugged open the drawer that held my ibuprofen. The box slid forward, bumping against the front of the drawer. I popped out two pills, then grabbed a couple of Tylenols as well for good measure.

The yolk-smeared plate was still in the sink, and all my glasses and mugs were dirty. My tiny studio apartment was a microcosm of my life; things were getting on top of me lately. I'd just reached for a glass of questionable cleanliness when my phone rang. Vaughn's name lit up the screen, and my heart leaped. With the glass still in one hand, I grabbed my phone from where I'd left it on top of my blankets and stared at it for a second. I hadn't answered his text. Maybe I shouldn't answer his call?

Huffing at myself, I braced myself. If there was one thing I'd learned about myself this past year, it was that I was no coward. I swiped to answer.

"Vaughn" I greeted. "What can I do for you?"

"Hello, Alba," Vaughn responded, and I was glad he couldn't see the flush on my cheeks from the way my name sounded on his tongue. "I was just calling to let you know I've got an appointment with my tailor on Monday. I'd like you to come along."

Good. We weren't talking about the kiss. That was good. I straightened, relieved...and a little disappointed.

"I can do that," I said, turning back toward the sink. My aches pulsed with every heartbeat, and I needed water to swallow those pills. The sink was a slightly outdated style, with two plastic knobs on either side of the faucet for hot and cold. They were stiff, caked with green corrosion, and I knew I'd have to put some elbow grease into it if I wanted to fill my glass of water. "What time on Mond—ahh!"

"What? What happened?" Vaughn's voice called out from my phone, which now dangled from my hand near my thigh.

I screamed again, shielding my face from the spray of water coming from the sink. In my hand, I held a plastic knob with a blue ring around a black C. The cold water tap had snapped off entirely, with only a bit of the plastic remaining at the back, which directed the spray of water in a perfect arc toward my face.

I ducked and screamed again.

"Alba! Alba! What's going on? Are you okay?"

I put my phone to my ear again. "My sink!" I screamed.

"Your sink?"

"My sink!" I confirmed. "It snapped!"

"What?" Vaughn sounded like he was on the move. I heard the outdoors, the sound of traffic, then sudden silence. "What's going on? What do you mean, your sink snapped?"

"Not the sink—the—the thingy!"

"Slow down, Alba."

I sucked in a deep breath and watched the spray of water. It fell just short of my bed but had landed directly into one of those drifts of laundry. A puddle spread and soaked my toes.

"Now, tell me what's going on," Vaughn said, his calm, warm voice piercing through the shock.

"I'll show you," I rasped, and my hands shook as I swapped the call to video. I filmed the fountain of water, then lifted my other hand into the frame to show him the knob.

"Turn the water off," Vaughn exclaimed, like it was obvious.

I stared at the piece of plastic in my hand, then at the water. Feeling dumb and confused, I tried to plonk the knob back in place, which sent a spray of water blasting in all directions. I screamed.

"Under! Under the sink, Alba! There should be a shutoff valve!"

I dropped to my knees, opened the cabinet, and shoved away all the things I'd let gather there—cleaning products, odd pot lids, tomato-stained Tupperware—and looked at the network of pipes. It looked horribly complicated. White pipes and then copper ones. There was a flexible one snaking around the whole thing—

"There should be a little brass valve," Vaughn's calm voice sounded from the phone in my hand. "Can you show me? Move out of the way so a bit of light comes through—there. See that little valve with the blue on the end of it?"

I blinked water away from my face and pretended it wasn't a tear. I couldn't even turn on a sink properly. Gulping, I focused on Vaughn's voice and reached for the valve. "This?"

"That's it, princess. Should just take a quarter turn—yep. Good work."

The arc of water shrank above me, soaking my back and head, then turned to a dribble that went down the sink. I sighed out my exhale, then slumped onto the floor. Without thinking, I flipped the camera around and was momentarily stunned by the sight of my red cheeks, bloodshot eyes, wild hair half-plastered to one side of my head, and worn-out sleep shirt hanging off a shoulder, the other side of it soaked through. Another scream slipped through my lips and I slammed the phone on the ground, face down so the camera would be covered.

"Alba!"

"I'm fine," I said, shouting at the phone without moving it from its spot on the floor. "Um. So what time did you say on Monday?"

There was a pause. "Appointment's at eleven. I'll send the address."

"Great. Yep. Thanks! See you then." Being careful not to let any part of myself come into view, I flipped the phone around and hung up. Then I slumped back against the cabinets and half laughed, half sobbed in relief. The puddle had grown. I stretched out my legs, not caring that I was sitting in it.

When I finally gathered myself and stood, I stared at the carnage on top of my scant few square feet of counter space, the water on the floor, the mess of pot lids and cleaning products strewn all the way under my bed, and stomped to the bathroom to take a shower.

Everything would be easier after a shower.

Except it wasn't.

As I stepped out of the bathroom in a cloud of steam, curling the ends of my towel around each other to tie it around my chest, there was a knock on my door. I jumped, glancing across the carnage of the studio apartment to the front door on the opposite side of the room.

"Alba!" a familiar voice called out. "Are you okay? Answer me."

My eyes went wide. Vaughn was outside my apartment door. I blinked, momentarily speechless, trying to understand how this could possibly have happened.

My phone rang. It still rested on the bedsheets where I'd placed it before heading for a shower, and I glanced over to see Vaughn's name on the screen. My pulse jumped. I glanced from my phone to the door, feet glued in place.

What... was...*happening*?

Vaughn was *here*. Here, in my dumpy studio apartment, right outside the door. If I even cracked the door, he'd see the mess of laundry everywhere, the puddle of water that had soaked into everything. He'd see how tiny this room was, how filthy, and he'd finally realize just how far I'd fallen.

It was a messy, moldy, musty *wreck*. Kind of like me.

My heart hammered so hard my extremities tingled, and as Vaughn pounded on the door again, I was frozen with inaction. I could call out and tell him to go away, but I suspected that would only make him more insistent on coming in. I could stay exactly here, completely quiet, and hope he'd go away. I could—

"Open it," Vaughn's voice barked, and a moment later, a set of keys jangled.

The door swung inward, and the building's grumpy, ancient superintendent, Mr. White, stood in the opening, his eyes landing on my legs and climbing all the way up to the towel I held clenched at my breast. Behind him, Vaughn loomed, tall and broad, his brow wrinkled with worry, his blue eyes snapping to mine.

I made a noise, a pathetic little *eep*, which seemed to make Vaughn spring into action. He glanced from me to the super. One hand came up to clamp on the super's shoulder while his other slapped over the other man's eyes.

"Hey!" the old man said, and Vaughn hip-checked him out of the doorway. The old man made another outraged noise, but I barely heard it, because I dove back into the bathroom and locked myself inside.

My front door closed, and for a second, I thought I was alone, and a sigh of relief slipped through my lips.

Then, footsteps.

Vaughn's voice came rolling through the closed bathroom

door. "I was worried," he said by way of explanation. "You weren't answering my calls."

"How did you get my address?"

"Your employee file," he said.

"That's a breach of privacy."

There was a pause, then Vaughn said, "I thought you were in trouble."

Still clutching at my towel, I slumped against the vanity. I stared at the closed door, biting my lip, trying to pretend that my heart wasn't melting. He'd come to my rescue because he thought I needed it. No one had ever come to my rescue before. "I'm going to come out," I announced. "You have to close your eyes."

Vaughn hummed like he was considering his options.

I glared at the door.

"Fine," he said, and I cracked the door. Vaughn had his back to me, and I noted the presence of a big tool bag by the front door. I slithered out of the opening and grabbed my bathrobe from the corner of the bed, wrapping it quickly around myself. I tugged the towel out from under the robe and hung it up on the hook just inside the bathroom door.

Then I exhaled, crossed my arms, and said, "Okay. Now tell me what you're doing here."

Vaughn took one step and was across the room from me. He bent over and unzipped his tool bag. "I'm going to fix your leak."

"You can't just come here and fix my leak," I protested, planting my hands on my hips as I kicked a mound of laundry under my bed to hide it. It was wet, and I grimaced. I'd have to wash it all again, which would probably end up in me ruining everything I owned and burning the building down as well. I picked up a couple of pot lids and a bottle of multipurpose cleaning spray and let them clatter onto the countertop. The smear of egg yolk on my dirty plate stared back at me like an eldritch smile, cackling at my predicament.

Vaughn glanced over his shoulder and arched a brow at me. "I can, and I did." He stood up, holding a tool in one hand. I had no idea what it did, nor did I care. I was overwrought and over-whelmed. On the one hand, it was sweet that Vaughn had rushed here to save me from whatever he thought was attacking me. But on the other, his presence was making me feel things.

Like the sweet, mournful yearning of wanting him to come to my rescue all the time, forever. And the hope that now that he was here, everything would be okay. And the mortification of him seeing my cramped, filthy living space.

And, as he crossed the distance between us and stood before me, eyes steady on mine, cologne temporarily banishing the musty smell of my apartment, I became keenly aware that I wasn't wearing any underwear.

I gulped. "I, um, was in the middle of cleaning," I said, waving at the spray bottle on the counter.

His lips twitched. "Uh-huh."

"I'm usually very tidy," I lied.

The twitch turned into a curve. "Oh?"

"You caught me on laundry day, is all," I finally said, huffing.

Vaughn shifted, bringing his chest almost to mine. His free hand lifted up and pushed a strand of wet hair off my temple, which sent a zing of heat arrowing down my stomach. "I'm going to take a look at your sink," he said.

My heart—traitorous, silly thing—sank when he didn't lean down and kiss me again. Even though it was a good thing. A very good thing. Kissing him was bad. I couldn't quite remember *why*, but I was sure it was.

I busied myself tidying up the rest of the tiny apartment while he hunched under the cabinets of my kitchenette, but his presence was impossible to ignore. Anywhere I stood, I could see him from the corner of my eye. I caught hints of his cologne if I got too close. The sound of his breathing made my heart thump harder.

I'd just started folding some of the clean clothes on my sofa where there was a loud bang, and then a tearing sound. I jumped, then turned to see Vaughn crawling out from under the counters, holding a big piece of my cabinet.

"Oh my God, what are you doing? Put it back!" I said, flapping my hands.

Vaughn held up the piece of melamine to display a disgusting black patina crawling up the face of it. "Put it back?" he asked.

"I'll never get my deposit back!"

"Alba. This is mold." He held up the piece of cabinet.

I blinked at it. Then at him. Despair yawned open in the pit of my stomach, and I felt the mortifying urge to cry. Mold meant I'd *definitely* never get my deposit back. How did I deal with mold? How much would it cost?

Problems that would have previously been fixed with a phone call now seemed insurmountable. My chest began to feel tight. Breaths came faster. The landlord would blame me. I'd have to pay to fix it, and it would drain my savings and then some. I'd be kicked out. I'd be homeless. I'd have to—

Suddenly, Vaughn was there, a wall of warmth and safety. His hands clamped around me, enveloping me in their warmth. "Alba. Breathe."

"I can't."

"*Breathe*," he commanded, leaning his face right up into mine, his big palms coming to cup my jaw on either side, his bulk shielding me from the view of my horrible, dank home. I inhaled and exhaled with him, and the tightness in my chest began to ease. The warmth of his hands soaked through me, and before I could stop myself, I was burying my head in his chest, sighing as his arms wrapped around me once more.

Nowhere had felt safe for almost a year and a half—longer. Nowhere except Vaughn's arms. Tears prickled at my eyes, and as Vaughn's hand stroked my back, I let them soak into his shoulder.

"Sorry," I said, my voice muffled in his bulk.

"Don't be," he replied. Once I'd gathered myself, Vaughn pulled away slightly, but he didn't let me go. He guided me to the bed and sat down, pulling me down onto his lap. His thumb stroked the tears from under my eye. His gaze was utterly serious as he said, "Pack a bag, Alba. You're not staying here tonight."

I stiffened on top of him, my forearms resting on his shoulders. "What are you talking about?"

"It's a health hazard," he said, tipping his head toward the kitchenette, where the moldy cabinet stared at us from on top of the counter.

"I don't—I haven't—" I shook my head. *I don't have anywhere else to go.* Straightening, I shook my head. "This is inappropriate. You're my boss. You shouldn't even be here, and I can take care of myself."

"Alba—"

I screamed as another loud bang went through the apartment. I jerked. Vaughn caught me, and we slid off the end of the bed and tumbled onto the floor. One deep breath later, I looked over to see one of the feet of my bed had snapped, and the whole thing had collapsed.

Vaughn looked at the broken bed frame, then at me. "Pack a bag," he repeated, and his tone brooked no argument.

"The landlord...the mold—"

"I'll handle it." His tone was final.

For a fraction of a second, I considered protesting. I considered pushing him away, because getting any closer to him would no doubt end in heartbreak and disaster, just like everything else. But I was utterly drained—and I had nowhere to go.

It would feel so good to let someone else take some of the weight, for once.

I nodded.

Vaughn exhaled, like my agreement was a relief. "I'll wait downstairs." He helped me to my feet, and with my hand still clasped in his, he pulled me in and gave me a hard, demanding kiss. Then he pulled away and speared me with an icy, angry look. "You have twenty minutes. If you're not in my car by then, I'm carrying you out of here."

I scowled at him and opened my mouth to retort, but he kissed me again and made me lose my train of thought. Then he grabbed his tools and stalked out the door, leaving me in my bathrobe, panting, wondering how the heck I was going to resist him now.

SIXTEEN
ALBA

LIKE ANY SELF-RESPECTING BILLIONAIRE, Vaughn had properties dotted all over the place. This I discovered when he brought me to a luxurious tower on W 57th Street. We rode up the elevator to the penthouse, and Vaughn explained that he'd bought this place a couple of years ago, renovated it, and hadn't quite decided what to do with it.

"You'll be comfortable here," he declared as the private elevator opened directly into the vast apartment.

My heart thundered as I stepped out, floor-to-ceiling windows giving me a view of the snow-covered Central Park. We were on the southern end of it, looking straight up the length of it. It was like the apartment I used to live in—full of gorgeous furniture and finishes, pristinely clean, and absolutely enormous. I was a sad, dirty lump of despair by comparison. I didn't belong here—not anymore. Besides, I couldn't accept this kind of generosity from my boss. Not after we'd kissed. Not when I was supposed to be keeping my distance and figuring out my next steps. Gulping, I turned to him and gave him a sharp nod. "I just need a couple of nights."

He frowned. "You can stay here as long as you want, Alba. It's empty most of the time."

"I just need a couple of nights," I repeated, a little more forcefully.

He held my gaze for a moment, then shrugged. "The master bedroom's through here. It's got a great view of—"

"Oh, that's okay. That would be your room, wouldn't it?" I gave him a tight smile and gestured to the closest door, where I could see a large space with a plush-looking bed. "This one should be fine."

He opened his mouth as if to protest, then closed it again. With a nod, he said, "If that's what you want."

I walked over to drop my bag inside the door, feeling his gaze on my back.

Sure enough, when I turned around his frown had deepened. "Are you limping?"

"What? No. Well—yes. But it's just my hip. From the accident." I waved a hand. "It's fine."

"I'll get the concierge to bring some food up," Vaughn said, crossing to the kitchen where he glanced in the refrigerator. His eyes slid back to me, and I tried my very best to walk normally as I joined him in the big, marble-covered room, crossing to the opposite side of the massive island. Putting physical distance between us seemed like a necessity.

"I have to get back to work. I've still got my daughter, so I won't be able to—"

"That's fine," I said. "I'll be fine."

"Call me if you need anything," he demanded.

I nodded. "Will do."

"I mean it, Alba."

"So do I." I gave him my best smile, which only made his scowl deepen. After only a brief hesitation, he nodded, said goodbye, and made for the door.

"Vaughn," I called out.

He paused, the distance between us vast. "Yes?"

I didn't know how to put into words what I wanted to ask. We'd kissed, and now he'd swooped in and brought me here... "Is this... Thank you for this, but I..."

"Just say what you need to say, Alba."

"I'm worried that you think that because we kissed, I might owe you—"

"You owe me nothing. I need you fully committed to the job, and you can't do that if you're sick with inhaling black mold."

"Right. Yes."

"Is that all?"

The distance between us shimmered with all the things I wanted to say to him. That he was the first man I'd wanted in over a year. That he made me believe in hope again. That he terrified me. Instead, what came out was, "I still don't think we should have kissed."

His blink was slow, and the curl of his lips a little bit wicked. "Understood. It won't happen again."

I straightened, nodding, pretending his words didn't fill me with disappointment.

"It won't happen again until you beg me for it. Then I won't let you go so easily."

I opened my mouth to shout a retort, but the door snicked shut behind him, and I was alone. Exhaling, I spun in a slow circle. Everywhere I looked, there were incredible views and beautiful items. I ran my fingers over the back of the sofa in the vast living room, then poked my head into all the rooms. It felt familiar and strange at the same time.

Apparently, I'd gotten used to living in squalor. This apartment was just like my clothing: it felt like it no longer fit me. It was so nice that it made me think it would all be snatched away as soon as I took a wrong step. I was afraid to enjoy it.

I jumped at the buzz of the doorbell, then shuffled across the beautiful timber floors to open the door. A tall, thin man gave me a slight nod, his cart laden with enough food for a small army. "Ms. Enders?"

"Yes."

"For you," he said, nodding to the cart as I opened the door wider. "The masseuse is running a few minutes late," he said, rolling the cart inside the apartment. "I've given her your phone number."

"The masseuse?" I asked, staring after him.

"Mr. Avery organized it," he explained, and started unloading the groceries into the refrigerator.

I made to help him, then stepped back when he gave me a confused frown. It took me a few moments to slip into my old skin, where I was used to other people doing things for me. I drifted over to the sofa and scrolled mindlessly on my phone, then stood when the man told me he was done.

As soon as the door closed, my phone buzzed. Vaughn had messaged.

VAUGHN

Have you eaten?

I bit my lip to hold back the smile that tried to break through. It shouldn't have felt so good to have someone take care of me. I *wanted* to be independent. I wanted to stand on my own, to never be as vulnerable as I was before I was disowned.

But maybe, just this once, I could let someone take care of me again. I drifted to the refrigerator, and grabbed one of the pre-prepped meals, snapping a photo of it to send to Vaughn.

ALBA

Thank you

The masseuse arrived when I was done with my meal, apologizing profusely for her tardiness—apologies that I waved away. By the time she was done with me, my aches had faded to a low background buzz.

That night, I slept like the dead.

I ALLOWED MYSELF THREE DAYS. Three days of comfort. Of luxury. Of daily massages and beautiful food. Three days of winter views from my perch on top of the world, so my muscles could unknot and I could take a breath.

Then I forced myself to pack my bag and leave Vaughn's apartment, because it was too much like my old life. If I got used to it, it would hurt just as much as the first time when I got kicked out. I didn't know how to turn off a broken faucet, but I wasn't stupid. I'd learned my lesson: I couldn't rely on other people to be the safety net that I trusted to catch me when I fell.

Vaughn called me before I'd even left the building. "You're leaving," he said.

I glanced up at the corners of the lobby. "You got cameras on me, or something?"

He huffed. "Alba. Stay."

My heart thundered. We hadn't seen each other since the day he'd brought me here, and even the sound of his voice was weakening my resolve. I stared at the wintery street outside the lobby door and straightened my shoulders. "Thank you, but no. I've got a home."

Vaughn was quiet. "Fine. But you'll take a car."

"The subway—"

"It's already waiting for you."

My gaze shifted to the black sedan parked outside the building. I bit my lower lip, knowing I should refuse. Knowing that every time I accepted something from him, some of my resolve weakened. But one little car ride wouldn't be so bad, would it? It's not like I was kissing Vaughn again. It was just accepting a courtesy. "Thank you," I whispered.

His sigh ruffled the speaker. "Are we still on for tomorrow's lunch?"

"Yes," I said.

"I'll see you then."

"See you then," I replied. After I hung up, I clutched my phone to my chest, pretending that the warmth in my ribcage was simply the result of three days' rest. Then I stepped outside and waved to the driver, who opened the back door for me and took me back to my apartment.

Except I never made it to my apartment. I made it to the building and was intercepted by a spry, middle-aged redheaded woman in the lobby. She exited the office tucked in the corner next to the elevators and marched toward me. "Alba Enders?" she called out.

I paused with my finger on the elevator button. "Yes?"

"Here are your keys," she said, thrusting a new set at me.

I frowned. "My keys? What keys? Who are you? Where's Mr. White?"

"Retired," she announced. "New management. Name's Gina. Nice to meet you." She pumped my hand, then slapped the keys into them. "Your things have been moved to apartment 815. We've started work on your old studio. The mold—my goodness. Have a good day!"

I blinked at her back. "Wait!"

Her door slammed just as the elevator door opened. Dazed, I stepped inside, my finger hovering over the button for the fifth floor, where my studio was, before moving to the eighth. I pulled out my phone and found Vaughn's number, sure that this was something he had done...

But how? He'd whisked me off to his apartment and booked a few massages for me, but he'd have no control over my apartment building. I hiked my bag higher on my shoulder and made my way to the door marked 815. Half expecting the key not to work, I slid it in slowly and turned.

The door swung open to a clean, bright apartment much, much bigger than my studio. My things had been packed in boxes and left in the corner of the living room. There was no hint of my old, two-seater sofa. Instead, a long three-seater faced two armchairs, all surrounding a coffee table on top of a plush rug. The kitchen was tucked in the corner next to the front door, and through three doorways, I spied a bathroom and two other rooms. Upon closer inspection, one had been furnished as a bedroom, and the other as a small office. The furnishings were nowhere near as luxurious as Vaughn's penthouse, and there were no decorative touches or any artwork on the walls, but it was solidly built and ready to move into.

I wobbled on my feet as the walls closed in. A two-bedroom apartment...furnished...

How much would this cost me? Why had they moved me? What was going on?

Back downstairs, I banged on Gina's office door and was

greeted with silence. I spun around in a circle, hyperventilating, then I pulled out my phone.

Vaughn answered on the first ring. "Hello, princess."

"What did you do?"

"You'll have to be more specific."

"What did you *do*, Vaughn?" I repeated, leaning a palm against the wall before placing my head on the back of it. "You did this."

"Again, you'll have to—"

"My *apartment*!"

Vaughn paused, then said, "I might have called the building management and impressed upon them the importance of having habitable accommodations—"

"I can't afford the apartment they've put me in, Vaughn."

"Your rent isn't changing, Alba."

"But—"

"You need somewhere clean and safe to live. Now I need to get back to work."

"I—"

"Yes?"

I gulped. "Do you do this for all your employees?" My voice was small.

The silence between us stretched, and I wondered if Vaughn would answer at all. Then, finally, he said one word: "No."

"Oh," I whispered.

"I'll see you tomorrow," he said, gently.

"Yes."

I hung up, my head still leaning on my hand on the wall, then slowly straightened. When I stepped through the door of my new apartment once again, I couldn't help the sardonic huff that blew through my lips. He must've known I wouldn't stay at his place, and he organized this. Strong-armed the landlord, no doubt. Maybe even paid for it.

As I sank into the brand new sofa and stared out the window at the building opposite, I couldn't help the easing of my muscles.

THE NEXT WEEK and a half passed in a haze of winter and Vaughn. We had late afternoon dance lessons, with the space between our bodies kept at a professional arm's length, just as I'd requested. The warmth of his hand cupped mine and the press of his fingers tingled at my back.

At night, beyond the windows of my new apartment, snow swirled under the streetlights, and I came to the thought of those hands on my body.

We met for lunch at all my previous favorite restaurants, and I pretended that I didn't find the dining rooms stuffy and pretentious while I scanned for old enemies. I watched him become more comfortable as I squirmed, the touch of his foot against mine sending sparks dancing through my legs.

He presented his elbow for me to hook my arm through when we entered and exited, and I ignored the way his scent made me want to lean closer. He held my jacket and slid it on over my shoulders, his knuckles brushing the sides of my neck. The perfect gentleman.

I went home, collapsed in bed, and pretended the wetness in my underwear hadn't been there since the moment I saw him. My clit ached, engorged, throbbing, needy.

I sat on the couch at Mr. Koval's shop, watching the older man pin the beginnings of a tuxedo on Vaughn's frame, then went with him to an Italian shoemaker to get his foot measured for a pair of bespoke shoes. He stood close to me, his fingers brushing mine as he took a display boot from my hands, the scent of leather and Vaughn making me dizzy.

He didn't kiss me. He barely touched me. I felt like I was starving. I was in too deep already.

SEVENTEEN
VAUGHN

CHARLOTTE'S PLAYDATE was entering the ear-piercing shrieks portion of the afternoon. I sat at my desk in my home office, going through emails that I'd neglected during the week. Saturdays should've been reserved for my daughter—especially during the weeks that I had custody of her—but the extra time I'd dedicated to my training with Alba meant that some of my work spilled into the weekends.

"Daddy!" I looked up from the computer screen in time to see Charlotte skidding to a stop in the doorway. Blue paint smeared her cheek, and one of her pigtails had lost its tie. She brandished a paper covered with not-quite-dry paint. "I made this for you!"

I pushed my chair back and turned to face my daughter as she circled my desk. Taking the painting in one hand, I curled the other around Charlotte's shoulder. "I love it," I said. "Reminds me of Van Gogh."

"I used blue because it's your favorite color."

"Is it?" I asked, smiling faintly.

"Duh. Your new suit is blue."

"You chose my new suit."

"Because blue is your favorite," Charlotte replied, looking at me like I was dense.

I laughed. "Fair enough. Where should we hang this one?"

"Daddy, it has to dry first," she said, plucking the paper from my hands. "You're so silly."

I huffed and turned back to my computer. Time passed, and I heard my daughter running down the hallway toward me. "Daddy!"

"I'm working, turkey." The lawyers had sent through the latest communication with the troublesome subcontractor, and—

Charlotte's shoulders dropped. Her face was pure disappointment. "Okay," she said, and disappeared around the corner to rejoin her friends.

Pain shot through my chest, and I stared at the half-read letter on my screen, cursing myself. All this work—for what?

My wife had divorced me for this. She kept vying for more custody time because she insisted I wasn't spending enough time with Charlotte when I had her. But if I didn't work, then we wouldn't have all these nice things.

It was a justification I'd recited to myself a thousand times, but it felt hollow now. I thought of Alba, thrown out on her own, the bitter twist of her lips when she compared my words to her father's. My throat was tight. My hand snapped out like a striking snake to shut the top of my laptop. Charlotte would be going back to her mother tomorrow, and I could answer emails then.

I followed the sounds of high-pitched squealing toward the second living area, which had been transformed into a play space for Charlotte. The table was covered in a plastic tablecloth, smeared with various colors of paint. The children were feral.

Billie herded them toward the bathroom one at a time, calling out a cheerful, "Time to wash our hands!"

"Daddy!" Charlotte called out as she walked out of the bathroom, her fingers leaving a trail of drips of water from the bathroom back to the playroom, her face splitting into a huge smile. "Sit down. I want to paint your nails." Imperious, she pointed to one of the child-sized chairs in the playroom.

I complied. What else was I supposed to do? Five-year-old children swarmed me, brandishing kid-safe nail polish bottles at me.

"Matilda," Charlotte said, "he likes *blue*." She held up a bottle of sparkly blue polish.

"Because he's a boy," Matilda said, nodding in understanding.

"I'm a boy, but I like purple," another child said.

"Purple is nice," Charlotte agreed, wrenching my hand toward her. I sat back on the too-small chair, smiling, and let my daughter smear polish all over my fingertips. When she concentrated, her brow furrowed and her tongue stuck out at the corner of her mouth.

It took her ten minutes to cover my nails (and surrounding skin) with glittery blue polish, while her friends put clips in my hair and wrapped swags of fabric around my body. When she capped the polish and proclaimed the job done, she gave me the biggest, most beaming smile I'd ever seen. "You're pretty," she told me, and I laughed.

Later, when the other kids were gone, Billie had gone home, and I had finished reading Charlotte her favorite bedtime story, she threw her arm over my chest and planted a kiss on my cheek. "I love you, Daddy."

"I love you too, turkey."

She nestled next to me and let out a sigh. "Today was the best day ever."

I stayed with her until she was asleep, then crept out of the room and went back downstairs. I sat on the couch, a huge piece of wildly expensive artwork behind me, a custom-built coffee table in front, my toes wiggling in the imported, handwoven rug that framed all the furniture...and I realized that Alba had been right.

None of this stuff mattered to Charlotte. She wouldn't care about private tutors and luxurious vacations. She just wanted me to be there to let her paint my nails.

Later, maybe, when she was older, she'd appreciate everything I did. She'd have a home of her own, a good career, anything money could buy. She'd know how hard I worked for her.

Or...maybe she'd remember days like today, that had hardly cost a dime.

THE NEXT TIME I saw Alba was on Tuesday evening at the dance studio. She sat cross-legged at the far end of the room, black leggings cladding her bottom half, a loose white tee giving me a glimpse of a black sports bra beneath. She looked up, blond hair glinting, and nodded.

"Good," she said. "You're here."

My eyes dropped to her lips, then away. "I'm here."

She stood up and faced me. "Next time, bring your date."

"My date?"

"To the gala. So you can practice dancing together."

I nodded. "Right. Um...about that."

She arched a brow. "Don't tell me you don't have a date."

"Noble bullied me into buying a table. I just figured I'd fill it with people from the office."

"*Vaughn.*"

"What?"

"You are unbelievable."

I loved it when she got exasperated with me. I'd only gotten glimpses of it these past couple of weeks. She'd put her walls up, and I told myself it was for the best. At least she'd allowed me to take care of her living situation. That had calmed the part of me that needed to control, protect, and watch over. But I loved her like this, open and annoyed and real.

I shrugged. "Look, it's a business dinner. I'm bringing business associates. What's the big deal?"

"What am I even doing here?" she demanded. "Have you learned *nothing*?"

"I've learned I should use the side plate to butter my bread and keep my grubby fingers off the wine glass bowl."

She grumbled to herself, then turned back to me. "You find yourself a date. The gala is in three weeks!"

"You don't think I can get a date in three weeks?"

"Someone who won't see it as an excuse to get drunk on champagne and embarrass you."

"I agree. I'm perfectly capable of doing that myself."

Her jaw hardened, and her eyes flashed. She clenched her fists, then took a deep breath. "It's your funeral. Or should I say—your business's funeral."

"Arlo Noble doesn't seem like the kind of guy who would stand on ceremony."

"That's not the point."

We'd moved closer at some point, as we always seemed to do. I could smell her shampoo, see the glint of the lights against the gold necklace she always wore. I canted my head and arched my brows, just because I knew it would annoy her. "And what is the point?"

"You," she said, poking my chest, "are a debutante. This is your ball. Your entry into society. The appearance that will shape people's opinions of you."

"How exciting."

"You're not taking any of this seriously, are you?"

"Five hundred dollars an hour is pretty serious to me."

She shrugged. "Not to these people."

The way she said "these people" made me pause. Her gaze slid away from me, and I studied the stubborn tilt of her chin, the muscle feathering in her cheek.

I wanted to kiss that frown away. I wanted to drop to my knees and worship her until she was boneless in my arms.

"There's only one person who could be my date and not embarrass me," I finally said.

Her eyes, blue, slitted, unimpressed, blinked back to meet mine. "Don't even think about it."

I took a step forward, and she took a step back. "Alba," I started.

"Absolutely not."

"The only other person I could bring is my mother."

"Wonderful. A family man."

"She'll *definitely* get drunk on champagne and embarrass me."

Her stubborn chin lifted. "Maybe that's exactly what you deserve." I'd backed her up against the wall of mirrors, and now she pressed herself against it.

My palm landed next to her head. "Come with me," I said.

"No."

"Show all those people who turned their backs on you that you aren't broken."

Her eyes sparked. God, she looked good when she was furious. "You don't know anything about me."

"I know that you hate the way you felt when you ran into those assholes at Rebellieux."

Her jaw clenched.

"You hate to be made to feel small and weak and scared."

"You don't know anything about me," she repeated through clenched teeth.

"I know that's how you felt, because that's how I feel every time I have to walk into one of these business meetings and pretend I respect the person on the other side of the table. Rich, pretentious assholes who don't know anything about hard work."

She turned her head to look at the darkened windows. "So what? I go to one event on some oaf's arm—"

"Ouch."

"—and then suddenly I'm back in? I don't even want to be back in. I just want—" She stopped.

"What? What do you want?"

Her chest rose and fell with a breath, and she turned to meet my gaze. Tension pulled tight between us, my fingers curling against the mirror by her head. The flash in her eyes was what did me in. I could keep my distance when she put her walls up, but this? When she was real?

Irresistible.

Alba's gaze flicked between my eyes, her brow wrinkling. We'd circled each other for weeks, and I was so sick of holding back. But I wouldn't push her. Not when I knew it might push her away.

Instead, I waited. The silence hummed between us, and I thought about how badly I'd wanted her to stay at my apartment. How much it had soothed me to know she was there, safe, taken care of.

Maybe she read that thought in my face, because she finally whispered, "I just want to feel like the rug isn't going to get pulled out from under me." Her throat clenched as she swallowed. "I just want to feel safe."

I could give her that. I would live to give her that. If she let me.

But Alba had thick walls, and I knew it would take a long time to get through them. But I could try.

My free hand slid to her hip, thumb tracing the bone that protruded there. Her breath caught.

"Tell me to stop, and I will."

She opened her mouth—but nothing came out. A mouth I'd dreamed about every night since I'd tasted it. A mouth of razor-sharp words and wry smiles and desperate kisses.

Slowly, studying the fluttering of her eyelashes and the pulse thrumming in her neck, I moved my palm from her hip to her inner thigh, sliding it up so I could feel the heat of her beneath the stretchy, smooth fabric of her leggings. She shivered, stepping her feet a little wider, and I curled my hand to hold her there, where she was hot and damp. My heart rattled.

"Are you wet, Alba?"

She glared at me.

"Have you been waiting for me to touch you all this time?"

"I haven't been *waiting*—"

She gasped as I ground the heel of my hand against her clit, hands scrabbling at the mirror.

"You want me to stop?"

She bit her lip, closing her eyes. I took my hand away from the mirror and gripped her chin, tilting her head until she opened them back up again and met my gaze. Her eyes were liquid, desperate.

"Do you want me to stop, Alba?" I rubbed at the gusset of her leggings, heart pounding so hard I wondered if she could hear it.

She sipped in little breaths, and she shook her head.

"You want me to make you come?"

Alba nodded.

"I need your words, princess."

"Yes," she whispered.

"Yes, what?"

She huffed, frustration flashing across her features. "Yes, I want you to make me come."

The words sent a jolt through me. She was burning hot against my palm, wet enough that I could feel it through her clothing. She was mad as hell—and she wanted me.

EIGHTEEN
ALBA

I WASN'T SUPPOSED to be doing this. And I definitely wasn't supposed to enjoy it. It had happened so fast, but, but...

Maybe just this once—

Vaughn's hand gripped between my legs, and heat pulsed through me. I gasped, clinging to his shoulders, my head falling back onto the mirrored wall with a thump. His scent was all around me. Heat rolled off his body, warming me through. His hands were big and scarred and possessive, and I didn't have the will to fight my attraction anymore.

There were so few things in my life that were enjoyable these days. A rare vanilla latte at the café near my apartment. The few weeks of later sleep-ins I'd enjoyed since working for Vaughn. Yoga on the only available patch of living room floor—though these days, the living room was bigger and I had a dedicated yoga space in my home office. But who knew how long that would last?

I'd endured more than a year of drudgery, scraping by without the skills or resources required, with nothing but my own willpower and sheer stubbornness to see me through.

And I was *tired*. I wanted to let go.

That's why I didn't back away, why I ignored the voice in my head that told me I shouldn't give in to the pull of Vaughn. His touch felt too good.

That, and I wasn't sure I would've been able to stop. There was a pounding desire inside me, some other force that made me into a selfish, needy creature. Tension pulled tight below my navel, the promise of release.

I wanted to give in.

Vaughn cupped one hand over the side of my neck, his thumb running along my jaw. Then he kissed me, the heel of his other hand pressing harder against my clit. I squirmed, panting against his lips, and I felt him smile against me.

"So impatient," he murmured.

"Vaughn," I whined.

His chuckle was dark, and it sent little sparks of sensation detonating in my gut. Then he slid his hand to the waistband of my leggings and tugged it down, catching my underwear along the way. My hips rocked forward with his yank, and when I leaned back, my ass pressed against the cool mirror at my back.

Vaughn let out a groan when his fingers touched my core once more. I was slick, his fingers sliding against me as he pressed me harder against the mirror. My leggings pinned my legs together, but I rocked my hips forward to try to give him more access.

I was wanton, desperate. I'd completely lost control.

And I loved it.

The heat of his touch against my center made me tremble. The scrape of his teeth against my jaw made me cling to him with my fingernails.

"Look how wet you are, princess," he said in a low voice. "How much you need this." His fingers slowed, circling my clit with teasing touches.

"Vaughn, you promised you'd make me come." The back of my head knocked against the mirror as I pulled back to glare at him.

His smile was bright, and the pressure of his touch didn't change. "I did promise. And I will."

"Stop messing around."

He dipped his fingers back to circle my opening. "What if I like making you pant like this?" he asked, head ducking to kiss my ear, the corner of my jaw. "What if I want to see just how demanding you'll get?"

"You're such a jerk."

He hummed, one finger sliding inside me. The heel of his hand pressed where I needed it, and I trembled against him. He pulled back to watch me, his eyes half-lidded, as he pumped his finger inside me—and then added another.

My breaths became shorter, faster. His touch felt so good. I wanted to come. Wanted to feel that rush of relief, that flush of heat and pleasure. I squirmed and sighed and clung to him, and it seemed like my orgasm got further and further away. When he pulled his fingers out to circle my clit, his hand slick with my arousal, I gulped down breaths and squeezed my eyes shut, willing myself to let go.

But I'd been on edge for over a year. Longer. It was hard to relax, to let my guard down long enough to get there. I wasn't supposed to be doing this. This man, for all intents and purposes, was my boss. My one lifeline to stability.

And I was ruining it. I'd already ruined it when I agreed to let him touch me. I'd been selfish and stupid and reckless, just like before—

"Alba, stop." His fingers stilled.

My eyes flew open. "What?"

He kissed me, then pulled back. One hand was still on the side of my neck, holding my chin up so I'd have to meet his eyes. "Turn that brain of yours off. Stop thinking so hard."

With the fingers of his other hand, he entered me again, slow and steady, until his thumb was nestled against the side of my clit. Then he stopped and kissed the corner of my mouth. "Let me do this for you."

I gulped, nodding. "I'm—it's okay if I don't—"

"Let me do this for you, Alba," he repeated, voice rough. "I've imagined it too many times to fuck it up now."

A huffed laugh fell from my lips. If only he knew how much I'd dreamed of him these past weeks. How many times I'd touched myself, wishing it was him.

But imagining him, solo in my bed or my shower with my hand between my legs, was different from the reality of being here, in a studio where we definitely weren't supposed to be doing this, with his scent and his warmth and his size.

It was too real.

With Cole, sex had been a commodity. I knew, on some level, that he didn't really want me. Our sex life became mechanical, transactional. Whenever it had been too long, I'd hear my mother's voice in my head on repeat: *You'll need to take care of your husband. You'll have to keep him happy so he has nothing to complain about at home. At least until you've given him a child.*

I'd been trained to be the perfect little wife, hadn't I? From a young age, I'd been trained to treat sex as something to be used to exchange power. It wasn't for my pleasure; it was to keep my future husband happy. If I gave it away for the wrong reasons, my value in society would plummet. If I somehow gained the reputation for being loose, then all hope of marrying well would disappear. Even in this day and age.

Sex wasn't a rush of relief and pleasure. It wasn't the union of two people. It was something to be used.

And here, in this dance studio, who was using whom?

Vaughn's eyes flicked between mine, and his movements slowed. He pulled his hand from between my legs, but he didn't back away. I stood against the wall of mirrors, trembling slightly, trying to push away all the thoughts that swamped out my desire.

But Vaughn saw it all in my eyes. Saw my conflict, felt my tension, heard my ragged breaths—and knew they weren't from pleasure.

"You're not enjoying this," he said, and straightened slightly.

"It's not—" I gulped, my hands still on his shoulders. I curled my fingers, holding him there. "It's... I don't know, Vaughn. Maybe —" I squeezed my eyes shut. "This was a bad idea."

I wanted him to touch me. I wanted him to look at me like I mattered. But I couldn't get out of my own head. I couldn't stop thinking about the fact that having sex with him right now would ruin something.

After all, hadn't I learned my lesson with James? I'd given him everything—sex, love, money, power—and I hadn't realized he'd been the one using me all along.

It always came down to using. Being used.

How was I supposed to have sex when that was all I knew? When the one time I thought I'd found someone to love, he'd only been with me for my family's money? For access to that world that was so hollow and false?

Vaughn's body was still close to mine, and my fingernails curled into the shoulders of his shirt. I expected him to back away, to leave me cold and alone. Wasn't that the easiest thing to do? I'd rebuffed his advances. I hadn't put on a show of loving his touch, of wanting to reciprocate. I'd ruined this, just like I'd ruined my engagement and my affair and my life. Rejection was incoming; it always came after I screwed something up.

But he didn't back away. His thumb stroked my jaw, and his

other hand slid up my hip to rest on the bare skin of my waist beneath my shirt. "Talk to me," he said.

I huffed a bitter laugh. My bare ass was still pressed against the mirrors. The wetness between my legs had turned cold, and I was trembling in front of him. The situation wasn't exactly conducive to conversation.

Vaughn didn't seem to care. He widened his stance, eyes flicking between mine, and held me there.

I gulped. "I'm sorry."

"No. Don't apologize. Just tell me what's going on in that beautiful head of yours."

Oh, God. I was going to cry. Could this get any more mortifying? My gaze slid over his shoulder, and the thumb on my jaw stilled, then pressed until I met his gaze again.

"Alba," he said, voice low. "I'm not the kind of guy who ignores it when a woman looks like she isn't enjoying herself. Is it something I did?"

"What? No." I shook my head. "It's just me. I'm messed up."

"Tell me."

"I..." I opened my mouth, but no words came out. His thumbs stroked my jaw and my waist, soft and comforting, but I still couldn't work my voice past the lump in my throat.

Vaughn waited, patient, steady, unmoving.

Finally, I said, "The last guy I had sex with turned out to only want me for my family's money."

"That coward from the restaurant."

I nodded, dropping my eyes to his chin. It was easier than looking at his eyes. "I... All my life, I knew that I would marry someone, that I'd have to appear in society as that man's wife. So I had to learn what that meant. How to act. How to dress. How to make him look his best."

"Like tying his tie."

My gaze flicked up to his, and I found his eyes serious. I nodded. "Yes."

"And sex?"

"I wasn't trained in the art of seduction, if that's what you mean," I said, voice tightening. "But sex was never...for me." On the last word, my voice was a bare whisper. My body was hot and cold, my fingers twitching on his shoulders. I couldn't meet his gaze. My heart pounded, but I felt it only distantly.

Rejection shimmered nearby, a ghost ready to make itself known. Vaughn would surely take one look at me right now and decide that I was too much work. He could get his rocks off with someone else. Someone who was easier. Someone who wasn't so messed up.

Instead, Vaughn stepped closer and shifted his hand to grip my chin between his thumb and forefinger. He tilted it up so I had no choice but to meet his gaze. In a low voice, with no hint of judgment, he asked, "What do you need, Alba?"

The question terrified me. I needed a lot of things—shelter, security, food, a job—but I knew that wasn't what he meant. His gaze was steady, his body unmoving. I knew he wouldn't turn away from me until I told him the truth. There was something so utterly comforting about that that I had no choice but to tell it to him: "I need to stop thinking so much."

Understanding flashed across his eyes. He dipped his chin. "Do you want me to help you? Tell you exactly what you need to do, and nothing more? You won't lose control, Alba. All you've got to do is listen to me."

Yes. I wanted that. I wanted to let go only as far as he would let me. Sucking in a sharp breath, I nodded.

Vaughn leaned forward and brushed his mouth against mine.

With his lips still touching me, he said, "You stop this whenever you want. Got it?"

I nodded. "Yes."

"Good. Now get on your knees."

As my knees hit the polished wood floor, the feeling that rushed over me was relief. Relief that he hadn't turned away from me. Relief that he hadn't tried to fix me. Relief that all I had to do now was exactly what he said.

His belt jingled, knuckles and tendons shifting as he pulled it out of its buckle and unfastened his pants. Then his cock was there, hard and veined and throbbing.

"Put those pretty lips on my cock and suck, princess," he commanded, and I did. I licked the tip of him and wrapped my mouth around his shaft, listening to him groan above me.

All I had to do was exactly what he said. I didn't have to wrestle with my own body, with my mind, with the ghost of rejections past. I could just wrap my lips around his cock and take him deeper in my mouth, and everything went quiet in my head.

He tasted like salt and man, and I groaned as the thick vein against my tongue pulsed. Vaughn's thumb stroked my hollowed-out cheek before his fingers tangled into the hair at the nape of my neck, gently urging me to take him deeper.

"That feels good, princess," he said, voice interrupted by his panting. "You'll make me come if you keep doing that."

I hummed, nodding, then wrapped my hands around the base of him and started bobbing my head.

"So pretty," he said, fingers tightening at my nape. "So fucking pretty with my cock in your mouth. Been dreaming of those lips around me. Been wanting to paint them with my cum and watch you lick it off."

My heart stuttered to a stop, eyes flying open.

So—Vaughn was super dirty. I glanced up to see him dark-eyed and heavy-lidded, watching my every move. He kept talking, telling me all the things he'd imagined with me over the past weeks, his fingers tightening in my hair until my bun fell apart, his cock hard and hot in my mouth.

I gripped his thighs and took him deeper, my eyes watering as he groaned above me. My mind was blessedly silent. All that mattered was this act. The ache of my knees on the hard floor. The need to focus on my breath so I could take more of him. So I could please him. So I could just do what he said and not *think*.

"Are you wet, princess?" At my nod, Vaughn hummed. "Show me. Touch yourself."

My leggings were still halfway down my thighs, so all I had to do was reach between them. I was slick with my own desire, my fingers coming away glistening.

"Good." Vaughn was panting hard now, his hand on the back of my head clenching and releasing, as if he was holding himself back from being too rough with me. "Keep that hand between your legs, princess. Get yourself nice and wet so my cock can slide right in when I decide to fuck you."

It was easy to touch myself in front of him when he said that, when I was only getting myself ready for him. I didn't have to orgasm. I didn't have to chase some climax that kept getting further away. All I had to do was make sure I was wet and ready. Make sure I would be good for him.

I didn't even have the mental space to judge myself for enjoying this. For *loving* this. For wanting him to use me whichever way he wanted to.

This time, it was my choice to be used. I decided if this ended —he'd said it himself, I could tell him to stop at any time. I was in control, even if he pretended to be.

So I let go of all those thoughts and insecurities and worries. I worked my hand between my legs until my arousal soaked my inner thighs, until I was trembling and humming with Vaughn's cock in my mouth. My existence narrowed to the taste of him, the salty beads already dripping from his tip. The feel of his hand at the back of my head, the strands of my own hair brushing the sides of my face, my neck. The ache of the hard floor against my knees. The slip of my fingers against my clit.

Vaughn groaned above me, and the sound sent spiraling pleasure through my body. "You suck my cock so well, princess," he praised. "Such a dirty, delicious mouth you have. Better than I could have imagined. Can't wait to get inside you. Can't wait to give you my cock. Relax, baby, let me take you a little harder."

His voice was low and dark, and his words chased away every inhibition I might've had. I eased my jaw open, and Vaughn had his way with me. My body was loose, my fingers frantic against my bud. Then Vaughn pulled out, his thumb on my chin, his eyes wide as his chest heaved.

"You're so beautiful," he said, watching me. "Did you make yourself nice and wet for me?"

I nodded, and then his hands were around my ribs and he was hauling me to my feet. I felt like a doll in his hands, empty of all thought, open, ready.

With one hand holding my chin, Vaughn reached between my legs. He let out a low noise at the slickness he found there, his eyes darkening as they held mine. "Good girl," he rasped. "Hands on the ledge."

He tilted his head toward the windows, where a low ledge stuck out a few inches. I shuffled over and bent at the waist, catching myself on it. My reflection in the darkened windows was clear, as was the shadow of Vaughn moving behind me.

His hands slid over my bare ass, stroking, worshiping. He held my hips, then slid his hands down, thumbs pressing at the juncture of my thighs. He stroked there, where I was wettest, his breaths growing ragged. One thumb dipped inside me, and then I watched his reflection bring the digit up to his mouth. He groaned as he licked his thumb clean, then met my eyes in the window's dark reflection.

"This is for my pleasure only," he promised, then got on his knees behind me and brought his mouth to my core.

I gasped as Vaughn's tongue lapped at me, delved inside me, then slid forward to tease at my clit. He spread me open with his hands and pushed me up so I was on my tiptoes, then he licked me from my clit to my ass like a man starved. My fingernails dug into the paint on the window ledge, my forehead pressing against the glass.

"Vaughn—"

"This is for me," he repeated darkly, and his mouth was on me a moment later.

I sucked in hard breaths, half expecting my mind to come back online so I could overthink this vulnerable position and the way Vaughn was devouring me. With other partners, I was never able to climax with oral. I was worried about the taste of me, the way I smelled, the way I looked. I was worried that they resented doing it, or that they'd expect more from me after they were done.

I'd always faked my orgasms, mostly to get them to stop. To save their egos, to avoid having to *explain*.

But Vaughn said this was for his pleasure. He—he was eating me out for his own enjoyment. The knot of tension in my gut eased, and then the sensations overwhelmed me. His hot tongue. His hands, gripping and spreading and holding. The rasp of his stubble, the press of his nose. The low grunts and gasped breaths.

And I let go. I stopped trying to resist the pleasure that grew in the pit of my stomach. I pushed back into his touch, chasing more. Needing more. Vaughn made encouraging noises, his fingers tightening on my thighs, his tongue stroking into me.

Then he pulled away, breathing heavily. "I'm going to fuck you now, princess. I'll do it hard and fast and you'll come when I say. Yeah?"

I nodded, strands of hair falling on either side of my face. My mind was deliciously blank, my body buzzing.

"Tell me that's what you want."

"Yes, Vaughn. Please."

He grunted appreciatively, one hand gripping my hip as he stood up. His cock pressed against my ass, hot and hard, and I trembled. With his hands on my hips, Vaughn walked me backward until my arms were extended, my head away from the window. There was the sound of fabric shifting. A crinkle. The reflection in the window told me Vaughn was getting a condom, sheathing himself with steady hands.

And then he fucked me hard and fast, just like he promised. My legs were still pinned by my leggings, and he shoved them together so the fit was tight and overwhelming. His thumbs pressed down on my lower back so I had to arch to take more of him, my arms trembling with the effort to hold myself up.

Everything was Vaughn. His hands, his cock, his breaths, the low murmur of his voice as he told me that I was beautiful, that I took his dick so perfectly, that he'd never had anyone as good as me.

"I want to feel you come on my cock, princess," he told me, his voice rough with need.

A thread of stress wound its way through me. It was hard for me to orgasm. What if I couldn't—

"I want to feel it," he said. "Want that perfect pussy clenching on me. Do that for me, princess. Give it to me, and then you can lick my cock clean."

A blush tingled over my lips, but I couldn't help the sigh that escaped me. I lost myself in the sound of his voice, in the words he used to command me. Vaughn hooked an arm around my waist to pull my upper body tight to his. He spun us around toward the mirrors, and I put my forearms on it while his hand slid down my lower stomach and over my mons. Then his thick, calloused fingers were on my clit, his cock filling me to the hilt.

His breaths were loud in my ear. His free hand reached up to grip my breast, thumb pressing into the soft flesh above my sports bra. I met his eyes in the mirror and realized I trusted him. I was as safe as I'd felt when we kissed. As safe as I'd felt in his apartment, for those three glorious days when I didn't have to worry about a thing.

Vaughn gave me that, and he was giving me this too.

I came, my head falling back onto his shoulder, my legs shaking as he thrust into me. His groans were wordless, but they told me how good he felt. How good *I* felt to him.

I was still feeling the rush of orgasm when he hardened inside me, the hand on my breast flying out to brace himself against the mirror. His thrusts were rough and deep, and another rush of pleasure went through me. I'd done that to him. For him.

My eyes closed, and my body went limp. He banded his arms around me and kissed my neck, breaths gusting out of his nose to wash over my skin. When he pulled out of me, a warm rush went with him. A moment later, something soft wiped over the skin of my inner thighs and my intimate flesh.

I looked down to see one of his pristine, expensive silk ties being used as a makeshift handkerchief and snorted out a laugh. Vaughn smiled at me in the mirror, kissed the side of my neck, and then lifted the waistband of my leggings back up to where it belonged. His hands lingered on my hipbones, fingers teasing the creases of my thighs. It was a possessive touch, and I discovered I didn't mind it at all.

"You're coming home with me," he informed me, and arched a brow at me in the mirror as if in expectation of a fight.

It probably should have sounded warning bells inside me when I rolled my lips inward and nodded, agreeing far too easily. But I wanted to go home with him. I wanted his soft, tender ministrations and his hard, mind-blanking sex. I wanted him, and I was too far gone to resist.

NINETEEN
ALBA

I WAS surprised when we didn't go to the penthouse. Vaughn had said he was taking me home, but I hadn't thought he meant *home*. Walking into Vaughn's townhouse felt like putting on an old pair of favorite jeans. It was beautifully decorated but maintained a cozy vibe. Much nicer than my current accommodation, and more in line with the places I used to live when I was part of my old world, but not so cold and impersonal. Evidence of his daughter dotted the space, from a few drawings pinned to the refrigerator to a playroom full of toys just off the main hallway.

Where the penthouse had felt familiar and uncomfortable, this was a beautiful melding of comfort and luxury. I loved it the minute I stepped through the front door.

We found our way to the kitchen, where Vaughn pulled down two wine glasses from the cabinets and grabbed a bottle of wine from the dedicated wine fridge.

"I thought you said you weren't a wine person," I said, leaning against the marble countertop.

Vaughn glanced over, grinning. "I signed up for an online wine tasting course, and now I finally have a use for this wine fridge the interior designer insisted I needed."

Laughing, I accepted the glass he handed me. I wandered over to the big, stainless steel refrigerator and studied one of the drawings pinned there with magnets. It was a drawing of a little girl, her father, and another woman. Shamefully, a dart of jealousy went through me. I'd slept with this man exactly one time and I already felt like I had a claim on him.

"Billie, her nanny," Vaughn explained, shifting to stand behind me, and the jealousy faded. His hand coasted over my side, stroking. He'd touched me constantly since we left the dance studio. Even when I'd frantically wiped down the mirrors and glass, horrified at the butt and handprints we'd left there, Vaughn had laughed, stroked my side, squeezed my hip, and made sure that he was within touching distance.

It was...nice. Cole hadn't been like that, even though we'd been engaged to be married. He'd held my hand occasionally, and he'd put his arm around me at events, but mostly we lived parallel lives. James had touched me often, when we went out, but it felt more like he was treating me like an object rather than simply touching me because he wanted to.

With Vaughn, his touches were intimate and casual all at once. He'd rested his palm on my knee the whole way from the studio to his house. His hand found its way to my low back when he guided me through a doorway. His fingers brushed my shoulders as he took off my jacket.

I straightened from my study of his daughter's drawing and leaned back against him, knowing his arm would come around me—and it did. He banded his free arm across my stomach, his other hand holding his wine glass by the stem, exactly as I'd taught him.

Spinning in his arms, I caught him staring at the drawing on the fridge. He shifted his gaze to me and smiled, but I could tell his mind was elsewhere.

"Thinking about your daughter?" I guessed.

"Sorry."

"Don't apologize. I saw a picture of her in your office. She's adorable."

His smile was soft. "Charlotte's the best. You'd love her. She bosses me around the same way you do."

I laughed. "I wasn't the one doing the bossing earlier."

His eyebrows twitched upward, a teasing smile curling his lips. Then he pulled me closer and kissed the tip of my nose. "That was different."

"If you don't mind me asking... What happened between you and Charlotte's mom?"

He hummed, shifting to take a sip of his drink. We pulled apart from each other, Vaughn's hand sliding down my arm to tangle with my fingertips. He tugged me across the kitchen toward the front living room. "We were married for six years," he told me, settling on the gigantic, royal blue sofa. I looked at the huge piece of artwork behind, slashes of cream and blue and gold, then took a seat next to him and mirrored his position, with my legs kicked up on the no doubt extremely expensive coffee table, a view of the feature fireplace in front of us.

Vaughn slung his free arm around my shoulders, tugging me closer to him. A part of me thought I should maintain some kind of distance—this kind of intimacy should've been reserved for a serious relationship. I should've been protecting myself, especially after falling so hard for James and being burned by him. But after the intensity of what happened in the studio, I felt tender and vulnerable, and being held by Vaughn eased some of the ragged edges inside me.

"Tiff and I both wanted kids," he continued, "and we were

ecstatic when Charlotte came along." He swirled his wine, staring at the red liquid curving up the edges of his glass. "The divorce..." He trailed off. "It was hard."

"You don't have to tell me about it if you don't want to."

He glanced at me, his thumb making soft sweeps over my shoulder. Shaking his head, Vaughn said, "It's fine. I found out she'd been racking up debt on secret credit cards for years. This was when the money from a patent I developed really started building, and Charlotte was just a year old. I was blindsided. I felt like everything I'd been working toward was snatched away from me, like we'd never get out of the hole she'd dug for us."

I remembered what he'd told me about his dad and said, "History repeating itself."

Vaughn looked at me then. Really *looked* at me. "Exactly," he said. "It hurt me in a way that I don't think she ever really understood. I'd told her about my childhood, about how uncertain it was with my dad chasing the next big thing, not knowing if the lights would cut out or if we'd suddenly have to move. She just thought it was about the number. She kept telling me we could afford it, but it wasn't about that."

"It was a betrayal."

"Yes." He hesitated. "But... It wasn't just Tiffany's fault. That first year of Charlotte's life, I felt this urge to work harder, to build my business, to make sure I was providing for my daughter. I wasn't there."

I could hear the guilt in his voice as I leaned my head on his shoulder. "So your ex spent all that money to try to fill the void."

I could understand that. How many times had I dropped tens of thousands of dollars at a designer's flagship store on Fifth Avenue, just because it was the only thing that had given me a temporary feeling of fulfillment?

Vaughn hummed. "By the time it all came to light, I was too

angry at her for hiding the spending, and she was too mad at me for being absent. The relationship was unsalvageable."

Trailing my fingers over the hand he'd wrapped around me, I snuggled into the crook of his shoulder and hummed. He wasn't perfect, but I liked that he recognized his part in the breakdown of his marriage. And yet, he was still chasing this investment and the growth of his business, when all signs pointed to him already being a very wealthy man.

Had he learned anything? He still seemed to work himself to the bone. What was the end goal?

Not for the first time, I wondered if the paths we were on were just too different to be compatible. The world he was trying to break into still seemed like a pit of vipers to me; I wanted nothing to do with it. Even if my parents invited me back into the family fold with open arms and wide smiles, I couldn't see myself going back. That version of me was gone.

Vaughn, on the other hand, was doing everything he could to get his foot in the door. That was the whole reason he'd hired me.

I looked up at him, tracing the line of his jaw with my gaze. My study of him drew his attention, and he caught my lips in his. With the first touch of his kiss, my worries melted away. It was so easy with Vaughn. The conversation, the touching, the kissing. So easy to trust him, to fall for him.

It scared me—but it felt too good to stop.

When we pulled away, our faces close, Vaughn stroked the back of my neck with his free hand and asked, "What about you?"

"What about me?" I asked, leaning back on the blue cushions.

"You've told me about your exes, but how..." He frowned, searching for the right words. "How did your family end up turning their backs on you? Even after everything, I still look after my mom. I make sure my ex has enough, because I want Charlotte to have a present mother who isn't constantly worried about money. I couldn't imagine..."

"Leaving them out in the cold?" I let out a bitter snort. "You're not like them, Vaughn. My parents don't think that way." I leaned into his side, my eyes tracing the arch of the fireplace, the line of the mantel. "I'll tell you a story," I said.

Vaughn hummed, his hand back on my shoulder, his thigh pressed into the side of mine. I was warm and safe and comfortable, and I wanted to share.

"When I was seven years old, I was learning about the life cycle of plants." Pain darted through my chest at the memory, even all these years later. Taking a sip to hide it, I glanced at Vaughn. "I was *really* into it. Something about planting a seed in a little cup, watching it sprout, moving it to the planters outside, watering it, running outside every day to see if there had been any changes... It just captivated my little kid brain."

Vaughn smiled. "You like seeing progress. Like with me. I'm a project to you."

I clicked my tongue. "You're a lot more than a project, Vaughn," I blurted, then caught myself.

Vaughn's eyes softened, but he let me off the hook and didn't ask me to elaborate. Instead, he said, "So seven-year-old Alba had a little veggie patch."

"I had an *amazing* veggie patch. I planted green beans and tomatoes. There were zucchinis, and even though I hated zucchini, I vowed that I'd eat them just because I grew them. They were growing like crazy. I was so excited." I played with the stem of my wine glass and fell silent. Vaughn took a sip of his, waiting. Then I took a deep breath and continued. "I went over to Long Island to visit my grandparents for a couple of weeks at the start of the summer. By the time I came back, the first crop should've been ready to pick. I couldn't stop talking about it. I was obsessed."

"What happened?"

I glanced at Vaughn and half expected him to be laughing at me. I was talking about a little kid's veggie patch, after all. Not exactly the deep and lasting trauma that some people endure. Not financial infidelity and the breakdown of a marriage.

But he wasn't laughing. He was listening and waiting for me to finish, his eyes solemn, his fingers stroking my shoulder.

I smiled sadly. "When I came back, I ran out of the car and through the house, out the back door...and it was gone."

A frown tugged Vaughn's brows. "What was gone?"

"The garden. My mother had had it removed and replaced with a patio, decorated with furniture and lights and flowers for their upcoming wedding anniversary party." My voice tightened, and I cleared my throat to try to hide it. I could still feel the confusion followed by the disbelief of that moment. The devastation at seeing all my hard work gone... It had broken my little heart. "She told me growing vegetables wasn't for people like us. We hired people to do that work for us. If I wanted, I could have a rose garden and she'd have our gardener tend it for me."

Anger flashed across Vaughn's face. "So your crop—"

"Gone." I pinched a smile. "Replaced with pavers, cocktail tables, and outdoor lights."

"What the fuck?" he demanded, leaning forward to put his glass on the table. "They just destroyed it? Without even telling you?"

There was something so unbelievably validating about Vaughn's outrage. Something healing about it.

Yes, I'd been little, and it was only a few vegetables. But it had hurt me deeply, and it was a pattern that would repeat itself throughout my life. My agency had been taken from me. I was stripped of any aspect of my personality that was undesirable, and when I rebelled...

Well, I was shown that my wants and needs didn't matter. Eventually, I was thrown out of the family altogether.

"Your parents are evil," Vaughn said, his jaw tense. "I can't imagine... Charlotte... God, I can't imagine doing that to her. The way her face lights up when she's excited about something..." He shook his head, his eyes focused on the middle distance. Then he shifted to look at me. "You are so strong, Alba. To have endured that kind of childhood and turned into the woman you are... Wow."

His praise was uncomfortable. I shifted, putting my glass down next to his as I shrugged a shoulder. "I can't complain. I had wealth and privilege and comfort. I had friends, opportunities. Not that I made anything of them," I said bitterly.

"And how much do those things matter, in the end?" Vaughn asked. "How much did that wealth help you?" He shook his head. "It goes to show how strong you are that you turned out so good after an upbringing like that."

I blinked at him. He'd said it like my upbringing was bad. And yes, it was devoid of the kind of love and closeness that I needed. I'd always felt like a pawn on a chessboard, moved around for someone else's benefit. But I'd had everything I needed. All the food and shelter and clothes and luxuries...

Vaughn pulled me close and wrapped his arms around me, and I realized that things would never feel as good as this—all the designer clothing in the world would never warm me up the way his arms did when they held me.

I was allowed to mourn the things I'd never had. The support, the love, the agency. I'd never been allowed to be myself. I'd never had the opportunity to make my own way in life—not until I left all the privilege behind.

"Hey," Vaughn said, wiping a tear away from my cheek. "None of that."

I rubbed the heels of my hands over my cheeks, laughing at myself. "I'm crying over a few zucchinis I wouldn't have even enjoyed eating."

Vaughn smiled, then pulled me closer so he could kiss my forehead. He said nothing; he just held me close.

I wasn't crying over zucchini, though. I was crying over the fact that I hadn't had the love I needed growing up. I'd never been treated like my own person.

"Thank you," I whispered, burying my face in Vaughn's neck.

He stroked my back and held me, and I indulged in a few more tears before taking a deep breath to pull myself together.

"Come on," Vaughn said when I'd straightened. He stood and stretched out his hand.

"Where are we going?"

His pale blue eyes sparkled in the warm light of the living room lamps. "We're going upstairs. I'm going to run you a bath."

I arched a brow. "Oh?"

"And I'm going to get in it with you."

I laughed and put my palm in his. "Deal."

TWENTY

VAUGHN

STEAM ROSE FROM THE BATH, and Alba leaned her head against my shoulder. Her back was to my front, her legs pressing against mine. My fingers made tight circles in her hair, the scent of my shampoo filling my nose.

Alba let out a groan. "That feels so good."

I hummed in response, tilting my head away as I used a small container to rinse some of the shampoo from her strands. Her chest rose and fell, the pink of her nipples poking out above the surface of the water. I knew she could feel me, half-hard behind her, but neither of us reacted to my arousal.

I wanted to take care of her in a way I hadn't really experienced before. Sure, I'd been in a position to step in and take care of my aging mother when my dad died. I stepped up for my daughter. My ex-wife had always relied on me. But Alba tugged at that instinct within me in a new way. She was so self-reliant. She'd picked herself up off the ground after being thrown out by the selfish monsters she called family, dusted herself off, and decided she could make it on her own.

She didn't run back to them. Didn't bend her morals in order to fit in.

I admired the hell out of that—and I understood why parts of her were so hard, so brittle. She had a sharp tongue because she needed it to keep her sense of self. She kept her walls up all the time, because that's what she'd needed to do to survive.

None of the other people in my life that I'd taken care of— mother, daughter, ex-wife—had that kind of mettle. And the fact that Alba had chosen me to lean on, that her body was limp and relaxed atop mine, that she'd trusted me earlier with her body... that meant something to me.

I cherished it. Cherished her. I wanted to be the man who took care of her always.

When my thoughts drifted to that sniveling idiot we'd met at the French restaurant, my pressure on Alba's scalp increased. She hummed, and I turned my attention back to the task, but not before my lips curled at the memory of him.

Never again would she be made to feel small. Never again would she have to run from a restaurant because someone else made her feel like she didn't belong.

Alba belonged with me now. She belonged *to* me. She was mine, and I wasn't going to let her go.

I rinsed her hair, then pulled out the only conditioner I had in the house. Alba cracked an eyelid when she heard the cap open, then snorted.

"My Little Pony conditioner?"

"You can't deny that their manes are lush and sparkly."

She laughed and let me work the product through her hair. It was slick, her hair darkened in its wet state, and my fingers ran through it with ease. Alba peeled herself off me to dunk her head, then turned around in the tub and settled herself on top of my lap, her forearms on my shoulders. My hands naturally found the curves of her hips, thumbs angled toward her navel.

We fit. There was no other way to say it. Her body fit against mine like it had been made to sit here, just like this.

"I've never had a man wash my hair with such care after screwing my brains out."

"Then you haven't lived."

Her smile was bright. The water sloshed as she moved to trace my temple with her finger, drips of water falling onto my shoulders and upper chest from her hand. "I don't think I've been this relaxed...definitely not in over a year. Maybe longer."

Satisfaction coursed through me. My woman, relaxed and satisfied, her body draped over mine.

But she wasn't my woman, was she? Or at least, she didn't know she was.

"Come to the gala with me," I said, my voice low.

Her eyes, which had been studying the movement of her fingers over my skin, shifted back to meet my gaze. "No," she said.

"I won't take anyone else."

Her brow arched. "Is that your way of telling me we're exclusive?"

Her tone was casual, and it sent tension stealing through me. "Are we not?"

She leaned back, the tops of her breasts exposed, her center pressing against my lower stomach, my cock. Her palms flattened on my shoulders, pinning me to the cold porcelain of my tub. "How very old fashioned of you, Mr. Avery," she teased. "One little romp together and you're trying to pin me down."

My hands moved over her ass, rocking her hips so my length was caught between us. "It won't be one little romp by the time you go home, princess."

Her eyes had a devilish light and a smile played around the edges of her mouth—but she didn't tell me what I wanted to hear.

"We're exclusive," I growled. "No other man gets to touch you while you're with me. Say it."

"That sounds very one-sided. What about other women touching you? Now that you've learned how to dress, don't think I haven't noticed how many heads turn whenever we go somewhere."

I huffed. "Alba, there hasn't been another woman since the day you mocked me for losing yet another investor."

Surprised flashed across her features. Her brows drew together —and I worried I'd said too much. Not wanting to give her a chance to question me, I lifted a hand to grip the back of her neck and pulled her in for a hard kiss. She melted against me, body wiggling, water lapping at both our bodies.

Her mouth was hot, and the water was getting cold, so I broke the kiss and pulled her to her feet. Grabbing a towel I'd laid on the counter next to the bath, I turned and draped it over her shoulders, stepped out of the tub, then picked her up around the waist and threw her over my shoulder in a fireman's carry.

She screamed, hands flying out to land on my ass, and started laughing. "What are you doing?"

"Taking you to bed. Seems like 'one little romp' wasn't enough for you."

"You domineering, egotistical, arrogant—ahh!" She landed on the bed with a scream, the towel flying open to give me a view of her beautiful body, beaded with moisture and red from the bath.

I pushed her knees open and climbed between them, not caring about the water that soaked through my duvet around us. Then I got down on my front, wrapped my arms around her thighs, and licked the heart of her.

"Vaughn—oh!" Her hands flew to my head, fingers curling in

my wet strands. She tasted like the best thing I'd ever had. I groaned against her skin, sucking and licking and devouring. Alba whimpered, her fists tightening, and pressed her thighs into my shoulders.

I glanced up to see her chest rising and falling with panted breaths, her stomach hollowed out as she arched back, soft flesh trembling below her navel. She was so beautiful it was almost unbelievable.

I wanted to take care of her like this too. Get her to the point that she was boneless and sated. Worship her body the way she deserved. But I knew Alba would struggle to accept that. I saw it in the tug of her brows, her forehead wrinkling as slight tension gripped her body.

She'd been made to feel small her entire life, and I intended to spend the foreseeable future fixing that misconception. She was strong and smart and funny and sexy and brave. She deserved to be eaten out morning, noon, and night.

But right now, she'd gone somewhere in her mind, and I wanted her right here with me.

"Alba," I growled, rising up onto my elbows and then straightening onto my knees. "You're thinking too much."

Her brow smoothed out, and her eyelids cracked open. A small smile curled the corners of her lips. "I do that sometimes."

"Do you need me to fuck you so hard you can't think?"

Her chest shuddered, and I reached up to feel the softness of her breasts, the hard points of her nipples. She nodded. "Yes, please."

I held her gaze for a moment, wondering how I'd gotten so lucky. Vowing that as long as she was with me, she wouldn't be worrying about whatever all those other people put in her head.

My hands swept down her body. I marveled at the softness of her skin, the perfect shape of her. I touched the mole above her left hip and the stripes of white stretch marks that shone on her thighs when she spread them open. Beautiful woman.

I couldn't help my groan when I entered her. Couldn't help the catch in my breath when I was seated to the hilt. Her eyes were wide, her pupils blown out. My palm landed on the bed next to her head, and her hands swept over my shoulders to curl around my neck.

I kissed her and pulled back. "No other man touches you while you're with me," I repeated.

Her eyes sparkled, and then she gasped when I thrust into her.

"Say it, Alba." I punctuated my sentence with another thrust. Her lips fell open, her thighs pressing against my haunches. I brushed my lips against hers and stilled. "I need to hear it," I said, voice low.

Her eye roll was pure sass, but some of the tension that had tightened her muscles earlier eased beneath me. She tilted her hips and took me deeper, her fingertips playing over the nape of my neck.

"Only you," she whispered.

"No one else gets to touch you."

"No one else gets to touch me—oh!"

Points of pain on the backs of my shoulders where her finger-nails dug in. The gratifying gasp that fell from her lips. A perfect moment.

"You belong to me, Alba," I said in a low voice, and I knew I was pushing it. Knew that this headstrong woman wouldn't take too much more of this kind of talk, but I couldn't help myself. I wanted her for myself. I wanted her to belong to me, mind, body, and soul. I wanted her to know it.

Alba surprised me by relaxing, her face easing into a soft smile as I drove my cock into her the way I knew she wanted it. "I belong to you," she whispered, eyes on mine, hands gripping, hips rocking.

I could've come right then, just from her saying those words to me with that look in her eyes. Instead, I dipped my head and kissed her, hard and wet, and then got to work.

My woman needed her mind cleared. She needed me to chase away all the demons that plagued her. She needed to be fucked hard and fast and dirty, so that all that was left was her and me and pleasure.

TWENTY-ONE
ALBA

I WOKE from the best sleep of my life with Vaughn's arm around me, his body a warm wall at my back. His hand was moving gently, palm spread on my upper abdomen, thumb brushing the underside of my breast. His cock was hard.

"Did you even sleep?" I asked, groggy, a smile in my voice. I wiggled my butt so he knew I was teasing.

"I slept plenty," he replied, voice full of gravel. His hand moved to cup my breast, thumb and forefinger tweaking my nipple. I sighed into the touch, eyes closing again, wanting this moment to last forever.

"Want you just like this," Vaughn rasped as he pressed a kiss below my ear. "Soft and relaxed."

"Mm?"

His hand slid down my stomach and between my legs. He groaned at the wetness he found there, and I leaned my upper back into his chest.

"Don't move, princess," he told me. "Let me have you just like this."

I let my body relax against his. The light from the windows was soft, and it was easy to keep my eyes closed as his hand moved between my legs, circling my clit, sending sparks through my thighs.

It was hard to believe it had only been about twelve hours since we'd come together the first time. I felt closer to Vaughn than I had to anyone else in a long time. Even with James, I realized, there had been some space between us. The pause when the check at a restaurant arrived, and I had to dig through my purse while James sat back and watched. The way he'd make me wait for his text messages, even though he was always on his phone. The way he'd rolled away from me that last time and kicked me out of his bed.

It had been agony when it happened, when he made it clear that there'd been no love on his side.

With Vaughn, it was different. He'd met me at my lowest—and he still wanted me. He still wanted *only* me. When had a man—or anyone—wanted me even when I couldn't give them anything? With James, I'd been the holder of the purse strings. With Cole, I'd been the gateway to respectability in the upper echelons of society. I'd been the bridge to make his father happy after the estrangement they'd gone through.

But with Vaughn, I was just...me. Terrifying. Wonderful.

"You going to let me in?" Vaughn asked, sleep still muffling his voice, his hand still moving slowly, leisurely, between my legs.

I hummed, shifting against him. Slight pressure from his palm told me he wanted me to spread my legs. I lifted my top knee, and Vaughn's breath gusted out as he dipped his finger just inside me.

A moment later, his cock was pressing against me, pressure and stretch and heat at my core. Vaughn stroked my body, telling me to relax, telling me that he wanted me just like this, that I didn't have to do anything but stay where I was.

A soft moan slipped through my lips as he slid inside me, slow and inexorable, filling me up completely. It felt so good to be joined with him like this, to know that he would tell me exactly what to do to make it feel good.

I didn't have to think or wonder or spin out in my own mind.

Vaughn's hand slid over my hip, gripping softly. His lips brushed the pulse point on my neck, and I kept my body soft, relaxed, accepting more of him inside me. He grunted, fingertips digging into my flesh, his hips rolling against me.

I let myself fall into the moment with him, my mind going blank. It was just skin and pleasure and Vaughn. His hand shifted between my legs as he entered me slowly, rhythmically. There was no pressure for me to perform or to be something other than who I was. I didn't have to orgasm for him. I just had to be.

"So perfect," he groaned, the pressure of his fingers increasing on my clit. "So wet and perfect, princess. I could keep doing this for hours."

My head fell back against his shoulder, and then he was fucking into me a little harder. A little faster.

"You make this so good for me," he continued, nose brushing my neck, teeth scraping at my shoulder. "Letting me take what I want like a good girl."

I sighed at his words, relaxing into his touch. There should have been shame that I enjoyed being used like this, that I wanted it, but there was nothing but sweet blankness and mounting plea-sure. No undercurrents of stress. No wondering if he was genuine or not. No need to perform.

When he rolled me onto my front and caught my wrists in his, I let out a sigh. He held them fast to the bed, his calves pinning my legs. My hips rocked up to meet his, and then I couldn't have formed a coherent thought to save my life. Vaughn took me hard and deep, and the sweet blankness gave way to the pleasure. I came with a cry, shuddering beneath him, then whimpered when I felt him pull out. A moment later, hot spurts painted my thighs and ass as Vaughn moaned above me.

I panted, my heart racing, as Vaughn stroked my sides and caught his own breath. Then he climbed off the bed and came back a minute later with a wet washcloth to wipe me off. I sank into the mattress as I enjoyed his ministrations, my eyes closing, then hummed as he gathered me into his arms and held me.

———

I STAYED at Vaughn's for three days. He went to work when he needed to and worked from home when he could. We did etiquette lessons at his dining room table and learned the rumba in his living room. He fucked me on every available surface. It was a bubble of sex and happiness, and on some level, I knew it would pop. Things didn't keep going well in my life. Vegetable gardens got demolished. Relationships ended. Bubbles popped.

I just didn't know when it would happen.

Finally, when I got sick of hand-washing my underwear only to have it ruined a couple of hours later, I made a trip to my apartment while Vaughn went to one of his worksites for some important concrete thing. His subcontractors had screwed him over, and he needed to go there to fix...something... I didn't really know. I'd tried to listen when he told me about it, but he hadn't been wearing a shirt and I'd gotten distracted by his chest. He'd noticed, and I'd ended up bent over the side of the couch.

Although my apartment was clean and much bigger than the studio a couple of floors below, walking into it still felt like waking up from a perfect dream.

Then my phone buzzed. I smiled as I dug through my purse, thinking that Vaughn hadn't been able to go more than a couple of hours without speaking to me. I could relate; I'd planned on sending him a message as soon as I'd showered properly. But when I looked at my phone, it wasn't Vaughn's name that popped up.

The number wasn't saved as a contact, but it didn't take me long to figure out who it was. James had changed his number, apparently. I'd blocked his old one.

> Haven't been able to stop thinking about you since we saw each other.

I stared at the message, heart pounding. It felt like I'd just caught sight of a venomous snake in the corner of the room, and now I had to figure out how to get it out of my life.

I could delete the message, pretend it didn't exist. The way he'd written "since we saw each other" made it sound like something other than running into each other in the lobby of a restaurant.

My phone buzzed again.

> Miss you.

It buzzed again.

> I want to talk to you, Alba. Can I see you?

I stared at those words, and my stomach turned. A couple of weeks ago, that message would have sent me rushing back to him. All the fantasies I'd had of running off and making a life together, just the two of us, would've come flooding back, and I would've jumped at the chance to make a fool of myself again.

Now...

I wanted to hurl my phone at the tile wall.

My hands trembled as I unlocked the phone and tapped my

messaging app. The message sat in bold at the top of the list. My thumb hovered. I could swipe to delete. I could block him.

I could answer.

I chose to do none of those things. I tapped on the second number down: Deena's. Within minutes of asking her if she was free, I had scheduled a date with her at the coffee shop. I got dressed, locked my apartment, and headed over.

She was waiting for me on that old velvet couch, her hair a wild mess of curls, her ears bejeweled with gold rings and studs, her clothing oversized and fabulously chic. She stood when I entered and said, "Get over here, you little horndog."

I laughed, embarrassed, as a few heads turned. My new friend wrapped me in a hug and sat me down beside her, where I noticed there was a vanilla latte waiting.

"Thank you," I told her, gesturing to the drink.

"I didn't want to waste any time." She smacked the side of my thigh. "Now. Start from the beginning. You and Vaughn...?"

Deena and I had been messaging back and forth ever since we met, so I'd told her about my adventures. She knew I was working for Vaughn and knew that I found him attractive. Now her eyes glimmered, and I worried she might be a bad influence on me.

I told her the whole sordid tale and ended by giving her my phone so she could read the messages from James.

"Are you sure it's him?" she asked, eyes traveling from my phone screen to my face.

"Who else would it be?"

Deena bit her lip, and the skin below her teeth went white. Then she blew out a raspberry and shook her head. "Girl, this is a mess."

I groaned and slumped on the couch. Unbidden, my mother's voice echoed in my mind: *Sit up straight, Alba. Cross your ankles. You look like a slob.*

I'd shifted into a proper seated position before I even registered what I was doing—and then cursed myself. I couldn't even have a conversation with a friend without being judged by the memory of my mother.

That's when I noticed Deena was typing on my phone.

"What are you doing?" I screeched, reaching for the device.

Deena cackled, angling her body so I couldn't grab the phone. "One second! I'm just answering him."

"Stop! Don't!"

My phone buzzed in her hands and she hummed, throwing me a mischievous look over her shoulder. Her thumbs flew over the screen.

"Deena," I growled.

"Calm down," she said, handing me my phone back, a giggle slipping through her lips.

I blinked at the screen. Three new messages had appeared in the chat: two from me (Deena), one from James.

ME

Sure, I'll see you.

JAMES

Time and place, babe. I'm there.

ME

When we're both dead I'll see you in hell. Asshole.

I slammed my phone down on the couch cushion beside me and slapped my hand over my face. Deena cackled, leaning her head against my shoulder. Despite my best efforts, a giggle slipped through my lips. Laughing would only encourage her...but then again, laughing felt good.

I smacked the back of my hand against the side of her thigh, and Deena laughed harder.

"You're awful," I complained.

"I'm awesome."

"That too." I grinned at her, shook my head, and leaned forward to take a bracing sip of my coffee. I turned my phone around and took a peek at the screen. There were three dots below my last message, indicating that James was typing. Not wanting to hear anything else from him, I quickly tapped his number and blocked him. Then I let out a sigh.

Deena bumped me with her shoulder. "Good job."

"Should've done that before handing my phone over to you."

"But then you wouldn't have the satisfaction of having the last word." She beamed at me, then tilted her head. "So, more importantly, are you going to do it?"

My heart was still racing, so I couldn't follow her thoughts. "Do what?"

"Go to that charity event?"

"The Noble Foundation Gala?"

Her eyes glimmered. "Sure. Why not?"

"Um, I can think of about ten thousand reasons right off the bat. Like for example all the people that will be there who know exactly what happened to me this past year."

"And wouldn't it feel so good to throw it in their faces?"

I crossed my legs and leaned back, not caring that the pose made me slouch against the busted-up back of the velvet sofa. Then I blinked at my friend. "Have I ever told you what a terrible influence you are?"

Deena smiled, looking decidedly evil. "I know. Isn't it great?"

TWENTY-TWO
VAUGHN

THE MIDTOWN JOB was hanging on by a thread, but walking around the site and talking to the site superintendent didn't fill me with the kind of dread it had a month ago. I went to the office and talked to Jim about the dire straits our company would be in if I didn't find an investor and wriggle out of the legal battle that seemed almost inevitable at this point.

And I hardly cared.

All I wanted to do was get back to Alba. Lock myself in my house and spend time with her. Watch that genuine smile spread over her face. Kiss every inch of her body. Get to know all her secrets.

I made sure she was free for dinner, but even the few hours that we were apart seemed too long. I threw myself into work to distract myself.

I called Charlotte at the usual time when I was still in the office, smiling when she answered, the video shook, and her gap-toothed smile came onscreen. I'd called her daily when Alba had been at my house, ducking into my office to make the call. It would be just over a week until she was back with me.

"Hey, turkey."

"Hi. Me and mom and Dale"—that was Tiffany's new husband—"had a snowball fight and I got snow all down my back, but I got Dale good."

"I didn't think there was enough snow for a snowball fight," I said, glancing out my office windows. This high up, I felt disconnected from the world.

"Duh," Charlotte said, smiling. "Maybe you and me can have one! I'm good at making snowballs and Dale said I have a pitcher's arm."

"Did he?" I forced a smile, something like disquiet slithering through me. We spoke for a while longer, Charlotte telling me all about her day. Then I said, "All right turkey, put your mom on. I need to talk to her about something."

"Okay. Love you!"

"Love you too. See you soon."

"For a snowball fight!"

"For a snowball fight," I confirmed. The phone shuffled, and a new face came on. "Hi, Tiff."

"Still at work, I see," she said, seeing my background. Her brows arched; she wasn't surprised.

"It's a busy period," I said defensively, heat rising up the back of my neck.

"I thought winters were the slow time for you?"

"Do we have to do this again?"

Tiffany took a deep breath, gathered herself, and shook her head. "No. We don't. What's up?"

"I've got an event to go to in a couple of weeks. I was hoping you'd take Charlotte a week early."

"You want to swap weeks?"

"Well…" I glanced at my computer screen, where emails poured in. Once this subcontractor was dealt with, and I'd bagged Noble as a new investor, and the lawsuit was handled…

Tiff sighed. "Of course I'll take her. What's the event?"

"Just some charity thing. It's for work."

"Uh-huh," my ex-wife replied, looking unsurprised and unimpressed. "Fine. You know I love having Lottie here. Just send me the dates and I'll shuffle things around."

"Thanks, Tiff."

"Yep." She gave me a closed-lipped smile and hung up the phone.

Sighing, I turned back to my computer, but my fingers hovered over the keyboard and mouse. That conversation had been familiar. Me, needing more time for work. Tiffany, being disappointed but not surprised.

But I was doing this for them, I reminded myself. Growing the business was for my kid. I worked to make sure she had everything I needed. Tiffany benefited from that.

Bolstered by the familiar thoughts, I blocked out the doubts that tried to creep in. Doubts that told me I already had more than enough money to provide a good life for my child. I'd already secured my legacy. Saving and growing the construction company was simply a matter of my pride.

Brushing those thoughts away, I turned to my computer and got back to work.

A COUPLE HOURS LATER, I picked Alba up at her apartment building. She walked out the front door wearing a dark orange silk dress with her jacket thrown over the top, open to reveal the liquid fall of the fabric of her dress. Gold jewelry glittered at her neck and in her ears. I straightened from where I'd been leaning on the side of the car, dazzled by her beauty.

"You look amazing," I said after I kissed her.

She smiled. "It's nice to be able to wear some of my old clothes." Her fingers touched the dark orange fabric, then moved to adjust my jacket's collar. "Where are we going? No driver today?"

"It's a surprise," I said, grinning, then opened my car door for her. "I figured I could drive, for a change." She moved gracefully, tucking herself into the seat and checking that her dress had cleared the doorway before looking up at me and smiling. I closed the door and circled to the driver's side. When I'd pulled into traffic, I placed my hand on her thigh. The fabric of her dress was soft and buttery beneath my touch, and her leg was warm.

She let out a sigh, leaning against the headrest.

"You okay?"

In my peripheral vision, I saw her turn to glance at me. "I'm good," she replied. "It was weird going back home after being at your place for so long."

I hummed. "I couldn't wait for the day to end so I could take you out," I admitted.

Her smile was soft but bright, and she shifted to rest her hand on top of mine. It was easy to touch her, to feel the intimacy building between us.

I parked a couple of blocks away from our destination in a parking garage, then helped Alba out of the car and threaded my fingers through hers. Our steps echoed against the concrete walls, and we made our way down to street level together. The wind was cold, and I enjoyed the way Alba tucked herself against me as we walked.

Finally, we reached our destination. A window gave a view into a crowded restaurant, with families and couples sitting at small tables sharing gigantic pizzas. Gold lettering arched over the window, proclaiming the name of the owner. We'd arrived at Ralphie's.

Alba watched me pull open the door for her and arched her brow. "I might be overdressed," she noted.

"You look perfect." My hand found the small of her back as I followed her inside, and we stopped at the hostess stand where I gave my name.

A moment later, an old man with tufts of white hair sticking out under his worn, black baseball cap came out of the swinging kitchen door. "Vaughn!" Ralphie called out, smiling wide. He dropped a pie on one of the tables, slapped a patron on the shoulder, then turned toward us. "When you called, I thought someone was pranking me. Back to the old stomping grounds, hey?"

I grinned. "Had to come by and see if you'd finally fixed this place up."

"Never," Ralphie promised, then turned to Alba. "Vaughn told me I had to pull out the red carpet for you."

Alba's gaze slid over to me, and she arched a brow. "Did he, now?"

Ralphie grinned. "But he didn't tell me you were a stunner. Wow! What are you doing with him? I've got a grandson—"

"All right, all right," I cut in, laughing. "That's enough."

Ralphie's eyes twinkled as he met my gaze. "You've finally cleaned yourself up," he noted.

"Can't say the same about you, old man."

He guffawed and turned to Alba. "I met this guy when he was this tall." Ralphie held up his hand at about eye level. "He was all elbows. Cost me a fortune every time he knocked something over."

"It happened twice," I said, rolling my eyes and fighting my smile. "And I knocked over a can of tomatoes that cost a couple bucks."

"Like I said, a fortune."

Alba laughed and looked at me. "First job?"

"Had no idea what I was getting myself into," I said, nodding. "But Ralphie introduced me to his brother, who got me into contracting. Got a soft spot for him even though he's hard to put up with."

Ralphie groaned. "Don't listen to him. Full of shit as usual. Pardon the French."

Alba laughed and glanced around the dining room at all the busy tables, and I knew she was wondering where we'd squeeze in. Not one single chair was unoccupied, and no one looked like they were leaving anytime soon. Then Ralph swept his arm toward the swinging door where he'd first appeared, and Alba glanced at me questioningly.

"Best seat in the house," Ralphie promised.

The old man led us through the kitchen, where the cooks shouted and worked, the wood-fired oven crackled, and the heat made sweat dot on my forehead. Alba's dress swirled around her ankles, her heeled boots clicking on the tile flooring. We followed the old man around a corner to a solid black door.

He paused with his hand on the knob and turned to face us. "There's a secret to perfect pizza," he said, and I settled in for a familiar speech. "Tomatoes straight from Italy, picked at their ripest and canned immediately to concentrate the flavor. Italian type oo flour, milled to perfection. New York City tap water. And the freshest ingredients for toppings, year-round."

He opened the door, and Alba's shock cleared the lingering smile from her face. Beyond the doorway, instead of a dirty alleyway full of snow, gravel, and rats, was lush greenery and warmth. Ralphie waved her through the door, and I followed close, watching the way her eyes widened as she looked around the space.

"This greenhouse has been here longer than I've been alive," I told her, and Alba met my gaze. "It's one of the reasons the food here is so good."

"Please," Ralphie said, gesturing us forward. A small table had been set up a few paces ahead, in the middle of the greenery, with a line of basil plants on one side and a rosemary bush on the other.

"It smells amazing," Alba said, wandering over to brush her fingers over the rosemary. "This is incredible."

"Vaughn told me you had a green thumb," Ralphie said, pulling out her chair.

Alba laughed. "Not quite. Thank you," she said as she sat down, leaning back as he laid a white cloth napkin across her lap. I hadn't even known Ralphie had cloth napkins in this place.

"This is great, Ralphie," I said, genuinely impressed. The table was dressed in a white tablecloth, with a tea light flickering in a glass jar between us. To my left, a wine bucket sat in a stand, ready to receive whichever bottle we chose.

"When an old friend calls and asks me to make space at a table for him, I do my best," Ralphie said, his hand landing on my shoulder. He handed us both menus, took our drink order, and wandered back into the restaurant. Despite myself, my throat felt tight. Ralphie had been the first man in my life who was in any way reliable. He'd been a hard man to work for, but he'd always been there for me.

And he still was, I realized. When so many other people let me down, the old man was there.

Alba took off her jacket; the greenhouse was comfortably warm. Her skin gleamed under the fairy lights that had been strung up around our table, her earrings glinting as she took another look around. "This is incredible." She looked at me. "Thank you."

"Just as a fair warning, Ralphie will probably want to give you a tour of all his plants after we've eaten. I made the mistake of telling him you had a vegetable garden when you were younger. He'll want to tell you optimal growing conditions for each plant."

Happiness shone on her face. "I would love that. Maybe one day I can put the knowledge to use." She smiled, and it was tinged with sadness, but she shook her head and cleared it quickly. "You organized all of this today?"

"I can't take too much credit. I called Ralphie, and he did the rest."

"Still," she said. "Thank you."

TWENTY-THREE
ALBA

I'D BEEN WINED and dined before—but not like this. Not in a secret hideaway garden, with the noise and chaos of the city muffled, and the scent of fresh herbs making me forget we were still enduring the tail end of winter. Vaughn chose a rich Syrah wine and made a big show of talking about the notes he could taste in it.

"That online wine tasting course is paying off," I said, grinning.

"It's a bit floral," he continued, smacking his lips. "Must have been grown in a cool climate."

I pursed my mouth and plucked the bottle from the silver bucket where Ralphie had placed it to save space on the tiny table, squinting at the label. "'...grown in our highest-elevation California vineyard, the cooler climate allows our Syrah to develop the full-bodied flavor with hints of floral notes'—you memorized this label, didn't you?"

"You are so rude, Alba," Vaughn replied, laughing. "I can taste the blackberry and the new oak! And anyone could taste the violet blossoms in this. I mean, come on."

"Uh-huh," I said, scanning the label as my lips curled into a smile. "I bet you can also taste how the difficult growing conditions have made this an oft-undervalued grape."

"One of my favorite things about it," Vaughn replied, his eyes on me.

My cheeks warmed, and I placed the bottle back on the table. Ralphie had left us some fresh bread with olive oil and good balsamic vinegar, and I mopped some of the dip up on a hunk of chewy, wood-fired bread. Delicious.

Our pizza arrived not long after, when the wine had filled my belly with a buzzing warmth. Or maybe that was because of Vaughn's smile, illuminated by the fairy lights strung over our heads. He gestured for me to serve myself, then hummed when the cheese pull to end all cheese pulls came with my chosen slice. I laughed, throwing all my etiquette training out the window as I opened my mouth and dangled all the melted cheese into it before taking a bite of the tip of the slice. A groan went through me as I chewed mozzarella- and marinara-flavored bliss.

This was, hands down, the best date I'd ever been on. I'd laughed more in the hour that we'd been sitting here than on the rest of the dates in my life combined. I felt at ease and happy and light. We were hidden away here, with lush greenery, warm lighting, and good food. It was easy to get carried away.

That's why I didn't have my guard all the way up when Vaughn topped up my glass, looked me right in the eyes, and asked, "Will you go to the gala with me, Alba?"

My refusal didn't come as quickly as it had before. Instead, I fingered the stem of the wine glass and bit my bottom lip.

"Is it because of me? You don't want to be seen with me?"

I rolled my eyes. "Don't be ridiculous."

"So why not? Don't you want to show all those people that they haven't broken you?"

"You sound like my friend Deena." I took a sip, watching him across the table.

He leaned forward, reaching over to put his hand on top of mine. "I wouldn't ask if I didn't think you could handle it."

"I didn't handle seeing Yvette and—and James very well," I said, stumbling over his name.

"They caught you by surprise. This time, you'll be ready."

"Why do you care?"

Vaughn huffed, frowning at me like my question made no sense. "Because it kills me to see you shrink yourself, Alba. You're the most driven, strong, stubborn woman I've ever met. And you're going to let a bunch of rich assholes make you feel small?"

"Might I remind you that one of those rich assholes is going to be offering you a fat wad of cash for part ownership of your company?"

"That's work. This is different."

"Hmm."

Vaughn cleared his throat. Then he said, "I want you to come with me. I want you there by my side, Alba. What would I do there on my own? It's like all these fancy restaurants we've been to. What would be the point of me going to them if you weren't there?"

His words made my heart stutter. I took another sip of wine to calm myself, then set the glass down on the white tablecloth and blinked my gaze up to meet his. "You don't mean that," I whispered. Once he was through with me, he'd move on to bigger and better things. Wasn't that what always happened?

Things were blissful now, but they would end. They always did—and I was always left out in the cold. Engagements, love affairs, family. They meant nothing. Why would this be any different?

And I was speeding toward the end right now by refusing him. I wasn't doing what he wanted, and he'd leave me by the wayside because of it. I had to twist myself into knots for people to love me, to care about me, and even then it was never enough.

Vaughn brushed my hand with his fingers, then leaned back and grabbed the last slice of pizza. "Maybe you're right. If you don't want to go, you don't have to." He took a bite, chewed, and swallowed. I ignored the pit in my stomach that told me he would pull away, that the fairytale romance would die right here in the middle of a pizza restaurant's greenhouse.

The lights glinted off the surface of my wine. The smear of marinara on my plate looked almost black in the dimness.

My whirlwind with Vaughn was coming to an end. Rejection was incoming. I could feel it like an arthritic woman feeling a coming storm in her bones. I'd gotten a temporary reprieve, but the end was nigh. I'd refused him, and he would reject me.

Then Vaughn finished his piece of pizza, brushed the cornmeal off his fingers, and said, "I think you should meet my daughter."

TWENTY-FOUR
ALBA

I BLINKED. "WHAT?"

"My daughter, Charlotte."

"I know who your daughter is, Vaughn. But you said..."

"I think you should meet her."

"But...*why*?"

Vaughn frowned at me. "What do you mean, why? She's my daughter."

"And you want me to meet her?"

He stared like he wasn't understanding. "You don't want to?"

"No! I mean, yes!" I shook my head. "I want to. But I don't understand... You want *me* to meet her?"

"Obviously."

I cleared my throat. Nodded. "Yeah. Obviously."

Inside, I reeled. Sure, he'd made me say those things when we were having sex. Possessive things. He wanted to be exclusive. But meeting his daughter?

I had to quickly rearrange my train of thought. I'd believed we were about to break up. I thought he was getting bored of me, that if I didn't behave the way he wanted—by going to Arlo Noble's gala with him—he would toss me aside.

But I'd said no, and now he wanted me to meet his daughter.

I had to clarify. "So, even if I don't go to the gala with you, you want me to meet Charlotte?"

Vaughn frowned. "I'm not sure what one has to do with the other."

I laughed, feeling fizzy and floating inside. "Right. Sorry."

He wanted me for me. He wanted a *relationship* for me—even though I had no money, no connections anymore, nothing to offer him but some advice on how to dress himself. And he still thought I was worthy of dating. Him, the man across from me with the square jaw and the sparkling eyes and the broad, scarred hands and the construction empire.

He wanted *me*.

"Are you okay?"

I nodded, saved from answering when the door swung open and Ralphie reappeared to take our dishes. He cracked jokes as he cleared our table, and I was able to settle myself down. Still, when Ralphie insisted on giving me a tour of his greenhouse, my hand found Vaughn's. With his fingers braided through mine, we followed Ralphie and listened to his explanations about humidity and temperature and light. He showed us his grow lamps and gave me advice on fertilizing various herbs.

I absorbed none of it—but I still couldn't stop smiling. Finally, when our wine was done and Ralphie had been called back inside, I leaned my head against Vaughn's shoulder and hummed as he wrapped his arms around me.

"Ready to go home?" he rumbled, lips brushing my temple.

I liked the sound of that. *Loved* the sound of that. Home—with Vaughn. Nodding, I tilted my head up for a kiss, and I couldn't help the way my lips curled into a smile against his.

Ralphie sent us home with a container of his famous tiramisu, and we headed back to the darkened townhouse.

We made it three feet into the door before I jumped on Vaughn, wrapping my legs around his hips as he laughed and caught me. His broad hands slid down to my ass, and the paper bag containing our dessert hit the floor with a dull thud. Then my back was against the wall, and Vaughn's lips were devouring mine. The fabric of my dress rucked up between us, and cool air kissed the tops of my thighs. Vaughn groaned, clawing at the fabric until he felt my skin.

Then he froze and pulled back. "Are you—" His fingers moved slightly. "Are you telling me you've been sitting across from me all this time with no underwear on?"

I smiled. "Surprise."

The sound that came from his lips was pure, rough desire. His hands shifted, and then a finger was inside me. I gasped, rolling my hips toward him, clinging to him with my knees and thighs. It was awkward, with his arm curled around my leg and my back pressed against the wall, but I didn't care. I clung to him, pushing at his jacket, trying to get access to his skin. I wanted to run my hands over his shoulders, feel the prickle of his chest hair, soak up the warmth of his bulk.

My core was slick with desire—it had been since he'd held my hand and stood patiently by my side as his old boss rattled off feeding schedules for his plants. And when we'd driven here, and he'd placed his palm on my leg, I'd imagined how it would feel to have him touch me through the silk of my dress.

This was better.

We made it to the couch in the next room. I laughed as I fell back against the royal blue cushions, my knees falling open as Vaughn tugged me to the edge. His jacket fell to the ground. His belt jingled. His cock sprang free. He produced a condom, his eyes dark with need.

Then he positioned himself in front of me—and thrust in.

I cried out. It was intense and burning and beautiful. My fingernails sank into the rich cotton of his shirt, tugging so hard the top three buttons came free. Vaughn grunted above me, hooking his arms under my legs to deepen the position.

I could feel him everywhere. I was trapped here, against the couch, my back bent and my head buried between two big cushions, and I didn't want to be anywhere else. My existence was simply Vaughn and pleasure. Safety and heat and the sizzling lightning coursing through my veins.

"You feel so good," he groaned, the rhythm of his thrusts gaining a needy edge. "Alba—princess—the things you make me want—"

"I'll go," I panted.

He pulled back slightly, one hand on the back of the sofa, the other hooked around my knee. He batted at the couch cushions until he could see my face. "What?"

"I'll go to the gala with you—oh!" I threw my head back as he drove himself deeper inside me.

"You will," he said, snapping his hips.

"I will."

"You'll stand by my side," he growled, his pace increasing.

"Yes—"

"You'll make all those assholes wish they were me."

I laughed, hands finding his sides, sliding up underneath his shirt so I could stroke the hard pack of his stomach muscles. "If that's what you want."

"I'm just telling you what will happen," he said, a bright, almost boyish smile flashing across his features. Then he shifted his arm to hike my leg up higher, and we both lost ourselves in the pleasure of the moment. I came hard, bent like a pretzel on his fancy couch, and then locked my legs around his back when I felt him go stiff above me.

Vaughn's lips ran across my temple, over the shell of my ear. He breathed hard, arms trembling as he held most of his weight off me, knees lowering down to the cushions. He swore, then kissed my cheekbone, then swore some more. I laughed, but it was mostly breathless.

"Sex with you makes me feel like I'm losing my mind," he admitted, pulling back far enough that he could meet my gaze before pressing a soft kiss to my lips.

"I know," I said. "Me too."

He gulped. "I won't—I won't hold you to your promise. The gala—forget it, Alba. I don't want to make you feel—"

"I'll go," I said, stroking his face with my palms. He was still inside me, going softer with every heartbeat. I smiled, feeling grounded and light at once. "I want to go," I told him, surprised to find that it was the truth.

"I thought you were hell-bent on refusing to go near that event," Vaughn said, wry.

I smiled. "I changed my mind."

His lips brushed against mine, then he moved to kiss the tip of my nose. "I'm afraid to ask why," he rumbled, his cheek creasing as he grinned, his eyes tracing my hairline, my features.

I finally let my legs uncross and slid my ankles down along the back of his thighs, all the way down to rest them in the crook of his knees. I loved touching him like this. Feeling so connected, like our bodies already knew each other.

"You make me feel safe," I whispered. "That's why I changed my mind."

Vaughn's gaze slid up to meet mine. He shifted so he was holding himself on his elbow, then used his free hand to stroke the side of my head, his thumb tracing my eyebrow. He exhaled slowly, his eyes soft.

I felt raw and open, like I'd said too much. But it was the truth—I was safe here, with him. His gaze was steady as he watched me, his features intent. He opened his mouth and for a moment, nothing came out.

Then he replied, "You can change it back anytime."

My heart did a cartwheel. Even now, when I'd given him what he wanted and promised to go to Arlo Noble's event with him, he was giving me an out. Making sure I felt safe. Taking care of me.

I wanted to tell him I was falling in love with him—because wasn't that what this was? This fizzy, too-big-for-my-chest feeling that made me want to smile and sigh and cry all at once? I wanted to say it out loud, to put a name to this ball of emotion that made me feel like I would explode.

But the last time I told a guy I loved him, it blew up in my face. Vaughn wasn't James—I knew that. Still, I was afraid.

So instead, I lifted my head, wrapped my arms around his shoulders, and kissed him. Vaughn groaned against my mouth, settling his body on top of mine so I could feel all the weight and warmth of him. I sighed, happy.

I'd go to the gala with him. I'd go anywhere with him.

As the reality of the situation sank in, my eyes snapped open.

I needed a dress.

TWENTY-FIVE
VAUGHN

MY EX-WIFE OPENED her front door, looked at me, and called out Charlotte's name. Then she turned to me and gave me one of those tight, cordial smiles I'd become accustomed to. "Hi, Vaughn."

"How was it?" I asked, as usual, referring to her two weeks with our kid.

"Great," Tiffany replied, then turned at the pitter-patter of little feet sprinting down the hallway toward her. Our conversations were always stilted now, but that came with the territory. The only thing keeping us together was the love we shared for the little girl currently barreling toward me.

"Daddy!"

I knelt and spread my arms, bracing myself for the collision. Charlotte launched herself at me. I caught her, stood, and spun, inhaling the scent of her shampoo and feeling all the tension in me drain away. Her hair was a wild mess, half of it sticky with some mystery substance, but her eyes were alight and her smile was wide as she pulled back to plant a kiss on my cheek.

"How you doin', turkey?"

"I'm so good. Mom and Dale and me went out to dinner last night!"

"Ooh," I said, hiking her up onto my hip. She was getting heavy to be held like this, but I was reluctant to let go of these moments. "What'd you have?"

"I had a piece of pizza as big as my *head*." She placed her hands on either side of her head to demonstrate.

I laughed, even though my thoughts flicked back to my last dinner date with Alba. We'd eaten oversized pizza slices too. Which reminded me—I had to have a chat with my ex-wife.

"Go grab your stuff," I said, "I want to talk to your mom."

"Okay!" Charlotte took off, and Tiffany leaned against the doorjamb, arching her brows. I didn't take offense to her not inviting me in; our coparenting relationship relied on these sorts of boundaries.

"I saw your company in the news. Midtown job still stuck in the ground?"

Sighing, I shrugged. "We'll get there."

"I can keep Charlotte longer if you need to be at work."

"No," I replied. "That's not necessary." I was only getting one week with her this time; I wouldn't give up both.

"She seems to spend an awful lot of time with that nanny of yours, and not so much time with you."

I bristled. "She spends plenty of time with me, Tiff. And I'm not here for you to take swipes at me."

My ex-wife sighed. "Well, what is it?" She straightened, frowning. "This isn't about money, is it? That job drained everything from your company and now you can't afford your child support payments?"

Frustration snaked through me, and I curled my fingers into my palms to dispel some of it. Tiffany was always worried about what she could get for herself—more time with Charlotte. More money. She was a great mom, but she was just a little too selfish to be a good partner. At least, that's how it had felt to me. Maybe, a quiet voice chimed, maybe she felt that way because I hadn't given her enough of me, freely enough, often enough. Maybe I'd put everything else first, and she had no choice but to fight for what I *would* give her.

I gritted my teeth. "I said I wasn't here for you to take swipes," I bit off. "The money'll come on the first of the month, like it has since the day our divorce was finalized."

Tiffany clicked her tongue. "So?"

"So, I've met someone. I'm going to introduce her to Charlotte."

Tiff blinked at me. "Oh."

Feeling defensive, I took a page out of Alba's book and went on the attack. "Don't look at me like that. You started dating Dale, what, six weeks after we broke up?"

"I'm not looking at you any which way, Vaughn, I'm just—"

"Everything okay?" Dale appeared behind my ex-wife, tall and lanky, his long-fingered hands landing on Tiffany's shoulder.

She relaxed slightly, took a deep breath, and filled him in: "Vaughn's dating someone and wants to introduce her to Charlotte."

Dale's eyebrows went up, and he nodded. "Happy for you, man."

My ex-wife's new husband was a calm, unassuming accountant. He kept regular work hours—even during tax season—and was apparently a great cook. From the moment they'd started dating, I could tell he was better for Tiffany than I'd ever been. He balanced her out when I only riled her up. She needed that kind of stability in her life, someone who wouldn't snap back every time she did.

I should've known to be better, but I was who I was. I nodded at the other man, backing down. "Thank you. Now, would you like to meet her before I introduce her to Charlotte?"

It was part of our custody agreement that we'd let the other parent meet new partners before introducing them to Charlotte, and Tiffany nodded. "Yes, I would. I assume Hillary will be in touch to work out the scheduling?" That was a not-so-subtle dig about how unavailable I was to her—had always been to her. When we were married, she'd get irate when my assistant would step in to make time in my schedule for her. With the benefit of a few years' distance, I could understand that. Tiffany's shirt crinkled around Dale's fingers; he was squeezing her shoulder.

Sighing, my ex-wife shook her head at me. "I'm sorry. It just always gets to me when I have to say goodbye to Charlotte. Hand-offs...are tough."

"I know," I agreed. "I'm sorry for springing this on you."

She huffed and gave me a half smile. An olive branch. "Four years isn't exactly springing it on me," she acknowledged. "This woman—she's good for you?"

I thought of the way Alba pushed me, and how she softened in my arms. The way her smile lit me up from head to toe, and how all I wanted to do was share every part of my life with her. I couldn't wait to see her interact with Charlotte. I hoped they'd like each other. Meeting Tiffany's gaze, I nodded. "She's great."

Tiff and Dale exchanged a glance, and she released a long sigh. "Good," she said, then we all turned to watch Charlotte barrel down the hallway toward us.

Tiffany's smile was strained as she said goodbye, and then Charlotte slipped her hand in mine, and I took her back home.

That night, I missed having Alba by my side. Like some sort of lovesick fool, I pawed at my phone and found her number. She answered on the first ring.

"Hello," she purred.

My body relaxed at the sound of her voice. "Hey. What are you up to?"

"Trawling through pages and pages of dresses looking for the perfect gala look."

I hummed. "Anything you wear will be perfect, Alba." I curled a hand behind my head and stared at the ceiling, imagining it. Alba, on my arm, looking like a vision in a beautiful gown. Being in a stuffy, uncomfortable tux wouldn't even matter when she was by my side.

"You are so wrong, Vaughn," she said, laughing. "The dress needs to be legendary."

"I mean it," I insisted. "You could wear my mother's old prom dress and be the most beautiful person in the room."

Her laugh warmed me, until she said, "Oh, my sweet summer child."

"What's that supposed to mean?" I mock-growled.

"It means you don't understand what will happen when I walk in on your arm, Vaughn."

"Heads will turn. Men will wish they were me. Women will wish they were you. And you'll be all mine."

She hummed quietly, like she was considering it. "Maybe," she conceded. "In a fantasyland of your making."

I laughed. "Okay. Tell me about your fantasyland, then."

"We'll walk in, and everyone from my old life will turn to look at me. They won't recognize you, but they'll dissect everything about you from the way you hold your head to the way you treat the staff to the level of shine on your shoes. I'll undergo the same scrutiny, but worse, because they'll all be wondering how in the hell I got a ticket."

Discomfort squirmed through me. This gala would be every-thing I hated. All the vapid fakery. All the pretentious airs and turned-up noses. I already knew I was going to feel uncomfortable from the moment the car door opened to let me out at the venue. My father, on the other hand, would've loved every minute of it. I rubbed my forehead. "So? Who cares what they think?"

"I do, Vaughn," Alba admitted. "I've been humiliated, and if this is going to be my big F-U moment, I want to make the most of it."

There was a note in her voice that pulled me back from my own discomfort. Alba needed me. I'd pushed her to come with me, because I wanted my moment with her by my side. But I was asking something of her that was bigger than me feeling uncomfortable.

The people at that gala had thrown her out and turned their backs on her. She said it herself: they'd humiliated her. If I wanted her to trust me—be with me—then I needed to make sure she knew I was there for her. Things with Arlo Noble had progressed; his team was trawling through our financials and making all the right noises. The gala was the final hoop to jump through. I could afford to step back and let Alba have her moment.

"So tell me about this dress," I said. "What does it have to do? Shoot fire from your nipples to destroy your enemies, or something?"

Alba laughed. "Close, but no. It has to strike a perfect balance between unbelievably memorable and not main-character-y. I have to look like I didn't try too hard while also being flawless. Timeless without being outdated. Trendy without being flashy."

"I'm regretting ever agreeing to go to this event."

"You and me both, Vaughn," she said, laughing. "And I've got a little over a week to make this happen."

"I believe in you," I said.

There was a short silence, and I could hear the shy smile in Alba's voice when she replied, "Thank you." It made me realize that she needed to hear these things. She needed to know how amazing she was and how highly I thought of her.

Which reminded me: "Are you free for dinner this weekend?"

"You want to go over the cutlery again?"

I huffed. "Not quite..."

TWENTY-SIX
ALBA

IF OUR LAST date had been one for the history books, this one was too—but for different reasons. Vaughn's ex-wife sat directly across from me, her eyes slightly narrowed as she scanned my face. Judging. Finding me lacking, evidently.

I resisted the urge to go on the offensive and smiled blandly at her. "The way Vaughn talks about your daughter, it sounds like you've done a wonderful job."

"What is it that you do for work again?" she asked, tilting her head as she ignored my compliment. Her tone made Vaughn sigh and Dale, her current husband, move his arm so it was slung around the back of her chair, his hand making soothing strokes over her shoulder.

My smile remained stuck on my face through sheer force of will. This reminded me of countless events where I had to make nice with someone awful because of their last name. People weren't so different, no matter how many zeroes they had in their bank account.

"I'm a consultant," I replied, nodding in thanks as the waiter filled my glass of water.

"Huh," Tiffany replied. "And what is it, exactly, that you consult on?"

"Tiff, come on," Vaughn said. "We're just here to get to know each other."

"Why do you think I'm asking these questions?" she shot back. "I'm trying to get to know the woman you'll be bringing around my daughter—"

"*Our* daughter—"

"—and make sure she's not some sort of sociopath—"

"Honey, come on—"

"I knew this would be a disaster the minute I suggested it," Vaughn growled.

"The minute *your assistant* suggested it, you mean—"

"Honey," her husband said, gentle warning in his tone.

"I'm just saying—"

"Well, say less," Vaughn snapped, then sighed as he rubbed his temples.

I sipped my water, and I wondered if this was worth it. Then Vaughn slid his hand onto my thigh, and I turned to meet his gaze. He gave me a tight smile, something like an apology in his gaze. The tension that had stolen up my spine dissolved away.

Yeah—it was worth it. Worth it to have Vaughn here beside me, touching me like I belonged to him. Worth it to make a life for myself, finally. To choose something for myself.

I leaned forward, and Tiffany's gaze snapped back to me. "I'm an image consultant," I told her. "I helped Vaughn update his look."

"I see," she said, eyes flicking from me to him. "I had noticed the haircut. You're not so scruffy-looking anymore."

"That's what she called me," Vaughn grumbled, tilting his head toward me.

Tiffany huffed, and it looked like she'd tried to hold back her laugh. "She wasn't wrong. You still have that old pair of clippers you bought for ten dollars?"

"They worked, didn't they?"

"Depends on your definition of 'worked,'" I cut in, which made Tiffany huff again.

"Oh I get it," Vaughn said, leaning back in his chair. "The way to get you two to get along is for you to pile on me. I'm sure Dale has his own clippers that—"

"Keep me out of this," the taller man said, lifting his palms. "I'm just here for the food."

Tiffany elbowed his ribs. "Liar."

He laughed, leaning over to press a kiss to the side of her head. Tiffany relaxed slightly, her smile turning softer as she glanced at her husband. He gave her a long look that seemed to say, *Give her a chance, honey.* She rolled her eyes. *Fine.*

Turning back to me, Tiffany took a deep breath, like she was preparing for a long and arduous session scrubbing scum from her bathroom tiles instead of an evening at a fancy Mediterranean restaurant getting to know me. Her smile was forced, but she was trying. "So—image consulting. How did you get into that?"

"Um," I said, frowning, "I kind of...fell into it."

"Barged into it, more like," Vaughn corrected, and it was my turn to elbow him in the ribs.

At Tiffany's questioning look, I shook my head. "Long story."

"I see," she said.

From there, the waiter came to take our orders. Conversation turned to Charlotte, then to sports, and to Tiffany's work (freelance copywriter for various online publications, including a fashion e-magazine I loved). By the time we turned down the waiter's offer to bring over the dessert menu, I felt like I'd run a marathon. We said goodbye to the other couple, and then Vaughn stood with me to wait for a cab.

"That was nice," I said as cold wind made me flip the collar of my jacket up.

Vaughn snorted. "You don't have to lie to me," he said, arm sliding around my back as he pulled me closer. "Thank you for coming tonight. It means a lot to me."

And how could I stop the way my heart melted at his words? I knew I was falling too hard and too fast for him—but he wasn't making it easy for me to slow down. Meeting his daughter, attending the Noble event with him, sleeping over at his place every night his daughter wasn't...

He made me feel like there was a future for me other than drudgery. Other than crawling back to the family fold so I could kill the part of me that thought for myself. I could have a life with Vaughn. Sure, he had a snippy ex-wife, a daughter, a business that took up so much of his time, and a thousand other things that would make life complicated...but it would be worth it, just to hear him talk to me in that dark velvet voice, telling me how much he appreciated me.

"I wish you could come home with me tonight," he said, leaning down to press his forehead against mine.

I smiled, touching the tip of his nose with mine. "Me too. But I'll see you Monday for your fitting at Koval's shop."

"Yeah," Vaughn said, pulling back. His arms were still around me, but his head was out of reach for kisses. The streetlights glinted over his hair, his cheeks slightly red from the wind. He was beautiful. And I was distracted by it, which is why his next question made me jerk: "How much money do you need for your dress for the gala?"

I blinked. "Sorry?"

His shoulders dropped. "You're still going with me, right?"

"The Noble Foundation Gala?" I asked.

"Yeah."

"Yeah, I'm going."

"Good." His smile was a flash of white teeth. "So what do you need to get a dress? All that talk about finding the perfect one sounded expensive."

"You don't have to—" I stopped. He kind of *did* have to pay for my outfit, since I was still pretty close to destitute.

But Vaughn just frowned at me. "Well, I'll reimburse you, obviously. You can just submit the purchase the normal way."

My brows jumped, and my heart dropped. "Are you—is this—" Familiar fears rushed at me—that he was pushing me away, that I'd misread the situation—but I forced myself to take a deep breath. "Is this a work event?" I asked, not liking the way my voice cracked when I asked the question. "I thought... I thought you wanted me there as your date."

"I do. What do you mean?"

"It's just—if you're paying me..."

It felt dirty. It felt like being used as a prop, which I kind of *was*, but it hadn't felt that way when he'd asked me, but—

"Hey," he said, tilting my chin up. "I just didn't want you to worry about the cost of the dress."

My shoulders dropped. Vaughn was being thoughtful, not dismissive. Sighing, I nodded. "Right. Okay. Thank you."

"Get a dress, shoes, whatever. Charge it to the company. I'll cover it."

I nodded, feeling silly. And it *was* helpful, because the gown rental companies I'd been trawling had a whole lot of nothing. A ton of gorgeous gowns, of course, but nothing that the keen eyes of my former peers wouldn't immediately identify as untailored, ill-fitting, and cheap by their standards.

But did Vaughn really mean it? The people at the gala would be wearing outfits that cost thousands. Tens of thousands. He probably thought I needed a few hundred bucks. That would cover the shoes—maybe.

I never should've agreed to this.

Vaughn kissed me softly, then pulled back. "I told Billie I'd be back before nine."

"Go," I said, forcing a smile. "I'll see you tomorrow."

He kissed me one more time, then hailed a cab and opened the door for me. I smiled at him as he closed the door, then exhaled and leaned against the squeaky leather seats.

Being taken care of like this took some getting used to. I had to stop assuming the worst in Vaughn. He was a good man, and he cared about me. Everything he did had proved that to me. Now I just had to stop doubting myself—stop doubting *him*—and enjoy our relationship blossoming. Sure, it was fast, but it was also good.

But this out-of-control feeling was a little too familiar. It was how James had made me feel when we'd met. When he'd taken me out on the back of his motorcycle. When he'd kissed me and made love to me and told me I was special, right before he dumped me.

As I leaned my forehead against the cool glass of the back seat window, I wondered if I was making the same old mistakes all over again.

TWENTY-SEVEN
VAUGHN

MY FITTING with Koval went well. The tux was coming along, and he bullied me into also ordering an overcoat for the big night. I asked what the point of that was when I'd take it off within three minutes of arriving, and he and Alba squawked at me until I backed down. Then I asked him if he sold women's clothes, and his judgmental, all-seeing eyes had slid to Alba. She'd given me a long look and shook her head. Koval had huffed and gone back to pinning the partially completed sleeve to my shoulder. The hunt for the dress continued. I still didn't quite understand what she needed. It was a dress. How hard could it be?

Instead of parting ways when we left the shop, I tugged on Alba's hand. "There's someone I want you to meet," I told her, and watched the smile bloom over her face.

That's how we ended up in my living room, surrounded by a mass of dolls and children's toys. Billie disappeared into the kitchen to prep some food for the week for Charlotte, which left Alba, me, and my daughter in the living room, free to play. I'd pulled her out of kindergarten for the day, hoping we could have some fun.

I thought this would be easier than dinner with my ex-wife.

I was wrong.

Charlotte ignored Alba for a full fifteen minutes. She mumbled a hello, then played with her dolls in the living room with a kind of intense focus that could only be deliberate. I didn't hold it against her, and I was happy to see that Alba didn't, either.

"Charlotte, do you want to share one of your dolls with Alba?" I prodded.

Charlotte glanced at me, then at Alba. "No," she said.

Alba gave me a look, her eyes glimmering with humor. "That's okay," she said. "I'll just sort out all the doll clothes and see what we've got here." She grabbed the plastic container filled to the brim with tiny clothing, sat cross-legged on the floor, and began laying all the pieces out, organizing them by style and color. A tiny pink skirt was set beside a tiny purple skirt. A long sparkly dress was laid out below the skirts, beside what looked like a wedding gown and another evening gown.

Charlotte's eyes slid to the array of clothing, then back to the dolls in her hands. She grabbed a brush and began detangling the doll's hair—then glanced at Alba's work again.

Alba said nothing; she simply kept organizing the clothes and occasionally making comments about how much she liked a piece. "I wish I had a dress like this," she said, smoothing her hands over dark red sequins. "So pretty."

"The purple one is better," Charlotte said, jumping up like she couldn't resist anymore. She dug through the container of clothes and brought out a handful of sparkly purple fabric with so many ruffles that I could hardly tell it was a dress. She presented it to Alba, whose eyes went wide.

"Fabulous!" Alba said, and Charlotte beamed. "Should we put it on your doll? Are they going to a ball?"

"A fancy ball like the one my daddy is going to. Are you going to go too?"

Alba glanced at me, then accepted the spare doll Charlotte handed her. "Yes," she replied.

"What are you going to wear? You should wear purple."

"I haven't found a dress yet," Alba admitted. "But that's a good idea."

I slid off my chair and down to the ground with them, and Charlotte thrust a third doll at me, followed by an outfit she and Alba chose together. Then I struggled to get the dress on the doll and fumbled with the tiny snap closure until Alba laughed and took pity on me, reaching over to help me dress my doll. Charlotte grinned, and I laughed.

Later, we went out for dinner. Charlotte chatted with Alba the whole time, and I got used to the strange tightness in my chest at watching them together. It felt like a future I wasn't allowed to hope for. I'd lost my chance at a solid family when Tiffany and I broke up—and now it felt like I might get a second chance.

Distantly, lurking at the back of my mind, images began to solidify: a diamond ring glinting on Alba's finger. A new baby. Charlotte's wide eyes as she held the infant for the first time, her first step in becoming the overprotective big sister. Alba, tired and deliriously happy, looking at me with shining eyes...

I blinked the images away. It seemed like too much to hope for when I'd already messed up my first chance at a happy family.

That evening, when Alba had gone home and Charlotte had had her bath and was snuggled in bed, I lay next to her and angled my head so it touched hers.

"What did you think of Alba?"

"Is she your *girl*friend?"

I turned to see Charlotte grinning at me, a little giggle slipping out. Frowning, I asked, "Where'd you learn about girlfriends?"

My daughter laughed, snorting and giggling and looking like the little girl she was—and wouldn't be for much longer. I wrapped her in my arms and tickled her until she squealed. Then I said, "Alba's my girlfriend."

"You said she was your friend."

"She's my friend and my girlfriend."

Charlotte frowned at me; she hadn't considered that possibility.

"One more book, and then bed."

Charlotte nodded, then got on her knees and reached for the shelf of bedtime books near her bed. She grabbed the thickest, longest book and handed it to me with a smile. I couldn't be too mad, though, because she blotted herself against me and snuggled in the way that never failed to melt my heart.

She was asleep by the second-to-last page. I lay there for a while, watching her sleep, then slid off her bed and tiptoed out of the room. With one last glance over my shoulder toward my daughter, I released a long breath and closed her door.

Leaning against the wall, I thought of all the decisions that had led to today. Returning to Carmine's even when I knew I shouldn't. Exchanging letters with my mystery cleaning lady. Staying late to work, and discovering she was Alba. Hiring her. Sleeping with her. Falling for her.

It all happened naturally, and it had been just as natural to see Alba and Charlotte together. Alba had a core of integrity that Charlotte could sense; I was sure of it. She'd come from a vapid, rich, horrible family, but she'd grown from it and now the amazing woman I knew.

I never wanted to let her go. I wanted a thousand days like today. I'd let my company burn to the ground, just for the kind of quiet happiness that I'd experienced by watching Alba and my daughter playing and laughing and chatting.

Except...would I? Or would I spend long evenings in the office, fighting for a company that no longer seemed to hold my interest?

I shook my head. Of course I would. I was a businessman, an entrepreneur. I didn't just abandon projects when they got difficult. I didn't flit from idea to idea, dragging my family down every step of the way.

Maybe I could have it all. The business. The partner. The family. Maybe things weren't destined to crumble the way I'd grown up thinking they would.

TWENTY-EIGHT
ALBA

A LOUD NOISE made me jump from my spot, nestled in the corner of my couch. I whipped my head around, looking for the source of the noise as my heart pounded.

Then I saw a little lit-up screen beside the front door. Someone had rung my buzzer. The studio's intercom screen had never worked, and as I walked up to glance in this one, I realized this was the first time that someone had come to my apartment to see me.

It was Thursday afternoon, and I hadn't seen Vaughn in three days. Even though we talked every day, it wasn't the same as being in his arms. I knew I should enjoy the time away from him and use it to settle my feelings down a little, but I couldn't help it. I missed him.

I studied the buttons next to my front door, and I pressed the one that looked like a phone receiver. "Hello?"

"Delivery," the guy on the grainy screen said.

"Who from?"

"How am I supposed to know? You Alba Enders?"

"Yes."

"Then I've got a box for you."

"I'll buzz you up." It took me a second to find the button to unlock the front door, but I did, and then I watched the delivery man open the door, a long box coming into view as he shifted to step inside. I unlocked my front door and waited until I heard the elevator door slide open, then pulled my door open and stood in the opening.

"Sign here," he said, thrusting a palm-sized device at me.

"What is it?"

The delivery man looked at me like I was the unfortunate owner of half a brain. "I don't know," he said, then thrust the box at me. It was huge and flat and had a big velvet bow holding it closed. There were little droplets of water on the velvet; it was snowing outside.

I opened my mouth to say something, but he was already rushing down the hall and ducking into the elevator. Sighing, I shuffled inside and let the door fall closed behind me. Frowning at the box, I turned it around, but there was no card on the outside. Just a simple white box with a black velvet bow.

Who had sent this? It looked like an item from my old life. Luxury for the sake of luxury. But from who? My parents? *James?* Why? None of them knew where I lived, so how could they?

I walked over to the couch and shoved off the blanket I'd wrapped around myself.

My pulse rattled. If this was a present from my old life, I could expect to open it and find a nest of snakes. Vaughn wouldn't send me anything...would he?

I knew the logical answer wasn't that my parents had discovered my address and decided to send me a mound of dog shit wrapped in a pretty black bow. I knew that most likely, this was from Vaughn. But believing that Vaughn had thought about me and had taken the time to send me a surprise present...that would mean believing that this thing between us was real. *Real* real.

That was terrifying. And wonderful. But mostly terrifying.

I huffed. It was a box. How bad could it be? The velvet bow fell apart with a gentle tug. I pushed the damp fabric aside, brushing off a few dots of water from the thick cardboard, then pulled off the top. Nestled in protective paper was a waterfall of lilac-colored fabric.

My heart began to thump—and it wasn't from nerves.

Someone had sent me a dress.

I touched the neckline, feeling the beading that had to be hand stitched. The dress fell to a deep V front and back, held up with thin straps at the shoulder. The bodice was almost completely beaded with thousands of twinkling sequins and stones, which dotted the dress through the hips and down to the bottom hem. Pulling the dress out of the box, I held it up and felt the satisfying weight of the fabric, admiring the way it swirled and danced against my legs.

I glanced at the tag: *Versace.*

Oh, my word.

This wasn't just a dress. This was A Dress. It looked like it was inspired by Claudia Schiffer's lavender Oscar's look from 1995. I frowned at the material, the stitching. This wasn't a new dress. Was it inspired by that dress? Or was it *the dress*?

How—

Who—

Not Vaughn. He had multiple pairs of steel-toed boots, and he hadn't gotten up close and personal with a decent suit until a few weeks ago. He'd buzzed his hair over the bathroom sink, for crying out loud. Vaughn wouldn't have the connections or the knowledge to get a vintage Versace piece released from the archives. He probably didn't even know that fashion houses had archives.

For him to send me this dress would mean he had to put in serious effort, and way out of his comfort zone. That wasn't... He couldn't, could he?

My mouth had gone dry at some point, and I was afraid of leaving sweat stains on the fabric from how damp my palms had become. I laid the dress back on its protective paper and shifted my gaze to the bottom edge of the box.

A card was secured to little slits in another, smaller box contained inside the big one. My name was written in swirling calligraphy. The card was thick and luxurious, and when I turned it over, there were a grand total of four words, followed by a name: *See me for alterations. Koval.*

I laughed. The grumpy old man had a way with words, that was for sure. And that meant this dress had to be from Vaughn. Of course it was from him.

Tears formed in my eyes.

And wasn't that just so typical of him? He'd seen the stress in my face when he'd mentioned expensing my outfit, so he'd taken it upon himself to fix the problem. I guessed he'd gone to Koval after the fitting on Monday and asked for a dress, and Koval had handled the rest. I wondered if Vaughn had requested purple, to make his daughter happy. It seemed likely.

I looked up, my eyes skimming the main room of my apartment. It was just like this place, wasn't it? He'd found the mold and had told me he'd handle it. And he did. I wasn't sure how he'd convinced the landlord to keep my rent the same for a place two or three times the size, but he'd done it. For me. He'd given me a safe roof over my head, somewhere to start fresh, again.

As my heart thundered, I stripped down to my undies and slipped the dress over my head. It felt like cool liquid falling over my skin, the straps at the shoulders sitting a bit wide, the hips feeling a little tight. The only mirror in this place was in the bathroom, so I stood in front of the vanity and admired what I could see. I spun around to look at the play of the light over the sequins at the back and sides and front, my hands skimming over the sides of the garment.

My phone rang. Vaughn.

"Do you like it?" he asked as soon as I answered.

"Vaughn." I twirled. "Where did you get this?"

"Mr. Koval is full of mysteries. I'm guessing that means it's the perfect F-U dress for a certain gala?"

"It's more than an F-U dress. It's a Diana Revenge Dress."

"A what?"

"Never mind. I need to call Koval to make an appointment."

"There's a car waiting for you downstairs. He's blocked out the rest of the day for you."

"*Vaughn.*"

He laughed. "Hurry up. I'm sick of sitting here on my own."

My heart kicked. I ran to the window, struggled with the painted-over sash, and finally heaved it up far enough to stick my head out. "What are you doing here?" I called out, down the eight stories that separated us. Snow fell on my head, over my shoulders.

Vaughn leaned against the side of a black town car, grinning up at me.

"You're crazy."

"Get down here," he said. "You know the old man doesn't like to be kept waiting."

I slammed the window most of the way down, then stripped off the dress and threw on the old leggings and shirt I'd been wearing earlier. Carefully repacking the dress, I peeked in the smaller box—beautiful lavender satin shoes—and replaced the top. I left the velvet bow untied, hauled the box under my arm, and flew down the stairs.

Vaughn caught me at the bottom, taking the box from me to

hand it to the driver, then swinging me around in his arms. I laughed, breathless, then tilted my chin up to accept his kiss.

"Where did you find that dress?" I mumbled against my lips. "You didn't even know what a Windsor knot was until I met you."

Vaughn grinned. "Do you really think so little of me?"

"You aren't real. This is a dream."

"I've been pinching myself since I met you," he said.

My heart fluttered. He was too good to be true—but he was right here in front of me, and I had no choice but to believe this was really happening. I let Vaughn guide me into the car and then sighed when he slid in beside me. The door closed, and I saw the darkened shape of the driver move around the car through the tinted windows. He'd placed the dress in the front passenger seat, and the privacy shade was up.

Vaughn slid his hand over my jaw, and as the car merged into traffic, he kissed me. My heart had already been racing, and his kiss only made it speed up. I clung to his lapels, kissing him back even harder.

"I take it you like the dress," he mumbled against my lips, his cheek creasing beneath my hand.

"The dress is beautiful. I love it. And—" I stopped myself. I wanted to tell him I loved *him*. That he made me feel special and worthy and whole. I wanted to tell him that my time with him had been the happiest in my life. He listened to me and never dismissed me. Even when he didn't particularly care about something—like a dress—Vaughn went out of his way to find the perfect one.

I'd never imagined life could be this good. Even when I had all the wealth I could have wanted, I wasn't as happy as I was now.

And it wasn't the fact that he'd found the perfect, priceless dress for me. It's that he'd tried. I was so important to him that he'd put in the effort. I *mattered*.

I hadn't mattered to my parents—not unless I acted exactly the way they wanted. I hadn't mattered to James—not unless I gave him access to wealth and prestige and luxury. And I hadn't mattered to Cole—not really. Not once he was given the option to walk away.

I'd always been on the end of a conditional bargain. I knew my worth in relation to what I could provide other people.

With Vaughn, it was different. Yes, I was teaching him skills to land an investor, to move in higher circles. But I believed him when he said that whatever I wore to the gala would be perfect. And I believed him when he said that if I changed my mind and decided I didn't want to go, he wouldn't hold it against me.

He valued me for me. No strings. No conditions.

When he pulled back from the kiss and placed his forehead against mine, he was still smiling. "I should buy you dresses more often."

I choked on air. "*Buy?* You bought that dress?"

He leaned back, frowning. "What else would I do with it?"

"Fashion houses don't usually sell archival pieces unless—"

"It was already in a private collection."

"Koval—"

"Started his career in the Versace workrooms. Apparently now, after a few decades, he's kind of a big deal. He has some nice stuff, actually. But when I explained the situation, he insisted that was the one," Vaughn said, tipping his head toward the front seat where the dress was. "And it was purple, which seemed fitting."

"Oh, my goodness." I couldn't breathe. "Oh...my *goodness*."

"Hey. Take a breath." Vaughn tilted my chin so I'd meet his eyes. "Breathe, princess. It's just a dress."

"It's not *just a dress*, Vaughn."

He laughed. "It is to me."

Because it didn't matter what I wore. He still looked at me the same way. Waitress's uniform. Cleaner's outfit. Priceless, vintage designer dress. It was all the same to him.

What mattered was me. For the first time in my life, I didn't have to perform. I just had to be.

The feelings roiling inside me were too big to contain. I leaned over and kissed him again, my hands trembling as they coasted over his shoulders.

"Hey," he mumbled. "Hey. Come on." He pulled back and brushed a thumb over my cheek. It came away wet; I was crying.

"You think it's silly to cry over a dress," I said, tapping into that old, familiar well of shame that had been kept full by every relationship I'd ever had in my life. I snorted at myself, wiping my face with the heels of my palms.

"I don't think that," Vaughn said, pulling my hands away. "But I think you need to breathe for me, Alba."

I sucked in a rattling breath and met his eyes.

"Better?" he asked gently.

I took another breath, then nodded. "Better."

"Good," he said. "Now come here."

TWENTY-NINE
ALBA

VAUGHN HAULED me onto his lap, his hands framing my hips. All it took for me to lean in and kiss him was slight pressure from his fingertips at the base of my spine. The car began to move and we swayed back into the leather seats, and Vaughn grinned against my lips when I yelped.

"This is dangerous. We're not strapped in," I said.

"Live a little, Alba," Vaughn replied with a laugh, tangling his fingers into my hair as he dragged me closer for another kiss.

It was a fitting thing to say. I hadn't really lived in so long. Ever since my disownment, I'd been trying to survive. And even before that, I wasn't really living. I'd been beaten into the box where I was supposed to exist and been told how to act, how to think. Even the clothes I wore—clothes that had remained mostly unworn in my closet now—were in service to an image that no longer felt like me. Yes, they were beautiful. Yes, I missed *feeling* beautiful. But did I really want to wear them? What about all those times that my feet had hurt in heels that were too high, or the times I'd declined dessert because I was afraid I would stop fitting into my pants?

When had I ever lived? For me? For the sake of it? For the pleasure of it?

Vaughn's lips tasted like freedom. He swept his tongue against mine and banded his arm around my back, his other hand still buried in my hair. I was caught in his arms, and I never wanted to find my way out of them. I kissed him back, hoping he'd hear everything I was too afraid to say.

That I was falling for him. That I wanted forever with him. That he had the power to destroy me.

This time, when I felt his hardness swell beneath me, I didn't feel that uncomfortable itchiness under my skin that made my mind want to spin out. I didn't feel like I needed to perform. I didn't want to be told what to do.

This man was safe in a way I'd never experienced before. I rubbed my cheek against his as I lowered myself down on top of him, fully clothed, feeling like my chest was split open and my heart vulnerable to him. And that's how I wanted it to stay.

He groaned, lips coasting across my jaw. "I should buy you dresses more often," he said.

"It's not the dress," I replied, catching his lips for another kiss.

His arm pressed against my back, and I ground myself against him. The car started moving again—I hadn't noticed it stopping—and turned. Our bodies swayed sideways, my shin on the seat stopping me from tipping over.

"What is it, then?" Vaughn asked, pulling away to look in my eyes.

I shook my head. I couldn't put into words how he made me feel like a new person. I didn't know how to say it, other than admitting that I was in love with him. And how could I say that, now, in the back of a car on the way to a tailor? He already had the power to destroy me. Admitting that I had already fallen for him would be inviting him to do it.

"You deserve it, Alba," Vaughn said softly, his thumb stroking my cheek. "You deserve that dress and a whole lot more. You hear me?"

My throat was tight. "I hear you," I said, and then Vaughn took pity on me and kissed me. It was a hungry kiss, one that didn't leave space for words or thought. A kiss that made my hands tighten on his shoulders, my knees clench against his hips. Vaughn slid his hand across my back and gripped my hip, his head falling back with a sigh as I ground myself against him once more.

It didn't matter that we were both fully clothed. The heat sparking between us was explosive. I could feel the steel-hard bar of his cock beneath the placket of his pants, and I rubbed myself against it with the kind of desperation that, with any other man, would've had my cheeks burning with shame.

Not with Vaughn—because Vaughn was right there with me, riding the edge of frenzy, gripping me like I was the only thing that mattered.

"I should've come up to your apartment and delivered that dress myself," he growled, his lips near my ear, his breath hot on my neck. "I don't have enough time to do all the things I want to do to you now."

My hips bucked, and his hand spasmed as it gripped my side. I smiled. "We've got all the time in the world."

Vaughn's smile was a wild thing. It was the kind of expression that told me he understood what I was trying to tell him: that I was in this for good. That I was *with him* for good. That this was real, no matter how it had started.

His kiss was hard and demanding, both his hands dropping down to frame my hips. He urged my movements on, guiding my hips to rock and buck against him. My body buzzed. My blood turned to honey. The friction of my underwear was almost too much. Through the thin fabric of my leggings, I could feel the hard press of his thigh muscles, the warmth of his hands, the thickness of his erection.

"Want you," I panted, my fingernails digging into his shoulders.

That savage smile reappeared. "I know, princess."

Before I could snap back at him, his hand was shifting and his thumb was where I needed it most. He pressed against my clit, and it didn't matter that there were layers of leggings and underwear separating us. It didn't matter that traffic rolled by outside the car windows. It didn't matter that the driver was just on the other side of a thin glass partition.

I gasped at the pressure of his thumb against my clit. I rocked against it, liquid heat building in the pit of my stomach.

For the first time since I could remember, an orgasm built inside me without the need for roleplaying and games. Without the need to get myself out of my head.

Because it was Vaughn sitting there, watching my face like he couldn't wait to see my expression. It was Vaughn's thumb catching the edge of my bud that he knew would send me over the edge. It was Vaughn's breath coasting across my cheek.

This wasn't transactional. I wasn't being used. I wasn't using.

This was something beautiful. It was the physical manifestation of my feelings for him. It was love.

"I—" The words stuck in my throat as a wave of pleasure crashed over me. I gasped, and Vaughn urged on with murmured praise and a frenzied look in his eyes. I ducked my head in the crook of his neck and mouthed the words that wouldn't come out as an orgasm made all my muscles clench: *I love you I love you I love you—*

The car slowed to a stop, and Vaughn caught my boneless body before I could fall off his lap. A strand of hair fell against my cheek, my breaths puffing out of my lungs in big gasps.

"We're here," he said.

I blinked, glancing out the window. The gold lettering on the front window of Koval's shop stared back at me, and I fought to catch my breath. "Oh," was the only response I managed, and then the door opened, and Vaughn's driver stepped aside to let us exit.

THIRTY

VAUGHN

I'D SILENCED my phone earlier, when we'd pulled up outside Alba's apartment. Now, as she ducked into the bathroom at Koval's, her cheeks still flushed with the orgasm I'd given her in the back of the car, I pulled the device out of my pocket and checked it.

Countless phone calls and emails and messages. The Midtown job had hit another snag. The price of materials had rocketed up between the time we bid on the job and now, and the team had been scrambling to find alternatives. But the lost time was costing us more than the price increase.

We'd hidden it from Arlo Noble's people, mostly, but they weren't stupid. This new wave of issues might be enough to make him walk away.

I scrolled through the call log and scanned the emails, and none of it seemed to matter.

Why was I doing this again? It had seemed so important to save this company, to find an investor, to keep on this trajectory of growth. But I had money—and it would keep coming until my scaffolding patent expired, or someone came up with a better one. By that point I'd have more than I could spend in a hundred lifetimes.

Alba emerged from the bathroom, looking much more composed than when she'd gone in, and I found it hard to care about anything other than getting this fitting out of the way so I could get her alone.

Koval bustled her into the back room. I took the dress box from the driver and followed. When I opened the top of the box, Alba let out a sigh like I'd only heard her make in private—but her eyes were on the shimmery purple fabric I'd just revealed.

"Mr. Koval," she said, "you've been keeping secrets."

The old man shrugged. "A dress is not a secret."

She gave him a sideways look, then accepted the bundle of fabric from him and followed his gesture to the curtained cubicle to change. A couple of minutes later, she reappeared, her hair twisted into a clip, her body clad in sequined purple.

She looked unbelievable. My heart began to clatter at the sight of her, and when her eyes lifted to meet mine, I could hardly stop from sweeping her into my arms and back into the car idling outside.

"Up," Koval ordered, flicking his hands toward the dais. "The hips are tight."

"The straps are a little long as well," Alba said. Koval hummed, then grabbed a pincushion and went to work.

"Are you sure you're okay altering this dress for me?" Alba asked. "It could be a museum piece..."

"It's your dress now," Koval said, placing the lavender heels on the dais for Alba to step into. "It should fit you if it's yours."

Alba was suddenly taller as she stepped into the heels, and she met my gaze in the mirror. The look on her face was one I'd never seen before. She looked moved by emotion, soft and almost overwhelmed. Then she gulped and moved as Koval directed, her hands skimming the dress when he wasn't in the way, her head tilting to and fro as she took in her reflection in the mirror.

It was almost unbelievable that this woman had chosen me. She was a goddess. She was so beautiful it almost hurt to look at her.

And I wondered...

Had I made a mistake in inviting her to this gala? What if she got there, surrounded by all the glitz and glamour she used to know, all the people she used to know, and she decided that some blue-collar guy who'd struck it rich wasn't good enough for her?

When the other guests saw the two of us walk in, they wouldn't be looking at me. And if they did, they'd be wondering what a woman like her was doing with an oaf of a man like me.

I'd be just like my father. Begging for scraps at the table. Invited but not welcome. Forever on the outside.

My phone buzzed in my pocket, and it struck fear in my gut.

Was I kidding myself? Was I just like my father? Trying to build my company to heights unknown—why? So I could be invited to events I hated? To watch the woman I was falling in love with leave me for another man? Because surely, once she got her foot back in that door, she'd want to step through. I could offer her a good life—but I couldn't offer her the pedigree, the privilege she'd grown up with.

Was she telling the truth when she said she never wanted to go back?

"Tomorrow," Koval announced, and pointed to the change cubicle. "You come back for the final fitting."

Alba nodded and, by the time she was back in her street

clothes, I'd mostly gotten hold of my racing thoughts. I say mostly, because after Alba handed the fabric to the old man, she crossed the room and stopped in front of me, frowning. "Are you okay?"

"Fine. We'll head back to your place. It's closer." I swept my hand down her arm and tangled my fingers in hers.

She blinked, then gave me a small smile. "Okay," she agreed.

I kept my hand on her thigh the whole drive there. Alba ran her fingertips over my skin, tracing my fingers, my nails, my knuckles. Her touch was soft and absentminded, and it grounded me slightly.

Maybe it was what we'd done on the way here. I was keyed up. I needed release.

But even as I tried to justify it to myself, I knew it wasn't unspent lust making me feel this way. I was the same desperate kid I'd been before, scrabbling to hold my world together. Back then, I hadn't been able to convince my father to make good decisions, to focus on giving us a decent life by forgetting about the riches he was chasing. I hadn't been able to convince my mother to stop enabling him and put me first, for once. Everything had always felt out of control, like I was in a dinghy on a stormy sea at night, hoping I'd make it until morning.

My marriage to Tiffany had given me a similar feeling. I'd thought it was perfect. It had the veneer of the white picket fence, of everything going exactly according to plan—and then it fell apart. Like the veneer of my father's success, right before we got evicted again and again. Tiffany had been the perfect wife, until I discovered the credit card debt, the months and years of lies and financial infidelity. Until I discovered that our values hadn't aligned at all.

That's what was roiling in my gut as we drove to Alba's apartment. My business was teetering on the edge. My identity as the raging success that my father never was hung in the balance. And

Alba was there, a beacon of everything I'd never had growing up—and all I wanted to do was to make sure she was really mine. I desperately wanted what we had to be true. It was a clawing need inside me, to claim her, to be sure, to *know* she wouldn't betray me the way others had done.

Her fingertips traced my palm, then moved up to feel the knobby bones of my wrist. I squeezed her thigh, and Alba shifted in her seat.

"Thank you for the dress," she said quietly.

I glanced over at her, losing myself in her eyes. I'd bought her the dress because I wanted her to feel good on my arm—but now I wondered. Maybe I'd bought it because I wanted to prove to her that I could move through her world. That I was worthy. That I had learned from the lessons she'd taught me, and I would be the right man for her.

"It looks beautiful on you," I said. "I'm glad you like it."

She smiled at me, and it was like a glimpse of the sun through the clouds. Her fingers tangled into mine, and she rested her head on my shoulder. I wanted it to be enough, the weight of her pressed in my side, the warmth of her hand on top of mine—but it wasn't. I needed her naked and panting for me. I needed her mindless, crying my name, telling me I was the only man for her.

My heart thumped, blood thrumming as we slid to a stop outside her building. The driver took an age to let us out. I slid out ahead of her and then took her hand and pulled her out of the vehicle, nodding to the driver as she jogged up to the building's front door.

Her hands were trembling—but then again, so were mine.

On the eighth floor, we crashed through her front door, and then I had her pinned against it. She let out a sigh, her arms around my neck a comfortable weight.

"How much time have we got?" she asked.

"What?" I replied as I ran my lips up her neck, inhaling the sweet scent of her.

"Before you need to go to work. Your phone's been going off like crazy."

I huffed, impatient, and pulled out my phone. I'd taken it off silent by accident at some point. I turned it off with a swipe, then tossed it across the room. Alba let out a surprised laugh when it landed on her kitchen's tile floor. "You'll break it!" she exclaimed.

"Don't care," I said, then hiked her up into my arms. Her legs wrapped around my waist, and I carried her across the apartment to the bedroom I spied through an open door. "Need inside you," I said, dropping us both onto the mattress.

She laughed, breathless. "You're insane."

"You make me that way."

"I guess we've got that in common, because that's how I've felt since the day we met."

I pulled back to grin at her, then couldn't resist the urge to kiss her. Her mouth was my downfall—always had been. I kissed her until I forgot who I was, where I'd come from. Until all that mattered was her soft body beneath mine. I ran my hand up her side, marveling at the softness of her skin. I lifted her top over her head, then unclasped her bra. Her breasts were perfect. Small and round with pink pearls for nipples. I ran my tongue over the left one and enjoyed the shiver that went through Alba, my hand moving to plump her other breast.

The frantic energy inside me calmed slightly as I ran my hands over her body, but I still felt keyed up, on edge, just this side of out of control. My hands framed her chest, then moved down to span her stomach. I inhaled the scent of her skin, tried to ground myself with her presence.

"Vaughn," she said, her hands clawing at my shirt.

I ripped it off. "I'm here."

"I need you."

Her eyes were blue, blue. Her lips were kiss-bruised. She was mine. I would never let her go. Not if she told me I wasn't good enough for her. Not if some other guy tried to woo her away with promises of riches and privilege. She was mine now.

THIRTY-ONE
ALBA

SOMETIME IN BETWEEN leaving Koval's and that moment on my bed, the energy between Vaughn and me had shifted. He touched me like a man starved. He kissed me like I was the only thing that mattered.

It fed the neediness inside me. Made me feel wanted, beautiful. I wrapped my arms around him and sighed at the warmth of his skin, the hard pack of muscle beneath my palms. I ran my mouth over the bulk of his shoulder and traced the line of his stubble on his neck.

"Vaughn," I repeated, shimmying as he pulled off my bottoms, underwear and all.

"You're mine, Alba," he said, his voice rough. "I'm not letting you go."

His words sparked something in my gut. Excitement. Pleasure. Hunger. I wanted to belong to him. I wanted him to want me so badly that he was deranged with it, because no one had ever wanted me like that before. It was easier to reckon with the size of my own emotions when he was wild with his own.

Then his mouth was on me, and there was no time to reckon with anything at all. His hands spread me, his lips devoured me, and I flew. I clung to his hair and rocked myself against his mouth, my heart thumping so fast I thought I might pass out. I cried out his name and arched when he entered me with a finger. Two.

It was a frenzied, delirious coupling. Vaughn flipped me onto my stomach and hiked my hips up, then licked into my opening as I moaned into the covers. He spread my arousal over my clit, back to my ass. He rasped that I belonged to him. That he'd keep me always. That I was his.

And I agreed. I was a raving, shameless woman. Putty in his hands. He knocked my knees wider and ran his hand between my thighs.

"Who does this belong to?" he growled, entering me with a finger. He curled it, rubbing inside me as I writhed on the bedsheets.

"You," I panted. "I belong to you."

"All of you."

"All of me," I agreed, my fists twisting into the sheets as he drove me to another shouted orgasm with nothing but a finger inside me and a thumb circling my clit.

I loved belonging to him. I loved giving him my body. I loved that he wanted me so badly he was incensed. That's how I felt too.

The bed dipped, and I gasped for breath while I tried to get my bearings. My arms shook as I propped myself on my elbows, sweat slicking my hair to my forehead as I glanced over my shoulder. Vaughn was behind me, a conquering warrior, all brawn and greed. I'd put that look on his face. *Me.*

His cock slipped between my legs, hot and hard against my flesh. He rocked his hips, an exhale slipping through his lips. "I want to take you like this, Alba." His hand smoothed up my spine and back down again. His eyes landed on mine. "Want to feel my skin against yours, finish inside you. Make you all mine, princess."

It was the kind of thing that, if a girlfriend had told me about it after, I would have rolled my eyes. Yes, he wants you so badly he just can't wear protection. How tired. How cliche. I wasn't that stupid—no way.

Except I was precisely that stupid. I felt his cock against me, felt the weight of his attention and his desire and his covetousness, and I wanted to be his. I wanted to feel him inside me and drive him as wild as he drove me. I wanted all of him—just as he wanted me.

My chin dipped. "Yes," I whispered.

He groaned, his hips rocking forward so that his cock slid against me. The hair on his thighs rasped against the back of mine. His hands tightened around my waist. "You want me to fuck you like this, Alba?"

"Yes," I repeated. The covers on my bed felt rough against my forearms, my knees. "Yes, Vaughn."

"Want my cock in you, raw and hard?" His eyes were nearly black with need. "My little princess needs to be taken care of, doesn't she? She needs me to fill her up and fuck her?"

My mouth was dry. "Yes," I rasped.

He shifted behind me, positioning himself at my opening. His gaze lowered, and as he entered me, I knew he was watching. My own head dropped between my shoulders, forehead resting on the pillows, and I exhaled. It felt so good. The stretch of him inside me. The weight of his hands. The heat of his body.

Vaughn shuddered, his hands sweeping up my sides and down my spine. They settled on my hips, his thumbs pressing near my spine, his fingers gripping me hard. He settled into a steady, relentless rhythm, and I clung to the sheets and moaned in the pillows.

"You feel like heaven," he said, his voice ragged. "You feel so good, Alba."

I gasped my agreement. My mind was blank, my body burning from the inside out. All I could do was cling on as he thrust into me, our bodies shaking and writhing and groaning. This was something other than sex. It was more. It was rough and feverish and greedy—and nothing had ever felt so good.

Vaughn draped his body over my back, his lips running over the back of my shoulder. My arms trembled, and he shifted to press his hands into the mattress to take most of his weight. His chest hair rasped against my back, his arms caged me in, and his hips snapped forward over and over again. All that existed was me and Vaughn. Our bodies. Our pleasure.

"Love you like this," Vaughn said, voice gasping, and his words were dangerously close to the ones lingering on the tip of my tongue. "Love the feel of your body. You grip me so good, Alba. Never felt this good in my life."

"I know," I panted out. "So good."

"Want to come inside you. Want to fill you with it, princess."

I shouldn't have wanted that, but I did. It shouldn't have turned me on, but it did. I reeled with it and managed to say, "I'm not on the pill."

"Don't care," Vaughn said, his arm coming around my stomach. He slid his fingers down to my bud and started stroking. "I could put a baby inside you." He exhaled, hips snapping. "I'd like that. Having you carry my child."

I huffed—mostly to cover up the rush of heat that went through me. It was wrong to be turned on by the frantic words he whispered in my ear, wasn't it? It was wrong to want this—to want to be wanted so badly he could hardly make full sentences, so badly he was talking nonsense.

"You're mine, Alba," Vaughn said, his fingers moving over my clit. I trembled beneath him, overwhelmed by sensation. "You'll always be mine, princess."

"Yes," I moaned, heat warping through me. It coalesced between my legs, around the spot that Vaughn teased with his fingertips. A fine trembling started in my limbs, and then I was gone. I cried out, muffling the noise in my pillows, lost to the pleasure of Vaughn's touch. A moment later, his teeth sank into my shoulder, and he came along with me. Another rush of hot sensation went through me, and I collapsed on top of the bedding with Vaughn on top of me.

He caught himself, shifting his weight so it wasn't fully on me, his mouth moving from my shoulder to my neck as he peppered my skin with clumsy kisses.

"That was nuts," I rasped.

He huffed, sending a strand of my hair flying through the air. "You drive me so crazy, Alba."

"Was that—" I stopped, shifting my head so my voice wasn't so muffled by the pillow. My thoughts were in tatters. I couldn't figure out what I was trying to ask. "Was that just dirty talk?" I finally managed.

Vaughn slid off me—and out of me—and shifted me so we were facing each other on our sides. His big hand coasted up my side and over my shoulder, reaching up to brush hair off my temple. "About putting a baby inside you?" His brow arched.

I blushed and bit my lip. "I should probably get the morning-after pill."

His eyes were solemn. "Would it be so bad?" His hand moved from my temple downward, the backs of his fingers brushing the space below my navel. "You carrying our child?"

My pulse sped. Yes, it would be so bad. We'd met only a couple months ago. He was rich, and I was destitute. He already had a child with another woman, and the relationship seemed strained. Having a baby with him would be disastrous. The possibilities that had opened up with my income from working for him would shut. I'd be entirely reliant on him. Vulnerable.

And it would also be wonderful. A sweet-smelling baby with soft, soft skin, bundled in my arms. The sight of Vaughn holding our child, his eyes soft. My features—or his—in miniature. The first gummy smile. A little white tooth poking through, sharp as a saw. It would be the best thing to ever happen to me—if my life were a fairytale. If things worked out for me, which they never did.

Or they never *had*...until I met Vaughn.

"You're not thinking straight," I whispered, mostly talking about myself.

"I know," he agreed easily, his fingers still stroking my stomach. "I know."

His release was still there, between my legs. Serious blue eyes stared back at me, and it felt like we were having an entirely different conversation without saying a word. A conversation that started with *"What if...?"*

I sighed, closing my eyes as I shifted and leaned my forehead against his lips. He kissed me softly, his hand moving from my stomach to my side and then up my spine. His touch was tender. We moved slowly, limbs wrapping around the other, lips coasting over skin. Afternoon sunlight slanted through the bedroom window, and I stared at the play of the shadows against the opposite wall.

"You want to come home and have dinner with me and Charlotte?"

I shifted my gaze from the wall to Vaughn's face and smiled. "That sounds wonderful."

He let out a sigh, like he was relieved to hear my answer. His fingers traced my hairline and the shell of my ear, and then he leaned in to kiss me. It was a chaste kiss, nothing like the frantic lovemaking we'd just experienced, but it still sent a tumble of heat through me. Heat—and comfort. He held me a while longer, and I felt as safe and comfortable as I ever had.

I felt like maybe my fairytale might be happening, after all.

And later, when I listened to Charlotte tell me about the goings-on at school, I couldn't help but think she'd make a good big sister.

I had officially lost my mind.

THIRTY-TWO
VAUGHN

THE DAY of the gala dawned with bad news. The subcontractor who had walked off the Midtown job was countersuing us, and the latest email from the legal team informed me that they might actually have a case. I was looking at a major loss—and I knew that Arlo Noble would find out about it sooner or later. His team had trawled through our books; they weren't going to miss this.

But I still had a shot. Noble's charity event would be my opportunity to speak to him, to impress upon him that my business was sound despite this hiccup. With his investment, we could go far. The pressure was mounting, but I couldn't let it get to me.

All my doubts had settled after I'd claimed Alba for my own. She was mine, and I could forge onward with my plans. An investor meant access to the true power brokers of the city. It meant securing my future, my daughter's future. It meant success —success that had eluded my father.

My townhome was quiet without Charlotte, who had gone back to her mother's the day before. I haunted the rooms, spending most of my day in the home office, sorting through legalese.

Then it was time to get ready and go get my date. Soon, we'd walk into the gala, and I'd leave my mark. I'd have my investor, I'd be a success, and Alba would stay by my side through it all.

Or...

Alba would use me as a stepping stone to go back to the world she knew. I would make a fool of myself. My life would come full circle, and I'd lose the investor, crash my company, and end up as much of a failure as my father had been.

The doubts rattled around my head all afternoon and evening, and only fading away when Alba's building's front door opened and I saw her step out onto the street.

She was a vision in lavender. The dress twinkled under the streetlights, dancing around her legs as she approached. She'd draped a shawl over her shoulders, and her hair was curled in big waves that fell, gleaming and golden, behind her shoulders. My mouth went dry as she approached, a soft smile on her glossy lips.

"You look—" I shook my head. "Wow."

Her smile widened. "Thank you, Vaughn." She lifted her hands to touch my cheeks, then pressed a kiss on my lips. Her thumb wiped away the gloss that had transferred to me, and then we spun toward the waiting vehicle behind me. My driver stood beside the back door, ready to close it once we entered.

Alba arranged her dress on the seat and clipped herself in, giving me a raised eyebrow look as I watched, as if to tell me that there would be no hanky-panky on the way to this event.

I settled in beside her and took her hand. My palms were clammy, and it wasn't just because I was beside the most beautiful woman I'd ever met. As the car slid out into traffic, I took a deep breath.

I had the woman of my dreams on my arm. All I needed to do to achieve everything I ever dreamed of was avoid making a fool of myself at this gala, bag the big investor, and let riches rain down on me.

But Charlotte's smile flashed through my mind, and I wondered if I was making a big mistake. She was supposed to be my *why*, my reason for doing all this...but I'd shunted her off to her mother while I worked. Just like I had all through my marriage. Then I glanced over at Alba and watched her transform into that cool, aloof woman who had walked into restaurants with me and taught me how to hold a wine glass.

Fear struck deep in my gut. What was I *doing*?

The woman beside me—did I really know her? Was she the ice queen born into privilege, or was she the warm, snarky woman I'd come to know? Would she use me to launch herself back into the society she'd fallen out of?

Maybe she was just like my father—always chasing something better. Maybe *I* was just like my father—lying to myself about what really mattered for the sake of a few extra bucks.

The seams of my new shirt itched my sides. My shiny black shoes were stiff and uncomfortable. The white tie at my neck felt like a noose.

"You okay?" Alba asked, squeezing my hand.

I gulped, feeling the pressure of my necktie against the front of my throat. "I'm good," I said. "Just a little nervous about making a fool of myself."

It was a half-truth. I was almost sure I'd make a fool of myself somehow. What I was actually worried about was that I'd blindly followed this path, thinking I wanted a cashed-up investor, thinking I wanted to grow the business to new heights, that I was a good father for providing...but I was actually barreling toward destruction. I was acting just like my own father. I *liked* having a barber make house calls. I loved my beautiful home. I enjoyed being able to wine and dine a woman like Alba, to buy her a one-of-a-kind dress and pretend I didn't know how special it was. I relished the ability to snap my fingers and make all her problems go away, even though I pretended not to.

I was as fake as my father had been, and tonight was proof.

And if I was as fake as he had been—how could anyone else be any different? How could I trust Alba to stand by my side? Why had she agreed to come here with me in the first place, if not to get a foot back in the door that had been closed to her just a few short weeks ago?

"Vaughn," Alba said, squeezing my palm. "You'll be fine."

She was so beautiful. Her makeup was perfect, subtle but enhancing. Her hair looked shiny and soft. Her shoulders were bare, as was her neck, but earrings dangled from her lobes. She looked like she'd stepped out of the pages of a magazine and for some reason decided to slum it with me.

"The fact that you bought tickets to his gala is all that matters," she continued. "Arlo Noble is one of the good ones."

"Oh?"

She smiled. "I'll put it this way: he wouldn't destroy his daughter's vegetable garden for the sake of an anniversary party."

I nodded.

"It's a formality. We'll go in, have dinner, dance a little. You'll go up to him and tell him that you're looking forward to working together, and then we can leave."

"That's all, huh," I said, leaning against the headrest and glancing out the window. We were getting closer to the venue.

"That's all," she confirmed. "You've done the hard work. This is just the final hurdle."

I wanted to believe her. I wanted it to be true. After tonight, Arlo Noble would inject the business with cash, and the Midtown job's problems would seem like little tiny bug bites instead of gaping wounds. Charlotte would still be with me every two weeks. Alba would be by my side. Everything would work out perfectly.

And yet, when the car slid to a stop and our driver opened the door, I watched Alba take a deep breath and don another persona, and I couldn't help the discomfort that slithered through me. If I continued to move in these circles, would I get used to slipping into a new role? Would I dismiss the fakeness of it as formality? Would I enjoy the glitz and glamour a little too much?

I got out of the car and turned to extend my hand to Alba as she exited behind me.

"Here we go," Alba said, straightening. Her chin lifted. Her shoulders rolled back. Her eyes went flinty.

The Alba I knew—the Alba I'd fallen in love with—was gone.

THIRTY-THREE

ALBA

I REGRETTED AGREEING to be Vaughn's date long before I stepped through the doors into the ballroom. And when I did finally step through and recognize two dozen faces around the room, my regret ballooned into something bigger.

My steps were stiff. I wore a mask that had once been as familiar as my own face, but now it felt rigid and uncomfortable. The remote socialite who judged people at a glance. The flighty girl who lived off her parents' fortune, who was trained to stand beside big, powerful men in rooms just like these. To all these people, I was Alba Enders, rich socialite who'd been whispered about for over a year.

But I wasn't that Alba anymore. The past year and a half had changed me. I wore a beautiful dress and I glided in my heels, but I knew I didn't belong in this room. Every cell in my body screamed at me to turn around and run away. The F-U moment of glory that Deena and I had laughed about was a lie. I didn't want it. I just wanted to leave.

Beside me, Vaughn exhaled, and I remembered the other reason I'd agreed to come here.

Vaughn was a good man—the best man I'd ever known—and I'd fallen fast and hard for him. I was here to stand at his side and support him. It was ironic that after fighting so hard against all the training my parents had put me through, I ended up doing exactly what they'd taught me to do. I was an accessory to Vaughn's big plans, here to make him look good.

But it felt different when I loved him. I *wanted* him to succeed. I was ready to endure some discomfort for his sake, because he'd done so much for me these past months. He'd made me feel like a person again. He'd reminded me that I had worth. That I deserved dignity.

So, as he stiffened beside me, clumsily grabbing two flutes of champagne from a passing waiter's tray, I steeled myself against the uneasiness flooding my senses and braced myself for a tough evening. It would be worth it to watch Vaughn flourish. I could endure a lot worse than this if it meant getting my happily-ever-after.

Taking one of the champagne flutes that Vaughn offered me, I filled my lungs, braced myself, and faced the people who had rejected me not too long ago.

And I realized that not *all* of these people had rejected me. Arlo Noble approached with his wife by his side, a broad smile on his face.

"Vaughn! You made it."

Vaughn smiled back at the other man, and it was only because we'd spent so much time together that I noticed the slight strain around the corners of his mouth. They shook hands, and I waited patiently for my moment.

It was a familiar dance to me, waiting to be introduced like this. Arlo was well-practiced, turning to the woman at his side as soon as he and Vaughn's hands came apart.

"My beautiful wife, Bonnie," he said. "This is the guy I was telling you about."

"The contractor with big dreams," Bonnie responded, smiling as she shook Vaughn's hand. She turned to me.

Vaughn picked up right where he was supposed to, sweeping his hand down my back. "This is—Alba." He stumbled over the introduction, evidently not knowing what to call me. His girl-friend? His employee? His image consultant?

In the end, it didn't matter. Bonnie and I had met several times before. "Hi, Bonnie," I said, nodding. "I love your dress." It wasn't a lie. She wore a long gold gown that emphasized her blond hair and goddess-like proportions. The dress flared out at the hips and shimmered under the chandeliers dangling above our heads.

Bonnie had never been catty to me. Not the way Yvette was. She was a kind woman who loved her kids and made a point to support her friends' business ventures. Once upon a time, when Cole and I were meant to be married, I'd thought that I wouldn't mind being her friend.

Now I braced myself for her reaction to seeing me here with Vaughn.

"Long time no see!" Bonnie said with a smile, gaze flicking between me and Vaughn. "I didn't know you two were—I mean after—" She cleared her throat.

We both thought about the reason we hadn't seen each other for so long. The end of my engagement to Cole. My ousting from society.

"We met at work," I explained, which sparked curiosity in Bonnie's gaze. It wasn't much of an explanation; I hadn't worked when she knew me before.

She'd just opened her mouth when a voice made us jump.

"Get *out!*"

The four of us turned to see a vision in black. A tall, dark-haired woman wore a figure-hugging gown with a gorgeous off-the-shoulder neckline. Her throat glittered with diamonds. She lifted her hands toward me, her stiletto nails painted a dark shade of red. Nikita Blakely, née Jordan, wife of my ex-fiancé's best friend, stared at me from a few feet away. Fingers of both hands spread toward me, she shook her hands in my direction. For a moment, I thought she was kicking me out and I thought, *That didn't take long.* But what came out of her mouth was a shocked, "That is *not* a vintage Versace dress, is it?"

Relief made me wobbly. A smile trembled at the corners of my lips. "What, this old thing?" I swished the bottom of it and laughed as the dark-haired woman gasped.

"Claudia Schiffer. The Academy Awards in...I want to say 1994?"

"Close," I replied, grinning. "'95."

"Replica?"

"Vaughn's tailor used to work in the Versace workrooms, apparently," I said, patting my man's arm as I wiggled my brows. "It's the real deal."

"Hold on," Nikki said, putting her hand to her forehead. "I'm about to die of envy. I need a minute."

Bonnie laughed. "We're going to need to know the name of Vaughn's tailor."

"I'll take it to my grave," I teased.

"The color is divine on you," Nikki said, reaching forward to feel the fabric of the skirt between her fingertips. "It wouldn't work on me. Well..." She frowned, humming. "No, it really wouldn't."

I laughed. "I'll let you try it on sometime."

Nikki brightened. "*No. Really?*"

I shrugged. "Sure." Smiling, I glanced at Vaughn, whose

eyebrow twitched. I gave him a look that said, *See? I told you it wasn't just a dress*. And he grinned back at me like he'd known all along.

This wouldn't be so bad. Bonnie and Nikki weren't treating me like an outcast—and why had I worried they would? My parents weren't good people. James and Yvette weren't either. But not *everyone* in this room was awful. Maybe this wouldn't be a big middle finger of an evening to all of them, a splash and a goodbye.

Maybe it would be a beginning.

"Babe," Nikki mock-complained as she glanced over my shoulder, "why have you never surprised me with a vintage Versace dress worn by one of the world's most famous supermodels?"

The false sense of ease that had begun to trickle through me turned cold. I stilled, spine stiffening.

The man behind me said, "I'm always looking for birthday ideas," and came into view beside me. Rome Blakely, advertising guru extraordinaire, crossed to where Nikki was still admiring my dress and wrapped an arm around her waist.

But it wasn't him that I'd sensed. It was the other man who joined our circle. Tall and dark-haired, Cole Christianson was as handsome as I'd remembered.

And he was with his new wife.

I nodded at my ex. "Cole."

"Alba," he said, gaze flicking to Vaughn.

"This is Vaughn," I said. "Vaughn, Cole."

Recognition flared in Vaughn's gaze at the name, and after a brief hesitation, he stuck out his hand to shake my ex-fiancé's. Meanwhile, Cole's wife clung to his other side and tilted her head at me. We'd met a couple of times, and now we studied each other silently. She wore a black dress and carried a gold clutch. In her ears, little gold earrings with dangling birds swung with her every movement.

"This is Carrie," Cole said, then cleared his throat. "Carrie, you remember Alba?"

I knew my smile looked stilted and forced. I knew I was completely failing at keeping my mask on, but I hadn't really expected to run into my ex within minutes of walking into the room.

I thought I'd been ready to be here, but now I wasn't so sure.

When I'd met Carrie, she'd been one of the many people in Cole's assistant pool, and I'd known—I'd *known*—there was something between them. It was in the air when they were in the room together. Electricity, snapping between them, static raising the hair on my arms.

I hadn't known their history—but then again, I hadn't needed to know. It was right there in every look they shared. Every touch they tried to avoid. Cole had been a good fiancé to me. He hadn't betrayed me. He'd simply treated me the way everyone else did: like I was replaceable. I was the one who'd had an affair. If not a physical one, it was at the very least emotional. I fell in love with another man, and I hit the eject button on our relationship as soon as I got the chance.

I hadn't expected to feel pain at the sight of Cole. We'd never loved each other—not really. But he had been such a big part of my life at that time. He represented The Right Way of Doing Things. Marrying him was what I'd been supposed to do.

And now I was reminded of how easily our relationship had broken down and the fall from grace that came afterward. I couldn't help the tightness in my lungs, the cold sweat that broke out between my shoulder blades.

Then—warmth.

Vaughn's palm swept down my back, over my upper spine, and then coasted down the glittering lavender fabric of my dress. He slid his hand around my waist and pulled me close. My shoulders relaxed, and I managed a smile. A real one.

"You look beautiful," I said to Carrie. I nodded to the ring on her finger. "Congratulations."

Carrie's smile was tentative, but it seemed genuine. She and Cole shared a look. The expression on Cole's face was one I'd never seen before. It was tender and so full of love that seeing it made me feel like I was intruding on a private moment. I glanced away and found Vaughn staring down at me.

His fingers tightened on my waist. "You okay?" he murmured.

I exhaled and reached up to straighten his white necktie. "Yes," I told him. "Thank you."

He held my gaze for just a moment, then dipped down and gave me a quick, soft kiss. Then he straightened, his arm still holding me firmly at his side. That one kiss was healing. It lasted only a moment, but it was enough to make me forget about the tension of my engagement to Cole, the fear that it would all fall apart—and then the horror when it actually did. Cole and I would never be friends, but that was okay. He didn't seem to have any hard feelings for me; he had bigger things to worry about. And he hadn't batted an eye at my being here, in this room, with another man. I wasn't an outcast to these people. I relaxed into his touch, a jagged wound in my heart beginning to knit itself together.

At that moment, my eyes met Cole's. His gaze skimmed over Vaughn's arm, and his lips curled into a kind smile. "It's good to see you, Alba."

I smiled back at him, leaning into Vaughn. "Same."

"You look happy," he added, and glanced at Carrie. She smiled at him, and his own smile grew before he turned back to look at me. "That makes me glad."

They were simple words, delivered genuinely, and I felt tears prickle at the corners of my eyes. I hadn't known that I'd wanted or needed Cole's forgiveness. But he was giving it to me now, and that wound in my heart scabbed over a little bit more. Throat tight, I nodded. "Congrats to you two again."

We said our goodbyes. I watched Carrie and Cole drift off together, and I felt like I'd just passed the first hurdle. It was overwhelming. These people, this event—it was like revisiting an old version of myself. A stranger. I hadn't realized how difficult it would be to stand up here as the new me, facing all the mistakes of my past—even if they seemed to be forgiven.

I took a sip of champagne from the glass I still held, but even the taste of it on my tongue made me dizzy. "I need to duck to the washroom," I murmured to Vaughn, who nodded, concern drawing his brows together.

A waiter took my glass, and I wove my way through the crowd, shaking off the jitters of my first interaction. The hallway to the washrooms loomed up ahead, and I kept my eyes on it as I crossed the ballroom. I needed the relative privacy of a stall of my own to compose myself again so I could be the woman Vaughn needed me to be for the rest of the evening. So I could brace myself for other interactions that might not go as smoothly as that one.

Then I heard my name—and I recognized the voice.

THIRTY-FOUR

VAUGHN

AS SOON AS Alba left my side, I felt untethered. She'd been glittering and gorgeous at my side, sucking all the attention away from me, which was exactly how I liked it. Now I stood on my own, surrounded by people richer and classier than I was, and I felt like my skin was suddenly on too tight. My tongue was clumsy in my mouth, and I didn't know what to do with my free hand.

I took a sip of champagne and tracked Alba's progress through the ballroom, hoping she'd hurry.

"I hear there might be some legal trouble on the horizon for you," Arlo said casually, his own gaze sweeping over the gala's guests.

Mentally, I cursed. Outwardly, I tipped my head to the side. "We'll see what happens. I think it's a lot of posturing from a subcontractor who didn't do his due diligence."

Arlo hummed. "My lawyers are warning me about you," he finally said, gaze flicking to meet mine. "They say I'd be taking too big a risk."

My heart began to thump. I said nothing.

Arlo shrugged. "But I don't make my bets on what my lawyers say," he finished, dropping his hand onto my shoulder. "Enjoy your evening. I'll be in touch next week."

We shook hands again, and then the group of people lingering around him drifted away from me and over to the next guest. I swallowed and realized I was parched—and I'd finished my drink. A waiter appeared, took my empty glass, and replaced it with a full one. I nodded my thanks and took a gulp. Bubbles exploded on my tongue, and I swallowed them down, enjoying the warm buzz all along my throat.

As I scanned the room, I meandered toward the edge of the vast space. Alba was nowhere in sight. I nodded at a man in a tux, and his gaze flicked over me and away as he dismissed me with a glance. Sourness gurgled in my stomach. I didn't belong here. Why had I come? Even Arlo had essentially told me he knew my company was about to be in a world of trouble. He was dangling the promise of more—but was he being honest? Was I being played?

And where was Alba?

I nodded my thanks to a waiter who gave me another fresh glass, surprised that I'd finished another one. I had to slow down, but I couldn't quite manage to get rid of my parched throat, and I wasn't sure how I'd make it through the evening.

Alba had slipped right in, surrounded by the people she used to know. She hadn't even seemed that uncomfortable. People who had never contacted her once she was disowned. Had Bonnie and Nikki known? Were they just being fake?

Was *Alba* being fake?

I resisted the urge to tug at my necktie. I knew I was fidgeting, moving my glass from one hand to the other, fussing with my cuffs, rearranging the stiff waistcoat under my jacket. My clothes fit perfectly, but they felt like they were three sizes too small.

What was I doing here?

Delicate classical music tinkled through the air, and the sounds of conversation filled the room. I heard snippets echoing from all around. *"We'll summer in Malta this year, of course..." "I sat down with the Governor last week..." "Living there was a nightmare. I had to fly the help in from three hours away every time I wanted the house cleaned..."*

I tried to block them out—all those conversations that had nothing to do with me. I was here for my business. I was showing my face, not making a fool of myself, and leaving with a hand- shake deal struck between me and Arlo Noble. That was the plan—but I couldn't help feeling like coming here had been a mistake.

I'd already spoken to Arlo Noble, and there hadn't been any sort of confirmation. Would we get the chance to speak again before the night was over, or had that been my one chance? Anxiety twisted my guts, made my vision blur around the edges.

And where was Alba? It couldn't take that long to go to the bathroom.

Scanning the room, I thought of the way she'd straightened before coming in. The way she'd held her hand out to shake, the way she'd laughed with those other women. There'd been a hint of the woman I knew, but she'd been trapped in the aloof ice queen of her socialite persona.

But...what if it wasn't a persona? What if that was the real Alba?

Carried on the river of champagne I'd already ingested, old fears rushed me. Did I really know Alba? Was she just using me to gain access to this world again? Had I been played?

I'd felt like I was falling in love with her, but what if it was all a lie? What if she'd fooled me?

"You're Vaughn Avery, right?"

I turned to see a blond man, my height, eyes sharp as they studied me. He stuck his hand out. "Leif Sorensen."

"The developer." Leif's name was a big deal around the city. Many of the skyscrapers in Manhattan had been built by his company. We shook hands. My thoughts were still whirling, but I forced myself to focus.

This was why I was here, wasn't it? To mingle with people who could advance my business in ways I hadn't been able to do alone. But my heart still thumped unsteadily, and I found it hard to relax into conversation with someone I didn't know.

"I've been watching the growth of your company with great interest," he said. "Arlo told me you're looking for an investor."

My brows jumped. "He told you that?"

Leif laughed. "Not in so many words. But he started asking pointed questions about construction, and I did some digging. Excuse the pun."

"I see."

He grinned. "These things are awful, aren't they?" He tipped his head toward the crowd.

I huffed, taking a sip of my drink. "Not my scene," I agreed.

"If things fall through with Arlo, you should give me a call," Leif said.

"You're looking to expand? Seems to me you've already got an empire."

Leif grinned. "I'm always looking for opportunities," he said, settling in beside me as we watched the crowd go by. "I think you and I have got that in common. Excuse me."

As Leif re-entered the fray, with other attendees parting before him like fish before a shark, I was struck by the certainty that I didn't belong here. I didn't *want* to belong here.

I never should've come.

THIRTY-FIVE
ALBA

I'D BEEN STRIDING toward the washroom hallway, and then James was there. It shouldn't have shocked me to see him—to hear his voice calling out my name—but it did. He was still as tall and green-eyed and gorgeous as usual, even more striking in his evening jacket and white tie.

When his hand closed around my arm to drag me down the hallway, his head ducked away from the crowd, I let him. It was muscle memory, maybe. We'd circled around each other for so long. He'd promised me the world, and I'd imagined scenarios just like this. Where we might steal a moment, where I might finally take the leap and be with him. I imagined walking in on his arm and making it public.

Instead, all I'd had were stolen conversations. Messages. Phone calls. Promises. I'd lived a life of fantasy, crafting a relationship between the two of us that never existed.

He'd only wanted me as a stepping stone into a life that he thought I could provide.

"Let go of me," I finally said, snapping out of my stupor.

"Alba, babe," he crooned, ducking his head. "I'm sorry, but you just look so beautiful, and—"

"What do you want?"

He had the audacity to look wounded. "I just wanted to talk to you. I miss talking to you. Things ended so abruptly between us—"

"Did you not get the message when I blocked you?"

"That was a joke," he said, blinking, looking completely innocent. He tilted his head, a hint of the smile I used to love so much curling his lips. "You didn't mean that. You told me you wanted to see me."

"In hell," I said, even though it was Deena who had written the words. "I told you I would see you in hell."

His eyes sharpened. "That was a joke," he insisted. "But it's okay. I forgive you."

"I think you might be insane."

"Alba."

"I can't believe this act worked on me before."

"What act? You look great, by the way—"

"I don't want to hear this." I threw my hands up. "Leave me alone, James."

"I didn't expect to see you here." His voice held a different note. Something that made the back of my neck twinge, like there was danger that my body sensed but I hadn't yet consciously detected. James took a step toward me.

I stood my ground. "And how did you get through the front doors? I'm guessing you were marked down on the list as, 'Yvette Williams...And Guest?'"

It was a catty thing to say, and I knew that the pop of my eyebrow would infuriate him. And I realized, in that moment, just how much I'd held back during our "relationship." I'd made myself small and pleasant and likable, because I was so desperate for his attention—for any attention. I'd hidden my true personality, because I didn't think I was lovable.

It took a year of being destitute, of picking myself up off the street and surviving, to learn my own worth. It took a man like Vaughn to show me that I could be loved even if I hid no part of myself.

But this man in front of me? He'd never known the real me. He'd been able to see how desperate for affection I'd been, and he'd used it to worm his way into my life.

I wasn't innocent; I knew that. I'd reveled in his attention—but I'd done it because my entire life up until that point had been an exercise in hiding my true self, in changing myself so I would finally be lovable.

No more.

James must've seen that truth written in my eyes, because his mouth twisted. "You were always so full of yourself, Alba. I heard you were washing dishes at a sandwich restaurant. How long did that last before you whored yourself out to the first man who could put you in a pretty dress?"

His words echoed my father's. That ugly, cutting insult flung at me with the intention to hurt.

A year and a half ago, I'd been wounded by it. Now?

Now, I was stronger. All I saw was a small man who had to bring people down to make himself feel better. I couldn't believe I'd cared about him. I couldn't believe I'd been swindled by him. I'd loved him. Now, having felt what I felt for Vaughn, the love I had for James seemed like a cheap imitation. James didn't cherish me. He didn't even *know* me. He'd preyed on my loneliness, my desperation, and made me feel special for the first time in my life.

But he didn't know about my childhood vegetable garden. He didn't grin when I sassed him, or listen when I talked about hemlines and lapel widths. James didn't know the first thing about me, except for my last name.

Shame boiled through me, but there was nothing I could do about my past mistakes. All I could do was be better. Do better. I could be the kind of partner Vaughn deserved: loyal and loving, ready to stand beside him always.

Cole had forgiven me, and I wondered... Would I ever be able to forgive myself?

In that moment, standing before the man who'd used me and discarded me, I straightened. I couldn't forgive myself quite yet, but I could draw a boundary that should've been drawn a long time ago. Chin high, I looked James in the eyes and said, "I don't want to see you or talk to you. Don't contact me ever again."

James's eyes narrowed, but I didn't give him the chance to respond. I spun on my heels and ducked into the bathroom. I strode to the middle of the tiled area in front of the mirrors and let out a shuddering breath. Pressing my hands to my face, I tried to gather myself, but my lungs heaved and my legs trembled with unspent adrenaline. Gasping breaths sawed in and out of me, and I tried to pull myself together. Soon, I'd have to go back out there and pretend that everything was fine.

"Alba?"

My head jerked up. Bonnie was there with another woman, one who looked vaguely familiar from her circle of friends. Dani, I remembered. Wide-eyed, I stared at the two of them before turning to the mirror to salvage my streaked makeup.

"Are you okay?" Bonnie asked quietly.

I nodded, hands trembling as I pawed through my clutch for my compact. "I'm fine. It's just—a lot. Being here is a lot."

"Can I get you a glass of water?"

"That's okay." I gave Bonnie a tight smile in the mirror. "I just ran into...someone I wasn't expecting to see again."

Dani came closer. She wore a dark blue dress and a glittering diamond choker. "Do we need to kick him out?"

I shook my head. "No. I just need a second."

Bonnie squeezed my arm, then pulled a tissue from her purse for me. My bottom lip trembled as I accepted it, and I shook my head, embarrassed. "I wasn't expecting you to be nice to me."

Bonnie frowned. "What? Why?"

"Cole and me...the breakup..."

"That's between you and him," Bonnie said, waving a hand. "He's never had a bad word to say about you. All he said was that you two weren't right for each other."

Throat tight, I nodded. "That's nice of him to say, all things considered. I wasn't a good fiancée to him. I thought I was doing what was expected, but..." I trailed off, not knowing how to explain.

"Well. That's in the past," Dani pronounced, pulling a small granola bar from her purse and thrusting it at me.

I took it, blinking. "Um. Thanks?"

"Ever since having kids, I've carried snacks everywhere. They really do solve ninety percent of problems. Eat it. You'll feel better."

It was such a small act of kindness—and so opposite to what anyone in my old circle of so-called friends would have done—that I couldn't help the teary laugh that burbled through me. "Thank you," I replied.

"Now. Do you need us to stay with you, or should we guard the door so you have a minute to yourself?" Bonnie asked.

"I'll take the minute," I whispered.

Bonnie squeezed my arm again, and the two of them walked out the door, leaving me alone. I fixed my makeup, inhaled the granola bar, and then stood in the mirror until I could stand straight and bear the idea of facing all those people. When I pulled the door open, Bonnie and Dani nodded at me, then accompanied me back into the main room. They greeted people and mingled while I did my best to paste a smile to my face, my eyes scanning for Vaughn.

All I wanted to do was to run back to him.

I realized, standing there in a throng of bejeweled people, that Vaughn was everything to me. I loved him so much it hardly seemed possible.

Cole had been the man my parents wanted me to marry. He'd been the "right" choice, the man who could stand at my side through events like this one. James had been the man I thought I wanted. Someone who made me feel special, who took me away from the gilded cage where I'd been trapped.

Vaughn wasn't with me for my money or my connections. He wasn't with me because that's what was expected. He'd found me at my worst, and I'd still been enough for him.

He made me a better, stronger person, because he knew the real me. I wanted to pay that back a thousandfold. I wanted to find him, drag him to a dark corner, and show him just how much it meant to me that he'd chosen me—the real me.

Buoyed by the rush of emotion, I separated from the pack of people surrounding Dani and Bonnie and drifted through the milling crowd. I scanned for a man a head taller than everyone else. My heart thumped at the thought of seeing him, watching the smile break over his face, and feeling the weight and warmth of his arm come around me. He was my safe harbor, my shelter from the storm of life.

A smile burst over my face when I saw him leaning against the wall about halfway down the room. He hadn't spotted me, but he was scanning the crowd just as I was. I sped up, but a crowd of people drifted in front of me, and I lost sight of him. I ducked around voluminous skirts, teetering on my lavender heels, trying to peer around broad backs and tall updos.

There! A flash of him, still scanning the crowd. My smile widened as my heart beat for him—because I knew that as soon as I was in front of him, I'd tell him how I felt. I'd tell him those three little words and hope that he wanted to say them back.

I was so intent on Vaughn and on the words that wanted to burst from me that I failed to sense danger approaching until it was too late. One second, Vaughn was in my sights, and the path to him seemed to be clearing—and the next, my mother and father were blocking the way. I stumbled to a stop, barely catching myself before barreling into the both of them.

My mother clicked her tongue. "Graceful as always, daughter of mine," she taunted.

My father said nothing. He just watched me with blue eyes that looked like mine, his white hair combed back from his face, his chin lifted high.

"Who is that man you walked in with?" my mother continued, her voice dropping as she flapped her hand at me. "Really, Alba, at Arlo Noble's gala, you—"

"You dared to show your face," my father finished for her, his deep voice resonating in my bones. He looked me up and down, his lips curling almost into a sneer.

The urge to shrink into myself was too strong to resist. My shoulders curled as my breaths came faster. All feelings of love and light and happiness seemed to evaporate. Vaughn was impossibly far away—too far to save me from this confrontation.

"Stand up straight. You're embarrassing yourself," my father hissed. "After over a year without a word, this is how you greet us?"

The situation was painfully familiar. The two of them, smiling at everyone else, hissing poison in my ears. My mother impressing upon me the importance of the man who stood beside me. My father making me feel like I wasn't good enough, then ambling off to talk about golf with one of his business associates.

It would be so easy to crumple. After all, that's what I'd always done before. I'd toed the family line. I'd gotten engaged to the appropriate man. I'd dressed and acted exactly as was expected.

But that was then—and this was now.

For over a year, I'd been on my own. I hadn't had their protection—or their voices in my ear to tell me exactly what they wanted me to do.

In that year, I hadn't died. I'd suffered, yes, but I'd accepted that as balance for the way I'd behaved before. But now I stood here, stronger, more resilient, and surer of myself than ever before.

They'd already done the worst. They'd cut me off from everything and everyone I knew. They'd shown me just how conditional their love was.

Now, thanks to Vaughn, I knew what love really felt like. I knew that there was safety in love. There was a home that would always be open, somewhere to go back to. Even if I hadn't wanted to come here tonight. If I hadn't performed for him the way he'd asked. Even then, he'd still accept me.

So I did as my father asked and straightened my shoulders. But when I met his gaze, I watched him frown at the look in my eyes, and I lifted my chin to match his pose. "Over a year without a word, and not nearly long enough for my liking," I said, hardly recognizing my own voice. It was the voice I'd learned in etiquette lessons, the glacial voice used for the worst putdown—but now it was infused with the strength I'd forged since I'd been on my own.

I looked down my nose at my father, then at my mother, who stared at me with wide eyes. Her cheeks were red, and she clenched her clutch with white-knuckled fingers. At least she'd stopped flapping.

Even if this was the last time I saw them, I would be at peace. The realization settled over me, and I knew that this was the end of their power over me.

I knew what real love felt like now. I knew I didn't need to stand in ballrooms and mingle with the monied class in order to be happy.

All I needed was my independence—and Vaughn.

Saying a silent goodbye to my parents—and to the woman I used to be—I gave them both the tiniest of nods. "Mother. Father. Excuse me. There's someone I need to speak to."

There were three important words I had to speak, now more than ever.

THIRTY-SIX

VAUGHN

SPEAKING WITH LEIF—AND drinking down my glass of champagne—succeeded in settling a lot of my nerves. If things with Arlo fell through, I had other options.

Alba had been right: all I had to do was act like I belonged, like I had investment opportunities to choose from, and options would open up right in front of me.

Leif had excused himself a few minutes earlier, and I scanned the room for Alba. There was a growing murmur in the room, and a few people seemed to be moving toward the dining room, as if some innate sense told these people that dinner would soon be served. An innate sense that I didn't have.

The hallway where Alba had disappeared showed me no hint of lavender, and the itchiness beneath my collar returned. She was taking a long time. Would I stand here until everyone had moved to the dining room, looking as out of place as I felt?

I closed my eyes and shook my head, regretting that last glass of champagne. *Deep breaths.* I heard Alba's voice in my head, calming me, and wished she were beside me to steady me.

In one corner of my mind, I knew this was just some fancy event, and it was ridiculous to feel as deeply uncomfortable as I did.

But to me, it wasn't just an event. It was everything my father had chased during his lifetime. Everything I'd rejected—or thought I rejected. I was vying for a spot at a table that I'd previously scorned. My early memories were peppered with instances of watching him dress in his tuxedo, my mother frantically clipping stray threads and hiding worn linings. My father would transform into a man I didn't recognize.

Kind of like the man in the mirror, in his white tie and coattails.

And in the end, my father's efforts had meant nothing. We still lived with the instability of near poverty. I still watched my mother pick up the pieces and make sure I had enough.

So, standing at the edge of the sumptuous ballroom, I didn't just feel anxious about not fitting in. I felt guilty for even trying. I felt like a hypocrite, a liar. I felt like the core of my identity as a hard-working man who sacrificed for the people he loved was laughably false, because in the end I was as fake as my father had been, driven by the desire to fit into societies that wanted nothing to do with. I was pathetic. A fraud. A cheap excuse of a man, standing here exposed on the fringes of a society that would never accept me.

For what?

A familiar refrain started up in my mind: I was here for my business. This was my one shot, the chance to make a good impression and bag an investor. An investor meant growth, and growth meant success. Success was the antithesis of everything my father had been.

As long as I was successful, I was not my father. As long as my business ventures worked out, I was better than him. I provided for my family instead of draining their resources.

That's what mattered. I could stand here and pretend to belong as long as it pushed me toward that ultimate goal.

That was the moment Alba's ex walked up to me. Her other ex —the one we'd seen in the lobby of the French restaurant.

"So you caught her," he said, his lips twisting in an ugly smile. "I should be giving you a round of applause. I tried to reel her in for months, and she didn't give it up until it was too late."

"Excuse me?"

"I think you're wasting your time, though. She'll never end up with a guy like you." He delivered the words casually, but in the sharpness of his eyes, I saw that he knew the blow had landed.

I licked my lips. "You have no idea what you're talking about."

"Look." He jerked his chin toward the restroom hallway. Alba was there now, her shoulders hiked up, tension visible across the room. An older couple stood in front of her. I could only see their backs, but judging by the look on Alba's face—the upturned chin, the ice-queen expression—I guessed they were her parents.

When she brushed past them, they both turned, and I saw Alba's features in the man's. Her parents stared after her in shock.

"She won't slum it with you for long."

"I think you should leave," I growled. Alba had disappeared behind a clump of people, so I speared the man with a glare.

"Don't believe me? Look."

Then his phone was in my face, and I had no choice but to read the messages on the screen.

JAMES

Haven't been able to stop thinking about you since we saw each other.

Miss you.

> I want to talk to you, Alba. Can I
> see you?

ALBA

> Sure, I'll see you.

JAMES

> Time and place, babe. I'm there.

I jerked, my hand snapping up to grab the phone, but James was quicker. He slipped the device into his breast pocket and gave me a victorious smile.

"You can't keep a woman like that," he said, his tone a mocking imitation of sympathy. "She just can't help herself." He reached out to slap my shoulder, his hand clamping down to give it a squeeze. "Better you know now, though, right?"

Before I could formulate a response, he'd dissolved back into the crowd. Then I heard a breath and turned to see Alba's shining eyes. Her face was flushed, as if she'd just sprinted here instead of the stately glide I'd observed. Her smile was shy, but it blossomed into something wide and bright.

And it was all a lie.

Like the snark, and the teasing, and the flirting. The touches. How long had she played me? How long had she planned this? Since I offered her a job? Earlier?

Maybe she'd seen me as a mark from the moment I sat down at her table at Carmine's, and I played right into her hand.

I realized with a start that it wasn't me who was like my father —it was her. Always looking for the next big win. Willing to transform herself into someone else, just to get what she wanted.

I'd been such an idiot. I'd fallen for this woman, and I didn't know her at all. She'd played the damsel, and I'd felt like such a fucking hero for plucking her out of her distress and taking care of her.

Now she was here, making a fool out of me on the one night it mattered most.

Did Arlo know? Did they all know? They watched me walk in here with her on my arm, and they didn't wish they were me. They felt *sorry* for me.

Alba's smile dropped off her face, and she took half a step back. "Are you okay? Why are you looking at me like that?"

"How long, Alba?"

"Excuse me?"

"How long have you been lying to me?"

She jerked back as if I'd slapped her. Her cheeks flushed, and hurt flashed across her gaze. For a moment—an instant—I regretted my words. Then her gaze hardened and she hissed, "What the hell are you talking about?"

"Your old lover just showed me some interesting text messages. Did you plan to meet him here? Is that why you took so long in the bathroom?"

"What are you talking about?"

"I'm talking about you meeting with the guy that you said used you, Alba!" My voice was too loud. People all around glanced over, curious and predatory.

Alba didn't even seem to notice. She stared at me like she didn't recognize me, gulped, and then her face shuttered completely. Even the flush drained from her cheeks, so she stared back at me from under arched brows, her eyes so cold I felt the chill of her look all the way down to my bones.

But I was too far gone. I leaned closer and said, "This is everything I've been working toward, and you've made a fool out of me. My business, Arlo's investment—they'll all be laughing at me."

Moving slowly, she undid the clasp of her purse and reached inside. With long, graceful fingers, she tapped on the screen, then turned her phone so I could see.

I saw the same messages James had shown me—plus an extra one.

ALBA

When we're both dead I'll see you in hell. Asshole.

Right below the message, there was tiny text indicating that the contact was blocked. The phone dropped, and my gaze snapped to Alba's face.

"I—" My voice died. Heat rose up the back of my throat, and I was suddenly lightheaded. "He didn't show me the last message," I said, but it sounded weak even to my ears.

Alba snorted. "No, he didn't, did he?" She tucked her phone away, not looking at me.

"Alba—"

"Save it, Vaughn. I know how little you think of me now."

"I thought you were lying to me. I thought you were fake—"

"I gathered," she answered, sardonic and unruffled. It was only the very slight trembling in her hands and the tight swallow she couldn't conceal that told me she wasn't as unaffected as she appeared. She lifted her gaze to mine once more. "Goodbye, Vaughn."

"Alba, wait—"

She walked away from me. She didn't run. She didn't push past the other guests. She just gave me her back and glided across the room toward the exit, never once looking back.

THIRTY-SEVEN

ALBA

SURPRISINGLY, it took me two whole days to break down. I took a cab home from the gala, stripped my dress off and hung it up, showered, and went to bed. Then I got up and lived in a strange, numb twilight. Breakfast, yoga, chores. Food had no flavor, but I chewed and swallowed anyway. My apartment remained pristine, because I cleaned more than I ever had before. I sat and stared out the window for an unknown amount of time, so long that my hip felt stiff when I stood, and I realized the sun had gone down. I existed somewhere outside my body, watching myself vacuum and scrub and cook and live like nothing at all was the matter.

Then, after two days, I turned my phone on for the first time.

It wasn't the messages from Vaughn that snapped me out of it, or the nine calls I'd missed from him. It was a single message from my only friend.

> DEENA
> How did it go??

I read those four words, and a flood of tears burst out of me.

Collapsed on the couch that didn't belong to me, in an apartment that wasn't meant to be mine, I cried until my body shook, until it felt like I'd drained myself completely and I worried the swelling around my eyes would never go down again.

Finally, as my bottom lip trembled almost as much as my hands, I picked up my phone and answered.

ME

It was bad.

She didn't answer for an hour, and I regretted even telling her that much. After all, we'd hung out a handful of times over the past couple of months. It wasn't a deep and lasting friendship. She was entertained by my antics, but she wasn't volunteering to be my shoulder to cry on.

I would forever be on my own. No one actually cared about me. I'd been such a fool to think that Vaughn did—that he might think highly enough of me that an attack on my character from James might not affect him.

That was the heart of my pain. I thought Vaughn saw me and respected me. I thought, finally, that I'd found a man who saw me as a real person, with flaws and desires and dreams. I thought he'd be the one to make me happy.

But he was just like the rest of them. I was useful to him, and as soon as it was inconvenient, he hurled insults at me and reminded me just how little he thought of me.

My phone buzzed, interrupting my pity party.

DEENA

Oh no. You okay?

My throat tightened. I answered a single word:

ME

No.

DEENA

Do you need to be alone, or do you want me to come over? What's your address? I just need to finish one flight booking for a client and then I'm free for the rest of the day.

I typed out my instinctual response, which was that I wanted to be alone. Then I stared at the words, my thumb hovering over the little paper plane that would send the message, and I couldn't make myself press it.

My back ached. My hip was clicking more than ever. I sat in my pristine apartment, feeling untethered and utterly alone.

Deena was reaching a hand out to me, offering her help, and it felt dangerous to accept. I'd accepted Vaughn's advances. I'd let myself fall for him, only to realize that he didn't feel that way about me at all. He thought I was some fake, vapid social climber. He thought I was betraying him.

And why wouldn't he? He knew I'd spoken to James while I was engaged to Cole. He knew I'd acted wrongly, and it wasn't a huge stretch of the imagination to think that I'd do it again.

Except—

Except it *was* a stretch, because my engagement to Cole hadn't been my choice. Not really. I'd been under my parents' thumbs, living a life that had been prescribed for me from the moment I was born. As long as I did what was expected of me, I could stay in the family fold. I could live a life of luxury and privilege. But I'd been on a leash.

With Vaughn, I'd been independent. Struggling, yes, but I'd made the decision to be with him on my own. That was so much more powerful to me. It meant so much more. I was *choosing* him.

But he didn't choose me back.

Except for those nine missed calls and seventeen texts you haven't looked at, my brain reminded me.

Swallowing past the constriction in my throat, I erased my message to Deena and typed out my address. An hour later, my buzzer rang, and I let her into the building. When I opened my apartment door for her, she greeted me with arched brows, a sympathetic smile, and two bulging bags.

"I brought ice cream, chocolate, chips, hummus and pita, and half a dozen takeout flyers. I wasn't sure if you eat your feelings with sweet or savory, so…"

I huffed out a watery laugh, and she set the bags down before wrapping me in a hug. I broke down immediately, my emotions off-kilter, my world bleak and miserable.

It took me an hour and a half to get the whole story out. Deena fed me chocolate and then ordered us some Thai food. I sat on the couch with my legs wrapped in a blanket, feeling oddly vulnerable yet happy she was here.

"I shouldn't even be mad at him," I said when our food arrived and I opened my container of tom yum soup. I inhaled the delicious aromas and then blew out a sigh. "He has every right to question me about James."

Deena gave me a strange look. "What do you mean?"

"He knows what happened between me and Cole," I explained.

"Is this more of your karmic retribution bullshit?"

"Excuse me?"

"You think you need to be punished?"

I squirmed, dipping my spoon into the soup and swirling around. "Well…yes. I had an emotional affair, Deena."

"And Cole didn't?"

I jerked. "Well—he—I don't—" I snapped my mouth shut, frowning. "I wouldn't say that."

"He gets to have his happily-ever-after, even though he drifted away from you as soon as...what's her name?"

"Carrie."

Deena blinked at me, her head moving back. "Wait. Are we talking about Cole Christianson? Carrie as in Carrie Woods?"

"I don't know her maiden name—"

"I *know* Carrie!" Deena exclaimed. "I worked with Carrie! She's amazing! You've been talking about Carrie and Cole this whole time?"

I forced a smile. "Oh, um—yes. That's great that you know her —ha. What are the chances..." Inside, I wilted. The one friend I thought I had was loyal to someone else. She might not believe in karma, but the pattern in my life seemed pretty consistent. I'd gone against what I was supposed to do, and now I was suffering for it.

"And she started dating her boss..." Deena laughed. "Oh, you *really* don't need to feel bad."

I started. "What?"

"When Carrie went back to work for her old boss, she and I had lots of time to talk. I handle all his travel arrangements. She told me all about what happened at their work retreat thing. Were the two of you still together then?"

Mind reeling, I frowned. "Um. Well, that's when we broke up—"

"So it took your ex-fiancé about four milliseconds to jump into bed with another woman. And don't get me wrong, they had their reasons. And I'm happy for them. And I *do* think Carrie is amazing. But that's riding a fine edge of acceptability, don't you think?"

"I—"

Deena set her food down, then took my bowl out of my hands

and put it next to hers on the coffee table. Then she took my hands and squeezed them. "Your relationship with Cole wasn't built on anything real, Alba. Not the kind of thing that can withstand the arrival of true emotion."

That stung, even though I knew it was true. I gave her a tight smile.

Deena squeezed my hands again. "I'm not saying this to beat up on you. I'm saying it to set you free. You need to stop punishing yourself for the failure of a relationship that was never going to work in the first place. Let it go, babe."

My bottom lip trembled. "I'm just so ashamed, Deena," I whispered.

She sighed. "It's messy. But life is messy. Sometimes you just gotta deal with it."

"I wish I could go back in time and slap the phone out of my hands when I got that first message from James."

"I wish I could do that too," Deena answered, smiling. "But then—would you have broken up with Cole if you hadn't had James? Would he have broken it off with you? Or would you two be locked in a bad marriage right now, slowly drifting apart, doing your best to keep up appearances? Maybe it all happened for a reason."

"I thought you didn't believe in that stuff. You said karmic retribution was bullshit."

"I'm a complex person." She shrugged, grinning. "I can believe whatever I like."

A weak little laugh tumbled out of me, and I sighed. "Cole seemed happy."

"He's certainly forgiven himself for not being all-in on your engagement," Deena agreed.

"If he can be happy, maybe one day I can too."

"That's the spirit." Deena smiled encouragingly and picked up her food again. "Step one: forgive yourself. Step two: find a job. Step three: be free."

"Just like that, huh."

"Just like that."

I drank a spoonful of soup, then glanced at the only person who was willing to sit with me and tell me she believed in me. "And Vaughn?"

"What about him?"

"What should I do? He's called and texted me a bunch."

Deena hummed. "What do you want to do?"

"I don't know," I whispered.

"You still love him?"

Tears prickled at my eyes. "Unfortunately, yes. But if he thinks so little of me, what's the point?"

It had felt so good to finally confront Cole, James, and my parents at the gala. It felt like breaking chains that had been keeping me in place. I'd finally found the courage to live my life for myself. I'd thought that life would be with Vaughn by my side.

Now I wasn't so sure.

"Sleep on it and decide tomorrow," Deena suggested.

BUT TOMORROW CAME, and I was no closer to figuring out what I wanted. My conversation with Deena rattled around my brain while I ate breakfast, and I finally pulled out my phone and tapped on Vaughn's messages.

They ranged from apologetic to frantic. The last message simply read:

> VAUGHN
> Please call me.

I'd received that one almost two days earlier, and nothing since.

My heart wanted Vaughn. I wanted those lazy mornings in his bed, with his arms wrapped around me. I wanted the warmth of his hugs, the tenderness of his kisses. I wanted that feeling of safety and home.

But I didn't want to get the rug pulled out from under me again like I had with my parents, and James, and Vaughn at the gala. I didn't want to hand him the power to hurt me again.

After my confrontation with my parents at the gala, I knew that door was fully closed now. I could never go back to them. I was on my own.

Sipping a coffee as I curled myself into my favorite corner of the couch, I glanced out the window at the blue skies and realized spring had arrived. Soon the world would burst into life, and I'd be able to go outside and feel the warmth of the sun on my skin. I clambered off the couch and pushed open the window—the same one I'd poked my head through to yell down to Vaughn when he'd given me the dress—and peered through a gap in the buildings at the blue skies above.

I was on my own—but that wasn't a bad thing. Being on my own kind of felt...wonderful, actually. Scary and dangerous and unknown. But also a little bit wonderful.

The sounds of the city rattled up toward me, and I took my spot on the couch again, grabbed my mug, and sighed.

I knew what I had to do.

THIRTY-EIGHT

VAUGHN

WAITING WAS AGONY. I tried to work, but legal issues and construction snags only made my temples pulse with pain. I couldn't even spend time with my daughter, because she was at her mother's place for the week I'd given up. I checked my phone incessantly and forced myself not to send Alba a barrage of messages.

Finally, she answered. She wanted to meet for coffee.

Dread walked its cold fingers down my spine as my driver approached the coffee shop on the Wednesday following the gala. Then I walked in, and a temporary burst of hope lifted me up as I saw Alba sitting next to the window, her eyes lifting to watch me walk in.

That hope withered and died when my gaze landed on the seat next to hers, where a garment bag had been draped. Even without the little clear window in the front of the garment bag showing sparkly purple fabric, I already knew what was inside.

Alba was returning the dress.

This wasn't going to be a reconciliation.

She stood when I reached her table. "I haven't ordered you anything," she said by way of greeting.

"That's fine," I said, then nodded to the dress. "I'm not taking that back."

Alba squared her shoulders. "You are."

"It's yours."

"I don't remember paying for it."

"It was a gift, Alba."

"Give it to your daughter when she grows up."

"No."

We faced off, a little square table between us, until Alba released a sigh and dropped into her chair. I sat down more gingerly, as if there was a bomb under the seat of the chair that might blow up if I moved too quickly. When I was settled, Alba took a deep breath—but I had things to say before I let her break things off between us.

"I'm sorry, Alba."

Her mouth clamped shut. She swallowed, eyelashes fluttering as she blinked, then dipped her chin. "I appreciate you saying that."

"I shouldn't have accused you of going behind my back to meet with your ex. I know I shouldn't have jumped to conclusions. You deserve better than that."

Her eyes were watery, and all I wanted to do was jump over the table to wrap her in my arms. She took a deep breath and whispered, "So why did you?"

I swallowed convulsively, searching my blank mind for the right words. I didn't know how to explain my state of mind that night. The anxiety. The feeling that I wasn't being true to myself. The doubt. All the work that had gone into finding an investor, the months of meetings and effort, hinging on that final gala to close the deal with Arlo Noble. "I was intensely uncomfortable, and you didn't seem to be," I finally started, speaking slowly. With the thumb of my right hand, I dug into the fleshy part of my left hand between my thumb and forefinger. The slight pain helped me focus, and I continued: "You'd said all those things about your family and peers, how awful they were, and then you seemed to be thriving. I started thinking—" I pressed my thumb harder when my voice stuttered to a stop. "I started thinking that maybe I didn't really know you. That you weren't the woman I'd gotten to know, and instead you were one of them."

"One of them," she repeated softly, her eyes glistening with tears.

"Not that they're all bad," I rushed to add. "Just—" I stopped, not knowing how to continue. Then I said, "There was a lot riding on that evening, and I guess I cracked under the pressure."

There was a silence. Alba's drink steamed between us, but she made no move to drink it. Then she took a deep breath. "When we walked in, I was uncomfortable too. But I told myself that I was there for you."

"Alba—"

"Let me finish, please." She paused, then said, "I put on a mask that I used to wear when I had to go to those types of events. When I ran into Cole and his new wife, all the guilt and shame of my actions came rushing back to me."

"He didn't seem angry."

She shook her head. "He wasn't. But I needed a minute, and that's when James confronted me." She straightened. "For the first time since I met him, I told James to back off. I felt like I was seeing through the charm for the first time, and I stood up for myself. I was so proud, but all that guilt and shame just compounded and weighed even heavier on me. When my parents cornered me, then, it was like this rush of strength went through me. I felt like I was finally free. All I had to do was cross the ballroom and get to you, and I would be okay. The one person who knew the real me. The one person I could rely on."

Sourness rose up the back of my throat. "And I accused you of —of—"

"Of trying to cheat on you. The way I did with Cole."

"Alba, I never thought—"

"I understand," she interrupted, smiling sadly. "I probably would've thought the same thing in your shoes. But your reaction made me realize that I can't put myself in a position to be hurt like that again. I was relying on you for safety, for support, for everything. It's time I rely on myself."

"You've been relying on yourself for over a year. Let me help you."

She smiled sadly. "No, Vaughn. Thank you, but no. On Saturday, I went to the gala for you. I faced all those people and was determined to stay there and make a good impression—for you. But you weren't there for me. You were there for your business. And that's fine—that's your right. You built your empire, and you deserve to see it grow. But I've realized that I'd rather be alone than second on someone's priority list. It hurts too much when I inevitably become collateral damage."

I couldn't speak, because she was right. I should have seen the toll that event was taking on her. I should have been there beside her every step of the way. Hell, I should have shielded her from James and her parents, instead of letting her face them alone.

Instead, I stood on my own and stewed in my own insecurities, thinking about how her actions would affect my business. I was afraid of looking stupid to a bunch of people I didn't even know.

Cold spread through my chest, and I saw my chance at making amends slipping away. I opened my mouth, but no words came out.

Alba gathered her things and stood.

"Take the dress," I finally commanded.

She looked at me, then at the garment bag.

"Take it," I said. "Sell it. Wear it. I don't care, but I don't want it."

A heavy sigh slipped through her lips, and then she reached for the bag and draped it over her arm. She circled the table and ran a finger over my temple. "Goodbye, Vaughn. Thank you for everything. You gave me an opportunity and a way out when I thought I had nothing."

I could give you more, I wanted to scream. I could take care of you. I'll never hurt you again.

But her hand dropped to her side, and my tongue stayed still. She walked away from me for the second time, and this time I knew it was for good.

IT LOOKED like I also wasn't going to get the chance to fix the Midtown job. A week after my meeting with Alba, Arlo Noble sent his regrets. He was taking his legal team's advice and declining to invest in my company. Ever since the news of the legal battle had spread, we hadn't won a single new project. The Midtown project was bleeding money and not progressing. No one wanted to touch us—not an investor, not a new client, not a replacement subcontractor. The company was in free fall.

I almost wanted to laugh.

I'd blamed Alba at the gala, but it was my own fault this was happening.

Then, that afternoon, I got another email—this time from Tiffany's lawyer. She was petitioning the court for a review of our custody agreement for Charlotte. I stared at the words, not under-standing. Then my phone rang.

"Tiffany," I growled as I picked up. "What's this about our custody agreement?"

"I'm trying to do right by our daughter, Vaughn. You work long hours, and you've asked me to take her on your weeks regularly. I don't want her being raised by a nanny, no matter how great Billie is. And I'm not going to be asking for more money, if that's what you're worried about."

"I'm not giving up time with my daughter," I barked.

"You won't have to," Tiffany answered, sounding tired but calm. "I've kept track of all the times you asked me to take her during your custody time, and I'm just asking for our agreement to reflect the current status quo. I've let the nanny thing slide too long as well. Our current agreement has the right of first refusal. When you can't be there to take care of her after school, she should be coming home to me. That's what my lawyer said, and that's what I'll ask for in court."

I stared at my computer screen, not understanding. The lawyer's letter jumbled before me, and I rubbed my eyes to try to make it make sense.

Tiffany filled the silence, her voice soft but unyielding. "I'm doing what's best for Charlotte, Vaughn."

"You're talking to me like I don't care about my own daughter."

"I'm doing what's best for Charlotte," she repeated. "If you can't be there with her, she should be with me. And you'll be free to work on your businesses as much as you need to."

There was nothing else to say, so we hung up. Heat burned the back of my throat, and my blood rushed through my veins, making my body tremble and shake.

I was losing everything—I'd already lost everything.

My business. My daughter. Alba.

All the things that mattered to me were slipping through my fingers, and even with a fortune at my fingertips, there was nothing

I could do about it. Tiffany would win in court, no doubt, because she was right about how little time I spent with our daughter. Alba had walked away from me without looking back.

But my business could be saved—maybe. If I felt like bankrupting myself.

I sat in my corner office as the sun went down, setting the skyscrapers of the city ablaze. I sat until the lights came on, until the hum of the cleaner's vacuum started up down the hall. The noise made me think of Alba, and I finally pushed myself back from my desk.

I stood, and then froze. Where would I go? Back to my empty house? To the penthouse apartment that had never felt like home? Over to Alba's, so I could stand outside her window and beg her to take me back?

Every option seemed terrible, so I took none of them. I sat back down, woke my computer up, and worked.

Maybe if I saved my business from ruin, I would feel better. Maybe if I did one thing right, it wouldn't feel like the entire world was crumbling down around me.

THIRTY-NINE
ALBA

IT TOOK me three weeks to notice that both of my most recent rent payments had been returned to my account. I needed the extra cushion now that I was jobless again, but the thought of owing money made me itchy all over.

Gina, the redhead building manager who'd taken up residence in the lobby office, clacked on her keyboard and squinted at her screen when I asked her. "We've received your rent payment already. You said it was returned?"

"The last two rent payments. Ever since I moved into the bigger apartment."

"I've got your rent marked as paid through to the end of the year." Gina spun around, her office chair squeaking with the movement.

"What?"

"It says it right here."

"That can't be right."

Gina shrugged.

"And when am I going to be moving back to the studio? Has the mold been removed?"

"You're not moving back to the studio," Gina said, frowning. "We've got your lease updated for apartment 815."

"But—"

The phone rang, and Gina held up a finger. "I've got to take this." She waved me out of her office then closed the door in my face, and I stood there, gaping at the closed door, wondering what the heck was going on.

The next four times I went down to ask her, she told me the same thing.

Deena was the one who suggested I email the landlord directly, whose contact details were on my original lease. But when I did, the landlord answered back that the building had been sold, and management had been handed over to a new company. He suggested I talk to Gina, the building manager.

Deena read the email the following day when we met up at the coffee shop. She hummed as she handed my phone back. "Strange."

"I feel like this is going to blow up in my face. I can't just live there without paying rent. They'll come back and ask me for it all at once. I'm trying not to spend the money, but my savings are dwindling. The money I made working for Vaughn is almost gone."

"And no hits on the website yet?"

Deena had helped me set up a website for image consulting work. It seemed farfetched and ridiculous that someone would hire me based on a landing page, but Deena had seemed confident that I'd get some bites.

I shook my head. "Nothing. Not that it's a surprise. Who would hire me?"

"Plenty of people," Deena said as she waved a hand. "I mean, if people are going to hire me to do their travel arrangements, they can hire you to do their image."

I smiled at her confidence, but didn't believe it.

"I'll talk to some of my clients, see if anyone is interested," she promised.

"And I'll keep looking for a job in the meantime."

Deena nudged her shoulder against mine. "And everything will work out. Maybe the free rent is good karma for your terrible last couple of years."

"That's not how it works," I said, laughing.

We parted ways, and I went back to the apartment that felt luxurious compared to my old studio. I loved living here, except for the fact that every time I walked through the door, it made me think of Vaughn. He'd said he'd handle the mold problem, and—

I frowned as I tossed my purse onto the kitchen counter.

Had Vaughn paid my rent? I grabbed my phone and found his number—and stopped. That was crazy. He wouldn't have paid my rent for a year as a way of "handling" my problem. He'd bullied them into moving me into this apartment, and then some wires had gotten crossed somewhere. I'd eventually get a big rent bill, and I had to be ready for it.

The thought of Vaughn made me feel hot and prickly all over. All the feelings that I'd pushed down wanted to come rushing back up again. My phone was like a venomous snake in my hand, ready to bite as soon as I found his number and hit "Call."

I thought of the twist on his lips when he accused me of meeting up with James. The pit that opened up in my stomach in that moment, when I realized that he didn't feel the same way about me as I did about him. If he had loved me like I loved him, he never would've doubted me. He would've stood up beside me that night, the way I was ready to stand up beside him.

Moving slowly, I set my phone down and took a deep breath.

I'd jumped into my relationship with him too fast. I thought he was going to save me from a life of drudgery, and that's where I'd gone wrong. No man—not Vaughn or anyone else—would save me. I had to save myself.

There was no safety net now. My parents weren't one phone call away anymore; I'd burned that bridge. I was well and truly on my own—but for the first time in my life, I felt like I could handle it.

This time, I hadn't been thrown out of my life and my home. I hadn't been cut off from all the relationships that had given me stability.

I'd chosen to walk away, and I *would* make it work.

Cracking the door open for Vaughn would only make things harder, even if I did have to figure this rent thing out, and he was the person I had to ask for more details.

I wasn't ready for that.

Better to give myself more time.

***

TIME, however, was not on my side. Not when I realized I couldn't remember my last period, and I bought a pregnancy test to settle the nagging fears that kept swirling around my mind. I squinted at the little window, wondering if it was a shadow of a second line I could see, my heart beating out of my chest.

No. Definitely not.

But I took another test the next day, just to be sure. And the next day. And the next.

And all of a sudden, there were two lines where there had been none before. I stared at them in denial, looked up to stare at my shell-shocked face in the mirror, then tucked the pregnancy test into the bathroom trash can and walked out into the apartment's main living area.

My blood pumped so hard my face tingled.

I was pregnant with Vaughn's child, and I had no idea what to do about it.

FORTY
ALBA

ELENA SAT BACK in her chair, tapping the end of her pen on her chin. She looked me up and down, and it took all my muscle memory not to fidget. She was as intimidating as anyone I'd met at a white tie affair, and I'd just asked her for a huge favor.

"I need coverage for the brunch crowd on Sunday. You can do a shift, and then we'll talk."

"Thank you!" The words burst out of me, and I forced myself to take a breath. "Thank you. You won't regret it."

"Mmhmm," she replied, turning to mark my name down on this week's schedule. "Be here at seven a.m."

"No problem." I turned toward the door, relief making my knees weak.

"And Alba?"

I met her dark gaze. "Yes?"

She glanced down at my midsection, giving me a small smile. "Congratulations."

She was the first person I'd told, so it was the first time I heard the word. I swallowed thickly, then dipped my chin. "Thank you. For everything."

"If you talk back to customers the way you did before, I won't hesitate to take you off the schedule again. Baby or not."

"Understood." A broad smile spread across my face, and I darted out of the office before she could change her mind.

It wasn't my dream job, but it would give me a lifeline. I said goodbye to the cooks and made my way outside, lifting my face to the spring sunshine.

I still didn't know what to do. I didn't know if it was possible to make it on my own. I didn't know how to talk to Vaughn when even thinking about him made my chest feel tighter.

But I had a job. That was a start.

ELENA DIDN'T TREAT me like I was made of glass. After my second double shift in a row during my third week back at work, I stumbled through my apartment doorway and collapsed on the couch. My feet were killing me, but Deena had gifted me a foot spa bath after listening to me complain about it every day for three weeks. As my head lolled on the couch, still nauseous even though it was evening, the sight of that little tub sitting next to the couch was my salvation. I smiled, hauled myself off the couch, filled it with water, and then soaked my feet and fell asleep where I sat.

I TURNED sideways in the mirror, running my hand over my lower stomach. If my pants hadn't been a touch harder to button this morning, I might have thought I was imagining the slight swell of my belly. I bit my lip, heart thumping. There was no way I could do this on my own.

I had no choice but to do it on my own.

I would do it on my own.

THE SONOGRAPHER TAPPED her keyboard and angled the ultrasound wand, the clear jelly warming on my skin with every passing minute. The whooshing sound of a tiny, fast heartbeat echoed in the room.

"Do you want to find out the sex?" she asked, moving the wand so the black-and-white image on the screen sped to a new view.

My heart clogged up my throat. "Yes," I whispered. "I'd like to know."

SWEAT DRENCHED MY BACK, my front, my underarms, and my unmentionables. Summer had blasted into the city, mugging us all with humidity and heat. I pushed open my apartment door and propped it open, then turned to drag in my latest purchase.

The bassinet was used, but it was serviceable. It was a soft gray with a thin white mattress, and the woman who'd sold it to me had thrown in a few sleep sacks she no longer needed. I hauled the whole thing to my home office—soon to be nursery—and tucked it into the corner.

It was still early to be buying things—I was barely out of my first trimester—but I hadn't been able to pass up the deal. With most of my time spent at Carmine's to save up what I could in what little time I had, I knew I couldn't afford to wait until the last minute.

After I'd guzzled a glass of water, I tiptoed back into the room and picked up one of the sleep sacks. It was soft green, with darker green leaves dotted over the fabric. It looked impossibly tiny. I carefully folded it, put it back on the pile of baby things, and then closed the door and went to get ready for work.

I READ the email three times, and still I couldn't believe it.

"Deena!" I screeched when she picked up my call. "One of your clients just emailed me through the website you set up!"

"Which one?" she asked.

"Brian Hull."

"Oh yeah, he needs your help, big time," she said, and we both laughed.

I LAY on the grass and watched the leaves of a nearby tree flutter in the warm breeze. To my left, Deena licked a drip from her ice cream cone before it reached her fingers, then used the pinky finger of the cone-holding hand to turn the page of her book. I closed my eyes as a child screeched and laughed on the other side of the park, my palm resting lightly on my stomach.

A NOTIFICATION POPPED up on my phone. The payment from Brian Hull had come through. A minute later, an email came through from him. He'd written an email testimonial and attached before-and-after photos of his new look, giving me permission to add them to my website.

Three days later, one of Brian's coworkers sent me an inquiry, requesting more information about my services.

IT WAS hard to fall asleep after a late shift at the restaurant. Exhaustion made me loopy, but my brain wouldn't shut off. I stared at the wall in my bedroom, curled on my side, knowing that every minute that passed was one less minute I'd get to sleep before my opening shift at Carmine's. The dreaded clopen.

In the stillness of the night, while my mind raced, there was a flutter. I frowned, unmoving, wondering if I'd imagined it.

And then it happened again. I put my hand to my belly and the flutters stopped, but tears had already sprung in my eyes.

"Hello, baby," I whispered.

IT WAS twilight when I got home from my day shift, which meant the days were getting shorter. As I pushed open my apartment door, the baby somersaulted inside me. It was still a foreign feeling, the movement of a separate being within me, but I'd come to rely on the movements to mark the passing of the days.

But the days were indeed passing, and I still hadn't done what I knew needed to be done. The longer I left it, the harder it was to think of the right words, to brace myself for the conversation I owed to Vaughn.

I'd become braver these past months. Without the weight of my shame and hurt, life away from the people of my past was hard but worthwhile. My emergency fund was growing, my belief in myself with it.

If I could survive the gauntlet of this pregnancy on my own, I could tell Vaughn about the baby. I wasn't the broken, resentful woman that I'd been when we met. I faced my problems head-on—for the most part. I could look at myself in the mirror and be proud of how far I'd come, be comfortable in the life and future that had opened up before me. Some days, I was terrified of that future—terrified I'd made one too many mistakes, and I'd be paying for them soon.

But mostly, I believed in my own abilities. I wasn't bested by laundry or bills or a difficult customer. I had bigger things to worry about now—and bigger things to look forward to.

But some of my old cowardice still remained, because I found myself unable to pick up my phone to send him a message.

Instead, I found a piece of paper and I began to write.

FORTY-ONE
VAUGHN

I PULLED my gloves off and brushed a smudge of dirt off my thigh. Glancing over the tops of the townhouses lining the street, I paused to take in the sunset. Clouds drifted across the sky in soft brushes of white, their undersides limned with fire. The sky was awash with color, deepening to a dark purple above my head.

I'd watched the sunset from up here every day this week, my face pointed toward the west, my skin goosepimpling in the cooling night breeze. As far as retirement went, this wasn't a bad way to start.

Charlotte would be going to her first day of first grade on Monday. She was at her mother's place now, as she had been for most of the summer. We were due to go back to mediation in a couple of weeks, and I was intending to prove to Tiffany and the mediator that I was serious about setting work aside for the sake of my daughter.

No more late nights. No more handing Charlotte off to the nanny because I had to get a project over the line. I would make sure that for the rest of Charlotte's life, she knew that I was there for her.

Funny how a few months of existential panic and all-out misery changed a man's point of view.

Not for the first time, I wished Alba were beside me so I could thank her for making me see things clearly. If she hadn't walked away from me, I wouldn't have felt the pain I needed to clear my head. I would've kept on working, kept on giving all my time to reach some mythical success that didn't really exist—all to prove to a dead man that I'd succeeded despite his best efforts to ruin our family for the duration of my childhood while he chased his growing ego.

But I was a father now. I wouldn't let Charlotte grow up with the same feeling of abandonment and instability. If that meant burning my business to the ground so I could make more time for her, then that's what I was prepared to do.

If it meant growing old by myself, because the best relationship of my life was the price to pay for that lesson—well, that hurt, but I'd accepted that I had to pay it. I'd lost Alba, but I wasn't losing my daughter.

As the light dwindled to the soft gray of twilight, I cleaned up my workspace with the small brush and dustpan I'd left here for that purpose. A car rolled down the street below. A door slammed. Someone called out to their child down the street.

Then there was a noise that was more familiar. I brushed the last few bits of soil off the workbench, frowning. It was a slight squeak, barely audible over the other sounds of life and city, and it took me a few seconds to place it.

My mail slot. Someone had just dropped something off at my house.

Idle curiosity made me glance over the low parapet wall of my rooftop terrace, peeking down at the steps that ran up to my front door. No one was there, but my gaze snapped to the lone figure of a woman darting down the street away from my house.

A blond woman, above average height, bundled in a long, knitted cardigan that brushed against her calves as she hurried away. Her hair was piled in a high bun that I'd recognize anywhere.

"Alba!" I called out, hands curling against the brick of the low wall—but a car honked at the same time, and she didn't slow, didn't stop. "Alba!" I called out again.

Her steps faltered, her head turning slightly. It was her. She was here, at my house.

After all these months, Alba had come back.

My heart thundered, and before I knew what I was doing, I was shooting down the trapdoor and down the rickety ladder that led to my attic space. Then I flew down the attic stairs, landing hard on the wood floor outside Charlotte's room, and I ran to the main townhouse stairway. Two flights of stairs spat me out at the front door, where an envelope lay waiting for me in the foyer. It was a normal letter-sized envelope, and Alba had written my name in block letters on the front.

I snatched it up and crashed into the door, swearing as I tugged on it and found it locked. I threw the lock and sprinted down the steps, vaulting over a dog on a leash while its owner yelled at me. I'd left my front door wide open, and I didn't care.

"Alba!"

She turned a corner, her cardigan fluttering around her legs. I redoubled my speed, legs and arms pumping, breaths gusting out of me. Finally, I turned the same corner and saw that I'd gained on her.

This time, when I yelled her name, she turned around. Her eyes widened, shock and panic flashing across her face, and she made to spin around again.

"Alba, wait!" I crashed to a stop in front of her and watched as she took a deep breath and turned to face me fully. My lungs burned, my legs trembling from the all-out sprint.

Her eyes snapped from my face to my right hand, where I held the crumpled envelope she'd slid through my mail slot.

I held it up. "What's this?"

She gulped. "A letter. I—I have to go."

"Wait," I said, and took another deep breath. "Wait. What does it say? Why a letter?" It hit me then, that she was right in front of me, wide-eyed and blond-haired and beautiful. My throat clogged up, and all the feelings I'd tried to ignore for months came rushing back at me. All these months, I'd tried to forget her. I'd done my best to clean up my life, but she'd left a big, gaping hole in the middle of it.

And now she was here. Out of nowhere, she appeared at my doorstep. I couldn't let her go.

"Just read it," she replied. "Read it and get back to me."

"Don't go," I pleaded. "Please, Alba. Just give me a second."

She closed her eyes, shoulders dropping, and nodded.

I tore the envelope so aggressively it ripped nearly in half. Pulling out the folded piece of paper, I glanced at Alba, who was staring across the road at the leaves on a tree—the first tree on the street with its leaves beginning to change.

My gaze snapped back to the letter. She wrote:

Vaughn,

My cowardice hasn't allowed me to face you in person, and even the thought of hearing your voice over the phone or seeing your name pop up on my phone screen fills me with fear, so I find myself planning to drop this at your house before I scurry and hide.

Maybe it's for the best, because it'll allow you to process the news on your own.
I'm pregnant—

My gaze stumbled over the word, and then I looked up at Alba, who was still staring at the tree, then down at her midsection. She wore a loose, flowing dress that hid her shape—until a gust of wind blew against her. The outline of her stomach bulged slightly, a curve that confirmed what her letter proclaimed.

She braced herself, squaring her shoulders the way she had before entering the Noble Gala Foundation, and shifted her gaze to meet mine. Her expression was steady, but I saw the doubt and fear hidden behind her eyes. Her chin lifted slightly, and she said, "We can get a DNA test once the baby is born."

"What?"

"I haven't been with anyone else, but I don't expect you to believe that after how we left things." Her hand cupped her lower stomach protectively, and she gave me a tight nod. "I'd like you to be in his life, but I understand—"

"His? It's a boy?"

Her brows tugged. "Did you read the letter?"

I looked at the letter again, but my vision was jumpy. My heart thumped a little too hard, and I was afraid that if I took my eyes off Alba, she'd disappear.

I'm pregnant. It's yours. My due date is December 1st, and I'm having a boy.

I understand that this may come as a shock to you, and I'm not sending you this letter because I'm looking for money from you. I simply think it's my duty as a soon-to-be mother to tell you about the child and ask you to be part of your son's life.

Take all the time you need, and contact me when you're ready. My number hasn't changed.

Alba

When I looked up again, Alba's gaze slid away from me. She'd been watching my face as I read, so she saw the myriad of emotions that swarmed me. The shock. The bolt of happiness. The crushing despair.

We could've experienced this together if I'd been a better man. If I hadn't screwed up and turned on Alba when I was supposed to support her. If I hadn't been so selfish.

"So," Alba said as she gave me a tight smile. "Now you know. I'll give you some time—"

"I don't need time."

Her brows jumped, and pain flashed across her expression. Then she took a bracing breath and nodded. "I see. Understood. You won't hear from me again." She turned to walk away.

"I love you," I blurted out to her back.

Alba froze, then whirled around. "What?"

"I love you, Alba. I've been in love with you for so long I don't remember when or how it started. Maybe it was the moment you walked into that private dining room for our first lesson. Or maybe it was when you ran your fingers through my hair that first time. When you told me I was scruffy looking. Maybe I loved you the moment you walked up to my table at Carmine's and called me a failure."

"I don't recall using those exact words—"

"I haven't stopped loving you these past months, even when you walked away from me. But now, with this?" I held up the letter. "I won't let you walk away again. Let me fix what I broke, Alba. Please."

Her mouth pinched, and I suspected it was to stop her bottom lip from trembling. Her eyes went watery, and she looked at me like I'd just handed her the first bit of hope she'd felt in a long time.

I closed the distance between us and lifted my hand. Hesitating for only a moment, I cupped her cheek and tilted her head up so I could look in her eyes. "I love you, Alba. I love how resilient you are. I love your strength, and your sass, and I love that you give as good as you get. You make me a better man, and I'm not talking about teaching me how to hold a wine glass."

She huffed, a tear falling down her cheek.

"You make me a better man by challenging all the things I always believed to be true."

"Like what?"

"Like my belief that my success in business defined me. That I needed to push and push just to prove something. That letting go of my business was failure, because that's what I'd watched my own father do time and time again. But I let it go, Alba. I sold the business and walked away, and I'm no less of a man, no less of a father."

"You sold your business?"

I stroked her cheek and smiled. "I met a guy at that gala after all. Leif Sorensen, the property developer. We came to a deal, and I officially retired a week ago."

Alba's mouth opened and closed like she didn't know what to say.

"You told me you wouldn't be someone's second priority. Let me put you first." With the fingers of my free hand, I touched the slight swell of her stomach. My voice cracked, so the next words came out as a whisper: "Let me put you both first."

"I thought—I thought you'd tell me to leave," she whispered. "After I said I didn't want to be with you, I thought you'd throw it back in my face when I told you about the baby."

Lifting my hands to cup both sides of her face, I looked into her eyes and said, "I'm not your parents, or your lover, or your ex-fiancé. You had every right to be angry with me. I'll take your anger, Alba, and I'll cherish it if it means I get to be near you. I'll take it all. Anger. Frustration. Guilt. Fear. Hurt. Everything you can fling at me will be worth it if it means I get to spend a lifetime making sure you stay by my side."

"Vaughn—"

"I've been cursing myself for what I said to you that night, and for not getting on my knees and begging for your forgiveness when you tried to give me the dress back. So let me do it now. Forgive me, Alba. Forgive my harsh words, and let me spend the next several lifetimes making it up to you."

Tears fell freely from her eyes, and she shook her head. "This isn't how I thought this conversation would go."

"What did you think I would say?"

"I thought you would tell me that you'd moved on. That we'd had our fun, and that it was over. I thought I would feel used and tossed aside, like I've felt with every other relationship I've ever had."

"It's not over," I told her. "It'll never be over between us."

Her laugh was watery. "Do you remember what you said to me, before?"

I leaned my forehead against hers. "When?"

"When you put me up in your penthouse."

"You told me you didn't want me to kiss you."

Her lips curved, her cheek shifting under my palm. "Yes. And you said it wouldn't happen again until I begged you for it. And you wouldn't let me go so easily."

My heart thundered. "I meant it."

She pulled back, met my gaze, and traced my upper lip with her index finger. "I'm begging for it, Vaughn. Kiss me, and never let me go."

Relief swept through me, washing away the hurt and the pain and the despair I'd felt since she left. I angled her head, gripped her chin, and kissed her with all the love, the passion, the need that was inside me. She flung her arms around my neck and gave as good as she got—as usual.

"I want to show you something," I said, panting, when we pulled apart to catch our breaths and stood swaying on the sidewalk.

"What's that?"

"Come," I said, tangling my fingers with hers. I floated back to my townhouse, stopping every few feet to wrap Alba in my arms and kiss her. She laughed, finally batting me away and shoving me toward the house. I grinned; the curiosity was getting to her.

I put my arm around Alba as we went up the steps, my gaze dropping to make sure she didn't lose her footing. She was carrying precious cargo, after all.

She gave me a flat look. "Don't start. I've made it this far without being treated like I'm made of glass."

"Can't help it," I said, grinning.

"Why is your door open?"

"Left in a hurry." I tugged her over the threshold and guided her up the stairs to the third floor, then over to the attic ladder staircase. I stood behind her as she climbed, my heart rattling as she made her way up the narrow staircase. She sneezed at the top, and I hurried her across the plank I'd laid over the rafters to the ladder.

"I'll make a proper walkway," I told her, and gestured to the ladder. "Careful as you go up."

Her eyes were bright as she looked back at me, and then Alba started up the ladder. I wasn't far behind—close enough to hear her gasp when she cleared the trapdoor. We clambered out onto the rooftop terrace, Alba's eyes on my summer project, my eyes on her.

"Vaughn," she whispered, staring at all the greenery, the raised planters, the rich dark soil. "Vaughn—what is this?"

The sun had gone down fully, and the stars were beginning to blanket the sky above. A nearly full moon hung low over the tops of the buildings in the distance, bright and beckoning. I crossed over to the power point in the corner of the terrace and plugged in the orange extension cord I'd left hanging there.

Dozens of buttery yellow bulbs came on, crisscrossing above us, and Alba let out a delighted laugh. I crossed the terrace and wrapped my arms around her, pulling her back to my front.

"You built a veggie garden on your roof," she finally said. "Look at that cucumber! Oh my God. The mint! It's huge!"

"And invasive, apparently. I'm going to have to put it in its own pot. It killed off my parsley."

"And green beans!" In her voice, I could hear the delight of seven-year-old Alba, who never got to pick her first harvest. "Vaughn, this is incredible! You did this?"

My throat was tight as I said, "Ralphie helped set it up. After you left, I had to take a long, hard look at myself. At my priorities. I knew I'd lost you, but I decided I needed to make changes to make sure I wouldn't lose my daughter too. And I guess building this garden, it was kind of a...a message to the universe. That sounds lame, I know, but I thought, maybe..."

"Maybe I'd hear the message, and I'd come back." She turned in my arms, her eyes bright with unshed tears.

"Maybe you'd hear the message, and you'd come back," I repeated softly, leaning down to kiss her.

She tolerated my kiss for about three seconds, then pulled back and asked, "Can I pick one of those green beans? I always wondered how they'd taste fresh off the vine."

I wanted to keep kissing her, but I couldn't refuse when she smiled at me like that. We crossed over to the raised planter containing my green beans, and I watched Alba lean in to inspect the plant, choosing her green bean carefully. She picked two good ones and handed one of them to me. Then she crunched down and chewed, and I had the privilege of watching those beautiful blue eyes light up like she'd just won the lottery.

"I love you," I couldn't help saying as I watched her hunt through the growing beans for another good one.

She abandoned the task, turned into me, and pulled me down for a long, hard kiss. "I love you too," she finally replied. "And most importantly, I love your rooftop veggie garden."

Laughing, I leaned down to kiss her—but she stopped me with the tips of her fingers.

"Oh," she said. "That reminds me. My rent. Did you pay my rent until the end of the year when you were 'handling' my mold problem?" At my expression, Alba reared back, frowning suspiciously. "What? What's that look on your face?"

"I didn't *exactly* pay your rent," I admitted.

"But...?"

"But I might have bought the building."

She gasped, then smacked my chest with her palm. "Vaughn!"

"What! You were living in a shithole, Alba. I knew you wouldn't stay in the penthouse, so I had to come up with another solution."

"Another solution? That's what you call buying up an entire

building just to save me from a little mold under the sink? You can't—that's not—no! That's crazy! You can't do that!"

I caught her around the waist and pulled her close. "Try and stop me, princess."

"I'll move out," she warned.

I gave her a sharp, victorious smile. "I know you will."

Her brows tugged, confusion flitting across her expression. "What's that supposed to mean?"

"Because you're moving in with me, here, today."

"I—"

"I told you that when you came back to me, I wasn't going to let you go so easily. And I meant it."

She opened her mouth to protest, but nothing came out.

"Besides," I continued more softly, my nose nudging hers, "I need someone to help me up here with all these vegetables."

"You're blackmailing me with green beans."

"Is it working?"

Alba's eyes sparkled under the fairy lights. "Yes," she admitted, and began to laugh.

I caught her laugh between my lips and kissed her as deeply as I'd been craving since we walked up here. Then the kiss became a touch, and the touch became a moan, and then I got on my knees and begged for forgiveness the way I should've done all those months ago.

EPILOGUE

ALBA

MY SON ADAM was born a few days before his due date, on November 27. It was the most intense, painful, beautiful moment of my life. Watching Vaughn hold him for the first time was a close second—and seeing Charlotte's eyes go soft when she finally peered into the clear bassinet beside my bed was up there at number three.

The months that followed were exhausting, beautiful, emotional, and rewarding. It seemed like a dream to have a growing family and the kind of happiness that I hadn't known existed.

When Tiffany agreed to go back to a fifty-fifty custody split for Charlotte, the little girl took to her big-sister duties with the kind of enthusiasm that made me think of Vaughn. She had his drive and his single-mindedness, wrapped up in a cute, chaotic package. The weeks that she was with us were lively and fun, although I did appreciate the quieter moments when she was with her mother.

Tiffany was protective of Charlotte, which I appreciated. Our relationship grew into mutual respect, and she was a huge help when Adam was born, sending over home-cooked meals and lots of Charlotte's old baby things.

I stopped working at Carmine's. As much as I had appreciated the independence, and as much as I had needed those months of work to prove to myself that I was capable of surviving on my own, it just didn't make sense for me to keep waitressing when I was in a relationship with a billionaire.

I did, however, keep pursuing the image consulting. I didn't take any new clients when Adam was very little, but by the time he was six months old, I had a steady stream of a couple of clients per month. The business kept growing, and Vaughn was my biggest cheerleader.

For his part, Vaughn remained retired. He threw himself into fatherhood, cared for me, and carved out time with Charlotte. I saw that same single-mindedness as his daughter in the way he researched vegetable gardening. Eventually, he picked up furniture making as a hobby and had the whole basement of the townhouse redone into a massive workshop. He was not the kind of man who would sit around doing nothing, even if he was officially retired from being a business mogul.

Deena was a regular fixture at our house until she got a new job for a demanding boss who insisted she be on call for all his travel needs. We saw each other less, but we still spoke almost daily. I would never give up that friendship—not as long as Deena still wanted to speak to me. She'd been the first person to treat me like a person when I was at my lowest, and she was the one who'd stuck by my side through it all. Secretly, I thought of her as a sister.

Nikki did end up trying on Claudia Schiffer's lavender dress, and she'd been wrong; the color looked great on her. That was the start of a tentative friendship, which spread to the rest of her girl gang. I kept myself apart, though, and I used Adam as an excuse. I told them life was busy with a baby, which they all knew. In reality, though, I had no interest in being part of the world of the monied class in Manhattan. All I wanted was to build a quiet life with Vaughn, Adam, and Charlotte, grow my business, and keep myself to myself.

I'd had enough of putting on masks and trying to fit into a mold that never really felt right. It was time that I admit to myself that I was a homebody who liked wearing leggings and loose tops, who got more joy from the first harvest of the year in her veggie garden than the fanciest gala in the city.

I'd found myself—and found my family.

So, it was by chance that I discovered that Yvette and James were engaged. Their announcement popped up on my social media feed, and I felt compelled to click on the link and scratch the itch of my curiosity. As I read about their upcoming nuptials, I was surprised to feel nothing. No pain. No outrage. No joy. They were living their lives, and I was living mine. I closed the article and mentally wished them the best, and then I never thought of them again.

My parents reached out when they heard about Adam's birth. I hemmed and hawed for a while, and eventually decided that I wasn't ready for them to meet him. My little bubble of safety and happiness with Vaughn felt too precious to invite them into it. Maybe one day, I would want to reach out. But for now, I decided to choose myself—and to choose peace.

ONE YEAR to the day after that evening on the rooftop, when Vaughn and I had come back together, he found me in that same place, weeding. Adam had just turned nine months old, and I'd set him up with some toys in a playpen nearby. Vaughn crossed over to our son and picked him up, blowing a loud raspberry on Adam's neck and making him break into squealing giggles. Then he walked over to me and pressed a soft kiss on my lips.

"I've been thinking," he started, spinning Adam around to hold him facing out.

I pulled off my gardening gloves and shoved them in my pocket as I turned to face them. I pressed a kiss to my baby's head, then leaned against the raised planters and arched my brows at Vaughn. "Oh?"

"About making an honest woman out of you," Vaughn finished.

"Is that right?"

"I think it's time."

"Start over, honey. This time, say it like you mean it."

Vaughn's face broke into a smile. He got down on one knee, balancing our baby on top of his thigh against the crook of his arm, then dug into the pocket of his pants and pulled out a black ring box. He flipped it open and turned it to face me, a glittering solitaire diamond nestled in velvet inside.

My heart began to thump.

"Alba," Vaughn said. "You are the love of my life. The mother of my son. The person that makes my life worth living. I have loved you since the moment I met you, and I'm begging you, please, will you make me the happiest man in the world and tell me you'll wear my ring and be my wife?"

A breeze blew through our garden, bringing scents of earth and growing things, the tang of herbs and the sweetness of blooming flowers. Vaughn kneeled before me, holding our baby, and looked at me with the open vulnerability of a man whose heart was on the line.

"Yes," I whispered. "Yes, of course I'll marry you, Vaughn."

Vaughn blew out a relieved breath, then grabbed the ring and slid it over the third finger of my left hand. The metal warmed against my skin, and the diamond threw off sparks of fire and rainbow in the last rays of the sun. I admired it for a moment, then threw my arms around my two boys. Happiness was a fizzing, wild thing inside me. Tears leaked down my cheeks, and when Adam saw them, he began to fuss.

"Happy tears, baby," I whispered to him, bundling him into my arms and holding him close. "They're happy tears." I soothed him until he settled, then met my future husband's gaze. "I need to call Deena," I said, "and ask her if she'll be my maid of honor."

"No need!" a voice said from the doorway on the far side of the terrace. Vaughn had replaced the trapdoor with a real set of stairs and a door when I was pregnant, even though I insisted I could negotiate the ladder. After having a baby, I was glad he'd made the switch. And through the door he'd installed, Deena's head popped out. She beamed at me. "He called me in advance, and I accept. Congratulations!"

Laughing, I hugged my best friend, kissed my baby, then crossed the terrace to stand in front of the man who held my heart captive. He wrapped me in his arms, and I leaned my head against his shoulder as our baby squirmed to get free. Deena swooped in and took Adam, and I had the chance to run my fingers through my fiancé's hair, my thumbs tracing his hairline as I smiled up at him.

"I love you, Vaughn."

He leaned his forehead against mine, his cheeks creasing with a soft smile. "And I love you. Forever."

"Forever," I agreed, feeling the weight of my new ring on my finger, solid and permanent, binding us to each other the way we were meant to be.

BONUS EPILOGUE

ALBA

I'D ALWAYS IMAGINED my wedding would be a big society affair. My father would walk me down the aisle; my mother would dab her tears with a handkerchief. I would be resplendent in a custom designer gown, and my husband would stand tall at the altar, a man my parents would look at and approve.

The only thing that ended up being accurate was the gown.

My fingers skimmed over the silk crepe of my skirt, the fabric diaphanous and so light it felt like spun moonlight. It was gathered at the bust, giving the dress a subtle waistline while still being airy and effortless. I felt beautiful in it, and as the hairdresser spritzed me with one more bit of hairspray to make sure my soft waves held for ceremony and the pictures, I rolled my shoulders back and turned to smile at Deena.

Tears shone in her eyes as she smiled at me. "And to think this all started with a spilled vanilla latte."

I laughed, dabbing my fingers under my eyes and inhaling to keep myself from crying, then accepted a hug from my best friend.

"I wouldn't be here without you," I said, my voice more blubbery than intended.

"Stop it," she said, squeezing me in another tight hug. "You look beautiful, Alba."

"I can't believe I'm getting married."

Her smile was bright. "About time."

Laughing, I straightened, flapping my hands near my face to try to dry the tears that tried to leak out of my eyes. Then I turned for the hotel room door, smiled at my best friend, and took the first step toward the rest of my life.

The hotel was gorgeous and smelled faintly of lemongrass. Outside, the sounds of the sea crashing against the shore were the steady backdrop to the faint music that floated up from the beachfront. We were in Thailand, at a private resort that Vaughn had booked in its entirety. Palm trees shimmered in the wind, the sky was impossibly blue, and the path beneath my feet was dark, solid wood leading me to the future I never thought I deserved.

A hotel worker in his pale blue patterned uniform gave me a little half-bow as I passed, a broad smile on his face. He waved me along the path, which snaked along ferns and palms and gorgeous white flowers and finally opened up to the private beach reserved just for us.

My eyes snapped to Vaughn, framed by the arch of flowers at the end of a white aisle. He held Adam, who was a wriggling ball of fifteen-month-old energy dressed in a tiny, adorable tuxedo. When they spotted me, Vaughn's face went slack, and Adam's went ecstatic.

He wriggled out of his father's arms and came sprinting down the aisle toward me—or what served for a sprint for a little man who'd only taken his first step two months earlier.

Laughing, I caught him in my arms, and this time there was no holding back the tears that fell from my eyes. My son's arms came flying around my neck, crushing all those perfect, carefully styled waves. He smacked a big, slobbery kiss on the cheek that my makeup artist had spent so much time dabbing and brushing and blending.

"Mama!"

"Hi, baby," I whispered, nuzzling my nose against his.

My son patted my cheek in that awkward, toddler way, then slobbered another kiss on my cheek. Then the light caught the delicate gold necklace dangling between my collarbones, and Adam made it his mission to grab and yank.

"Okay, buddy," Deena said, swooping in to save me. "Let's let your daddy see how good your mama looks before you tear her to pieces."

Laughing, I glanced up and caught Vaughn staring at me.

The look on his face made my heart explode. It was soft and tender, and it held all the happiness that I had thought would forever be lost to me.

Love you, he mouthed, then turned his head to try to hide the fact that he was dabbing at his eye with his thumb.

"Here," Deena said, thrusting a tissue at me. "You're leaking."

"I can't stop," I said, doing that hand-waving-at-my-face thing again.

"Get down here so I can make you my wife," Vaughn called, a broad smile on his face.

A little hand slipped into mine, and our son looked up at me with his father's eyes. "Mama," he said, then tucked his head against me.

My heart couldn't take much more of this. With nothing else to do, I smiled at Deena, who started our little procession, and then walked hand-in-hand with my son toward the man of my dreams.

"Come to Auntie Deena," my best friend said, scooping Adam into her arms without a care about sticky toddler hands on her gorgeous bridesmaid's dress. The two of them sat down in the front row beside Charlotte, Tiffany, and Dale. Vaughn's mother was there, waving a fan toward her face to ward off the sticky heat.

That was it. I considered inviting my new-old friends Nikki and Rome, Bonnie and Arlo, Leif and Layla, Dani and Emil, and Penny and Marcus, but if I invited them, I'd have to invite another swath of people on the edge of friendship, and then their partners, and maybe family members. Would I have to invite my parents? What about aunts and uncles? People that had dropped me when I was broke and had suddenly reappeared when I was with Vaughn?

I didn't want that. After stressing about it for ages, Vaughn had kissed me on the lips and leaned his forehead against mine. "Invite who you want," he'd told me. "If that's one person, make it one person. If it's a hundred. Make it a hundred. If it's no one, and you, me, and Adam go down to the courthouse tomorrow, then we do that. But Alba, sweetheart, don't do this to yourself. Don't give up your power and your happiness to people who don't care about you."

It was one of a thousand reminders he gave me about forgetting social expectations and doing what *I* wanted. I was still growing into the person I wanted to be. Someone strong and confident and independent—someone loving and soft and compassionate.

In the end, it was just our tiny group, in this gorgeous, sun-drenched paradise, celebrating the fact that Vaughn and I had found each other.

His palm was warm when I slipped mine against it, and he tugged me a few inches closer.

"I'm the luckiest man alive," he murmured. "I can't believe I get to have you as a wife."

"I'm the luckiest woman alive," I replied. "I can't believe I get to have an amazing rooftop vegetable garden in the middle of Manhattan."

He laughed, loud and apologetic, then banded an arm around my back and crushed his lips to mine. I squawked and batted at him—and then I gave in. He kissed me like he never wanted to let me go, like everything he'd ever wanted was right there in his arms.

I could relate.

Flushed and bubbling with happiness, I pulled away and turned to the officiant. She was a long-haired woman in a linen pantsuit who had moved to Thailand decades ago and now made her business officiating destination weddings. Arching a brow at the two of us, she lifted the little notecards in her hand. "You skipped a few of the necessary items before we get to that part," she noted, eyes glimmering.

"Let's get them out of the way, then," Vaughn said, not moving his arm from my waist.

That's how we were married. I was wrapped up in Vaughn's arms, promising to love, honor, and protect, feeling the most loved, honored, and protected I'd ever felt in my life.

The next time we kissed, we were husband and wife. And that night, when champagne bubbles burst all over my tongue and my cheeks hurt from laughing, I knew that the true joy in my life had only just begun.

LOOKING FOR YOUR NEXT READ?

ONE
FIONA

A TIRED GROAN shudders out of my best friend's rusty old Toyota. That...doesn't sound good.

On the bright side, Simone's hooptie has successfully gotten us three hundred miles north of Los Angeles and into our destination vacation town. Unfortunately, it doesn't look like it's going to make it much farther.

I grip the worn plastic door handle as if it'll help keep the car together. If Simone's worried about her car breaking down, she doesn't show it. With wild red hair tied back in a messy bun on top of her head and thick, black-rimmed glasses framing her pale blue eyes, Simone looks far younger than her forty-four years—a fact that has often needled at my own insecurities. Time hasn't been so kind to me.

Another screechy noise escapes the hood of the car as we turn onto the main drag of Heart's Cove, and I start hunting the signs on the street for a mechanic. Even if Simone isn't worried about this hunk of junk, I need a way to get out of here at the end of our two-week stay.

We make it about fifty more feet before the engine sputters, the car rattles, and the whole things dies right there on the street. Simone expertly navigates the coasting car to the curb as smoke curls out of the hood in thick black puffs. Parked in a semi-appropriate spot and acting like nothing at all is the matter, she pulls the handbrake and tucks a strand of flame-red hair behind her ear.

I throw my best friend a glance. "We should have taken my car."

"We couldn't take your car. It reminds you of Voldemort."

"Voldemort?"

"He Who Shall Not Be Named. That shiny white Mercedes is the only thing that asshole left you in the divorce and looking at it reminds you of his cheating ass. I see it in your eyes every time you turn the key in the ignition. There was *no way* we were taking your car. Big Bertha did just fine." She taps the dashboard fondly, as if there isn't a plume of dark smoke coming from Bertha's hood. My best friend gives me a meaningful stare. "This vacation is about us, about pampering, about being the women we were always meant to be. Besides, we made it, didn't we?"

"Barely," I grumble, fighting the grin trying to curl my lips.

"I'll find a mechanic this afternoon. We won't need the car for the next two weeks, anyway—everything in Heart's Cove is within walking distance from the Heart's Cove Hotel. It's in the brochure."

Through the windshield, past the smoke, I spy a faded green-and-white awning above the hotel door. A screen door hangs slightly crooked and lace curtains frame the interior of every window. Paint is peeling on the old siding, but neatly trimmed grass lines the front of the hotel and baskets bursting with colorful flowers hang from every post. A low hedge lines the sidewalk leading to a small parking lot, the other side of which is a well-maintained path to the front door.

This accommodation is quaint, though a bit worse for wear. It isn't exactly what I'd put as my first pick.

Or maybe it's not what John, my ex-husband, would have liked. Do I *actually* mind this place? It's kind of cute, in a lost-kitten-with-patchy-fur-and-three-legs kind of way. If Simone's to be believed, it's got great reviews and a killer continental breakfast.

John would've taken one look at this place and complained nonstop until we found someplace else, maybe even canned the whole vacation—but he's not here. He's in his swanky office in L.A. with whatever hot, young assistant he's decided to stick his junk into. Or maybe a paralegal. Or a junior partner. Or an intern. Or all of the above.

Deep breaths.

Simone must see my pursed lips, because she punches me in the arm. "Quit sucking lemons, Fi. Come on. We have art to create."

"How many times do I have to tell you I'm not an artist? Why did you have to choose an art retreat for our big self-actualization getaway? I'm a precision gal. Organizing. Planning. Why can't we have a vacation job hunting or something? At least it would be useful."

Simone lets out a snort and exits the car, casting a quick glance at the smoke still escaping her hood. She kicks a tire for good measure, then slings her purse over her shoulder and waves me forward. "Come on! The sign on the door says to check in inside."

Pushing thoughts of my ex aside, I follow Simone out of the car. The air tastes fresh here, if you can ignore the smell of Bertha's dying engine. Full of floral scents and a hint of salt from the sea, the smell unwinds a knot of tension between my shoulders. Simone's right. I need a vacation—and why not do something that I never would have done before? Why not try something new?

It's not like there's anything for me back in Los Angeles. Now that the fancy penthouse was transferred to John's name last week and my half of its worth has finally hit my bank account, I'm officially homeless. The divorce is settled, so I'm officially single, too. My dream of moving to the hills and getting my picket fence and perfect little family are gone with the penthouse, but I'm trying not to think about it too hard. Starting over at forty-five isn't something I'd planned on.

Simone decided I needed some time to figure myself out, so I'm here. About to do two weeks of art, yoga, and meditation classes in the hope of *finding myself*, even though I'm terrified of what I might discover. I find myself in the mirror every morning, and I'm not sure I like what I see. I'm on the other side of forty-five, with new wrinkles appearing every day. Things are sagging where they never used to, and soft where they were once taut.

Compared to John's younger, prettier, more docile playthings, I feel positively dumpy. I'm not sure a week of painting and *ohm*-ing will help any of that.

Simone's already halfway to the door by the time I take a step. She turns around and plants her fists on her hips, arching her brows at me. "Um, earth to Fiona! Get a wriggle on, girl. Our first class starts in half an hour."

I pause, tilting my head. "I thought you said tomorrow was day one."

"I lied. Deal with it." She pushes a stray piece of red hair off her forehead, looking zero percent remorseful. Her eyes sweep down the street then back to me, shoulders dropping slightly. Speaking more gently, she says, "I knew you'd never get in the car if you knew you had to try drawing something today. Your comfort zone is doing its best to keep you hostage, so you know, desperate times and all that."

"Who are you calling desperate?" I pop a brow.

Simone grins, but before she can open her mouth to answer, a rumble sounds from the asphalt separating us. My best friend's eyes widen as she looks at the ground where a crack is splitting the pavement apart. I take a step back, a hand on my chest.

Then the parking lot of the Heart's Cove Hotel explodes.

No, really. It explodes.

Asphalt everywhere. A geyser of water shooting fifty feet into the air, cascading down on top of us. I scream, putting my purse over my head while I crouch down. Rocks and bits of asphalt rain down around me, biting my skin as they land. I put a hand on the back of my neck, pull it back, and see blood.

What the...?

Water's still raining down on me as shouts erupt. Doors open, and a siren sounds in the distance. I'm still crouched on the sidewalk, staring at the blood on my fingers.

What in the name of self-actualization is wrong with this town? Where the heck did Simone bring me? Maybe I should hightail it out of here, but how would I even do that? Our car is out of commission.

I'm stuck, stuck, stuck. Just like I was stuck in my marriage. Stuck in a penthouse I didn't like. Stuck in a city I never wanted to be in. Stuck around sycophants and snobby housewives preening and gossiping while I felt like I was dying a slow and painful death as life passed me by.

Water seeps into my dress, soaking my back. I curl myself into a ball, worried another stray chunk of asphalt is coming for my skull. My thoughts rush around me, and my comfort zone constricts inside my head.

I should have stayed at home. What if John needs me for something? I should be apartment hunting and trying to find a job. A vacation is the last thing I need. Why would I even deserve a vacation? I need to get my butt in gear and start figuring out how to start my life over.

Emotion chokes my throat, and I feel silly. I'm not the kind of person who falls apart. I'm the rock. I'm the one who keeps the family together.

That didn't go so well, did it?

Tears threaten to spill onto my cheeks and I fight my rioting emotions to hold myself together. It's just a burst water main. I have a shallow cut on the back of my neck, but I'm fine. Just wet and weirdly emotional.

Then, a shadow. The water stops, and I hear the pitter-patter of a geyser hitting an open umbrella. The lack of water raining down on me allows me to take a full breath. I lift my head to see the owner of the umbrella currently helping me maintain a shaky hold on my own sanity.

Holy *ohm*.

Heart's Cove might not be so bad, judging by this vision in a wet t-shirt.

Tall, dark, and handsome doesn't even cover it. This guy looks like he belongs in every forty-something woman's wet dream, not in a sleepy town called Heart's Cove. He's broad, and by the way his wet shirt clings to his chest, I can tell he's packing serious muscle. My eyes sweep over the curves of his pecs and shoulders, down his arms and over his trim waist. Snapping my eyes back up before they reach dangerous territory, I see a hint of a smile on his full lips.

"Um, hi," I stammer, standing up as I brush my hands down my navy wrap dress. The back of it is soaked. My dress clings to me as much as his shirt hugs him, and I catch my mystery man's eyes heating as they take me in. A strange kind of warmth knots in the pit of my stomach as I tuck a strand of black-brown hair behind my ear. I gulp, still staring at my savior.

He has dark hair and rich, tan skin with two patches of grey hair above his temples. The rest of his hair is piled to one side in short, loose curls, one of which slides down across his forehead.

I watch in fascination as he lifts a broad hand to sweep the stray piece of hair back, his grey-blue eyes still studying me. Is he even real? I'm not sure people this good-looking exist in real life. Maybe I finally snapped after the last horrendous fifteen months. The geyser was the last straw. Something in Bertha's engine fumes has turned my brain to mush. I've finally lost my marbles.

"I'm Grant." His rich, deep voice sends a tremor shivering down my spine. It sounds real enough.

I barely manage to croak out a response. "Fiona."

His lips curl into a smile, as if the sound of my name pleases him. A curl of heat beads in the pit of my stomach and I place a hand over the offending spot. I feel... I'm not...

I haven't felt this in a *long* time.

Grant lifts a hand toward me, and I suck a breath through my teeth as he reaches around the back of my neck. As I close my eyes, I imagine him pulling me close, crushing me against that glorious chest of his, and taking my lips in his.

A man like him would take control. I can sense it in the electricity zinging between us. He'd pin me to a wall and show me what I've been missing for the past twenty years. He'd light up every nerve ending in my body and be as rough, as commanding, as demanding as he'd need to be.

And I would melt like freaking butter on his tongue. God, his tongue—I wish I could melt on it. Preferably when his hands grip me tight and I feel the raw power coiling in his huge body. *Wet and weirdly emotional*, huh. Yup, still accurate.

But Grant's touch is feather-light when the pads of his fingers brush across the back of my neck. They're calloused, rough. Not at all like John's doughy, soft hands were when he palmed my skin back in the days when we actually touched each other.

Grant's skin may be rough, but his touch is soft. A silent gasp escapes my lips before I can stop myself, heat flooding between my legs, spreading through my core, and all the way up to the tips of my ears.

This is... Oh, no. Is this menopause? Did I just have my first hot flash under a geyser in the middle of a parking lot?

But when I open my eyes, Grant's expression is soft. "You're bleeding," he says, almost to himself. Before I can stop him, he hands me the umbrella, then grabs the edge of his shirt and rips off a strip.

The man *rips his freaking shirt apart* and uses it to dab at my admittedly very minor wound.

I might faint.

This is a fever dream. This isn't real life. It can't be.

I stare at the strip of skin now exposed by the rip, just above the waistband of Grant's pants. His stomach is hard, and the unholy desire to run my tongue over that bit of flesh bubbles through me without warning.

"Fiona!" Simone's voice cuts through the lust fogging my mind. My best friend runs over, shielding her face with her hands as she laughs. "Can you believe it? I think it's a sign."

"Of what? Poor municipal plumbing?"

Grant lets out a chuckle at my words, and the desire to make him laugh again overwhelms me. I steal a glance at him as Simone walks up to me, her eyes widening as she takes in the specimen standing next to me.

"Well, hello there, handsome. I'm Simone." She wiggles her eyebrows at me, then drops into a curtsy in front of Grant.

A freaking curtsy, as if the man is the King of England.

My best friend is a maniac.

"Grant," he replies with a smile, not at all bothered by the fact that Simone is insane. "I'd better go check on the twins. They've been having trouble with the hotel maintenance lately, and I'm sure they could use a hand." I make to give him the umbrella, but he shakes his head. "Keep it. I don't mind getting wet." A flash crosses his eyes as his gaze drops to my lips then away, so quickly I wonder if I imagined it.

Call me the Wicked Witch of the West, because I'm about to melt right where I stand.

Simone squeals as she hooks her arm through mine, and we watch Grant stride around the geyser, his white shirt soaking through and clinging to every muscle in his back. "He is *delicious*. It's definitely a sign."

"A sign of what?"

"That this vacation is *exactly* what you needed."

"He's just a friendly local."

"I *hope* he's friendly," Simone answers, the word sounding *very* different when she says it.

I shake my head, laughing, and nod to the hotel. "Should we go find out what's going on?"

"Yeah, but first let me grab some tissues. I don't want to drool all over the hotel floor if I'm going to be in the same room as that *friendly local*."

Rolling my eyes, I fight the smile off my face and jerk my head toward the green-and-white awning, setting off in the same direction as Grant went as if there's a tether pulling me toward him.

Maybe Simone's right. Maybe this vacation was a good idea, after all...

Fiona is only in town for a vacation, until a flooded hotel room sends her to look for alternative housing arrangements...with the town's hunky handyman.

Get DIRTY LITTLE MIDLIFE CRISIS!
HTTPS://GENI.US/KTWYR

ABOUT THE AUTHOR

Lilian Monroe adores writing swoonworthy heroes and the women who bring them to their knees. She loves making people laugh and is eternally grateful to have found people who share her sense of humor.

When she's not writing, she's reading (or rereading) a book, walking, lifting weights, or attempting to play the guitar with very limited success.

She grew up in Canada but now lives in Australia with her Irish husband. He frequently asks to be used as a cover model for her books, and she's not quite sure whether or not he's joking.

ALSO BY LILIAN MONROE

For all books, visit:

www.lilianmonroe.com

Manhattan Billionaires

Big Bossy Mistake

Big Bossy Trouble

Big Bossy Problem

Big Bossy Surprise

Forbidden Boss

The Wrong Boss

Dirty Boss

More surprise babies!

Knocked Up by the CEO

Knocked Up by the Single Dad

Knocked Up...Again!

Knocked Up by the Billionaire's Son

Yours for Christmas

Bad Prince

Heartless Prince

Cruel Prince

Broken Prince

Wicked Prince

Wrong Prince

Lone Prince

Ice Queen

Rogue Prince

Small Towns are the best towns

Four Steps to the Perfect Revenge

Four Steps to the Perfect Fake Date

Working with the Enemy

Faking It with the Firefighter

Conquest

Craving

Combat

Calamity

Small Town + Later-in-Life Romance

Dirty Little Midlife Crisis

Dirty Little Midlife Mess

Dirty Little Midlife Mistake

Dirty Little Midlife Disaster

Dirty Little Midlife Debacle

Dirty Little Midlife Secret

Dirty Little Midlife Dilemma

Dirty Little Midlife Drama

Dirty Little Midlife (fake) Date

Filthy Little Midlife Fling

Merry Little Midlife Matchmaker

Brother's Best Friend Romance

Shouldn't Want You

Can't Have You

Don't Need You

Won't Miss You

He'll do anything to protect his woman

His Vow

His Oath

His Word

Enemies to Lovers/Workplace Romance

Hate at First Sight

Loathe at First Sight

Despise at First Sight

Fake Engagement Romance

Engaged to Mr. Right

Engaged to Mr. Wrong

Engaged to Mr. Perfect

Mountain Man Romance

Lie to Me

Swear to Me

Run to Me

<u>Doctor's Orders</u>

Doctor O

Doctor D

Doctor L

Made in the USA
Middletown, DE
09 January 2026

26831623R00229